OLA

ALBERT WENDT

University of Hawai'i Press

Honolulu

© 1991 Albert Wendt

All rights reserved

First published by Penguin Books 1991

Published in North America by University of Hawai'i Press 1995

Printed in the United States of America

95 96 97 98 99 00   5 4 3 2 1

Library of Congress Cataloging-in-Publication Data

Wendt, Albert, 1939–

Ola / Albert Wendt.

p.   cm.

ISBN 0–8248–1585–8

I. Title.

PR9665.9.W460343   1995

823—dc20   95–7329

CIP

University of Hawai'i Press books are printed on acid-free paper
and meet the guidelines for permanence and durability of the
Council on Library Resources

Designed by Richard King

For Jan and Pita Taouma
and
Bill Pearson

Foreword

What is a life? Can it be contained in three used beer cartons, taped up, and bequeathed to a stranger to shuffle, like a pack of cards, into some meaning?

About a year ago, on 26 February, such a 'life' was abandoned, like an hermaphroditic orphan, on my front verandah, with an unsigned, undated, typed note informing me that the 'life' had been bequeathed to me by one Olamaiileoti Farou Monroe (a pseudonym obviously), who hoped that I, being a writer (and she was an admirer of my work), would use it as the basis for a novel or, if not a work of fiction, a biography (which is fiction anyway, she said), or, if I considered some of it worthy, could publish it as my own work. Her only condition was that I wasn't to try to find out who she was 'in real life, which is fiction too'.

'Out of your reshaping of the jumbled contents of my three cartons I hope to read / find a meaning to my wasted life,' she wrote. 'If you find little or no value, even literary, in my life, please burn it.'

The contents of the cartons had been thrown together rather haphazardly, and I had to spend some weeks sorting them out into: diary entries (all undated); extracts from her life — some incomplete; what appear to be stories about events / happenings in her life but could also be fictional short stories she wrote; poems — others' and hers; random jottings made whenever they sprang to her attention; newspaper clippings / menus / theatre programmes / travel itineraries / old tickets / bills / lists of things she had to buy and do; copies of her letters to others and letters received; a detailed journal of her pilgrimage with her father to the Holy Land; and finally a record of her father's last years, and their return to Sapepe, the village of his youth. All totalling much less than what she must have lived out, but everything that is missing from her collection of papers is part of her life too.

Out of this stuff of a real life I've tried to reshape Olamaiileoti Monroe, resurrect her as fiction / art. As Ola says in her testament: art ain't life; history is recreation / fiction.

Gripped more and more by a huge excitement (and reverence) as I sorted through and thought about the possibilities of the life in the cartons, I decided not to rewrite any of Ola's records, or to write fillers to join the fragments, but to rearrange the pieces in such a way that

7

the readers (including Ola) could see *the connections, a unity. (All art is selection, says Ola. And I hope my selection does justice to her life.)*

My selection/arrangement, of course, makes me part of Ola's life: she is perceived through the way I've ordered her life. In a way she's my creation based on her memories as she recorded them. (Conversely, I too now perceive myself through her.)

I've left out what I consider to be repetitious and unnecessary to the unity of the work. Someone else would have selected and ordered the selections differently, and Ola and the leftovers, like the wood-chips from a carver's chisel, would have been different.

I've also broken up and used the journal of the pilgrimage to try and tie the whole life together.

My wife was the first person to read the final manuscript. Powerful stuff, she said, but parts of it, especially the sexual episodes, couldn't have been written by a woman — it's not the way a woman would view or write about sex. All I can say is, I've tried to remain faithful to what Ola sent me and how she saw herself (and her life). Although I must admit that, at times, I've thought sections were written by a man pretending *to be a woman (or by a woman who was a man as well). Those sections could also be purely imaginative.*

Anyway, you be the judge.

And, Olamaiileoti Monroe, if you read this book I hope I haven't mutilated you beyond your recognition.

1

Many of us want our lives to unfold like a novel.

Over the years I've written these bits and pieces and tossed them into these beer cartons alongside bills, notices, correspondence — a tangled heap of refuse, the stuff out of which to make a 'life'/novel. 'We are what we remember,' I recall reading in one of Albert Wendt's short stories. To which I now add: 'A society is what it remembers. The self is what one remembers, and the loss of memory is the loss of self.' For a foolish moment there I elatedly believed that to be original, but, aue, I'd read it in one of Kundera's novels. Much of what I am and remember is second-hand and from books —the fate of too much book-learning.

I keep adding compulsively to my refuse heap; why? 'If ya know ya history then ya know where ya're comin' from,' sang Bob Marley. A very apt description of what I'm doing: this refuse heap is my self — and every bit that I fish up out of my ribcage tries to reaffirm/understand where I'm comin' from. Some day I'll turn it into an autobiography/novel — no difference.

Sometimes when I reread some of the bits, I'm surprised by what I've fished up, or, should I say, what I've freed from the depths through the act of writing. I've often felt, with some dread, that instead of being the fisher I've been the fished-up, a creature born out of the imaginations of the creatures in the refuse heap; that I'm their captive taulaaitu/songmaker/shaman, the vehicle for their awakening.

Carl Jung said, *'One does not dream, one is dreamed. We undergo the dream, we are the objects.'*

Though I own what is commonly known as 'a bad memory', I'm shit-scared of losing it. My refuse heap is the result of trying to record who I am before I forget.

I can't hope to remember all that I was/am becoming. My vanity also determines what I hide (from myself and others) or want to forget.

Like most mortals, I don't have total recall — and I don't want it either, because I'm not masochistic enough to want to be like the deranged but holy wanderer in Albert Wendt's novel *Pouliuli*. He could remember every detail of his past: every taste/smell/word/fantasy/event/action committed and action contemplated but not carried out/every missed opportunity and regret, every thought he'd ever thought and, most unbearable, all his suffering and the suffering of those around him. And all he wanted to do, as he wandered from village to village constructing his forgiving circle of pebbles, was to forget. Total recall was his curse, his albatross, his fa'asalaga. As long as *Pouliuli* is read he will wander over our suicidal planet, like the Ancient Mariner, trying to hold it together in his simple circle of pebbles.

If I had the power of total recall I'd either self-destruct or turn my refuse heap into an awful Everest of vanity.

2

The pilgrimage was to be our surprise gift to my father, Finau, for his seventy-fifth birthday.

Everything was ready: the air tickets, passports, hotel bookings, the clothes he needed; I'd written to the Schneiders, my friends in Israel, and they'd arranged for us to be guests of their government; I'd got my father's doctor to agree that if the need arose he'd persuade my father to go, for although most of my father's generation dream of visiting the Holy Land, if actually offered the chance they would be frightened of it — after all, they'd never been outside of Samoa.

Nearly all of us Samoans are raised on the Bible, and after over a hundred and fifty years of Christianity (mainly fundamentalist) we know almost nothing of *our* ancient religion. My father's generation knows more about the biblical Holy Land (geographically, historically, spiritually) than our own country, and more about it than the modern Israelis. The biblical prophets, heroes and villains, the courageous saga of the Israelites, Jesus and His disciples, are a vital part of their everyday lives.

For them the Christian Heaven (and Hell), the deserts, plains, rivers and cities of the Holy Land, as depicted in the Bible, are covered eternally with a magic aura — and still exist today. My father *knew* there was a modern Israel but that was not *his* Israel. No, ma'am! His Israel (and its environs, so to speak like my old geography professor) was the one in the Holy Book, which the brave LMS missionaries had transported and replanted in the Darkness of a pagan Samoa to give it Light, a holy Israel which still flourished in the hearts of all *true* Christians. I too was raised on that diet, that Holy Land.

I drove to our family home in the Vaipe, arriving as planned after their evening lotu and in time to eat with them. (As was the custom, none of his children was to eat with us.)

'I've got something for you,' I said. I took the thick pouch of tickets out of my handbag and placed it beside his dinner plate.

'Air tickets? Who for?' He opened the pouch. I glanced at Penina. She smiled.

'For you,' I replied. 'From us, your family. A birthday present.' He looked puzzled.

'It's your birthday next week,' Penina reminded him.

'But — but I've never travelled before!' The fear was setting in.

'Ola is going with you. You'll be all right,' Penina reassured him.

'Where to?' he asked.

'Look at the tickets!' I urged.

He pushed them away. 'You tell me.'

'To the Holy Land,' said Penina.

'I'll think about it!' He shut the pouch as if locking up a creature he feared.

'Everything has been prepared, you don't need to worry . . .' Penina tried to say.

'Bring the food now,' he called to his children.

During the meal, we talked about everything but the trip.

I didn't want to watch television afterwards, and Penina accompanied me to my car.

'Don't worry,' she said, 'he'll go. I'll tell some of his friends and they'll tell him how fortunate he is to be going to the Holy Land. He won't let *them* down: he'll go on their behalf.'

He rang me after the weekend and thanked me. 'But it's so expensive,' he said.

'I can afford it,' I joked.

'Is Carl coming with us?' (Carl was my husband.)

I hesitated and then lied, 'No, he's got to go to Australia on business.'

'Is everything all right?' he asked.

'Yes. He tells me to wish you a happy visit to the Holy Land.'

A worried pause. 'I'm afraid of the journey,' he admitted. I wanted to hug him, for he rarely admitted to weakness.

'Don't worry, Dad,' I said in English. 'God will take good care of us, so will the Israeli authorities. I have some very influential Israeli friends.'

'What about the wars there?'

'What wars?' I laughed. 'Anyway, God's our bodyguard!'

'My doctor says I *should* go. He says I'm very lucky to be visiting Jesus' country.' Worried pause. 'And my friends are full of envy. They're giving me a list of the holy places they want me to visit and things I have to do for them.' Another worried pause. 'And our pastor says I should go. We'll be all right, won't we, Ola?'

'Of course,' I tried to laugh. 'We'll be on a jumbo . . .' He had never been on a plane, so I spent a long time explaining the kinds of planes we were to use.

Next morning I took an atlas to him and, with Penina, traced our route from Samoa to Athens to Tel Aviv. I also turned to a map of Israel and showed him the places on our itinerary, knowing he would spend the next few days memorising them. Now that he was committed to the pil-

12

grimage, he was going to file every detail of it in his orderly mind and, on our return, he was going to dazzle everyone with vivid tales of his exploits. His pastor had already won an agreement from him to describe his pilgrimage from the pulpit. Not that he was an expansive boaster or loquacious teller of tales. But he could, in his own quiet comfortable manner, hold the attention of an audience.

The news of our trip got to the *Apia Times*, which headlined DIVINE PRESENT: PILGRIMAGE TO HOLY LAND. I laughed to myself when I read it, knowing my poor dad wasn't going to be able to back out of his pilgrimage now.

'Carl should come with us,' he pleaded the next day when I visited him.

'Don't you think I'm strong enough to take care of you?'

'It's not that.'

'Our marriage is still all right!' I said.

I then gave him the piece of paper on which I had typed this quotation from Elie Wiesel's *One Generation After*: 'But Israel for me represents a victory over absurdity and inhumanity. And if I claim it for myself, it is because I belong to a generation which has known so few.'

I left while he was reading it.

3

I was born *after* my mother died. A scientific impossibility, you say. But it *was* true, so my father and aiga told me as soon as I was able to understand them.

While my mother was carrying me, the doctors discovered she had a terminal illness. My mother, against her doctor's advice, refused to have me aborted — bless her. To save me she agreed to a caesarian delivery two months before I was supposed to start living in this terrible century. Her heart stopped unexpectedly while she was undergoing the operation. Technically she was dead before the surgeon rescued me through the incision in her abdomen.

My mother's mother (with my father's agreement) named me Ola-mai-i-le-Oti, Born-from-Death, to commemorate the circumstances of my birth and my courageous mother's death. Everyone calls me Ola, Life, for short.

My mother's parents have described my birth to everyone as divine proof that my mother had led an exemplary Christian life. My father's parents, humble village folk now gone to God, have described my birth as 'a resurrection, our beautiful daughter's rebirth' — meaning, I am my mother, one and the same person. (Reincarnation, Hindus would call it.)

Throughout my early life people expected me to blossom into an extraordinary person because of the unique/miraculous circumstances of my birth.

When I was a young child my unusually superstitious Aunt Fusi, who brought me up, observed (minutely) every physical change in me or on me, expecting me to be transformed into some fabulous creature, an angel with fiery wings even, like the beautiful messenger who informed Mary that she was to be the fortunate receptacle (incubator?) for God's only Son.

Others, mainly those who disliked my aiga or who had envied my mother's beauty, hoped (and probably prayed) that I would metamorphose, so to borrow from Kafka, into an earthworm or a fly or one of those hideous monsters in cheap science fiction movies.

I sensed early that my father was mortified that his enemies' nasty hope would eventuate. Whenever he held me he would whisper, 'I know our loving God will keep you as beautiful as you are now.' I never let him know that I knew of his fear, and vowed, with all my little heart, that I would not allow myself to become the monster he feared. And in case it did happen, I would self-destruct.

Other people expected me to develop ESP or some healing powers. My more sadistic relatives wanted me to reveal diabolical powers and proceed (with total immunity against retaliation) to eat (literally) the hearts of our aiga's foes.

The gamblers in my aiga and neighbourhood 'consulted' me before betting on anything. This consultation took the ridiculous ritual of running their hopeful hands through my black hair (curled like a gorgon's) and then using those hands to bet with, or asking me to describe, in great detail, my previous night's dreams, which they then 'interpreted' for lucky omens. In my impish moments I enthralled them with the most fantastically involved dreams I could conjure up. They never blamed me if they lost their bets; the reason being that they had *misread* my dreams.

My teachers kept expecting me to reveal super-human intelligence. In my school reports they made comments like: 'Does not work to capacity, could do better,' or 'One day Ola will decide to show her true ability.'

Growing up within such an *expectant* atmosphere, I came to expect unusual, abnormal things of myself. According to one of my uncles, a school principal, 'Ola *has* to become an extraordinary person because, like Jesus, she overcame death!' That uncle considered himself an extraordinary person because, like Jesus, he was born at five minutes to midnight, 25 December. Poor Uncle, he never did show he was extraordinary. He served as a loyal teacher for almost forty years, was divorced by his wife and soon after was hit by a mighty coronary thrombosis, which killed him instantly.

When I was about twelve, I believed I was carrying within my womb (wherever that was) an insatiable foetus which, as it developed, was assuming my mother's forgiving features. Today when I remember that, the foetus becomes a blowfly's egg, which in the moist and fertile warmth of my womb will burst into ravenous maggots growing, growing.

Out of my mother's brave depths I was born/rescued.

I have carried that miracle all my life.

At times it is what sustains me.

As a child I hoped to reincarnate into my wonderful mother and be more than what I was.

Today I still want to be more.

4

Most of our relatives and my father's friends were at Faleolo Airport to see us off. I've never liked large aiga gatherings, especially tearful ones — and this was a real weeper. Penina, the children and grand-children, most of the women, and a few of his friends wept copiously. (Anyone would think it was a funeral!) There were tears in his eyes, but he had to be the brave consoler, tear-wiper and reassuring embracer. Me? I tried to be inconspicuous so they would not see I too was melting into tears.

To end the sobbing flood, he called for a farewell prayer and then, with one of his most poetic efforts, dried our tears and dispelled their fears of the not-to-be-trusted, accident-riddled, war-torn, violent, once-Christian-now-pagan world which my father and I had to traverse to get to the Holy Land. Their concern was for him, not me; after all, I'd trav-elled often and without harm; he was going for the first time, and what a long and difficult journey it was to be. 'To Jerusalem for your birthday,' I heard one of his friends whisper to him. 'And the Cross,' the unwelcome thought popped in my head.

He nearly lost his nerve at the door of the plane. He turned to me. I held his arm, turned, and waved to everyone. He did the same. (His face was diamonded with beads of sweat.) Then I steered him into the belly of the plane, which smelled of a mixture of frangipani, mildew and aerosol spray.

I got him to take the window seat and, as I helped strap him into his seat, noted again that, despite my having told him that experienced travellers dressed casually, he wore a white shirt and tie and a navy-blue suit. I was to watch him shed his 'formality' during our pilgrimage (with help from me, of course). He started at Honolulu, our first stop.

We stayed in a hotel in Waikiki, but he refused to let me take him for a walk over the 'most expensive grains of sand in the world' (my descrip-tion to him) or have dinner in the hotel dining room, so we ate in his room, and after I left him he watched TV until midnight. I gave him time to fall asleep and then crept into his room and laid out a summer shirt, light trou-sers and sandals for him to wear.

Next morning I caught him preening in front of the mirror. (He looked almost twenty years younger than his seventy-five years.) I complimented him on his *casual* dress. He smiled and said he was very hungry.

'To the dining room?' I asked.

Straightening up, he said, 'Why not?'

I've always considered my father a very handsome man who could've won the hearts (and the other vitals) of innumerable women and men, if he had chosen to. Yet he never revealed to me (or anyone I knew) he was aware he had this power.

The Athens International Airport lounge was bustling with passengers for flights to other parts of the globe. Finau sat beside me clutching his travel bag in his patient lap. He was the most patient person I knew, and I sensed (and resented it a little) that he wasn't so afraid anymore.

I was tense with anxiety, my belly a swarm of agitated hornets. Pre-flight time for me is always a battle against fear: a plane has to defeat the forces of gravity and I feel safe only when it has done so. And flights to and from Israel were under constant threat of hijackers and terrorists. Two weeks previously at Athens Airport, a preflight search had un-covered a plastic bomb in a passenger's suitcase.

I was wiping the sweat off my face when my father said, 'Don't worry, God's looking after us.' Some consolation, I thought, and tried to smile.

Even before we checked in at the airline's counter, our suitcases were searched, which annoyed me but my father observed the whole method-ical process, fascinated. Later his fascination deepened when we had to wait while three officials checked the body of our aircraft with what I thought were sounding devices. 'Very thorough, aren't they?' he whispered as we boarded.

He insisted that I take the window seat and, after he put our hand lug-gage in the locker above us, strapped himself in and then smiled at me as if to say, 'You'll be all right.' And though I resented his switching of roles from chaperoned to chaperone, I *did* feel safer.

Thirty or so minutes later, suspended in the blue crystal emptiness above the pastures of cloud, I relaxed and noticed he was singing to him-self in his head. I knew because his right hand was beating a barely visible rhythm on his thigh. I knew also that the song would be an ancient one out of his rich storehouse of old songs, his favourite music and poetry, acquired during his childhood and youth in Sapepe.

And while he sang, he observed in detail the strangers and strange-ness around us, making them familiar and part of his perimeters.

Lunch was served. He said grace and ate hungrily. I gave him my meal as well, and tried not to watch him. He seemed obsessed by a new

17

hunger to consume everything, and I was happy for him, and happy to be with him as he explored.

I fell asleep. No dreams visited, none that I could recall, anyway. Only a dull aching in the furthest corner between sleeping and waking, an annoying regret — what about, I didn't know. In my middle-aged sleep I was waking often to cold sweat, inexplicable fears, guilt and regrets, and wishing to be forgiven for them, or hoping to relive my life and undo all the harm (both real and imaginary) I had done, or be allowed to live the life I should have lived. We live with guilt, always, Kafka knew, so did Dostoevsky, Camus, Frame, Becker, and my father, though he would never admit it to me.

He woke me as our plane broke down through the clouds, and we were above the orange, burnt-out landscape shimmering with rising heat waves. 'Fasten your seat belt,' he reminded me. (I was again the daughter and he the confident, caring father.)

A short while later we were landing at Ben Gurion Airport, where everything was bristling with a fierce light. ('Like the sharp noonday sunlight on a calm sea,' he would describe it that night.) The hornets began stirring in my belly. No matter how guiltless I am, immigration officials always make me feel guilty. (We should travel with Kafka's *The Trial*.)

Five young security officers gathered at the foot of the gangway; a bus stopped a short distance behind them; an army jeep came and parked near the tail of the plane: one of the soldiers sat cradling a submachine-gun. My hornets were now stinging.

We stepped out of the plane's air-conditioned comfort, and the smothering heat started squeezing the sweat out of us.

One of the security officers, a petite blonde, scrutinised us closely as we came down. I tried to control my trembling.

'Are you with a tour group?' she asked me. I said no. 'May I see your passports?' Just behind her, hovering over her like Al Capone's baby-faced bodyguard, was a young man who was watching our every move while she flicked through our passports. 'You've travelled a lot,' she said, handing me our passports.

As we hurried to the bus, I said, 'We must look like Arabs!' My father looked puzzled. 'That's why they watched us more closely than the palagi passengers.'

Israel was under siege; the military traditions of ancient, biblical Israel were still operating; the nation had been on military alert since its rebirth in 1948, after two thousand years' extinction; but I couldn't accept the tight security, the numerous checks and searches we were to undergo during our trip. 'It's for our safety and protection,' my father would insist, but every time it occurred, I would quiver with fear and he would narrate (proudly) the heroic deeds of Joshua, King David or any other Israelite

18

warrior he fancied at that moment. 'The Israelites (he avoided using "Jews") weren't (and aren't) cowards!' he would end his tales.

And so onward to Jerusalem.

We shared a cab — an extended black Mercedes — with an elderly rabbi who sat beside the driver and who, soon after we left the airport, started joking about getting lost in New York during the six months he'd just spent there and how he was equally *lost* in Israel, his *unfortunate* country, where rampant inflation made it impossible for poor rabbis (like his humble self) to pay even the taxi fares. The dark sinewy driver participated eagerly in the banter, telling the rabbi, whose white earlocks and winter-pale skin were wet with sweat, that poor taxi drivers (like his humble self) were also finding it hard to make a living now that the almighty shekel wasn't worth a biblical shekel anymore. We enjoyed their humour as we observed the countryside.

The land was dry, burnt grass·and shrubbery with numerous rock outcrops and limestone protrusions, and out of the earth brimmed a quivering stream of heatwaves. However, wherever irrigation had penetrated, the country was green with orchards, fields of vegetables, pines and cypresses.

The cab windows were open, but the wind was almost oven-hot and my dress was clinging wetly to my body. The rabbi's black suit was now drenched with sweat, and I admired his stoical refusal to take off his coat and hat. My father seemed too preoccupied with the landscape to be bothered by the heat.

As we climbed over some steep hills and then down through a gorge we began to see signs of the last war: wrecked armoured cars and other war equipment; a few memorials to dead soldiers.

'Do you have wars in your country?' the driver asked us.

'No,' I replied.

'With the present inflation, victories aren't worth having,' said the rabbi.

'But we *have* to survive!' countered the driver.

'True, true!' the rabbi said.

Then we were on the outskirts of Jerusalem, among the new suburbs of apartment buildings and houses, which looked like severe surrealist constructions perched precariously on moonscapes. Around us (and as far as the horizon and up to the sky) was the thick creamy haze that we were to see throughout Israel every day from mid-morning on. In that haze everything looked unreal, without body and weight, and it reinforced the sensation that we were caught in a slowly unwinding dream, and not in the Holy Land, heading for its sacred centre, Old Jerusalem.

'It's so modern,' my father whispered in Samoan.

'This isn't the Old City,' I said.

A few minutes later the cab stopped in front of the Schneiders' apartment building. The rabbi, sweat dripping off his nose, shook my father's hand in farewell. 'Don't expect too much,' he said.

Nearly all of Jerusalem, both old and new, is constructed of the flesh-coloured stone dug up out of the city's core, and I'd read that in the evening, as the sun sets, Jerusalem and its surrounding land exude a golden light which emanates from the heart of this Jerusalem stone.

That evening, as we stood with Daniel and Rani Schneider on the front balcony of their apartment, we watched the city and hills glow like a healing fire.

'Welcome to Jerusalem!' Daniel said to us.

'Yes, welcome to our home,' Rani emphasised.

'Thank you,' my father replied in English. (It was the first time he'd spoken to anyone else on our trip.) In his eyes was reflected the fire of the city.

I had become friendly with the Schneiders on their visits to Samoa when he'd been Israeli ambassador to the Pacific. I'd warmed to their honesty and nobility, qualities born out of enormous suffering. From Germany they had fled to Israel before the war, had lost nearly all their close relatives in the Holocaust, and had fought for the establishment of Israel and watched many of their friends die in that struggle. 'I'm tired,' Rani had admitted one evening as we sat on the verandah of Aggie's Hotel in Apia. 'We just want peace.'

'But not at any price,' Daniel had said.

After a dinner of cold meats and vegetable salad, Daniel offered to show us the Old City.

'Shall I shut the windows?' I offered. 'It might rain.'

'It won't rain for at least four months,' Rani said. They must have seen our disbelief. 'It won't rain — not tonight, definitely!' We laughed and headed down to the car.

During our stay we were to find it difficult adjusting psychologically to the fact of a rainless four months. 'Strange how we adapt to certain climatic conditions and then expect those to hold true elsewhere; even our skins unconsciously yearn for rain when it is *supposed* to rain,' my father would explain to me later. Months afterwards I would realise he'd been referring to what *is* real and what we want or *expect* to be real; how we bend and see reality according to what we believe. Confronted with the real Israel, including its climate, he was disoriented because he wanted to see — and not lose — the biblical Israel he had grown up with and felt at home in.

5

'All our journeys are through myth to what is, though we may not like what we find. Each journey is a circle out of the self back to the self and towards God . . .'

'Dad, you're sounding like Herman Hesse.'

'Who's he?'

'A very sentimental German novelist who *isn't* anymore.'

'You don't believe in anything, do you?'

'That's not true.'

'What do you believe in then? And don't offer me your usual jokes or cynicism.'

6

Daniel drove us slowly through the empty Jaffa Gate, up a narrow street and parked above the Jewish Quarter. In the dark quiet everything seemed timeless, and as soon as we got out of the car the heat grasped us.

Daniel and I moved ahead. When I realised my father wasn't with us I looked back to see him rising from where he had been kneeling. (To kiss the earth of Jerusalem?) I looked away before he could see me.

Few people were about; above us the upward-sucking sky was a forest of stars. As we strolled down towards the Western Wall through the burrow-like streets and alleyways, Daniel explained that during the Jordanian occupation the Jews had been expelled from their Quarter and the synagogues destroyed; now the Quarter was being restored and reno-vated to preserve its original architecture. My father was now beside me and his walk seemed to have acquired a dance-like strength, a spring quality of renewed hope. My body was tired from the flight but my mind was alert, eager to see. We were flowing in the river of those generations who had come to the Temple and had passed on; I sensed their presence around us.

At the end of the labyrinth was a security checkpoint manned by an unsmiling soldier with a bald spot at the top of his head. As he bent over my handbag and searched it, the circular spot was like a shiny eye inspecting me. I had to stop myself from reaching down and shutting it.

Before us the cobble-stoned Temple Court sloped down to the floodlit Western Wall, which rose squarely up to the plateau that is the Temple Mount with the Quabbat al-Sakhra (Dome of the Rock), built by the great Umayyard caliph Abd-al-Malik, and the al-Aqsa Mosque, both made holy by the prophet Muhammad on his sacred Night Journey. (Daniel gave us this information.)

'So modest a Mount, yet holy to three great religions. Source of so much bitterness, object of endless bloodshed,' I said to my father in Samoan. Such terrible beauty to fight and die for, with the promise of sal-vation, whole generations convinced of the rightness of their cause.

A movable chest-high wooden barrier divided the Court from the Wall. We walked up to it.

A few pilgrims were kneeling in prayer in front of the Wall, their shadows like huge nesting blackbirds. And as a mounting awe gripped me, the immense night sky pressed down on my head.

'Are you cold?' my father asked.

'Yes,' I lied and edged closer to him.

'I come here often, at night,' Daniel said. 'I just stand here and let myself drift into the Wall to become part of its solidity, drawing strength from it.'

So for a long time we watched the soft light rippling like a film of water across the Wall, searching out all its crevices, testing and measuring its ability to keep on enduring beyond pain into forgiveness. The night released me, finally.

As we left the Wall, I told my father, in Samoan, that when the hardened Israeli paratroopers had recaptured the Wall in 1967, they had kissed its stones and wept: they had returned home to the capital of the Kingdom of Israel after two thousand years in exile.

Soon after, we were walking along the outer wall of the Old City, overlooking the deep gorge in which the remnants of the ancient City of David are located. From the Wall's highest point we gazed across the valley to the Mount of Olives.

'It isn't very big, is it?' my father said.

'The Mount?'

'Yes. And I didn't think it would have that hotel on it,' he said in English for Daniel's benefit. In its neon outline, the Intercontinental Hotel seemed to be pushing down the Mount, with distasteful arrogance.

'The Jordanians built it,' I told him when Daniel chose not to divulge that information.

'That was where the Saviour accepted His Cup of Pain and chose to overcome Death,' my father reminded me.

That night before going to bed I went into his room and found him sitting cross-legged on his bed, in a red lavalava and white T-shirt, praying silently. I sat down beside him and, though I still refused to pray, bowed my head and tried to be the daughter who hadn't lost her faith.

'You must *learn* to pray again,' he said. 'It should be easier here in the Holy City.'

'I'll try,' I heard myself say, and was surprised I meant it.

'Already I'm missing Penina and the children and Samoa. But I *am* happy to be here. My old body feels no pain tonight.'

In a dream, during the early morning hours, I watched ice-cold water swirling loudly over the black lava fields of Savai'i, washing them until they glistened like my father's eyes and the carapaces of giant sea turtles, and heard my mother whispering (in my voice), 'If only I had lived . . . if only.'

23

I woke at dawn and, for a puzzled moment, didn't know where I was. Quietly I hurried to my father's room and peeped in.

His sleeping face and hair were burning with Jerusalem's early morning light.

7

I've often wondered what my life would've been like if my mother had lived. Would I have become who I am now?

I mustn't forget though that *her absence* — the presence of that throughout my life — has been a telling influence in my becoming what I am. (Which is what?)

More importantly, if she had lived, would my father be who he is now? Would their love have survived the boredom, infidelities and squabbling that plague most marriages?

Our histories concern what could've been just as much as what has been. They are dimensions of what is and could be. Each life contains the possibility of all possibilities; a life is all the possibilities it can be.

8

Monroe was my mother's maiden name. (Her father's father was an American.) My father's surname is Lagona, an ali'i title in Sapepe, our village on the western tip of Upolu.

Leifi'ifi School was considered the best primary school, but it was reserved, by the colonial administration, for Papalagi and Afakasi children. So, to get me into that exclusive school, my astute father registered me under my mother's maiden name. I wasn't aware of that until two weeks before starting school, when my father explained he wanted me to use my mother's surname so we would remember her always. 'Apart from that,' he continued, 'I want you to have the best education possible. Your mother's name will get you into Leifi'ifi, where all the brightest children go.'

'What's my new name?' I asked.

'It's an American name,' he said. 'Monroe.' Because I knew no English, it sounded like a drawn-out grunt. 'Monroe,' my father repeated slowly. 'M-O-N-R-O-E,' he spelled it. And with that, I heard it for the first time.

'Monroe!' I sang, clapping my hands.

'Yes, that's correct. You're very bright.'

That day I skipped everywhere, singing to myself, 'Monroe, Monroe, Monroe.' I varied the pronunciation and tune, rolling the syllables, like hard round sweets, around in my mouth.

Next day, when three of my friends came to play, I told them proudly, 'I have an American name!'

'What?' Ianeta said.

'Yes, I have my mother's American name!' They gazed at me. 'Monroe,' I revealed. 'That's my name.'

'Liar,' Ianeta whispered, without malice. (They just didn't believe me, that was all.)

'It's true!' I insisted. 'My father told me yesterday.' They refused to believe me. 'I can spell it in English!' I boasted.

'Spell it then,' Ianeta demanded. (Ianeta wasn't my favourite friend.)

I concentrated hard, my eyes shut tightly. Then I spelled it. I opened my eyes to their sighs of envy. 'Monroe was my mother's grandfather, who came from America a long time ago,' I pressed home my attack.

'So you're an Afakasi!' Malia, my most perceptive friend, remarked. I nodded, but before I could boast more about my American ancestry, they skipped off to play under the shady gatae trees behind our house. I followed them.

For a while as we played hopscotch, they succeeded in not voicing their envy. But eventually, Salome, the youngest, couldn't hold it back any longer.

'But you can't speak English!' she said.

'So how can you go to Leifi'ifi?' Ianeta attacked.

'The Palagi teachers will find out and send you back home!' Malia snared me further.

I was trapped. 'I . . . I *can* speak a little English.'

'Say something in English then!' Salome challenged me.

'You're just jealous!' I changed tactics.

'I'm not!' said Salome.

'I'm not!' chorused Malia.

'And I'm not!' echoed Ianeta.

I was hooked by their accusing silence. 'You are!' I snapped, miserable because they *were* telling the truth. I started walking back to our house.

'MA-NI-ROU!' Ianeta chanted, parodying me. The others echoed her.

I fled home as fast as I could.

So until I married (for the first time) years later, Monroe was my surname.

Throughout my life I've often pondered (with a sense of irony) the combination that is my name: OLA-MAI-I-LE-OTI MONROE, ancient and poetic Samoan and plain New England backwoods American.

I never got to know my relatives on my mother's side and never acquired detailed information about Alexander James Monroe, my great-grandfather. Only that he had appeared in Apia at the turn of the century; had married my great-grandmother from Neiafu Village, Savai'i; had sired fifteen children; had died poor. I've imagined him as all sorts of wonderful characters. My favourite has remained that of an adventurous sea captain who had given up wealth to go contentedly native in paradise. And strangely enough, whenever I feel I've been abandoned by everyone else, his mellow presence eases out of the emptiness and wraps its comforting hands around my heart.

27

I never knew him. Yet I feel I *know* him better than many of the people who've moved in and out of my life.

*

My father, Finau Lagona, was sent by his parents, at the age of twenty, to the LMS Maluafou School, in Apia, where after four arduous years he graduated with a Proficiency Certificate* that got him a job as a clerk in P. H. Thurroughs Ltd, a merchandising firm owned by a fierce Englishman. Proud that he was the 'first full-blooded Samoan' (Mr Thurroughs' description) to hold *that* job in *that* firm — the other employees were part-Europeans — my father worked harder than any other employee and, within eight years, became senior clerk, with the demanding Thurroughs lauding him as possessing 'the best English in Apia, of all non-Papalagi, that is'. With a loan from Mr Thurroughs, my father bought a piece of land in the Vaipe only a short distance behind the firm. On it he built a fale to which he brought some of our Sapepe relatives to live and serve him. (His parents refused to shift there permanently, though they visited often.) Mr Thurroughs also got my father admitted into the English-speaking Protestant Church, which was dominated by the English merchants in Apia. My father insisted that our relatives continue to attend the Samoan LMS Church next door; in no way were the English going to have natives in their church.

Soon after Mr Thurroughs put him in charge of the firm's central office, my father married my mother, Martha Monroe, who, at the time, was a shop assistant in the firm. She was twenty, he was twenty-eight. With another loan from Mr Thurroughs he built a modest Papalagi house, with two bedrooms, a large sitting room, and a shower and flush toilet outside, behind our Samoan fale, a house befitting his wife and his status.

For almost two years there were no children.

Then I came along.

To be their only child.

(By the way, my second name is Farou, a Samoanisation of Thurroughs, a man my father admired and tried to emulate.)

No one can understand fully the sorrow one has to endure/survive after losing a loved one, unless one has experienced that loss. Throughout my childhood, my relatives, especially my grandparents, tried to convey the depths of my father's loss (of my mother, that is) to me. I tried to understand, but it wasn't until last year that I came across its most apt description: a poem written by one of our poets, and through which I will always be able to *imagine* and re-experience my father's pain.

---

*He had this framed. It's one of my most treasured possessions.

28

WE HAD A DOG ONCE

We had a dog once. (It belonged
more to Dad than to us.)
Large, vicious, his fiery red member
nearly always erect, his breath
the stench of a swamp,
he was more myth than dog.

When hungry the hairy brute
would snap repeatedly
at the air, his huge jaws
and fangs clicking
like rifles being cocked.
We suffered nightmares
of vanishing down his gullet
— one SNAP and we'd be gone —
and steered clear of him.

He obeyed only our father.
At home whenever Dad wanted
to be left alone to pick
at his sorrow, he would call
his devoted beast to lie
at his feet. This kept
us at bay.

I recall Dad acquired the creature
soon after our mother died.
(He never told us from where.)
I remember that Cerberus
guarded the gate to Hades.

9

Gideon Meir is to be our liaison officer. Oren Berkov, our driver. Allocated by Daniel to protect and guide us through Israel.

First it is to Yad Vashem.

'It was intentional that we should see and *experience* Yad Vashem before we visit any other place in Israel,' my father said that night when we were alone in the apartment. 'Now we will always see Israel (and the world and ourselves) through the Holocaust and its suffering.' He spoke with his usual measured deliberateness, imprinting each of his observations in Jerusalem's stillness and shaping forever my memories of and feelings about Yad Vashem. As he talked, his meanings soothed my pain and rescued it to become a treasured part of the mythology that is my life. '. . . We have to understand and come to terms with the Holocaust if we are to understand modern Israel (and ourselves) in this century of terror.' He pondered and continued, 'But even now I can't quite accept It. Why? Because It will reduce my Israel — the one I was brought up with — into insignificance. And, as yet, I can't let that happen. (Or, should I say, I don't *want* that to happen.) . . .'

As he described our visit that morning to Yad Vashem his description moved through my head like a silent film in slow motion. I was out-of-body observing my father and myself *experiencing* Yad Vashem, the Memorial on the Hill. And even then I was re-experiencing it *through* the Holocaust, through Yad Vashem.

To recapture an experience is to recapture the experience of that experience, and the more times we do that, the more the experience becomes myth. And to describe it in words, symbols, is a poor substitution, for symbols are not the experience, they merely represent it. It is an illusory reality, but it is the only one we have.

The sharp copper-coloured light of mid-morning is trapped in the black hood of our car; it is trapped on Gideon's right cheek and Oren's forehead and in my father's inquisitive eyes; the trees lining the road up the hill are bristling with it. (*Why has my memory selected only that theme of the copper light?*) It is as if we are wombed in an emotionless light emanating from our primeval origins in the eternity of space. (Pita tried explaining that to me once.)

I am afraid of my lack of comprehension, my self-complacency, which, throughout my pampered life, has prevented me from admitting to myself that I too was part of the universal indifference that permitted the Holocaust to happen. I'm not guilty, I'm from Samoa, a tiny country thousands of miles away from Europe and Hitler and the Nazis —it had nothing to do with me! But as our sleek black Oldsmobile noses up towards the summit of the inevitable hill, my heart beats in my dry mouth. A patch of my left arm is burning; it's the feel of my father's hand.

'What is this memorial?' he asks in Samoan.

'It is to the Jews who were killed in the war.'

'Killed?'

'In Hitler's concentration camps and prisons. About six million of them.'

For a frightened pause I think he has stopped breathing. 'I . . . I didn't know. I have little knowledge of *this* Israel and the modern Israelites.'

It's better you don't know, I want to tell him. For not to know is not to be guilty.

'So many,' he whispers. And in his remark there is the question, why? Our car stops in front of the office and I'm saved from having to answer him.

On the office steps stands an attractive young woman in a plain white dress that gleams in the copper light (like the angel who visits Mary in Pasolini's film *The Gospel According to St Matthew*). 'Your guide,' Gideon tells us.

We get out of the car. Smiling, the woman hurries down to us. Striking make-up. An American, I can tell immediately. Her hand feels cool. 'I'll not come with you,' Gideon whispers. 'I've seen the Memorial many times.' (I sense other reasons: fear, sadness?)

As we walk up the narrow avenue to the Memorial complex, our guide tells us she is a researcher at Yad Vashem, helping to reconstruct the history of the Holocaust so no one will ever forget it, or reorder it, or erase it. I notice that each small tree beside the avenue is a memorial. To individual non-Jews who died helping Jews during the Holocaust, she informs us. (Why do I keep looking for blemishes on her immaculately white dress? Is it too perfect, too pure?)

'It's all right,' my father whispers to me.

'I'm all right,' I insist.

On the outer wall of the Memorial building is a massive relief mural depicting the heroes of the Warsaw ghetto uprising. She explains each figure to us; her voice is laced with an irrepressible anger.

Everything has slowed down.

31

We enter the lobby. A smaller mural. She tells us it was designed and cast by a camp survivor; it portrays the Jewish passage into the camps and gas chambers, and their ultimate victory over terror and suffering. A numbness is filling me (like a thick liquid), and I can't feel my father's grip on my right arm. My vision is now confined to seeing only what our guide is pointing out. I don't see or hear the other people.

Now we're moving through the gauntlet of panels and displays about the rise of Hitler and the Nazis and the war: Nazis in metal-black uniforms; upraised arms and hands like arrogant phalluses; frozen in their goose-stepping. Mindless, spellbound crowds. Heil! Heil! Heil! they roar in my head. Our guide's voice, as she explains each panel, is the anger of the prophets; she refuses to hide her bitterness.

We're moving towards the Camps and Ovens, the mountains of bones and skulls. I know the sequence and don't want to experience it. No.

Unexpectedly our guide's voice is gone from my hearing, like a breath that's been cut off abruptly. Why is she looking at me? I stop. Why is my face wet? Dad? Dad? He presses his handkerchief into my shaking hands and steadies me with his arm. An exhaustion, close to one experienced after a bout of drunkenness, has invaded me and I can't move my body anywhere. 'I am sorry,' I tell our guide.

She puts an arm around me. 'Don't worry, it happens often here,' she says.

I'm again aware of the other people: through the galleries move slow, solemn groups of schoolchildren, soldiers and tourists. 'I'm sorry,' I tell our guide. 'I can't go on.' They steer me to the caretaker's office. My father sits me down. I refuse to look at him.

'I'll go on,' he says. 'I'll go alone,' he tells our guide, and is gone before I can stop him.

We wait in silence for him to return.

Our guide sits opposite me, sipping a cup of tea, the light from the window emphasising the whiteness of her dress; a clock ticks ponderously in the centre of my head; all else is thickly silent, their tongues have been cut off; once again I'm suspended and almost motionless, floating, unwilling to be born, yet expecting the surgeon's knife to rescue me.

Our beginnings are water, clay and cosmic dust. We still sway to their tides. Also to the moon's and sun's pull.

But where did our pain come from?

And where do we go from here?

Is evil programmed into our DNA?

When our first ancestor killed for the first time, did she enjoy it? Did she thrill at discovering that she had the power of life and death? Did she enjoy her first suck of blood, her first taste of meat?

Was it after feasting on (and enjoying) her sister's flesh that she experienced guilt for the first exhilarating time?

Torture/rape/violate/murder/erase/strangle/poison/stab/shoot/execute/hang/bomb/gas/electrocute/terrorise/starve/garrotte/guillotine/etc/etc/etc. Our tongue is most inventive with such killing verbs; we are rich in methods of dispensing/inflicting pain and death.

For our individual selves we deny death, yet inflict it on others readily, easily. Why?

Each day, as the La conquers the long Ao and the deep Po, millions are killed our planet over. I continue to die (comfortably) in my expensive squalor and watch the television versions of their slaughter. I am not a witness, I am a spectator.

What is evil?
Sin? Goodness?
Psychosis?

Since Einstein, even right and wrong have become relative.

'I've known for a long time that evil is everywhere, but I never thought it would be of this ferocity and greed. Did God desert us then? Did He forsake His chosen people? Why? The Holy Land in my soul now has almost no meaning measured up against this evil.'

'You knew nothing about it, Dad?'

'Now I do, and feel guilty for not having known.'

'But you can't be held responsible for something you didn't know about!'

'Who's to be held responsible then?'

'The Nazis, the people and the nations who knew but did nothing to stop it.'

'All of us are responsible for our history and our future, for all the evil deeds that were, are, and will be committed — or left uncommitted.'

'What about God?'

'What about Him? He *is* God. His justice is more.'

'He must have a very sick sense of justice!'

'No, a very rich one . . . Every time we kill someone, we are killing Him.'

*

33

Every Jew walks in the shadow of the Holocaust; her footsteps are a defiant light.

What about us Gentiles?

'. . . I'll never forget their eyes: still beacons in their sunken faces; thousands of accusing eyes stretching back and forward into eternity. As I passed through the galleries I felt as if I was walking on water; kept afloat by the magnetic pull of their eyes. (Strange, but could there have been such miraculous hope in all that indescribable suffering?) The eyes were those of owls. And, Ola, our family god in pagan times, was the owl . . . Inevitably I found myself in the last gallery, where the numbers of the victims are listed on miniature pillars. Square and still I stood in front of the middle pillar, which is made of transparent glass. In the pillar, on a small black shelf, is the well-used shoe of a child. A worn-out, utterly helpless shoe watching me. And I fled. Rushed out onto the roof of Yad Vashem and the endless, silent scream of God's universe . . .

'. . . That shoe will be worn by my heart for the rest of my days. It is a perfect fit.'

The eyes have it!
Their eyes.

Our guide at Yad Vashem smelled of Charlie perfume (and drying sweat). We embraced in farewell.

I envy her anger. She'll hunt Hitler for the rest of her life. That is her meaning, her purpose.

What is mine?

10

Ever since my grandparents took me to Sapepe for the first time, in 1945 when I was six, I've been afraid of the silences that fall in the evening in the villages.

Of that visit I remember little. What I can recall is of course shaped by hindsight and who I am now.

We travelled on a crowded bus. I sat on my grandmother's lap. The driver had a bulbous black mole on the back of his neck. We got off where the road ended and my grandfather piggybacked me through the dense bush — I remember it was cool — over the low mountain range. I slept most of the way in his warmth and rich earth smell, and remembered the hills were bearded with mist, a slow-weaving whiteness which, as I recapture it now, feels like a healing hand across my forehead.

Sapepe was a neat fringe of fale spread along the bay under palms on brilliant white sand, and it was never going to change, I believed.

That first afternoon, while I was playing on the black rocks and boulders on the beach in front of our aiga's compound, I sensed a threatening creature observing my every move. I turned swiftly. Nothing. But it *was* there. I wanted to run home, escape. Was too scared to move. Started crying. Heard the silence, its ominous breathing. Cringed in a crevice in the rocks to hide. 'Get up, up,' it whispered in my head. I forced myself up out of the rocks.

Sucked in my breath. A giant fireball, the sun, was falling into a sea that was splitting into slivers of burning light like golden veins bursting open.

Embraced by the silence, I sat down and watched the blazing horizon swallowing the fireball, and listened to the murmuring water talking to me about the mysteries of the silence as the sun dies. It told me I was alone, separate from other creatures and things. I scrutinised the palms of my hands, then my arms. I tugged at my hair; pinched my stomach until I felt the pain. Then rushed to a pool of water that was cupped in the hollow of a boulder and looked down at my reflection. Yes, it was me, I existed, I am, I am separate. I was myself.

For the next few days I wouldn't let anyone touch me affectionately, afraid their love would once again suck me into their being, dissolve my separateness, my aloneness.

O a'u, I, me.

O oe, you.

O tatou, we, us.

O outou, you.

O tatou uma, all of us.

That discovery, which we make as children, set me off on the individualistic kick I've been on most of my life.

We/us — I — is it ever possible to be the we/us again?

Another enduring memory of that visit is the smell of Sapepe. It wasn't until I gave birth to my only child, Pita, that I was able to identify Sapepe's puzzling odour; it was that of the birth sac bursting open.

Again I remember a poem:

TOWN AND VILLAGE

A town is made
of iron, stone and wood.
A village is made
of palm frond, people, and great silences.

I am attracted to the villages
but I live in the town.
Why is this? I always
ask myself.

In the town I can hide
from the great silences
that fall at evening.

Why do poems (not mine) continue to best explain the meanings of my life?

Where did it go? The we? The us? The all-of-us?

11

It is just before noon and we are in the Arab Quarter of the Old City, in the busy burrows of streets walled by stores and stalls selling an exotic assortment of wares and exuding the world's aromas, and I'm back in the 1940s and '50s adventure films about Arab bazaars and princes and princesses and black-eyed, gold-toothed caliphs mixed up in tall tales of intrigue that always end happily ever after. In one stall are stacks of carpets. I half expect one to detach itself from the stacks and fly out through the doorway and up into the Arabian Nights and harems of bored women and bald-headed eunuchs, billowing silk robes and diaphanous curtains dancing in the desert breeze and drawing envious sighs from me.

Halfway through the labyrinth, we come across small bakeries selling hot pita — the scrumptious smell of bread is that of the earth burning, and I can't resist it. I buy some pita and hand them to Gideon and my father. Ripping them apart, we eat eagerly. Very good, delicious, my father says.

I look down the alley and stop eating. Straight out of *Aladdin's Lamp* — a tale told to us often in standard four by our teacher Mr Lemoe and which we never tired of hearing — rides a white-bearded Arab in a real turban and robes, astride his valiant steed, a grey donkey. The crowd parts and lets him through. He bows and waves to many of the vendors, and I imagine him a magician on his magnificent way to advise the king about choosing a prince for his daughter to marry. I wave. He bows towards me.

Almost as if the donkey wants us to believe that he and his master are not myth but of this world and the now, the donkey drops a few lush turds: KAPASHHH! Then they are past us. The stench is powerfully real and right now! My father, who is usually prudish about such earthly matters, giggles. I smile at him and he laughs.

A few minutes later, as we leave the Arab Quarter, I remember that an Israeli soldier had been shot in the Quarter two days before, probably in retaliation for the bombings of two Arab mayors in the West Bank. An eye for an unblinking eye! says the Old Testament. And as we put out more and more eyes we get blinder, more unforgiving in our blind self-mutilation, in our vengeful lashing out, until we can no longer see the healing magician riding by on his wise donkey, only smell the death-like stench of the donkey's excrement.

Inflation in Israel is running at an unbelievable 120 per cent. Is the price of a life (whether Arab or Israeli) that inflated too?

Instead of bombing out the eyes, how about skilled surgery to restore to them a forgiving vision?

That would only serve to increase inflation because surgeons demand exorbitant fees. Bombing out eyes is far cheaper — anyone can do it; it needs no special skill.

Have you ever tried dy-
ing to see what it's like?

No, it's too perm-
anent a condition!

12

From the moment we're born we're fed on words/language; we're controlled by words; we're classified/described/identified, etc., by words; we're enslaved by language as prescribed by those who control our societies.

Females are *fed* to believe they mustn't use four-letter words, write/talk about sexual matters openly/frankly. For me this has been one of the most difficult taboos to break free of — it's like trying to be free of my very breath (my 'stereotyped' self) and to learn new ways of breathing and speaking. It takes a lot of courage (recklessness?).

So the following episode — my first real attempt to be free in my writing — took much embarrassment and a lot of painful revisions to trap on paper. It was like turning my skin inside out.

Once made though I felt clean, at home with myself (or the self my risk had taken me to).

I now understand a little of the fear, pain and exhilaration suffered by those pioneer writers and artists who challenged the censorship laws and the hypocritical public morality of our societies. Just a little of it.

Anyway, here's my first stumbling step into the puritanical heart of the censor.

It looks so vulnerable in the dull glow of the bedside lamp. Erect. Uncircumcised too. Middling size, like a miniature grass snake which has shed its skin and is now baldly pink. You're too fascinated by it to hear what its owner is saying.

His stubby fingers start playing absentmindedly with the snake. Tugging at it; nipping it; occasionally flicking it with a forefinger, and it springs forward and back like rubber.

Its owner talks on and on. The snake looks so funny, with a tangled mass of reddish hair at its base, slack balls veined purplish red, and its reddish head — the colour of a newborn chick — peeping out of the stretched foreskin. You want to reach over and, patting it on the head, say, 'It's okay, no one's going to hurt you.'

As you observe that skinless snake being crooned to by his fondling narcissistic hand, a tingling laughter starts stirring in your depths. You can feel it, hear it: laughter not aimed at him but at the snake, which looks so helpless. Soon you'll be brimming over with mirth, and, if he hears it, he'll be wounded to the insecure core of his manhood. No matter what your excuse is, he'll accuse you of trying to belittle his manliness.

You know what he's going to say: 'Do you want it?' All men say it in one way or another. Children in possession of clubs they believe can tame you, that you crave. He's offering you — whether you want it or not — a prize lollipop.

You cross your thighs and choke off the laughter.

'Well, do you want it?' It's an offer he expects you not to be able to refuse. (Bless the Godfather — at least with him it had been merely business.) Grasping the base of the skinless snake, he points it at you. There are to be no preliminaries, no lengthy foreplay (as recommended by the hygienic sex manuals). The bald snake's one slit of an eye is even oozing a large tear. 'Come on, I *know* you want it!' He says, right hand moving towards your pubic hair.

The laughter twirls around your insides and rolls you out of bed. You wrap your arms round your torso to still the laughter, your shaking body.

'Whatsamatter?' he asks. You dress quickly. Just in your dress. No shoes. Your back turned to him and the snake.

But you can't stop it. As you head for the door, the laughter bursts out of your mouth. One last glimpse of the bald snake. Poor unlucky creature to be owned by such an immature trainer! As you laugh, the snake wilts, collapses suddenly: KAACHUNG!

'You ungrateful bitch!' he shouts.

Periodically, throughout your life, you will try to reconstruct the man who was built around that erection, but you'll remember only that bald, vulnerable snake.

And sometimes in your dreams the snake will turn into a white, eyeless slug, a fat grub you can roast and eat. Sometimes its pink head will become the wizened head of a newborn baby still slickly wet with the birth fluids.

And this is what you'll say, when you're drunk at cocktail parties, to other pampered and bored wives: 'Prejudiced by my very Protestant, very Samoan upbringing, which considers other races as being inferior, I *prefer* portly, permanently sun-tanned and circumcised cocks.'

What am I doing here?
Why am I writing this?
Is it to save myself from myself?

What is wrong with me?

40

13

. . . To search for is to create what we find. All is an unbroken wholeness, a unity that is. Poor Einstein (my hero) tried but couldn't see that. He remained part-Newtonian to the end.*

---

*A quote from Pita's latest letter during his first year at MIT, USA. My son has left me firmly behind in the Newtonian world.

14

From the top of of the Mount of Olives we gaze down across the Old City at the New City, which is stitched on to the lower edge of the luminous yellow sky and is then swallowed up by the creamy haze. Rolling down the slope in front of us is the ancient Jewish Cemetery, rows and terraces of graves.

'The Jews believe they must be buried here to await the Messiah,' I tell my father.

'The Messiah *has* come,' he reminds me. I refuse to enter that debate.

Behind us the Mount drops sharply down to barren plains and hills that flow away to the Judean Desert and the swirling haze. 'How could the Prophets have come out of that hostile womb?' he asks (more a comment than a question). His remark reminds me that I am attracted to such places and their stark solitude (which heals) and their truth that they aren't anything else but rock and ferocious sun and thirst and death.

As I resurvey our surroundings I think: the desert strips us to our basic sinews and truths, and fires us with disturbing, compulsive visions which thirst for fulfilment. That is perhaps why the desert gives birth to lean prophets of very austere and demanding gods.

What about King Farouk? Gaddafi? Khomeini?

15

Love is a four-letter word. Though I now find I can use other four-letter words freely without embarrassing myself, I still find love most difficult to let myself go on.

Why?

My father remarried early in 1954, the year after I went to boarding school in New Zealand on a government scholarship. He wrote and told me about it. (I've kept his letter.*)

. . . I have good news for you, my beloved daughter. You have a new mother. Her name is Penina. She is a very kind Christian lady who, I know, will love you as your mother (bless her) did and as I do. I did not inform you earlier because I did not want to distract you from your studies . . .

I cried as I read his letter, my tears welling up out of a feeling of betrayal, and thickened by an anger directed at my stepmother who, I imagined then, was as vicious and as devious as Cinderella's.

I dropped the letter onto my bed, changed into my running gear, sprinted out of the dormitory on to our grass athletic track and, in that grey winter afternoon, I ran round and round the track, with tears streaming down my face, my ragged breath sounding like cardboard being ripped. Ran and ran, escaping to nowhere, caught in the groove of my betrayal, the winter track without end and brittle with cold as evening lapped up my frantic shadow. Until our house mistress, Miss Kall, brought a kind blanket and wrapped it around me and led me out of the groove, the track.

For two months I didn't reply to any of his worried letters begging me for forgiveness and (at the same time) lauding my stepmother's virtues to the tropical skies. Then I wrote and pretended I was delighted about the whole ridiculous affair of his marrying (without my consent) a girl half his age who was unworthy of my mother's sacred memory.

---

*The original is in Samoan. My father was never comfortable using English with me after I became fluent in it.

I had believed up to then that his love for my mother was the one unbreakable pillar in his life (and mine). And that that was why he hadn't remarried and had brought Aunt Fusi, his eldest sister, to Apia to look after me. In that time, as far as I was aware, I was the only woman in his life.

Now there was Penina.

As scholarship students we were to visit home at the end of every three years, so I didn't see my father and stepmother until the end of 1955, two years after their marriage and twenty monthly letters from her, and though my heart warmed to her letters, I deliberately cultivated a hatred of her. Such hatred reached its excruciatingly sweet, self-righteous peak in November 1955, when he wrote and told me that *she* had given birth to a son, and he was naming him Fiapese, after my grandfather.

Aue, my carefully manufactured and pre-prepared hatred disintegrated the moment she put her arms around me at the airport and whispered, 'Welcome home, Ola.' It was a warmth and voice out of my mother's womb, drawing me out of the loneliness deepened by three years in a spartan boarding school in Papalagidom.

Within a week, she was my closest friend.

16

It is noon, the sun beats down on the back of my neck. I straighten my father's hat and caution him about sunstroke. He waves me away. (I'm wilting in the heat; he's thriving in it.)

We join the line of worshippers and tourists and cross the causeway to the entrance into the Temple Mount. Muslim security guards search my handbag and drape a cotton shawl over my bare shoulders. Outside Mecca and Medina, the Dome of the Rock and the al-Aqsa Mosque are the most sacred Muslim shrines in the world.

The heat is buzzing in my ears. I head for the shade of the splendid cypresses and pines in the Mosque's courtyard. My father sits down beside me. We listen to the priest calling the faithful to midday prayers: his message floats, like a fabulous frigate bird, across the Old City and up to the Mount of Olives. I sink more and more into my inner calm and shed my skin of worries and a mind that keeps questioning, as I listen to his chant.

'They *look* poorer,' my father drags me back to the world.

'Who?' I ask. He nods towards the faithful who are washing their hands and feet in the basins sunk into the paved courtyard. 'Poorer than who?'

'Than the Israelites. But there doesn't seem to be any tension between them.'

Later, as we enter the Dome, I tell him that the pavilion houses the rock on which Abraham nearly sacrificed Isaac, his son. 'But God stayed his fearless hand and sent a sacrificial lamb to take Isaac's place,' he completes the tale.

'It is also the rock on which the prophet Muhammad rested his feet on his mythical Night Journey,' I add. He pretends he doesn't hear.

The clay-brown Rock lies open to the Dome, surrounded by a shoulder-high wall. We move around it as if we are inspecting a caged creature. No one else is about. The air smells of decaying flowers — jasmine? I look at the Rock again. The light shimmering over it gives it the sharp frightening blackness of the huge sacrificial stone altar I'd seen in a Hawaiian heiau/temple: fearsome stage for the priests' and gods' dance, shell knife ripping open the sacrificial belly, the steaming entrails tumbling out, then the probing hand pulling out the still-pulsating heart and holding it aloft, with the blood streaming down the priest's hand and weaving round his arm and down to his glistening shoulder. Before the Rock can break into blood, I retreat from it.

Outside, I breathe easily again.

'Once they were brothers,' my father says. 'Sons of Abraham — the Arabs and Israelites.'

An Arab lies against a low wall, fast asleep, oblivious to the cruel sun, his head bent to his chest, his thin knees to his chin, his arms resting on his knees, his gnarled hands dangling down like useless farm implements, his skin and tattered clothes ingrained with grease and dirt. No one seems to notice his wretched presence.

Clutching my father's arm, I steer him away from the Arab towards the exit.

That evening, after lotu, I confess to him that the Arab keeps confronting me, demanding an interpretation of his existence in relation to Israel's (and mine), offering himself as a key to an unknown door into Israel, a door and a lock I'll never find. I read to him from Elie Wiesel:

'The Talmud relates: when the temple of Jerusalem was set on fire, the priests interrupted the sacred services, climbed on the roof and spoke to God: "We were not able to safeguard Your Dwelling, therefore we surrender to You its key." And they hurled them toward heaven. Sometimes I think that somewhere the sanctuary is still burning and that the survivors are its priests. But they are keeping the keys.'

'I did not see the Arab you've described,' he tells me. 'But who's to say he's not a survivor, a guardian of the Temple's keys?'

17

Women are not supposed to fart, not in public anyway, and if they fart in private they're supposed to ease it noiselessly, smell-lessly, out of their delicate arseholes. (Or should I say, rectums?)

My first husband, Matthew Malcolm Browne (he never was a Matt), in our two years of marriage in Upper Hutt, New Zealand, never allowed his 'leaks' (his prim description) to find their true voice, as it were. Not even in the privacy of our bedroom. And even when he sensed I knew from the loud smell that he had 'leaked', he never once indicated (to me) that he *had* leaked.

During our seventh night as husband and wife, while lying in bed reading, I forgot he was there and shattered the prim silence with a short, clear blast. He didn't bat an eyelid, to use good Kiwi English. He continued reading his thick biography of John D. Rockefeller as if he hadn't heard my trumpet blast. Sweating with shame, I too pretended I hadn't broken wind and was inhaling my foul odour. (Never again, while awake or conscious, did I break wind audibly in his hygienic presence. I can't vouch I didn't do so when I was asleep or unconscious or drunk.)

Matthew was finishing his accounting degree and working in his uncle's accounting firm. I was studying anthropology. Rockefeller was his God; Matthew was set on becoming a wealthy industrialist. (Perhaps Rockefeller too had been a 'leaker', frugal even with his expensive wind, and Matthew was merely copying him.)

Why I ever married him, I don't know, only that he was handsome and well-off and every girl in our student hall was after him and I wasn't going to let them have him. But within a month of having broken audible wind in his presence, I concluded I was married to a 'leaker in everything', and a puritanically mean leaker at that. In money, laughter, joy, sadness, sorrow, conversation, and most frustrating of all (I was a very healthy twenty-year-old at the time), was most frugal with his Thing (his description). He was, so he argued, not to be ruled by his 'passions' — meaning, in my book, he was ashamed of Thing and the inexplicable upsets, inspired by my enticing presence, Thing kept plaguing him with.

Whenever I paraded past him in the nude, he never observed me directly, honestly. My nudity upset him. I swear he never once admitted to the existence of my Thing, described in a pornographic magazine I found in his study as the Hot-Box, the Snatch.

'Don't be silly!' he once remarked when alone in our flat — admittedly we were in the kitchen — I tugged at his Thing. (He was trousered too.) When I stamped off, he called, 'There's a proper place and time for everything!' Meaning, Thinging was for our bedroom and the night-time and restricted to the boring missionary position without foreplay, during play and afterplay.

Two years of noiseless farting, once-a-week Thinging in our rented flat, and over-proper moderation in everything else was too much for my immoderately frisky self. I found myself (or, put another way, I entangled myself) in the randy arms of a portly middle-aged poet.

In public John Velvetine wore a soulful mask, the look of profound pain, which attracted hordes of motherly women.

Within a solid, sweating, pornographic week — I loved it — I was cured of Matthew. I was also cured of the poet and his hairy, unwashed, perpetually erect machismo and BO; his Dylan Thomas bluster and drunkenness.

For Mr John Velvetine — and he was loved by the critics and academics and middle-aged groupies — I was merely his first Noble Savage Cunt; he was fucking Gauguin's earth-brown maidens, Margaret Mead's free-loving Samoans, Melville's Typee, R. L. Stevenson's housemaids, and most exhilaratingly noble of all, he was 'buggering Jean Jacques Rousseau without having to use some masturbating academic's vaseline' (his proud boast).

Sunday morning. I woke gasping. His bedroom was thick with his stench. Opened my eyes and recognised Mr Poet for what he was: a short, blubbery, middle-aged man who was going bald; who, in his snoring sleep, was dribbling; who was covered with ape-like hair which was turning grey, right down to his luxuriant pubis.

YOUR PEN IS A WILT AND NEEDS NEW INK AND A GOOD WASH,' I printed on a sheet of paper (meant for his nationally acknowledged poetry).

With one quick thrust of my erect forefinger, I made a hole in the paper, reached down daintily and shoved his slack pen, as it were, through the hole, smoothed down the edges of my note over his bush, and hurried out of his flat. Forever.

A month later I read in the paper that he was marrying Dr Marian Lusman, Senior Lecturer in New Zealand Literature, and wealthy. 'Lucky bastard,' remarked one of my friends. 'He now has his own literary critic to fuck, and her money to fatten on without having to work!'

I will remember him for the large brown mole, like a blob of rat shit, on the bottom of his left testicle. He displayed it to me proudly like one of his poems — and there were six volumes of them in the town library — but I found them full of empty wind and bluster and farm girls with buttery thighs and treasures rich with honey.

John Velvetine, unlike Matthew Malcolm Browne, was not a leaker. He gave profusely, loudly, dramatically, publicly, but aue, his poetry was bluster without substance.

Since Matthew and John (this is sounding like the New Testament), I've tried to live by farting honestly and accepting all my body odours, but now, even when I'm alone at home, I always (unconsciously) look east, west, south, north, up and down before farting. Immediately afterwards, I drown my foul smell with Mountain Dew aerosol spray.

I continue to fear my own smell. I am always deodorised expensively.

18

It's been only three days and I'm craving for Carl. Even on spiritual quests, my flesh (so to speak biblically) trips me up sooner or later.

'You've got a deliciously filthy mind.'
 'That's because I was born out of Death.'
 'You taste deliciously hot and frantic.'
 'Like melted cheese or rock cod?'
 'No, like the rich juice of the Angel of Death.'
 '*You've* got the filthy mind!'
 'Are we into metaphysics now, are we?'
 'No, just keep eating. It's delicious.'

Mental masturbation is certainly no substitute for actual masturbation.
 Actual masturbation is certainly no substitute for a real fuck (some of the time, that is, because a lot of fucks ain't worth it).
 For me that's the reality right now.
 Poor Pita, he's always trying to help me rise above myself.
 Wonder if Einstein was a good lover? Was he able to raise it, in his old age, beyond Relativity?

19

'... Since its creation, Israel has been on a military footing, but this hasn't forced the Israelis to establish a one-party state, declare martial law or impose censorship. The brutal rule of the Camps has become an eternal memory; any suppression of individual rights would be a return to the Camps. Israel refuses to do without democracy, yet, as a victor and conqueror, it now finds itself with over a million Arabs under its control. A moral dilemma: Israel does not want to rule an unwilling minority, but to protect itself it *has* to. Some Israelis are also demanding the expulsion of the Arabs from all occupied lands. "Good government is no substitute for self-government," an Israeli academic told us at lunch this week. "But in the war situation we're in, how can we give our Arab minority self-government without destroying our nation?"*

'... The Israelis may be caught in a moral dilemma, but what about the poor Palestinians?'†

---

*An extract from a letter Ola sent Pita from Israel.
†Pita's reply.

20

For your five years at boarding school you woke almost every morning to Gill exercising against Mount Taranaki framed in the window above your beds. Lean, angular, flat-chested ('One Christmas Santa'll bring me a neat pair,' she used to joke), with bony knees and elbows and long thin fingers and toes. She reminded you, as she stretched (tippy-tippy-toes) and bent (low-low-low), and swivelled (to an imaginary hula hoop), of a kotuku warming up for the arduous flight to the snow-capped summit of Taranaki, already aglow with the early morning light.

Gillian Prudence Smythe, only daughter of a Taihape farmer, with three older brothers she talked about incessantly. She was the one with the brains, they said, to become the scientist her father had wanted to be but couldn't, because of the Depression. Her talents and interests coincided with her father's wishes, so there was no conflict there. But she rarely mentioned her mother. At times when Gill talked of her family and 'the farm', you wished she'd invite you home for the school holidays, but she never did. Perhaps it didn't occur to her to ask you.

By the time you were in the sixth form, Gill was envied and admired by almost every student for her scholastic successes (they came easily), her understanding (she always backed the underdog), and her refusal to be anyone else but Gill. In her final school report your Principal, 'Melodious Mary' (in her birth certificate, Mary Marjorie Menzies), wrote that 'Nothing is going to deter Gillian from becoming an outstanding scientist, and a great credit to her school.' By that time Gill had become the sister you never had, the only Papalagi you'd allowed into your trust. And it began the hour you first met, on 21 January 1953, at the front door of your House, when Miss Willersey instructed her to show you and your hefty suitcase to your dormitory, bed and locker, and then to show you around the school and 'take good care of you'. This she did for five years.

You both enrolled at Victoria University, and stayed at Victoria House. Gill was voted House President, and she appointed you a House Committee member. Then you committed that disastrous error of marrying Matthew. Gill had argued against it (your father didn't know about it), but you still saw her frequently, especially when you were unhappy with Matthew. When you finally walked out on Matthew — Gill and your friends were jubilant (your father didn't know about it) — you flatted with Gill and two other women until you finished your BA (with very indifferent grades) and returned to Samoa, while Gill did her Masters (with First Class Honours) and started a PhD in molecular biology, something to do with the process of ageing.

You correspond regularly; she wrote and casually mentioned she was 'having a relationship' with a Julian Brakes. No further mention of him but she was thinking of breaking it off as she was badly behind in her research. You thought nothing of it until she wrote, just before the end of the university year, inviting you to their wedding on 3 December. It was to be a 'registry office job', she described it, and you knew she'd relented to a shotgun wedding so typical of your pre-Pill, pre-*Joy of Sex*, pre-Greer generation, and you wept for her and the mean ending to her enormous promise and courage. You'd expected her, the kotuku, to soar free of your society's destructive hypocrisies.

'Don't, please don't, Gill!' you wrote back. She rang you, in Samoa. At first she tried her usual cheery stoicism, but when you asked bluntly if she was pregnant, she exploded into a sobbing made more haunting by the echo and static of the long-distance line. 'Oh, Gill, Gill, Gill!' you cried back.

You suggested adoption — you'd adopt. She talked of duty to the unborn child, the responsibility of providing it with a good mother and a good home. You'd give it a good home, you countered. But it would be unfair on you, she argued. 'Do you love Julian?' you asked. Loud silence. The static answered for her. 'Do you *love* him?' you repeated. She talked of her father wanting her to marry and give the baby a name, a home. 'It'll be all right, Ola. I'll learn to bring up a loving family. I'll be a good mother,' she recited. 'What about an abortion?' You let her have it. 'No! Ola, I never dreamt you would ever think of that!' Loud sobbing. You didn't apologise or withdraw your suggestion, although abortions were still illegal, performed mainly by grubby backstreet butchers and therefore dangerous. It wasn't your life and future to be defiant with, either. Like Gill, you were still mired in the morality of the times, which was not far removed from a laced-up Queen Victoria (and the Samoan belief of placing the good name of your aiga above all else, including individual happiness), so you agreed and wept with her for the end of the clear, vivid view of Taranaki and the kotuku exercising for her bold flight to search the snows for a cure to our ageing and dying.

You didn't meet for about ten years but you corresponded regularly. Her lengthy letters became full of Shona Ola, George Monroe, and Karin Farou, the children she had in that time, as her family prospered and shifted to Remuera, suburb of the rich, overlooking Waitemata Harbour.

Her children were her life, that was obvious from her letters, which described every detail of their growing-up: breastfeeding's merits, weaning, first teeth, colds, first potty successes, accidents and illnesses, fights, first swear words, then kindy. The portraitures acquired definite personalities over the years. She didn't say much about herself directly. You had to discern her through what she said about the children. Also little about her community and country, not even the weather unless it had affected the children. She might have been living with and for her children on a planet without other people or geography or seasons. But you knew that when Gill devoted herself to something she loved, she did so almost to the exclusion of everything else.

You came to know her children far better than the children in your aiga except Pita, who was about Shona's age, and who you populated your Gill letters with, from his first 'brilliant scream' on confronting our hostile air, to his first 'brilliant' breast-suck, his precocious but 'brilliant' behaviour at kindy, and so on down the 'brilliant' unfolding of his mind, body, soul, personality, but even more fascinating, his 'brilliant' life in Sapepe with his wise great-grandfather, Lagona Fiapese, 'a great chief of our clan'. Not once did you feel you were boasting, turning your precious son into myth. Not once did you think Gill was doing the same with her precious heirs.

Mark Stripter, an American Peace Corps volunteer, came to teach mathematics at Samoa College and, more and more, found his way into your Gill letters as you allowed yourself to 'like' him (Pita liked him too), then to be 'fond' of him, then to 'love' him, then to marry him and find out, quietly because he disliked talking about it, that his maternal great-grandfather had amassed a fortune selling used cars and real estate, and later playing the futures market (you'd never understand futures); a fortune which Mark's mother, his only heir, tried to escape by being a social worker in the poorest districts of Chicago, then enlisting, through marriage, her penniless lawyer who was defending, free of charge, black activists in the Civil Rights movement, to help her evade her inherited wealth by buying a small unprofitable dairy farm in the nowhere middle of Iowa and keeping it unprofitable through their amateur efforts as farmers.

Mark worked his way through university and got a degree in agriculture, though he loved American literature, and, for about three years afterwards, helped his parents fail at farming. Vietnam erupted and the draft started killing a generation of Americans. Encouraged by his pacifist parents, he escaped to Canada, moving from one remote settlement to another until the end of the disastrous war saved him from a successful waiter's job in technicolour, picture-postcard Banff in the Rockies.

He returned to continue succeeding in keeping their farm unprofitable and spartan enough punishment for the fortune they'd inherited. Both his parents were still strong, but he could see them ageing quickly from the hard manual labour, the cold winters without central heating, a frugal diet, and a retreat from modern medicine and doctors.

'Why don't you give it away?' he suggested to them one particularly cold night.

'But it's our penance,' his mother replied.

'Punishment for what?' he asked.

She looked at his father. 'For inheriting it, and through it, our country's misuse and abuse of power, and for plundering our planet without conscience, so that we Americans can consume and consume and waste!' he said.

That night, as he lay listening to the sad howling of the wind, he decided his parents' form of penance was an endless, meaningless masochism — it helped no one, least of all the exploited of the earth. Grandpa's Piles (his mother's description) were still increasing in size and therefore in power and influence, which, if directed with conscience, would benefit the poor, especially in the Third and Fourth Worlds. (He'd read Mimme, Fanon, Mao, Ho Chi Minh, Ayn Rand, Gandhi, and a little bit of Galbraith and Marx.)

He needed time to experience the condition of the exploited and then devise a plan to help them using Grandpa's Piles. So he joined the Peace Corps, knowing, ironically well, that it *was* Jack Kennedy's painless cure (if only temporary) for the white middle-class guilt about consuming (and wasting) most of the world's resources.

Gill, Shona and George were at Auckland Airport to greet you at the start of your Christmas holidays and your first visit to New Zealand since you'd left university.

Over the years Gill had sent photos of herself and her family and you'd noticed her angularity rounding out into smoother, fuller curves, but you didn't expect the bulky woman with streaks of grey breaking through the brunette rinse, and the subdued manner so different from that of the kotuku. You hesitated for a moment. The woman smiled and she became Gill and you rushed into each other's arms, held tightly, and when Shona and George were introduced, you hugged them and cried some more and didn't give a stuff about the crowd watching you in the terminal.

You remembered Mark and introduced him.

'Neat car,' you remarked when you saw the Jaguar. 'A real beaut!' Gill looked awkward about it.

'Dad's got a Mercedes,' George said. Gill unlocked the boot, Mark put your luggage in it.

'Really up from our starving student days,' you said. Gill laughed softly. Mark held your arm. You got into the front seat while he got into the back with the children.

Their home was on the most prominent hill in the street. It was the plushest mansion (your only description for it) in a display row of mansions. It had been remodelled inside, and renovated on the outside to preserve its Georgian façade, with one noticeable innovation, the glittering expanse of black-tinted windows around the top storey overlooking the wide sweep of the Waitemata Harbour.

You parked beside the silver-blue Mercedes in the three-car garage under the house. You got out. The tiled floor sloped down to a wide lawn and a swimming pool, with bright beach umbrellas, wooden decks and a bar under a sheltering verandah. Behind those, on narrow terraces, were beds of roses, all neatly trimmed. For a moment you couldn't fit the gangly austere Gill of your youth into that expensive nest. She was looking at you. 'This is very beautiful,' you said.

'You like it, *really*?' she asked. At school she wanted your opinion on anything she had doubts about.

'Of course, silly.'

As you went up the circular staircase to the first floor you put your arm around her. 'Mum planned the whole house, everything,' said Shona.

'And supervised the building of it,' George said. 'Dad's not interested in such things.' You and Gill laughed.

Mark just stood in the middle of the guest sitting room as Gill and the children showed you through the rest of the guest quarters. 'Super!' you kept exclaiming.

Double-sized bedroom with white shag-pile carpet, massive bed with silk covering, two original landscape paintings on the walls. Adjoining bathroom with sunken bath and separate shower and wool-covered toilet seat and blue tiled floor islanded with thick fur rugs. Then back into the sitting room to the fridge full of beer (you'd told Gill in a letter that Mark drank beer) and soft drinks and fruit, the TV, the plush velvet-covered furniture, two more originals on the walls, and the wooden coffee table that glistened like marble, supporting a large bronze vase full of fresh red roses, which you smelled and sighed, 'Beautiful.'

'Welcome to our home,' Gill said.

'Yes, Auntie,' sang Shona. George bit his lower lip and looked at the floor. Mark reached out and held your hand.

Gill and the children retreated after telling you to unpack and then come out to meet Julian and Karin, who would by then be back from tennis.

Mark followed you into the bedroom, sat on the bed and gazed out at the burning sky aswirl with rivers of white cloud, while you unpacked the large duffel bag which had survived his Canadian exile. He'd refused to buy a suitcase for your trip.

'What do you think?' you asked.

'It's okay if you like this type of comfort.'

'Darling, remember we're on our first holiday.' (I'm glad to be away from our scungy flat!) 'Let's revel in the abundant waste and comfort and, if there's any decadence, I'll have a bit of that too.' As you talked, you piled his meagre 'wardrobe' onto the bed. 'You've been too long in that log cabin with your ascetic parents, pursuing the Puritan ethic. Be Polynesian — yes, be the stereotyped Polynesian — and enjoy tons of wine, song, and me. Grandpa's Piles can afford it! And look at this lot!' You held up his clothes.

'What's wrong with them?'

You lobbed his two pairs of faded jeans at him, his three faded shirts, his four faded T-shirts (two holey), his four pairs of ragged underpants, his worn-out running socks, his precarious pair of brown leather boots (his only footwear apart from the jandals he was wearing), his stained jacket and jersey, and his two lavalava, his only new clothes. 'Well, just look how awful they are!' you said. 'Tomorrow we'll buy you a new wardrobe.'

'No!' he whimpered. 'I like my old clothes. I like who I am.'

'Darling, I love who you are too.' You moved over and, putting your arms around him from behind, kissed his neck. 'Mark, buying new clothes and enjoying a few luxuries for a while won't change you into a rabid consumer; it won't corrupt you.'

'Are you sure?'

'Yes,' you whispered. He reached up and ran his hands through your hair. 'We could always shift somewhere else, somewhere that's as basic, as self-denying and scungy as our flat.'

'No,' he laughed, pulling your hair. 'Besides, you want to be with Gill and her kids. She's a very nervy lady but I like her.' He kissed you then.

You made love lingeringly. Afterwards you showered while he shaved — unusual for him. It was usual though for him to dress later in a lavalava and T-shirt, which you didn't want him to wear but didn't tell him, so, to make him less conspicuous, you dressed in a lavalava and T-shirt too.

You were correct about being conspicuous as soon as you entered the main lounge, with its high ceiling and walls that curved around to the tinted windows and sliding doors that opened to a spacious balcony and the sky towering above the harbour and Rangitoto Island.

Gill was busy at the bar in the far corner. You walked towards her. The carpet felt like air brushing against the soles of your feet. Mark held your hand.

The large room seemed intimate because of the way it was arranged, with movable carved screens as dividers and the spaces between furnished with different matching sets of furniture and art. You imagined their family spending different evenings in those different spaces.

Gill was perfectly made-up, and wore jewellery and a diaphanous white dress. 'Come, come!' she called. 'Just in time, I'm having my first (or is it second?) drink. What would you like?' You ordered a vodka-tonic. Mark ordered a beer. Gill's nervousness was gone; there was a healthy flush to her face. 'Cheers!' she said. You all drank. 'Julian's getting changed. Should be here in a minute.' She drank again, sighed, and said, 'It's really good to have you here.'

Soon you were filling in details about your lives and those of your mutual acquaintances. The kotuku was alive under that matronly respectability, as you laughed, talked, drank and forgot Mark, who drifted around the room inspecting the paintings, pottery and other art, and then went out onto the balcony.

'Here's Julian,' Gill said. 'About time!' she called to the short, trim man without much hair who was bouncing towards you, in his light grey suit, red-striped tie, white shirt and horn-rimmed spectacles that blurred his eyes slightly.

'You must be Owlar,' he greeted you.

'*Ola*,' Gill corrected him. You shook his correct hand.

'Means Life, doesn't it?' he laughed.

'Yes, and lots of it!' You all laughed at that.

'I'm no good at pronouncing Polynesian names, so may I call you Life?' he asked.

'Yes, if that's what you want to call me.'

'Your drink.' Gill placed a glass of tonic and ice on the bar in front of Julian. 'Julian doesn't drink liquor; it's bad for his ulcer.'

'Gillian tells me you're excellent at sports,' he said.

You couldn't help it. 'Yes, we Polynesians *are* great at sports. I used to be good. Now I'm into alcohol and cultivating fat.'

'But you're not fat!' Gill protested. 'And you still run.'

'Yeah, I try to keep up with Mark; he's an addict.'

'Speaking of the devil, here he is,' said Gill.

'I'm the addict but I can't beat Ola when we race,' said Mark. You introduced him to Julian.

'You're a volunteer, Mr Stripter?' asked Julian.

Mark nodded. 'I'm trying to find myself through teaching lousy students.'

He meant it as a joke but Julian said, 'That's very interesting.'

Mark accepted another beer from Gill and asked about the art in the room.

'All Gillian's choices. This room and just about everything in it and the way the things are arranged is like living in Gillian's imagination — I think that's how Janet Frame, Gillian's favourite novelist, would describe it. She's a very depressing writer, not that I read much fiction.'

You avoided looking at Gill. 'There are absolutely no imports in this room. Gillian has no — what do you Americans call it?'

'Hangups,' you rescued him.

'Yes, no hangups about the value of local art, products, and being a fair dinkum Kiwi. I tend to be like the other colonised Kiwis who still value imported stuff more. Frankly I don't give a stuff about being of the new rich and ignorant about art!' He stopped and sipped his drink. 'Anyway,' he continued, 'the furniture is handmade by Kiwi craftsmen, so is the pottery. The paintings are by jokers who Gillian claims are the first genuine New Zealand artists. Me, I don't know who's genuine; artists give me the creeps sometimes. Jokers like Toss Woollaston, Colin McCahon, Frances Hodgkins, and I forget who else. Gillian's also collected — and I hope they turn out to be worth the money I've spent on them — a lot of stuff by a new generation of Maori artists: Arnold Wilson, Matchitt, I think, Cliff Whiting, Ralph — I can never pronounce that joker's surname . . .'

'Ralph *Hotere*,' Gill saved him.

'Yeah. And Selwyn Muru, Buck Nin, and many other jokers with unpronounceable names . . .'

'Darling, why don't you take Mark and show him the paintings?' Gill interrupted him.

'Why not?' he said. 'You Americans may learn a little bit about us Kiwis from our art.'

Gill looked at you. 'I'm sorry about that,' she said.

'About what?'

'His remarks about the Maori artists and his not wanting to call you Ola.'

'I like him.'

'Ola, please don't be *nice* to me in your usual, polite Samoan way. You did it at school and varsity sometimes, even when I wanted you to scream at those condescending, patronising Pakeha racists! For this week, Ola, be kind to me, my children and my bigoted husband, and tell me — if not them — the truth about how you feel about whatever happens.' She started to mix another drink for you. 'Nobody apart from my children tells me the truth now. And I can tell that my kids, as they get older, are *pretending* with me. I don't even tell myself the truth. It's getting harder and harder.' She handed you your drink. You clasped her hand. She gripped it. 'Look at me, Ola, just look at the mess that I am!'

'I won't pretend or lie to you. We're sisters, remember?'

She nodded. 'Yes, I need that. Tomorrow I'm taking the kids to stay with Julian's mother so we can spend time together, uninterrupted.'

'Mum?' someone said from behind you. You turned.

'Karin, this is your Aunt Ola,' Gill introduced you.

'And in a beaut lavalava too!' you exclaimed. You bent down and kissed her on the cheek. No shy withdrawal.

'She saw a photo of you and Pita in lavalava and wanted one, so I made her a couple.'

'Good on ya, mate.' You hugged Karin. She was small for her age. On her T-shirt was the slogan *Bruce Lee Loves Me*.

'Dad didn't want me to wear my la-la-lavalava to meet you because you're guests,' she whispered.

'You look beautiful in it,' you praised her.

Gill pointed out the scratches, grazes and bruises on Karin's elbows and knees. 'I fall over a lot — you know that, Mum,' Karin justified her condition. She climbed up onto the next bar stool and asked for an orange juice 'and no ice'.

'Sure you don't want a Coke?' you tested her.

She shook her head and said, 'Bad for your health.'

You ruffled her hair and said, 'Where are you comin' from, mate? Are you for real?'

'Of course I am!' she insisted. 'I'm learning kung fu too — even though Dad says it's not for girls. And one day, Ola, I'm going to be a black belt like Bruce Lee!'

Hugging her again you laughed with Gill. 'See Mark over there?' you said to Karin. She nodded. 'He's hopeless at kung fu, perhaps you can teach him a few moves while we're here so he can defend himself against your aunt. Okay?'

'Right, but only if he wants to.'

As usual you woke at 5.30 a.m., dropped Mark's T-shirt onto his face to wake him and, in a few minutes, you were both out on the deserted road, heading down to the harbour and around to Mission Bay and the rising sun and heat.

Gill was in a bad way and needed your help, you said to Mark as you got into your stride. Would he mind being neglected for a week? He didn't object. He'd go to the museum and study the Polynesian artifacts there. Did he mind Julian? you then asked. A bit of a pain in the arse, he said. Julian wanted to take him golfing, yachting and playing tennis, you revealed. Shit, man, did he have to? No, but Julian, who never took holidays, was taking the week off just to show him around, you explained. He ran in silence for a while and then said he hoped Julian's friends weren't pretentious pricks like Julian.

You ran for almost two hours.

To prepare him for Julian (and Julian's circle), you got Gill to take you and the reluctant Mark to the shops where Julian bought his clothes. With

60

Gill around, poor Mark had to pretend he was enjoying your fussing over him as he tried on endless clothes.

Later, alone in your room, while you put his new clothes away he complained, 'Ola, don't you ever put me through that bullshit again. Okay?' You nodded. 'Those pretentious shop assistants! And the prices! Fucking daylight robbery!' You told him he could afford them, but he still insisted they'd been conned. And because they'd been in jeans the shop assistants had turned their long noses up at them, he argued. 'I can buy all the bastards and their awful shops!' he said. 'What am I saying?' he exclaimed. You told him he had every right to be vindictive and buy the pricks if he wanted to. He argued that Julian and his kind were changing him already.

So while you and Gill explored Auckland, shopped, drank and talked and drank some more, Julian immersed Mark in his tennis club, his golf club and his yacht club. Every night you asked Mark how his day had gone. 'Great! Just great!' he said. But you knew he was lying.

'. . . And your brothers?' you asked Gill, as you lay on sun chairs on the balcony, your sunglasses blocking out the vicious glare of the sun.

'John's married with two kids. Got a large orchard near Tauranga. Jeff lives with his Aussie wife, Martha, in Sydney; drives his own Road Warrior. Nick's in Gisborne with his third wife. He's been bankrupt goodness knows how many times. This time he's trying to make money out of freezing eels and exporting them.'

You recalled her romantic descriptions of their farm and asked her about it. 'Sold it,' she said. 'After Dad died.' You asked when that was. 'A year or so after Julian and I got married. Another drink?' She hurried off to refill your glasses.

For a long while you sipped your drinks. The sun burnt at your skins.

'Why don't you ask me?' she started.

'About what?'

'About my mother.'

'You've never said anything about her.'

'Was it that obvious?'

'Yeah. It was always your dad and your brothers.'

You waited. 'Mum was just an ordinary woman. Reticent, inconspicuous, the typical farmer's wife. But very loving. And she was keen on me doing well at school.' She waited for your response but you refused to save her from the silence. Just when you felt her ready to reveal her mother's truths, Julian and Mark entered and demanded cold drinks.

You waited nearly a week. She'd discuss everything else then veer towards her mother and, just when you expected her revelations, she'd veer off again into another gin and lemonade.

You were to leave on Monday morning for your two-week tour of the

North Island. On Sunday night they invited a large group of their friends to meet you.

'Are you a Maori?' the deep round voice challenged you. You turned. (Gill wasn't in sight.) 'Name's Tom, Tom Melson,' the slim man said.

'Ola,' you introduced yourself. With dyed hair and a clipped moustache, he looked like an inferior version of Errol Flynn.

He shook his glass in front of you to indicate it was empty. You just looked at him, then at his extended glass, and back at him. 'Ah, one of our angry ones,' he grinned. He waved and moved off.

You joined Gill and a group of women who wanted to know about your work as a teacher in Samoa. You answered their questions in detail, patiently.

You recognised the voice as soon as it broke above the general noise of the party. 'I don't care who hears me!' Melson was telling someone near the centre of the room. 'The trouble with this bloody country, which our English ancestors civilised, is that the natives are getting uppity again!' Your group fell silent. That silence spread through the room. Only a few people kept talking. 'Land rights, eh! That's what they're after.' You couldn't see Julian anywhere. 'We won the land fair and square. They never used it anyway. They didn't, and still don't know how to get value out of the land . . . They're buggering up one of my hotel developments up north . . .' Julian was pushing his way into the room. Many of the guests started talking again. '. . . And one of them is here tonight. I don't know what Remuera is coming to!' Gill was out of your reach as she rushed through the crowd.

Whackkk! The sound of Gill's slap was like a rifle shot, long, hollow, final. You hurried towards its target. 'Get out of my house!' Gill said to Melson, who was rubbing the side of his face. Julian put his arms around her. She pushed him away. 'I want this piece of trash out of my house!' she ordered him. Julian moved towards Melson.

'Don't you touch me!' Melson threatened, straightening his clothes. 'Needless to say, I'm not going to set foot in this — this *house* again!'

You got Gill and took her out to Mark on the balcony. 'I'm sorry, Ola,' she said.

The stars were silver spots of ice in the curving dome of the sky that stretched to the limits of your yearning and beyond.

During your travels around the North Island in the following two weeks, with the luxurious company caravan Julian insisted you use, you sometimes pondered the cause of Gill's guilt — yes, guilt you decided — and what it had done (and was doing) to her and her family.

*

You were sunbathing on the balcony. Mark, Julian and the children were swimming in the pool below.

'*I am Maori.*' The whisper seemed to have come out of the sky. You paused. Then continued rubbing suntan lotion into Gill's back.

'How's that?'

'Thank you,' she said and lay back on the sunchair and put on her sunglasses.

'You've got a great tan. And you've lost a lot of weight. What's happening here, eh? Been training?'

She shook her head. 'Spent about a week, while you were away, drying out.' When she didn't explain further, you asked if she was all right. 'Yes, I check in periodically to lose a few pounds and work a few depressions out of my head.'

'How periodically?'

'Oh, once a year, sometimes twice.'

'For how long?'

'Usually a week. One time, it was two weeks.'

You had to ask. 'What kind of clinic?' She was lying perfectly still, arms by her side, her dark tan sucking in the heat, her sunglasses pointing darkly up into the navel of the heavens.

'Psychiatric and for drying out the alcohol. It's voluntary. Very discreet. Everyone in my circle knows about it because many of them use it. None of them will admit to its existence, though. This is the first time I've admitted it to someone else — and to myself.' She was smiling, waiting for a continuation of your questioning. 'Ola, you're still the naive coconut you were at school and varsity!' She started laughing. 'The world's full of such clinics, Ola. In fact, it's one big overcrowded clinic with overworked doctors, all kinds of them, peddling magic remedies and potions and pills guaranteed to cure our pain — at least for a time. I'm just one of the millions of over-pampered, over-consuming, unhappy housewives who keep Valium, Tagamets, alcohol and Disprin the best-selling drugs in that clinic. And periodically, we need a rest from those cures and our husbands and demanding children and the skeletons in the stuffed cupboards of our heads. I just check myself into our little clinic. It's a very comfortable hotel, really, and Doctor Martin Balsman — yeah, that's his real name — and his sensitive staff *console* us with magic drugs that keep me on a high that's free of nightmares, husbands, children, dishes and watching your life being flushed down the plughole, and guilt, especially that.' She stopped. 'This time, I checked in but refused the dope. I wanted, but was shit-scared, to confront my skeletons clearly, head-on. Having you here gave me the courage. It was the most frightening, yet cleansing thing I've ever survived.' She sat up and hugged her knees to her chin.

Then she revealed the source of her pain. The laughter and splashing from the pool kept punctuating her lucid lament as it spread, like a long healing incantation. You found yourself holding her, your face nestled in the hollow of her neck, her arm wrapped around your shoulders. As her tears washed down her face onto your cheek, your head sang: *Gill, oh Gill, Gill.*

I am Maori, I'm part-Maori, my mother was Maori, therefore I *am* Maori.

Roimata Janet Aorangi was my mother's name. I found out from her birth certificate, which she kept hidden in the bottom drawer in her bedroom. I was about ten at the time. Everyone, including my father, called her Jan. Much easier to pronounce, to use to forget she was Maori. And she wanted to be called Jan. She was 'originally from Ahipara, up north, near Kaitaia' and refused any more details when I asked her. A very backward place, she said, best forgotten. To this day that's all I know about Mum's people: Ahipara, up north, near Kaitaia.

She was fluent in Maori. I discovered that when she took me to town one day and I heard her talk Maori to an old man by the post office. 'What did you say?' I asked her as we walked away from him. 'He wanted to find out where the station was,' she replied. 'Will you teach me Maori, eh, Mum?' I pleaded in the car on our way home. 'It won't get you anywhere,' she said. 'Please, Mum?' She just stared at the road ahead winding over the hills.

It was best to be Pakeha in a Pakeha world, she kept emphasising to me and my brothers. And because her life was mainly that of silence and being busy with her chores, that statement was a large philosophical guide burnt large into our consciences. And one which Dad bound us tightly with, though he never discouraged us from finding out, from Mum, about our 'other side'. We learnt early that in our house and in our lives we were *not* Maori or to *be* Maori.

Mum and Dad, but more Dad because he did most of the talking, extolled the virtues of self-reliance, hard work, thrift, honesty, the Pakeha way. Pioneer values, which Dad claimed had made this country what it was. 'What was it?' I asked one day. 'You'll find out when you're old enough, girl,' he snapped.

For Mum and Dad and my brothers, life was hard on the farm. Up at 4.30 a.m., winter or summer, work, work, work and more work for small returns, day in, day out. Frugal meals, a night out at the pub, the occasional dance. Skimp and save. A tough life, but in my present wealth I miss the sheer honesty of its severity, walking the thin edge between frugal meals and having no meals. It had improved by the time I was old enough to be out in the paddocks helping.

None of us kids *looked* Maori. But I sensed as we grew up that our parents were always on the alert for any signs of Maoriness. For instance, Jeff's hair darkened and became wavier, so Dad gave him crewcuts. John started using the expression 'youse jokers', and Mum banned it from our vocabulary. Mick, as a joke, used soot to paint a moko on his face. Mum nearly had a fit when she saw it. Dad got him to wash it off.

Ours was a country school. About forty kids at any one time. When I started there, there were four Maori kids, the Ponoas, who we referred to as the Poor-Noahs because they wore patched clothes, brought no lunches, couldn't afford shoes, and were always being told off by Mrs Sheffield for not doing their homework. We, that's John, Jeff, Mick and I, even joined the Pakeha kids when they made fun of them.

But the truth sometimes wins out. One cold playtime John, who was showing off to his friends, pushed Pat Ponoa and Pat grazed his knee on the asphalt. (I can see the bleeding wound now and the tears in Pat's eyes, and I ask for his forgiveness.) 'That'll fix you, hori!' John said.

'*And what are you and your family?*' Pat confronted us. I've carried that laceration since then. Deservedly so.

After that revelation, we kept away from both the Maoris and the Pakehas at school. I admit and accept that we even *resented* our mother for being the cause of our self-imposed isolation at school and for what we've had to hide all our lives. We became the feared Smythe quartet; no kid dared take us on. We retaliated together, swiftly and without forgiveness. Mrs Sheffield complained to Dad after we'd worked over Jimmy Mufflaw, son of the wealthiest farmer in the area. Dad promised to punish us but then congratulated us with, 'Good on ya. Don't ya ever show ya're scared of those Mufflaws, they're bloodsuckers!' For me that was Dad's saving grace, his sense of justice, of sticking up for the underdog and the other joker. A trait now peddled nationally and worldwide as our country's great virtue, though we still stomp on the Maoris and send our All Blacks to South Africa to play a simple game of rugby while the blacks die in the streets and prisons.

John, Jeff and Mick continued their proud isolation at high school, especially after Mick tried to break out of it by befriending Hemi Wharekura and bringing him home one afternoon, only to be told by Dad, after Hemi had gone, that it was best if Hemi stayed with *his* friends.

They hated school. It had much to do with having to survive in isolation, and they left, one after the other, when they turned fifteen. They were happier on the farm, where they were isolated from other people. Just like Mum, work and work as if they were trying to fill the silence with something solid, real, permanent.

They agreed to help Dad send me to boarding school. I was twelve and finishing Form One. I didn't want to go but Mum kept on at me.

'Make something of yourself. You've got the brains, girl. Do it for us who don't have the intelligence. Prove you're better than our uppity neighbours.' I noticed that she was thinner, more hunched up. *'Do it for me, Gill,'* she whispered. That plea keeps circling and circling and circling in my head. Why? Why did she want me to be better? For her sake? To make up for being Maori? To become Pakeha so as to survive the Pakeha world?

Two months into my first year — the year before you came, Ola — Mum wrote in her weekly letter that she had to go to Auckland Hospital for a check-up. Nothing to worry about, she wrote. I thought nothing about it until she wrote from the hospital a fortnight later saying she had to stay there for a few weeks; just a simple something wrong with her left thigh. I'm now going to offer a stereotype, Ola, so forgive me. Like most Polynesians, my mother's pain threshold was far higher than ours, the rest of the family. At school I admired your refusal to give in to physical pain, Ola. I wrote back to her, my usual boring letter about school, and forgot to mention her illness.

The next Sunday, and I can remember there was a snowfall on Taranaki (I refuse now to call it Mount Egmont), my father arrived unexpectedly at school and got permission for me to accompany him to Auckland to see Mum. In the car, on that long trip, he kept reassuring me that Mum was fine, only a swelling in her thigh but the swelling was going down. I maintained my silence, a posture I now recognise as Mum's when she was worried, and kept wishing I didn't have to see her and what I dreaded was wrong with her.

But, like every journey towards suffering, we have to confront it sooner or later. Shit, I'm sounding like Julian.

White curtains divided her from the rest of the ward. They were like something alive, the curtains. Dad pushed one aside. Bent down and kissed her. They rarely showed affection for each other in public. 'Gill's here,' he whispered. I stepped into the creature, the curtains, and her thin arms were open, wide, and I went into them, into the warmth that I'd been missing since I left for school, into her love and grief, which started welling up from the pit of her centre and, as she hugged me tighter, found a high-pitched voice, a quavering, in her throat and the long cleansing of the lament in her mouth burrowing for my warmth, the life in me that she didn't want to be parted from. 'Mum, Mum, it's okay.' I tried easing her sorrow. 'I'm here. I won't go away.' But I now know I'd left her the hour she'd denied me the language of the land. 'Stop, Mum, they'll all hear!' I cautioned her. 'Sorry,' she said, 'sorry.' She lay back on her pillows. I handed her my handkerchief and she dried her eyes with it. God, I was a monster. I was *ashamed* of her, of her lamenting like a Maori — what am I saying? She *was* Maori. I was ashamed — frightened of what the other patients would think of her being a Maori. Ola, what did I do to her?

What did they do to me? Last week in the clinic I wept: begged for her forgiveness.

Ola, what is a country, a society, a family, that turns you into despising your mother because of her colour, race? How could she have loved a man who was ashamed of the Maori side of her, who turned her into a Pakeha, an imitation of one, and who turned us, his children, into self-haters, exiled in our own skins? How could she have loved him? She was so patient with him, so caring, so tolerant. For over a hundred years now, her people have tolerated us and our crimes upon them: racism, large-scale theft, murder, rape, an attempt to destroy their way of life, assimilate them.

Mum died at 5.15 a.m. on Monday, 27 October 1952. I will never forget that time, that date.

Dad wanted her buried in Auckland but my brothers insisted on bringing her home. She's buried in the Taihape cemetery. It's not her real home among her people, but it is home. I've not visited her grave since I started university.

Every time I see or read about a Maori tangi I remember her miserly, lonely funeral. Just Dad and us and two neighbours and Reverend Johns. So miserable and undeserving of her.

In my nights at the clinic I rolled her name, Roimata Aorangi, over and over again over my tongue. Then around my mouth, sucking at the sweet beauty of it, and then swallowing it to illuminate my whole being with the strength of her that is the Land, the Earth. *Roimata Aorangi, my mother, I am Maori, forgive me.*

I haven't said much about my father, have I? And I won't. He deserves no history from me. He is the Pakeha New Zealand that continues to run away from its true history, that is rooted in blood and piracy and plunder and racism. Do you know how Dad finally persuaded me to marry Julian? He said, 'Think of what an illegitimate child would do to your mother's memory and her good name.' Meaning Pakehas would say I was still a Maori like my mother. Once a Maori, always a Maori! I fell for it. After all, I *was* a Pakeha.

Now I've worked out what I must do, to put back into myself and my children that side which my parents left out deliberately. I have to find her. I'm scared of what might happen out there. After all these years of living a lie comfortably, I may not have the courage to go the whole way, but I've got to find out. It may be too late for me but it's not too late for my kids.

Julian? He doesn't know yet. I'll have to find a way to persuade him to help me and our children. If he refuses to, I'll leave him behind. He'll fight for the kids. But I won't give in.

We married because of Shona. We're comfortable with each other most of the time. We don't demand too much of each other. He's got his business, 'the boys', power, and he needs his pretension — he's from poor, working-class roots and wants to hide that, same as I've hidden my Maori side.

And he *does* love the children, especially George, who's his obedient heir, to continue his name, business and genes.

By the way, Karin looks a lot like my mother when Mum was about Karin's age. I saw a photo in a drawer. Must be true that your dead always return to haunt you.

So, Ola, I've got a lot to do to correct the course of my life. Thank you for being here for me to admit to the truth of my ancestry. I hope you don't mind my using your shoulder, over the next decade, to cry on occasionally. I know it's not going to be easy for me in Kiwiland, colonial empire of racists, bigots, male-chauvinist rams, and rugby players who love South Africa and apartheid.

During your three-hour flight home you told Mark about Gill's confession.

'Julian's a real redneck,' he said. 'But I've got to admit he's generous under that pretentious Hollywood front . . . His cronies are going to castrate him if he goes 'native' with Gill and the kids. He'll fight for the kids, they're his investment in the future of his blue eyes and bald scalp. And if he wins them, he'll bring them up Palagi. Poor Gill.'

Strangely, right then, you were conscious for the first time that Mark, your husband, *was* Papalagi.

'Julian might disown the kids if they start growing permanent suntans, broader noses, thicker lips, blacker wavier hair, and taro-thick legs and thighs,' you said.

Gill, the kotuku, was ready to fly again. Mount Taranaki beckoned.

68

21

I search for meanings to sustain myself now that I am without the Atua and Freud, and I'm not an artist who creates her own meanings in order to live sanely with our most basic truth: that we are Atua with arseholes. We can imagine ourselves being immortal, yet know we have to die.

22

The automatic doors slid open and I pushed my cart of luggage out into the arrival area, into a staring sea of people waiting for passengers from our plane. I smiled at some of the Samoans I recognised as I pushed my cart up the roped-in aisle, searching the crowd for her. I hadn't seen her for four years, ever since she started boarding at Queen Elizabeth School.

I stopped at the end of the aisle. I sensed her before her hand touched my left shoulder. A hesitant, apologetic greeting. 'It's me,' she whispered.

It was as if I'd swallowed my tongue and couldn't breathe. I just gaped at the sixteen-year-old version of Gill who was fiddling with the pounamu pendant around her neck. Flat-chested, skinny, with narrow face and deepset blue eyes, light brown hair curling around her prominent ears; in faded jeans and black shirt and jandals. The kotuku. 'It's Shona,' she said. I sensed she didn't want to be slobbered over in public so I just shook her hand.

'Are you sure you want to come up north with me?' she asked as we went to the rental car counter. I nodded. She'd written to me in Samoa wanting to see me. I'd suggested holidaying together. She'd suggested up north, at her mother's home area.

I asked her to choose our car. She selected a Suzuki jeep with a cassette player. We loaded my two suitcases and her one canvas bag — she travelled light, she said. I confessed I was a nervous driver, especially in places like Auckland. She offered to drive — she had a licence, she said when I looked sceptically at her. God, she reminded me of Gill. I reached out and grasped her arm.

'It's okay, Ola. I'm all right. I was crook for a while but I'm fine now.' She opened the door for me. 'We'll take turns driving, okay?' I nodded.

She obviously loved driving, her long arms seemed a natural extension of the steering wheel and her movements flowed with the highway's long unweaving into the heart of summer. I relaxed as she drove but I couldn't stop looking at her. Framed against the open car window and the glare of the sun, she *was* Gill in front of Mount Taranaki. I'd brought the letters Gill had sent me since I last saw her, but decided it wasn't the time to show them to Shona.

'I'm no good at talking,' she said. 'My mates, teachers and George tell me that. But I'm a good listener. And read hang of a lot.' She glanced at me. 'So you'll have to talk or our trip'll be silent.' I asked if she minded the silence. 'No, but a lot of Pakehas do; they want to fill it up all the time. I'm used to it. But I want to hear you talk.'

'True? You're not pulling my leg, eh?' I mimicked her accent. She giggled.

Forty minutes later we were over the Harbour Bridge, on the highway heading north.

She suggested we overnight at Whangarei. Good fish'n'chips and beer there, she said. And added she'd been allowed beer as far back as she could remember.

'In return for doing the driving, you want me to talk, eh?' I asked. She nodded.

So I talked about Pita, my life in Samoa, my recent travels with Mark around the other islands, everything but her mother and sister. She'd nod, say Yeah or True or You're kidding? or Struth or Neat, especially that, Neat, eh!

At Whangarei we checked into the White Dolphin Motel on a hill overlooking the harbour. She chose it because she'd heard it wasn't 'a honky haven'.

'Pretty neat,' I said when we entered our unit.

She disappeared into the bedroom with her bag. I changed into jeans and a sweatshirt. 'How do I look?' she asked when she returned. Beautiful, I told her. 'I mean, do I look over eighteen?' she asked. 'Eighteen is the drinking age,' she reminded me. In her wide-shouldered sports jacket, calf-high boots, black slacks, hair pinned neatly into a bun, and light make-up, she did look older, and I told her so. 'Got to be careful about the pigs,' she said. 'Especially if you're a Maori. Even in one-horse towns like this the pigs can get tough.'

As we walked out of the motel she stopped and took something out of her jacket pocket. 'You want to wear my pendant?' I nodded. She clipped it around my neck. 'Mum gave it to me when I got my first ten per cent in Maori language. Looks real neat on you.'

'What about you?'

'Got this,' she said, holding out the bone pendant around her neck. 'My cousin Ropata carved it. The bugger charged me thirty bucks for it though. Beaut, eh?'

She escorted me to the nearest pub, where we avoided being picked up — she kept blaming my 'good looks' for attracting the 'local flies' — while we drank jugs of beer (I did most of the drinking) and ate piping hot fish'n'chips (she did most of the eating — four large pieces of fish and what seemed to be a mountain of potato chips overloaded with tomato sauce). Again we talked of everything else but her mother.

I woke in the middle of the night to find her in the sitting room, listening to her Walkman while she read Patricia Grace's *Waiariki*. She switched off the Walkman when she saw me. 'I can't go to sleep sometimes,' she said.

'Any good?' I asked about the book.

'Not bad. One of my teachers recommended it. A bit . . .' she tried to find the right word. 'Yeah, a bit sentimental about us but pretty neat.'

I made some tea and we talked about books and writers and poets. Literature was her favourite subject at school, oh, and Maori. I was surprised by her knowledge of New Zealand literature. She had a beaut teacher in that, she explained. Her favourite authors were Hone Tuwhare, Rowley Habib, Witi Ihimaera, Patricia Grace, Alistair Campbell, and Katarina Mataira and Arapera Blank because they wrote in Maori — beaut stuff! 'No Pakehas?' I asked. 'Most of them are intellectual wankers,' she said. I tried not to laugh. 'True,' she said, 'my English teacher described them that way.' I wiped the smile off my face. 'They don't understand the Land either. They're newcomers; they're not rooted in Aotearoa.' Here we had a budding Maori nationalist, not a sign of Julian anywhere in her.

I asked about her Maori. She rattled it off: 'Form two: 28 per cent; form three: 51 per cent; form four: 73 per cent; fifth form, a wipe-out; I was crook nearly all bloody year. This year, repeated my fifth form and got 87 per cent.'

'Bloody neat!'

'Yeah, blew the frigging minds of those girls in school who treated me as if I was Pakeha. Next year in the sixth form I'm going to be *the* best in Maori!'

Later, when I went back to bed, I couldn't sleep for thinking of Gill and Karin.

At dawn I woke to her sleeping head against my shoulder, her arms twined around my arm, her quiet warmth, an anchor of consolation.

I sipped orange juice at breakfast and watched fascinated as she devoured two fried eggs, a heap of bacon, three large tomatoes split and fried, a rack of toast with three pats of butter, then, remembering she'd forgotten the cereal, a hefty bowl of cornflakes and peaches and milk smothered with sugar. Just like Pita's ravenous appetite; a hollow body to be filled from toe-tips to skull-hair.

She asked if I wanted to go straight to Ahipara or take our time and visit some of her relatives and friends. She was the pilot, I said. 'First stop, Hikurangi and Matapouri,' she said.

I told her I was going to run on ahead. She was to wait for about forty minutes and then catch up to me in the car. 'Mum said you were a fitness freak,' she quipped. I remembered I was still wearing her pendant. 'You wear it,' she laughed. 'You're going to need it in this heat.' I jabbed her playfully in the stomach.

It was uphill and burning sun, with heatwaves brimming up from the road and weaving around my body, and no saving breeze, not a lick of it. But I forced my body to obey and keep moving ahead into the dread of what lay unsaid between Shona and me, and the decision I had to make about my marriage to Mark, that too.

'Good one, Auntie!' she congratulated me as I flopped into the car and lay back against the seat, leaking sweat from every pore.

'Next time, you run with me,' I suggested. I started drying myself.

'Bugger that,' she laughed. We started moving again. I changed into dry clothes. 'You're a year older than Mum, eh?' I nodded. 'You don't look forty at all.'

'And I don't dye my hair,' I said. She looked mischievously at me. 'Well, just a tint now and then.'

We laughed at that.

Just before Hikurangi we turned up an unsealed road shaded by thick macrocarpas, into a small farmhouse glittering with new paint and surrounded by fruit trees and a neat vegetable garden. Uncle Hemi and Aunt Hera, Mum's cousins, Shona said.

The air smelled of compost as Shona hurried me to the back and into Aunt Hera's arms and hongi and tears as she hugged Shona and cried, 'Ora, Ora, my Ora! Are you okay now? Are you well?' Shona kept saying she was well, okay now, fit as a fiddle. I felt she wasn't enjoying my watching her becoming sentimental in her aunt's abundant display of concern.

Aunt Hera ignored our having breakfasted already, herded us into the kitchen and soon we were drinking large mugs of tea and eating thick slices of bread and poached eggs. 'Eat, eat,' she kept encouraging Shona. 'You're too skinny. Always too skinny. Need muscles on your bones.' Shona ate obediently.

As we were leaving, Hera lifted a sack of potatoes and some pumpkins into our car. 'For Nanny Mataao,' she said. 'You give her my love. Tell her I'll come and see her soon. And, Ora, you look after yourself.' She embraced Shona and held her for a while. (In her letters, Gill spoke of Nanny Mataao and a cousin called Grace, who were now the centre of the Whanau Aorangi.)

'They call me Ora,' Shona explained as we drove out onto the main road. 'Maori for Ola. My second name is Ola, remember?'

'Great name,' I joked.

Fifteen minutes later we were at Matapouri, at Sandy Bay, in the home of the Hanaus, more of Gill's cousins. Uncle John and Aunt Rhonda taught at the school and had two boys much younger than Shona, who crowded beside her as soon as she sat down on the settee and insisted on monopolising her. Rhonda instructed them to go and fetch their father from the school. They grumbled as they left.

Within minutes we were given cups of tea and hot scones and strawberry jam. Rhonda, who was about my age, wore powerful spectacles that magnified her eyes. She fussed with her hair as she talked. '. . . You really look well, Shona,' she said. 'That place wasn't too bad?' Shona shook her head. 'And George?' Shona told her George was at home trying to be a yachtsman. Right then Uncle John came in and bent down and kissed Shona, who blushed.

'You're still skinny!' John laughed, feeling Shona's biceps. 'But you're okay now?' Shona nodded. 'Must've been awful.' Shona shook her head. 'Never mind, you're back with us, your family, now. Next holidays you come and stay with us.'

This time we left with a small sack of pipi for Nanny Mataao, and six or so paua for ourselves. 'Mum, I think, had a crush on Uncle John,' Shona said. 'He's neat, isn't he?'

'Yeah, really neat,' I replied. 'Wouldn't mind being a student of his.' She laughed and tooted the horn.

At midday, in Kawakawa, we were gorging ourselves on pickled mussels and Maori bread at the McKenzies', the parents of Jackie, one of Shona's 'best mates' at school. Jackie tried to talk her mother into letting her come with us. Her mother reminded her she had to mind the other kids (who at that moment were helping their Dad at the garage) for the holidays, while she worked.

Our farewell present was two large jars of pickled mussels. 'Good feed, eh!' Shona exclaimed as we headed for Paihia. 'Love mussels.' My stomach felt like a ton of rock anchoring me to the car seat, but I didn't mention it.

'Ladies and gentlemen, we're now coming to the picturesque historical Bay of Islands, Northland's most important resort,' Shona mimicked a tour guide. 'It was here, at historical Waitangi, on the sixth of February 1840, that some of our great and noble chiefs ceded the sovereignty of our beautiful country to great Queen Victoria. During Waitangi Day each year we celebrate that great occasion, and in doing so, celebrate the exemplary race relations in our great country.' She paused and then whispered, 'Absolute bullshit. The Treaty's a bloody fraud!' I gripped the back of her left hand.

'We don't have to stop here.'

'I'm okay,' she said. 'We can't go through without seeing the Mormon Aorangis, my favourite uncle and aunt.' She explained that Ioani was the oldest son of Grandmother Roimata's brother, Robert, who was killed in

France in the last war. As she traced the family connections, I was impressed by her detailed knowledge of her genealogy, her gafa, her whakapapa. '. . . Ioani and Keri are Mormons but not stiff ones; they're into Salt Lake City, Nanny Mataao described it. And Aunt Keri's got a crazy sense of humour.'

In Paihia we checked into a motel, soaked in the spa pool for a long time, dressed and went to the Mormon Aorangis. They weren't home. Shona knocked on the neighbours' door. We were told the Aorangis were in Wellington for a wedding.

Back in our unit I cooked our paua while Shona reluctantly made a salad (vegetables were yuk!).

We had our meal in the park by the beach, and watched the waves swing, twist, purr and coo under the night's caressing hands. The snow-white stars watched too. Difficult to believe that it was into that tranquillity the Pakehas had sailed to establish their first stronghold (of lawless adventurers, sailors, speculators, blackbirders, beachcombers) in Aotearoa.

A fraud, a fraud, a fraud! Shona's rage whispered from the waves.

Next morning we visited more friends and relatives in Kerikeri (Uncle Les pruning his citrus trees, his body striped with rivulets of sweat), Kaeo (toothless Aunt Thelma, who giggled nervously and held Shona's hand), Whangaroa (Ria Tuakana, 'a mate from school', whose Dad was a cray fisherman), Mangonui (Aunt Ruth's ramshackle house on the riverbank under willows was empty except for Rangi and Skipper, two nifty fox terriers which swirled like river rapids around our legs), and Awanui (well-groomed Moko and Tui, who owned a dairy and shouted us sundaes and milkshakes). Most of them inquired about Shona's health and continued filling our jeep with seafood, farm produce and gifts for Nanny Mataao, and promises of visiting her soon.

At mid-afternoon (I was drowsy from overeating and the heat) we were driving through the main street of Kaitaia. Shona waved and blew the horn at people she knew. Sometimes she stopped and leaned out of the window and hongied them.

She asked if I wanted a beer. I declined. She stopped in front of the St Justin Hotel and went looking for her Aunt Grace, who, she said, was taking care of Nanny Mataao. I didn't tell her Gill had already written to me about Grace.

I dozed off as I waited.

'Ola, this is Auntie Grace,' Shona was saying in my head. Startled, I woke to a large Afro coming at me through the open car window. I pulled back and was looking into the heavily made-up face of a tall, sinewy woman.

'Hi, Ola,' she said in a deep voice. Her strong arms pulled me into a jangle of bracelets and necklaces and her embrace of beer, sweat, Chanel perfume, and a bony chest — not a trace of fat anywhere. 'Shona's told me a lot about you,' she added.

I moved into the middle of the car seat. She got in beside me. At least six feet tall (she'd later say she was 'five feet twelve inches'), in a red blouse, skin-tight jeans and jandals. 'Right, kiddo,' she instructed Shona, 'let's head home to Nanny; she's probably expecting her afternoon cuppa.' Her accent was straight out of the Black American movies, her every gesture was exaggeratedly dramatic, and her array of rings, bracelets, anklets and necklaces jingled whenever she moved. She was a fabulous self-creation. Quite different from the person I'd expected from Gill's letters.

Winding a long arm around my shoulders — I didn't feel uncomfortable and was surprised — she talked almost nonstop. '. . . All those wankers in that pub, man, you'd think they were God's gift to women. Even old piebald Rangi, the decrepit eighty years of him, and still talking as if his pecker was laced with iron!' High-pitched laughing from Shona. 'As for Tama Shortstaff, well, he's all short slack!' More laughing and Grace's arm clapping against my back. 'Been here before, Ola?' she asked. I shook my head. 'Dead fucking country,' she said, 'but I like it. Got some juicy crayfish, paua and toheroa with enough iron to put strength into your soul (and your other muscles). Also a few gentle guys around, eh, Shona.' It dawned on me that Shona's accent was from Grace. 'Me, I got fed up with cities a few years ago and migrated back here to demanding Nanny and hard-hearted Tom Waitapu, who ditched me — the fucking sod! — for some fast bitch from Whangamata . . .' The ocean was now visible over the rolling hills, and its eternal sound awoke again in my ears and I felt at home, remembering: *the sea which cups my islands, washes each night through my dreams, no matter what shore I reach,* lines I'd written a few years before.

'Ahipara Bay coming up,' Grace announced. 'Home of lean tuatua, fast snappers and mullet, and paua as softly muscular as a baby's arse!'

Houses, baches and caravans lined the road that wove along the dunes sloping down to the sea. It was the height of the summer holidays so there were many people about. 'Just don't mind the Pakeha,' said Grace. 'To me they're invaders who'll disappear with the arse-end of the summer.' I breathed in the acrid, invigorating smell of the sea.

The Tasman was sweeping in. Heavy black waves thundered up the beach and sucked back loose pebbles, sand and driftwood. My sight followed the curve of beach and dunes and haze up the coast: Ninety Mile Beach stripped clean of trees, and dreaming under a sky as clear as Shona's eyes.

'The Mansion!' Grace said, pointing ahead to the end of the road. The

house and two shacks were locked among pohutukawa, pines and shrubbery. We turned in through the gate. Weather-beaten, unpainted, with a
wide verandah and a front garden of kumara, The Mansion, staring out
to sea as if it had always been there, waiting. For what? 'Righto, Shona-
baby,' Grace interrupted my thoughts, 'take Ola round to the front to
meet Nanny and sweeten her up before she sees me. I've been out nearly
all day and she doesn't like that.' She jumped out of the car and disappeared into one of the shacks.

During our trip up, Shona hadn't told me much about Nanny Mataao,
who was obviously the moa, the centre, of Shona's new life. Our pilgrimage north was to Nanny, that was how Shona had meant it. So I was
feeling anxious about meeting her, as we carried our luggage onto the
verandah.

'Aunt Grace's been saving up to go to New York,' Shona said. 'But
as long as Nanny lives, Grace won't be going; she's got to take care of
her.'

At first I thought the sitting room was empty because it was hushed
with a finger to its mouth, saying: Be quiet, the world is asleep. Even
Shona was tiptoeing across the floor. Then I saw the figure under the multi-
coloured quilt on the deckchair facing the large front windows that
opened out to the ocean. The muted glow of sun was spread over the still
figure, or, a better description, the golden glow was emanating from the
figure and up through the quilt. I moved closer.

The emaciated arms and hands folded across the belly shone like
ebony, and had reached that phase of ageing where they weren't going
to decay any more. So were the neck and face that now looked, because
they were so wrinkled, like unshaped clay.

I sensed she was blind. I couldn't reconcile the old woman in front of
me and the dynamic Nanny in Gill's letters.

I was afraid of old age, of watching people I love suffering the
humiliating ravages of ageing. When I've been with old people whom I've
not known well, I've experienced a fearful revulsion, as if their ageing
was a contagious disease which I'd contract if they touched me. So much
for the romantic myth that Polynesians accept ageing — and death —
gracefully.

So as I forced myself to search for the person in that face, I couldn't
believe that *was* the centre of Shona's family, because it seemed the mere
husk of what once was a human being. Now it was without sight, without
intelligible speech, without the sap and juices that kept the body supple
and questioning and feeling pain and joy, without the memory that gave
it an individual self.

As we approached, it raised its head of wispy grey hair. 'Nanny, it's
Shona.' (Was that a smile on its face?) Shona embraced it and kissed it

on the cheek. The figure's right arm rose up and around Shona's shoulder. They held onto each other for a long time. 'This is Ola, Nanny, from Samoa,' Shona whispered. 'You remember, Gill told you about her.' The hand beckoned me, touched my stomach and tugged at my belt for me to bend down. I kissed the cold, unpliable flesh. The arm held me down. I lingered and then, as I inhaled its subtle earth odour, I remembered my grandmother, Fa'afetai, and the love I'd felt for her, and I pushed my face deeper into the centre of Shona's strength, Nanny Mataao.

She released me, and her hand explored the whole of my face. She smiled, and I recognised that the unshaped clay had an individual self: Nanny, Nanny Mataao, sister of Janet Roimata (mother of Gill Prudence), grand-aunt of Shona Ola, and Eye of the Whanau Aorangi. 'She likes you,' Shona whispered.

Nanny's hand patted the wooden chair beside her. I sat down on it.

Shona brought her bag and unzipped it. 'Nanny, I brought you this bottle of Courvoisier brandy. She loves this expensive brand,' Shona whispered to me. Two boxes of chocolates. 'Your favourite,' she told Nanny, who waved her hand up and down appreciatively. 'And your favourite perfume, Joy.' Nanny's forefinger nodded imperiously.

'. . . And all these pipi, tuatua, crayfish and mussels,' Grace announced from the door. She entered with two sacks of the seafood we'd brought from their relatives. Nanny's hand uncurled upright, palm turned at Grace as though admonishing her. Grace stopped.

I looked at Grace, then at Shona, who was giggling at my astonishment, and then back at Grace. Couldn't be. But I looked again. Grace had washed off her make-up, combed her Afro into a slicked-back boy's cut, taken off her jewellery, jeans and jandals, and, now in a singlet and shorts, she was a man. 'Don't be cross, Nanny. I've got to have some fun sometimes,' Grace was saying. 'It isn't any fun day-in, day-out having to care for you. And I had to go and see your loving nephew about bringing your medicine this weekend.' Nanny's hand sagged, forgiving her. (I've never been able to refer to Grace as a man.) 'Thank you, Nanny, and please thank Ola and Shona for this food,' she said. She winked at us and sashayed her way out of the room.

Nanny's hand gripped mine. She was holding Shona's hand too.

Shona started telling her about our trip up. She concentrated on their relatives who'd given the gifts and love and promises to visit. Nanny's grip tightened every time Shona stopped, and Shona had to continue. In Shona's inventing, our trip became a pilgrimage, mythology to become part of the greater mythology of Nanny Mataao's life.

We smelled the raw shellfish before Grace was in the room with her two bowls of opened mussels, tuatua and pipi, and forks and bread. My mouth watered. There was a wistful, hungry expression on Nanny's face, and I imagined she was salivating too. 'Good, eh!' Grace said, placing the bowls on the table beside Nanny's head.

We couldn't take our eyes off Grace as she forked a tuatua into Nanny's eager mouth. We couldn't take our eyes off Nanny's chewing mouth. We waited, watched her swallow and nod her enthusiastic approval. 'She loves them,' Grace said. She forked in another tuatua. Then another.

Shona couldn't wait any longer. She dived into the bowl of mussels. I followed her.

'Delish! Delish!' Shona kept saying.

'Not too fast, you two!' Grace cautioned us. 'Leave some for Auntie Grace. You too, Nanny, not too greedy, it's bad for your tummy.'

Grace asked (instructed, more like it) Shona and I to cook that evening. What about Maori hospitality? We were guests, Shona argued. 'Guests, me left tit, you're family!' Grace said.

So, in Grace's neat attempt at a TV kitchen with a shelf stacked with cookbooks, another overflowing with herbs and spices, an impressive array of knives and kitchen implements (including a Cuisinart), pots and pans, wall charts of meat cuts and different types of fish, and a large poster which said GREAT COOKS ARE SLIM, we concocted a contradiction of dishes. Chicken soup out of a can (for Nanny), egg fu yung (Shona's speciality), pork and black bean sauce (my father's favourite), steamed rice, beans (easy to cook), peaches (out of a can) and strawberry ice cream, in quantities dictated by Shona's massive appetite. 'No Maori kai?' Grace would comment.

The only furniture in the dining room was a large oval kauri table and a matching set of carved wooden chairs, gleaming with polish and age. The walls were bare, and, as I set the table, I sensed them trying to say something to me. (I remembered that the walls of the sitting room, our bedroom, and the corridors were bare too.) Photographs? Photos of the people who'd lived there? None. Yet the walls were asking for them. I surveyed the dining room again. Light wallpaper, a history without faces. Strange for such an old family home to have no photographs of ancestors or of the living.

Shona fed Nanny her soup in the sitting room, switched on TV for her and then came to eat with us.

Grace entertained us during dinner with her risqué tales entitled 'The Ahipara Bay Frolics'. Sometimes Shona and I laughed so much we nearly choked.

'Not bad chow,' Grace remarked as an afterthought.

We washed the dishes and joined Nanny. I discovered they were, like me, addicted to the soaps, which Shona and Grace took turns, in Maori, to embellish for Nanny. They laughed, clapped, applauded the heroes and heroines, condemned the villains with snarls, belly-deep growls and gnashing teeth (Nanny still had most of hers), and wept during the tragic sequences.

I drifted out to the verandah, sat on the front steps, and gazed up at the stars that were fireflies illuminating the roof of heaven's cave that tunnelled out over the ocean to Samoa and Mark and our marriage which, unlike a soap opera, was dying without great gesture, drama and tears.

'You okay?' Shona asked as we got into bed later. I nodded. 'You don't mind Auntie Grace?'

'I like her very much. And Nanny's wonderful.'

'I'm glad,' she said, 'because they're my family now.' That reminded me that my problems were insignificant compared to the tragedy in her life. 'And you too, Ola, you're my family.'

After a delicious breakfast of orange juice, pancakes and syrup, and coffee, served by our chef, Grace, who fished for compliments which Shona provided with equal exaggeration and Grace fell for, we lifted Nanny on her deckchair out to the cool shade of the central pohutukawa that overlooked the beach. We propped her up with pillows and Shona read to her from the Maori Bible. Grace and I, in lavalava, lay on a mat on the sand beside them, in the shade. 'Only crazy Pakeha want to get fried out there!' laughed Grace. 'Me, I got a permanent tan.'

Every time Shona mispronounced or stumbled over the words, Nanny's hand stopped her, and Grace corrected Shona. Sometimes Shona pointed at a difficult passage, which Grace then read aloud, and Shona repeated to Nanny's smiling approval. It reminded me of how my grandparents, father, and Aunt Fusi had taught me to read in Samoan, during a childhood that now felt so far away.

'One day, kiddo,' Grace said to Shona, 'you may become as fluent as Auntie Grace, in Maori, that is. Only one other in our loving clan who's as good as me. Eh, Nanny?' Nanny pointed a laughing forefinger at her. 'Yeah, only Nanny, whose voice is gone, but which I've got here.' She jiggled her throat with her hand.

We took Nanny into the house for lunch. Nanny wanted me to feed her. After lunch while Nanny slept, we swam and fished for shellfish; lay in the shade and observed 'the tourists' (Grace's label for the holiday-makers who ventured up to our end of the beach).

Then dinner, television, bed.

This was to be our routine. Sometimes, however, while Nanny slept in the afternoons, we raced the jeep up Ninety Mile Beach, poached a kitful of toheroa, and zipped back. Sometimes Shona drove into town, got some beer and wine, and we lay under the pohutukawa and got sozzled. (We banned Shona from getting drunk but got too sozzled to notice if she did.) Other times, Grace drove us to her secret crayfish spots and while we watched with breathless admiration, she dived for the crayfish. 'Best fucking diver this side of Reinga and Hawaiki!' Shona echoed her aunt's boastful description.

Most days, friends or relatives brought food and other supplies for Nanny. We talked and provided meals for them. Before they left, Grace put a share of our seafood catch into their cars.

In time I learned much about their family from Grace, and as I learned, the inside walls of the house came to be peopled with photographs, faces.

Nanny's parents, the Reverend Matiu Rawhiti Aorangi (of Ngapuhi and Ngati Whatua) and Teremoana Rangi Jenkins (of Tainui and Ngati Raukawa), were married in 1899 and took charge of a parish in Kaitaia. Nanny Mataao Florence was born in 1900, Janet Roimata in 1905, and the three sons, Jacob, Abel and Rawhiti in quick succession after that.

Mataao never married and stayed with her parents, taking care of them when they retired to their family home in Ahipara, where her mother died of a heart attack in 1952, and her father, of a broken heart, two years later. Janet, their mother's favourite, disappeared in 1934 and they heard she had married a Pakeha farmer. Little was heard of or from her until Gill and her three children appeared at Ahipara in 1975 to say her mother had died in 1952. The three sons and their descendants were now scattered throughout Aotearoa and a few were in Australia. Many of them were the ones Shona and I had visited on our way up and were meeting when they came to see Nanny.

Grace wasn't sure when she was born because her birth certificate, as Matiu Moses Aorangi, wasn't issued until a year or so after Nanny brought her back from Auckland in 1945. Mataao told everyone she'd found her, one frosty morning, abandoned in front of a dairy in Wellington Street, Freemans Bay, where she was staying with relatives for a wedding. (According to Grace, the location of her abandonment explained her addiction to milkshakes, blue-vein cheese and pineapple chunks.) Everyone called her Grace because of Nanny's declaration that 'It was by the grace of Te Atua that the little bugger was still breathing after being exposed to the winter night.' She also came to believe Nanny's claim that, like the orphan Moses, she was a special person intended by Te Atua for a very special purpose. Reverend Matiu (he refused to be called anything else by his grandchildren) and Nanny Tere reinforced that conviction in Grace by giving her a unique education in Maori and things Maori, at a time when many Maori parents wanted the Pakeha way for their children.

She didn't start school until she was about nine, after Nanny Tere died and Reverend Matiu, her teacher, retreated into his prison of grief and refused to be freed from it.

Grace *saw* everything in Maori, for she knew little English, so when she was instructed on her first morning at school, by Mrs Thwaites, not to be speak 'Meoree' (because it wasn't allowed) but to learn English (because it would get her somewhere), Grace didn't take it seriously. She was puzzled by it and withdrew into observing the class activities that day. She told Nanny about it when she got home. Yes, best that she learn English quickly, was Nanny's reply.

On her second morning, Wiremu, her cousin, headlocked her while they were queuing up for class and in loud Maori she cried, 'Shit to you!'

Splittt! the sharp slap flicked off the back of her wrist. She winced and squirmed, looking up. 'No Meoree allowed!' Mrs Thwaites reminded her.

Next afternoon, when Mrs Thwaites twisted her ear (and the cutting pain screwed into her head) for bursting out in Maori again, Grace couldn't stop herself. After hours of not understanding what the others were saying, she screamed 'Shit!' in Maori at her tormentor and, in a flood of tears, swam home to Nanny, who dried the flood and told her there was nothing wrong or unclean about being Maori and speaking their tongue, the language of the civilised. No matter what *they* did to try to destroy that in her, she was to resist, and the best resistance was to pretend she was changing into a Pakeha, that she was one hundred and one per cent willing to learn English so as to survive as an ideal citizen in a Pakeha New Zealand. In Nanny's message she absorbed the anger, the pride, the refusal to be other than Maori.

Grace learned so fast, so willingly, to react like a Pakeha to everything that she became Mrs Thwaites's model pupil, held up to her other Maori pupils and any Pakeha deviant. With Nanny's complicity, Grace even learned to take 'Pakeha' sandwiches to school: thinly sliced bread with butter, Marmite, cheese or lettuce and tomatoes or meat, cut diagonally and wrapped in grease-proof paper. 'No newspaper-wrapped monstrosities for this house nigger!' Grace said.

At home Nanny continued teaching her Maori, and they attended church, where the sermons were starting to assume the English tongue because there were fewer people who were fluent in Maori. A few years later, while Grace was away at high school, Nanny stopped going altogether because, apart from one or two hymns and readings, the services were now in the tongue of 'the uncivilised'.

Grace topped her two-teacher school — Mrs Thwaites presented her with *Kidnapped* by R. L. Stevenson and shook her hand in front of the whole school, saying, 'Don't forget to be proud of your race always.' For her achievement (and being the grandson of the revered Reverend Aorangi) Grace was awarded a church scholarship to Te Ao Marama College, where her grandfather and many of the other Aorangis had excelled in rugby, good behaviour, Maori Studies and oratory, in that order. She had a family (and male) tradition to honour, be shaped by, within even more demanding school traditions which had produced 'our new warriors, such as Peter Mard, Rua Arapito, Tamihana James and Henare, my nephew, who refused to die in the Pakeha Second World War, and is still fighting, as a lawyer, to get back our lands' (Nanny's description).

Grace soon discovered, but would never tell Nanny, that though Te Ao Marama purported to instil in its students 'the best in Maori culture', that best was determined by a Pakeha principal, predominantly Pakeha staff and board; and one's ability to become a Pakeha gentleman with the virtues of godliness, hard work, thrift, short back'n'sides, individualism and being proud of one's race (in this case, of being Maori as perceived by the Pakeha). The aim was to shape a Maori leadership that would transform their people into 'brown-skinned Pakeha'.

Te Ao Marama also expected them to be men in the 'good ol' Kiwi tradition', tough, rugged, silent individualists who didn't flinch under physical pain; who could tolerate the absence of women (and sex), loneliness, unreasonable erections that weren't to be frigged away because that caused blindness; who weren't sissies, homos, shit-stirrers, commies, long-haired intellectuals, soccer or hockey players, non-conformists and pikers. The heroes they were to emulate were mainly Pakeha, rugby or military or colonial empire builders, including those who'd commanded the armies that had massacred the Maori people during the misnamed 'Maori Wars'. In fact, the history of New Zealand they were taught glorified Pakeha settlement, conquest and the assimilation of the Maori. Maori nationalists were cast as villains, savages, murderers and perpetrators of massacres. The Maori who'd aided in the missionising and conversion and assimilation into things Christian and Pakeha were extolled. (Reverend Aorangi, her grandfather, was in that select band.) Maori were to believe their subjugation had been a blessing; the 'new Maori' was to accept the colonised condition as the most desirable self to be.

'. . . Yeah, in that fish pond (forgive me, Mao!) I had to be a hori as cast by the Pakeha who ran, controlled and financed it; a pond which had been established by bastards who'd ripped off our land and made fortunes out of our misery and who saw their final victory in converting us into house niggers. In that bourgeois pond I had to be a "gentl'man", loyal, enthusiastic arse-licker of God, Queen and country. And for some time I was fucking happy in those roles because I didn't know any better. Yeah, I was a model Maori . . .'

Grace even played rugby thoroughly, if not with talent, and in her final year was in the Second XV. (No one could accuse her of being a sissy.)

And she excelled in things Maori because of Nanny's training. In language she won every oratory/essay prize; in haka she was a doubly ferocious warrior (but she never revealed her artistry in poi, which Nanny had taught her and her cousins); in woodcarving (but not in weaving, which Nanny had also taught her); and she was the best hangi-maker in her last year.

Of course it wasn't until she'd survived Te Ao Marama and was at university and into such writers as Frantz Fanon, Eldridge Cleaver, Albert Memmi, Albert Camus, Jean-Paul Sartre, Jean Genet, Che Guevara, Nkrumah, Sukarno, Kenyatta, Mao Tse Tung, Ralph Ellison and Richard Wright, and the student protest movement of the sixties, that she began to *see* her life (and through it the experience of her people) as one of the colonised, and to tell it like she was telling me.

She remained intact as Matiu Moses Aorangi, male, he-man, to the day she left Te Ao Marama, but during her last six months there she had to struggle to maintain that self, like a lizard refusing to shed its skin as a natural consequence of the seasons.

In 'good ol' Kiwiland' and much of middle-class Maoridom one was *allowed* to be only either male or female, because that was said to be 'the natural and divine order of things'. No in-betweens, or both, allowed. No queers, that was unnatural and, if tolerated or legalised, would corrupt 'the moral fabric of our society'. And at Te Ao Marama, bastion of that 'natural view of nature', she was Matiu, uprightly male like all the male Aorangi before her, 'no doubt about that, man!' She wasn't going to let the side down, disgrace the courageous masculinity of her family. She even 'fell in and out of love' with girls at their sister school; had long wistful romances — by mail — with them, stole furtive kisses and 'feels' at the chaperoned school dances, returned to her lonely male bed and had manly fantasies, while 'playing with herself', of experienced women, such as their buxom matron. 'Sometimes we doubled up in bed and pulled each other off, but we never dreamt — or admitted — we had 'homosexual tendencies' (our chinless principal, 'Bolt' Healy used to call it). And I was as creative as my other cobbers making up lurid stories about our sexual escapades with girls. I wasn't pretending to be male. It was for real!'

Until she 'fell in love' (her only description for it), in June of her final year, with Waka Graham, a friend but not up to then that close a friend. Nothing exceptional about Waka, average in everything, wouldn't stand out in a crowd; had a 'nice' smile; liked eating coconut drops and saying 'Geez', 'Cheesed off' and 'Fuck you too with a broom'.

And it happened, like a 'vision coming out of the blue'. One minute, while she was eating her breakfast opposite Waka, her feet tingling with the winter cold, she gazed up at him, and — BAM — she was almost flattened by the need to reach out and embrace him. The orange glow of the windows behind Waka was making him appear unreal, a figure of slow-burning vapour. A fork tinkled on the concrete floor. She blinked out of the vision and found she was nearly pissing herself with fear. She stuffed her food down to smother her guilt.

As soon as their House Master released them, she ran from the dining room into the gully and the tangle of ponga beside the swimming pool, where she tried to still the terror. Shit, God, jeepers, she was a homo! Queer. Unclean. Diseased.

She kept well away from Waka and tried burying herself in more rugby and other school activities, but the feeling (she refused to name it) persisted like a stomach ulcer that, when neglected, stung and burned to its own rhythm.

It was a hushed July morning, everything outside was covered with a dew that glowed in the dawn winter light, when she woke and looked out and realised she was *free* of Waka. Just like that. She was normal again. Clean. Well. She almost wept with the beauty of that feeling. But men don't cry.

Click. It happened again. This time with Spike Deakle, their shy, pimply history teacher, who'd graduated from university the year before and was a Pakeha. Shit, she was doubly sick: a homo and one who was driven enough to 'love a Pakeha' (and an ugly one at that). 'I can laugh about it now,' Grace said, 'but it was bloody awful at the time. One consolation, I suppose, was that I wasn't so frightened of my feelings. Getting used to them . . . Woke up one morning and Spike was back to normal as my boring, conscientious, fumbling teacher. Then just after the final exams there was Fred Rawene, a third former whose duties were to make my bed — I was a lordly prefect — polish my shoes and carry my Marmite and Weet-bix and jam to breakfast. A beautiful boy. Straight out of the Pakeha noble savage mythology about us. I almost, yeah, almost gave into my other side. But hung on like grim death and departed from Te Ao Marama as Matiu Rawhiti Aorangi, male, clean, natural, "Academically, the brightest Aorangi to attend our school; one who should excel in Maori Studies at university and prove himself worthy of the Maori people," so wrote Bolt Healy in my final school report.'

The late 1960s, when she was at Auckland University on a Maori Affairs scholarship, was a time of fervent rebellion against the Vietnam War, established values, mores, tastes and lifestyles, a search for a 'new morality' and alternative ways of living. For three years she was on a natural high generated by her energetic participation in that quest, in her studies (which she didn't neglect, though, like other students, she attacked university education as being narrow, totalitarian, élitist and irrelevant), and in the Maori movement for self-determination and the restoration of dignity, self-respect and language.

She zipped through her studies. Her Maori was better than that of most of her lecturers, but she let them believe otherwise and got very high grades. In Anthropology she argued for a more 'relevant' approach (meaning, a socially committed one) to other societies, and her Marxist head of department gave her excellent grades too. She also read everything she could find about her people. And saw hundreds of films, indiscriminately. Her favourites were those of John Huston and Alfred Hitchcock.

She was on the executive of the local Maori Students' Associaton and later the national one, where she advocated the destruction of the Pakeha power structures that were oppressing their people. Aotearoa was still under occupation, they agreed at one national congress. (Nanny Mataao loved it when she told her that.) Even rugby was a means of brainwashing their people. Look at Maori rugby players going to play in South Africa while blacks were being imprisoned, tortured and killed in the streets.

She composed militant haka and waiata for their association's public performances. She danced in the poi team and taught the women how to weave (and wasn't ashamed of it any more). Grew her hair long and styled it after the warrior's hairdo of pre-Pakeha times; wore faded jeans, denim shirts, greenstone pendants and earrings, jandals (or bare feet); talked Maori at predominantly Pakeha functions and corrected those who mispronounced Maori names and told them to get stuffed if they objected. A few fights resulted but she was 'adequate' with her fists, feet, everything; smoked marijuana and talked all night of world peace, banning nuclear weapons, which were obscene colonial weapons of oppression, ditching fat President Johnson and ending the Vietnam massacres and bringing the Vietminh and Ho Chi Minh to power (General Giap, victor of Dien Bien Phu, was a special hero), supporting guerilla movements in Third World countries (including Aotearoa) in booting out the CIA and their fascist, colonial allies, promoting Black Power and Black is Beautiful and the Black Revolution in culture. Frantz Fanon, Stokely Carmichael, Huey Long, Mao, Che, Eldridge Cleaver, James Baldwin, and Angela Davis were her mentors.

Life was lusciously full and exciting and promised a summer of justice without end.

Romantic love, once her fatal flaw at Te Ao Marama, she now condemned as another Pakeha invention aimed at misleading 'the natives'. Silly, swooning, sloppy love at first sight and forever was a fucking laugh! Once she saw that truth, she was free to zip through a series of lovers. Firstly women, then a few men, then a mixture, both Maori and Pakeha, and she wasn't unfaithful to any of them. She always ended one relationship before beginning another, though she hid her homosexuality from her women (the public and her family) and her heterosexuality from her men, exploring to the full her true bisexual nature. Nature or nurture was a debate she didn't give a stuff about. Her nature was *natural* and she was nurturing it.

She graduated with a BA in Maori Studies and Anthropology. Nanny Mataao and many relatives came down to her graduation, and Nanny and some of the elders wept as she went up to accept her degree. Afterwards they took her home to a marae welcome and feast, where she thanked everyone for her education and advocated the continuation of their struggle to right the wrongs inflicted upon them by the Pakeha. 'One hundred and one per cent!' Nanny Mataao congratulated her.

She was appointed a junior lecturer at university and, through her Maori language classes, promoted the cause of Maori rights. At the same time, she studied for an MA. Her flat at Herne Bay became a gathering place for Maori activists. Her natural high continued.

Frank Kahu first appeared — or she started noticing him — in her language class, in the front row, noting down everything she said. A mature student in his thirties, bearded, with an Afro and garbed after the fashion of Che Guevara, he exuded an air of vulnerability. Soon after, he started appearing in her flat as an ardent supporter of the Cause. He was gregarious and generous and they came to like him, especially when he became the main source of grass for their meetings and parties. He was good on the guitar and possessed a rich repertoire of popular rock and Maori songs, which made him welcome at student parties.

Before Grace knew it, Frank was in her life as naturally as her own shadow, and one night after a noisy party he was, like her shadow, in her bed and she was abandoning herself again to romantic love, thinking that after the first blinding passion it would vanish. But it dug in, right down to the bedrock at her centre.

He shifted in with her. They were careful not to reveal the truth about their relationship to the others. Frank kept declaring that he couldn't believe he was 'in love' with another man, but it was terrific to be free of his bourgeois hangups about gender, and to be 'in love' with someone so beautiful, so understanding. Grace marvelled at his 'innocence' — that was the only description for it, then at his ability to learn about love and 'making love' from her, and his willingness to experiment, explore, dare. Before she knew it, she was into cocaine and heroin in their daring exploration, and she never questioned where he got the drugs from. Her love for him became a hunger so compulsive it scared the shit out of her whenever he wasn't there or when she tried to put a solid shape to his personality and felt him escaping, becoming empty space. At parties she stuck to him because he was popular with the others and she didn't want him taken from her. She became so possessive that they started quarreling about it. She always ended up apologising, begging for his forgiveness, which he gave as a shot of what he called 'the White Death'.

He began having other lovers. At home she didn't seem to do any-thing right for him. At first his abuse was verbal: 'You lazy, fumbling bitch!' he'd whisper. 'Why don't you getta hold of yourself?' 'Look at yourself — you're a bloody mess!' Grace reacted angrily at first, but when he withheld her shots she accepted his abuse and begged to be forgiven. She knew he was deliberately humiliating her, enslaving her through the power of his White Death.

Verbal abuse became slaps, then punches, then beatings expert enough so the bruises wouldn't show. 'Why, why?' she kept asking. 'Cos you're a pretentious know-it-all, one of our Black Saviours,' he'd whisper.

It was a bone-cold morning, she'd cooked a breakfast of bacon, eggs, toast and tea, and as he ate it he seemed in a particularly good mood. He kept scrutinising her appearance, reaching across and caressing her cheeks, and smiling. 'Everyone, irrespective of race, colour or creed, is equal in the habit. They all grovel when they need it,' he said. 'Everyone is equal in the White Death.'

He led her into the bedroom and with unusual consideration made love to her for a long time. She cried, believing he was still in love with her.

Afterwards he told her about his life.

Like her, he'd been abandoned by his parents, but unlike her, his stepfather had kicked him out when he was about thirteen. His Samoan mother didn't do anything about it because her husband threatened to ditch her and her other children. Like her, he didn't know who his father was. So in their beginnings they were fairly equal.

But unlike her, for him there was no Nanny Mataao, family or tribe to go back to. The streets were his home, the city his marae, and his tribe were the other street kids. For three years they slept under Grafton Bridge, took part-time jobs, shoplifted whatever they needed. Winter was a most terrible time; the cold, when they couldn't get warm clothes or beds, was a killing hatred hurled against them by an indifferent society. Kutu, sores, ringworm invaded them during the unwashed winter.

Then he was convicted for burgling a couple of houses and converting the car they'd used to explore the Volcanic Plateau. In borstal he used his talent for fast talk and changed his personality to suit whatever circum-stances arose. He survived well, so well the warden recommended early parole.

A few months out with his tribe in the streets — they were better organised now — he was again caught and convicted of burglary. Four other jobs went undetected.

Now it was Mount Eden Prison, and he added sex to his repertoire of survival techniques. He wasn't a homo, they were paying for it, and he was doing it to survive.

Out again, more burglaries until he was convicted of burgling a teacher's flat. He didn't tell the police he'd been sodomised by that respectable citizen, who'd then refused to pay, and he'd stolen the video recorder as payment.

In prison he learned how to peddle drugs, controlled by Art Tamariki Boyd, who bragged he was a kingly Maori-Samoan-Irishman and a true nationalist and activist. Around Art gathered Maori prisoners who, under his teachings, became ardent nationalists. Frank joined the group, read the political literature recommended by Art, picked up the radical jargon and some of the fervour, but remained uncommitted. Causes were for fools, used by the powerful to mislead. However, he was committed in a strange way to what Art called 'the White Death', as a way of utu, paying back the Pakeha, and of course making a good living out of it.

'We are all equal in the White Death,' Art taught them. 'So don't use it. It's another Pakeha way of fucking us up.' This was Frank's philosophy when he left prison and became a pusher. Two years later he enrolled in Geography as Boyd Richards, transferred to Sociology the next year and, when he suspected the pigs were on to him, disappeared. He emerged at Otago University as Richard Tamariki, arts student, liked by his lecturers. He passed the occasional paper until things got hot and he shifted to Victoria University. Over a period of three years as Mana Boyd, he made the mistake of becoming too prominent a spokesman for the Maori cause and attracted the attention of the CIB, and had to shift to Canterbury and a new identity as Latu Ika, Tongan — there were too many Samoan students for him to pass as one and be the Samoan third of Art Tamariki Boyd.

During that time he made rich killings off Pakeha users, 'off their colonial arses' he described it, and banked the money under other aliases, in the university cities. He learned not to display that wealth, promising he'd retire one day and really live it up in Cannes or Hong Kong or Rio de Janeiro. He was mining the Pakehas' gold. And he wasn't being conned into any stupid, suicidal Maori fight for equality. True equality was through the White Death.

'So Frank Kahu isn't your real name?' Grace asked, realising she wasn't shocked by his cynical revelations.

'No,' he whispered, 'I wouldn't lie to you.' She believed him, or more correctly, she didn't care if he was lying because lying was a vital part of who *they*, the enemy, had made him become.

For a while everything seemed well between them. She'd given away her MA studies but was still teaching (and ashamed of the mess she was making of it). They couldn't sack her though; you didn't sack Maori in that political climate.

She'd stopped visiting Nanny and answering her letters. Her existence ticked to Frank and the White Death, but she refused to admit she was an addict.

Frank's rage was unexpected, inexplicable. He came home one afternoon and found her reading *The Golden Notebook* by Doris Lessing. 'Look at this pigsty,' he began. He hit the book out of her hands. 'Look at this filth! Don't you know how to clean up?' She said she was sorry but she wasn't well. 'So you shouldn't; you're a fucking queer who thinks he's better than me. Don't you?' He wrenched her face up. 'Look at me. You think you're brainy but you're just another white nigger. Get up and clean out your sty!'

She stumbled, suffered vertigo, and was drenched with a cold sweat as she cleaned the sitting room, while he slept in the bedroom. Later, needing her shot, she woke him. 'Frank, I've got to have it,' she pleaded.

Whipping off the blankets, he said, 'Okay, Miss Black Saviour, save me! Go on, save me!' When she refused, he forced her to her knees. 'I own you, Grace!'

The bouts of humiliation and sexual abuse became frequent and she hated herself for allowing it, but she needed the Death. The shot always came at the end of his rage, the Death that relaxed her, sent her into the calm eye of Ahipara Bay.

For over a year she was his prisoner, object of his overwhelming hatred of anyone he considered superior. She even had to buy the heroin from him, and her salary and savings went with it.

He started having affairs with other men, mainly young Pakeha addicts, and at first, when she was out, brought them to their flat. After she screamed at him for his infidelities, he brought one lover back and forced her to watch. She fled into the bedroom but he waited until she came out in need of the needle then he ordered her 'to perform' (his phrase) with his lover.

A week after, she found his cache of drugs in the back of their garage and waited for his return. Her fist crashed into the centre of his forehead as he entered; her kick crunched into his belly, and he tumbled down the front steps. When he staggered up, eyes wild with surprise, she punched at his throat. He gagged and stumbled down the street.

The supply lasted almost two weeks.

Then he was back, this time with two other addicts.

'. . . The next morning when I woke up from a sleep that felt like death and saw the hollow-eyed, pitiful, miserable skeleton that I'd become, and saw him sprawled naked on the bed with those miserable men beside him, I simply wanted to die, to end it,' Grace continued. 'The honour and history of my family, their aroha, and especially Nanny's, had been reduced to me, a miserable gay hooked on the White Death and owned by an evil creep who hated everything and everybody. Oh God, I was sick! I knew I had to go north, to the wellsprings of my life, to be saved . . . I can't remember how I got to Nanny but I did. I confessed it all to her. She got two of my cousins, who'd been nurses, and Patu, a nephew who'd been an addict after coming home from the Korean War. Together they eased me through the awful withdrawal.'

She was alone on the verandah, letting the sound of the sea wash through her head, as she lay in Nanny's deckchair, when the red car turned into their gate and slid, like a cheeky crayfish, up to the house, stopping a few paces from the verandah. She clutched the sides of the chair to hold herself intact against the fear of the car door clicking open and him emerging with that cocky, crazy grin of his.

She looked. He was leaning against the car, legs crossed, sleekly ominous in his windjacket, red scarf, Afro and dark glasses. She couldn't take her eyes away from him as he moved aside, opened the car door, bowed and invited her to enter that doorway.

Her mouth heaved gagging sounds as if she was drowning. And Nanny and her nurses were holding her, whispering aroha into her disintegration, fastening her together again, while Patu, like a slow net, was advancing on Frank, who was backing into the car. 'Next time I see you here,' Patu called, 'you're dead!'

The car revved, back wheels spinning on the gravel, backed onto the lawn and then, while they watched, it fled out the gate and down the road, churning up a tantrum of dust.

She cried as she told them who their visitor had been. Nanny sat beside her after they'd tucked her into bed. 'He is not of us,' Nanny whispered to her. 'He is of the uncivilised, created by the Pakeha and their sickness.'

Next day, Sunday, Nanny took her to their family church. She knelt in the front pew while Nanny, in black, stood in front of the crucifix before the pulpit, and chanted a karakia so old that Grace didn't understand the words, but she knew it was a call to atua more ancient than Jehovah, atua untainted by the invading gospels and out of which the voyaging canoes had come, with a ferocious beauty that knew no fear.

At lunch, while they ate, Patu drank only fresh water, saying that he'd eaten already at the Thompsons' down the road. Over the years, she noticed that Patu appeared whenever any of their elders were threatened. He didn't say much but he was always there, like an invisible shield. He'd spent years in the army; had gone to Korea as a sergeant; had returned with numerous decorations, but Nanny and her mother had to nurse him out of a heroin addiction; had shifted to Whangarei, married and established a trucking business. He brought his family to Ahipara every Christmas for a few weeks. Grace and the young people of Ahipara marvelled at his skills as a fisherman, sportsman, hunter. She noticed that the men kept clear of him whenever he was annoyed. It was as if Patu was a special tradition in their family.

That night before she fell asleep, she heard Nanny and Patu talking in the sitting room. Their voices sounded as if they were coming from a place, a time, far away. She dreamt of black horses thundering, snorting, rampaging over the dunes under a sky of molten lava and a dark wind ripping her clothes off and then, like painless scalpels, stripping off her flesh until she was white bone, free, floating, floating, while Patu sat on the crest of the highest dune, protecting her.

Three mornings later, she went to breakfast and couldn't get over how happy Nanny, Patu and their cousins were as they kidded one another. While the others were digging into piles of pancakes, sausages and fried eggs, Patu sipped a glass of water. 'Patu's going home to see how his wife and kids are,' Nanny told her.

'You okay, Matiu?' Patu said to Grace, who nodded. Patu got into his pick-up. 'Look after yourself,' he called. Grace waved.

As the pick-up drove away, gulls were wheeling and screeching over the bay.

Nanny reached over and embraced her. Grace buried her face in Nanny's invincible aroha, aware now that her special purpose was to protect the heritage and the knowledge his family had bequeathed her, to keep it alive, while the land was under occupation by the invaders. Though an orphan, he'd been chosen for that purpose, and it was wonderful to be alive, clean like the sea out of which their forefathers had come to Aotearoa to give it voice, shape, mana.

All was well, she was at a new beginning. Frank would never enter her life again.

The cousins returned to their families in Kaitaia that afternoon.

Nanny Mataao resumed her instruction shortly after. Grace wanted to write the knowledge down but Nanny forbade her. Nothing was to be written down, because the Pakeha would steal that too.

Over the next few years, Nanny took her to meet their other tribal kaumatua and keepers of the fire that had to be kept alive in the smothering darkness of the invaders. Even into the cities where most of their people now lived. Grace learned from them too. On other excursions Nanny took her to the tapu places that were important to their meaning, teaching her their tribal geography over which the invaders had superimposed their arrogant face.

And as Grace absorbed who Mataao was, the old woman lessened. 'Good, good,' Nanny told her, 'you are learning, taking the fire from me, as I took it from my elders.'

It was then that Gill and her children came.

*

Shona suggested to Grace that they take me camping up the beach, for a couple of days. Grace rang Patu's wife at Whangarei to come and look after Nanny. When they arrived we borrowed their pick-up because our jeep wasn't large enough to take our gear and the water and firewood we needed because the settlers had destroyed the forests along Ninety Mile Beach. I took Gill's letters with me.

Grace refused to heed Shona's encouragement to go faster. 'I don't want to be maggot meat yet,' she kept saying. The tyres hummed a high-pitched whine over the wet sand. Gulls broke up and away, squawking. The beach, which rolled up to the dunes that shouldered the creamy haze, stretched ahead as it swallowed our car, pulling us towards Cape Reinga and the meeting of the two oceans and the spirits diving for Hawaiki.

An hour later Grace turned our pick-up into a narrow entrance that led, for about fifty metres, into a horseshoe-shaped shelter formed by high sand dunes that were held down by marram grass, lupin and flax, and cut us off from the wind.

'This is Ringahina,' Grace introduced me to the shelter. She switched off the engine. A deep, restful calm. Even the sea sounded far off.

Islands of flax and marram grass spread over the floor of the shelter. We unloaded the pick-up.

I felt inadequate as I helped them pitch our tent, lay out our lilos and sleeping bags, set up wood for our cooking. They were expert campers, self-reliant livers off the land and sea, like my village relatives in Samoa, and when I told them that, Shona said, 'We got to be prepared.'

Afterwards we scrambled to the top of the dunes, Shona racing Grace (who let her win). That height enabled us to see unimpeded in all directions, and as I stood and sank into that space, that Va, of burning sky and earth and sea and the eternal humming silence that weaves all things together, I felt insignificant yet at peace.

'Every holiday Mum brought us to Ahipara, we came camping here,' Shona said, lying back on her elbows. 'To heal, Mum used to say.'

'Yeah, Gill and the kids loved it. Didn't you?'

'Every time, I didn't want to go back to Auckland.'

'Let's go get lunch,' Grace blocked us off from Gill, and she was forward-rolling down the dunes, with Shona chasing her, her legs sinking up to their calves in the bone-dry sand.

Within half an hour we had a kitful of toheroa and two crays Grace had dived for at the edge of the rock platform protruding into the sea to our right.

While the crays cooked in a large pot over the fire, we fed on the toheroa — raw, just steamed open. 'Delish, delish!' raved Shona.

'Yeah, yeah!' echoed her teacher.

'We going to outlast the colonial bastards!'

'Yeah!'

As the stars came out that evening we pulled our lilos and sleeping bags out of the tent, and lay on them beside the fire, talking and looking up into the heavens. Before, whenever I'd gazed up into the night sky for any length of time, I'd felt as if I was going to be sucked up into its black coldness, but that night I began to feel as if I was floating face-down on the trembling surface of a large well, gazing down through its dark green depths, at its bed of pebbles. Each pebble was being illuminated from its core by an inquisitive light that was swimming up through the water and burrowing into my body, trying to discover who I was.

And as the starlight set me alight a song was caught in my breath, and I sang it aloud:

> *Twinkle, twinkle, nosy star,*
> *why do you keep wondering who we are?*
> *Deep deep deep in the sky so dark,*
> *why don't you show us if you can bark?*
> *Twinkle, twinkle, nosy star,*
> *why do you keep wondering who we are?*

It caught the others and soon they were singing it too. Grace translated it into Maori and we learned that while Ringahina cupped us in her applauding hands.

Next morning we drove off the beach and up onto the main road that ran along the central ridge and up through Te Kao and Te Paki to the northern tip, to the Tail of Maui's Fish.

In front of us, the ridge sloped down to Cape Reinga, the finger of land that dived into the sea and out to the gathering of whirlpools formed by the meeting of the Tasman Sea and the Pacific Ocean, and further still to Hawaiki, the Spirit World. We didn't talk. The sky was immense as it swept out over ocean and more ocean and sun, and in that immensity I visualised the spirits converging at Reinga and finding the sacred passage that would take them to where their adventurous ancestors had sailed from, each step of their journey a reaffirmation of their belief in the Source, gathering strength from It as they journeyed.

'Most of our people don't believe in Hawaiki anymore,' Grace sennetted our silence. 'For them, our atua are dead. Consequently they have no protection against the illnesses of the invaders. They're lost in the cities of the Pakeha, with no compasses to find Hawaiki, the Source. The city is poisoning them — they have no immunity.'

'I believe,' said Shona. We looked at her. Arms folded, she stood with feet planted in the earth, staring out over Reinga, anchored against any new storm that might blow. Grace caressed her shoulder.

94

I told them that the Fafa, at Falealupo, Savai'i, was our Reinga pointing towards Pulotu, our spirit world, but no Samoans now believed in our ancient religion. Since the missionary conversion most of our people knew nothing about our pre-Christian atua — or cared. People even ridiculed them, relegating them to what they described as 'the Time of Darkness before the Light'. Without them we were exposed, without mana, to the maladies of the Pakeha. In truth, our new priests, leaders, politicians and educated élite were advocating those 'diseases' as ways for spreading the new religion they called Development.

'Perhaps the odds are against us,' Grace said. I half nodded.

'No,' said Shona.

We drove back to Ringahina in silence, the sun smarting on our skins, the light piercing our foreheads and foraging in our disquiet.

I changed into my running gear, took the three letters I'd received from Gill since the Christmas of 1974 when I'd last seen her — a letter each Christmas — and handing them to Shona, said, 'These may help explain why.' She glanced at me, then at Grace, but said nothing.

We watched her cross the beach and pick her way over the rock platform until she was at the edge, then sitting down and donning her sunglasses, she started reading. 'I'll keep an eye on her,' Grace said.

As I jogged up the beach I kept looking back at Shona, the kotuku on the rocks, stalking the prey in her mother's sea of words about a search for history, identity, aroha.

I pushed against the stinging heat.

I got back nearly an hour later. Shona was still perched on the edge, but now with her head resting in her hands, staring into the water lapping at her feet.

Grace was lying in the shade of her beach umbrella. I lay down beside her and told her what was in Gill's letters.

In her first letter, dated 20 December 1975, Gill described what had happened to her and her family since Mark and I last saw her in January 1975. She focused on Julian and the children.

The weekend after we left, while their children were at Julian's mother's, she told him about her mother. She didn't embellish it to soften the blow. It was simply stated, woven into a plain history of her family and Taihape. He just looked at her, no visible signs of being upset. She started to repeat it. He blinked, wincing at her every word, waved her away with one quick downward flick of his right hand, got up as if he was struggling to remain upright in thick liquid, glanced at her and hurried from the lounge into their bedroom. She heard him taking things out of the drawers and wardrobe.

A short while later he left in the Mercedes.

She couldn't sleep, worrying about him; examining the likely scenario he was going to put her through. Julian hated losing. If he ever *imagined* he had lost, he nursed the wound and always paid back. The quieter he was, the more wary you had to be. On this one he was exceptionally quiet, so the hurt was deep and his *utu* (yes, that was how it came into her mind) would be total. Yet she was not frightened. She was glad she had told him. Her confession had also committed her to a course of action she had been frightened of taking. No turning back now that Julian knew she was Maori, that she had lied to him. Never mind his lies about his family background.

About 8 a.m. next day he rang and told her he was going to stay at one of the company's apartments at Mission Bay for a few days. Matter of factly, as though he wasn't upset.

Sunday evening the kids came home and asked where he was. She told them he wanted a few days to himself to catch up with his work. Shona rang and he told her the same thing. They were used to his disappearing into a company flat whenever he quarrelled with Mum, but he always returned with gifts for everyone.

For a week he rang and talked to the kids in the evenings. He mentioned nothing about what Gill had told him. Then on Saturday morning, as if he had just remembered, he rang her and instructed her not to tell the children yet, not yet, *please.*

She waited for two days and when he did nothing, she sat the children down after dinner and told them. George's initial reaction was puzzled, unbelieving bewilderment; he just stared at her as though expecting her to become browner, more Maori-looking — but he wasn't going to believe it. Shona went and stood in front of the hall mirror and scrutinised her appearance. 'I don't look Maori, do I, Mum?' Gill shook her head. At first Karin didn't seem interested, but as Shona stood in front of the mirror fingering her skin, Karin said, 'See, I'm Maori!' She held up her right arm and showed them the area of dark tan under it.

When Julian rang that night, Shona said, 'Dad, we're part-Maori, that's good, eh!' (Karin told him the same thing. George refused to talk.) Julian ignored the girls' revelation and talked about taking them to the hot pools at Waiwera in the weekend.

Julian's 'few days' were becoming a permanent absence. The children sometimes spent weekends with him. George wanted to stay weekdays but Gill refused. One time, Karin returned to say, 'Dad reckons we don't look Maori.' 'We don't either!' George insisted.

Every time Gill rang Julian to discuss their future — she wanted a separation now that she knew she wouldn't be able to persuade him to accept her Maori side — he told her he needed more time to think about it. He still loved them, he said, and wasn't bitter about anything. She didn't care if he was lying; she just wanted to get the children away from his 'persuasion'. She knew that once he was convinced he couldn't win them he would use them as weapons against her.

Near the end of the first school term, the children's headmaster rang her and complained about Karin karate-chopping another girl. Gill asked why. He just said his school would not tolerate violence.

Soon after that, George came home and complained about people at school treating them differently *now*. Why did she have to tell everyone they were Maoris? He pushed her away when she tried to console him.

'See what you've done?' Julian accused her over the phone. 'Why didn't you just leave it alone? Why wreck our family? The kids were quite happy not knowing!' She put the phone down. She then rang the headmaster of Richmond Road School, a predominantly Polynesian school, and enrolled her children for the following term. A few days later she rented a comfortable flat in Ponsonby, not far from the school. She sold the Jaguar and bought a Toyota van, more camping gear, and told the kids they were going north for their May holidays. George refused to go; she was hurt but agreed to let him stay with his father.

Julian rang and warned her not to take *his* children north; she'd gone far enough in this 'stupid Meoree thing' and it was unfair on the kids. She didn't say anything so he threatened legal action. She rang her lawyers straight after and told them what was happening.

The 'war' with Julian was on. He was expecting no contest from her (she was a woman and a Meoree), but for months she had consulted her lawyer about protecting her property rights and gaining custody of the children.

As they drove north, fear gripped her in its teasing mouth and scared her silly every time she contemplated what she might find at Ahipara, and how hopeless she was as a camper, a fix-it-yourself leader of a two-children tribe venturing into the wilderness. With Julian they'd always stayed at hotels and motels or in business friends' opulent baches. Her demanding childhood on the farm was now mere rustic memory — the kotuku was matronly, unadventurous, safe in the confines of the status quo and the comfort of wealth. She couldn't even change a tyre. She confessed her fears to the girls. 'Don't worry, Mum, I can read the road maps,' said Shona. 'And I'll Bruce-Lee any joker who hassles us,' Karin offered. They laughed about that. 'You don't know our relatives, do you, Mum?' Shona asked. Gill shook her head, and the girls said never mind, the Maoris weren't cannibals anymore. They laughed about that too.

So, in this light-hearted fashion, they conquered some of their fear as they sped towards Kaitaia.

They checked into a motel and she looked up Aorangi in the phone book. Four were listed, so, hand shaking as she held the phone, heart threatening to leap out of her mouth, she dialled the first number. No reply. The second one, a woman, said she'd not heard of any Janet Roi-mata Aorangi; her husband might know but he was out. The third number rang for a long time and just before she gave up, someone picked it up and, in a gravelly voice, asked, 'What do you want?' She explained she was looking for the main branch of the Aorangi family. 'What do you want them for?' the man demanded. 'I'm a granddaughter,' she said. 'Are you sure, lady? You sound pretty Pakeha to me.' 'Yes, I'm sure,' she found herself saying, annoyed (but still frightened). 'You must be looking for Nanny Mataao, she's our kaumatua, our kuia.' Another heavy, suspicious pause. 'Yes, that's her,' she said, then jumping into the lucky dark, added, 'she's my mother's sister. My mother's name was Roimata.' He said, 'You're no Pakeha, lady. You'll find Nanny at Ahipara, last house on the beach road.' Another pause. 'Your mother was a beauty. Welcome home!' The phone went dead before she could thank him.

For a while she sat letting that voice of welcome run, like a soothing mountain stream, through her head.

'I have an aunt, your grand-aunt, Nanny Matty-ow.' She caught her very Pakeha pronunciation and said, 'Ma-ta-ao, Ma-ta-ao,' a few times. She got the girls to repeat it after her. Karin turned it into a rhyme and next morning as they drove to Ahipara, she recited:

> Ma-ta-ao, Ma-ta-ao, you're what we've found.
> Ma-ta-ao, Ma-ta-ao, we need you now.

Surprisingly, Gill's description of their first stay with Nanny Mataao at Ahipara was only two paragraphs long:

> It was beautiful. She is beautiful, so is my cousin. I still don't understand why Mum gave it up, ran away from it, denied it.
> It was difficult, very difficult. I was (still am) Pakeha, so were the girls. We were addicted to material comfort, privacy, private property. To adjust to 'The Mansion' (my cousins' nickname for their home), to the basic-ness of their lifestyle, to the food (and especially the kaimoana), to the lack of privacy, with everyone coming and going and sitting up all night — we helped Nanny feed everyone — was painfully difficult. Our Pakeha-ness kept springing up, protesting. Then Karin loved it, then Shona, and I swung into the rhythm of it and was glad to learn, to change. So much of who I was with Mum on that awful Taihape farm came back to me and stood me in good stead.

When they returned to their Remuera home she found it a second skin she wanted to shed — it was too large, a wasteful display. She discussed it with the girls and George, who returned reluctantly from Julian. The girls agreed to shift to the Ponsonby flat and their new school, but George protested, in tears, and rang Julian, who objected to any of the children going to 'that school'. She held the phone away from her ear. When Julian stopped, she said, 'The girls want to go there — they don't like their racist headmaster and teachers.' She put the phone down when he accused her of 'inverse racism', of being 'anti-Pakeha' and 'pressurising' their 'innocent' kids into disliking their Pakeha teachers and friends.

At dinner the girls told George about their holiday at Ahipara. They were so enthusiastic about it, George lost his sullenness and started asking for this detail and that. As she observed them, aroha (a new word for her) erased the fears that Julian had stirred up in her.

Julian got his lawyers to reinforce his objections. A compromise was arrived at: George would continue at his present school and live with Julian, while the girls lived with her and went to Richmond Road.

They shifted into their Ponsonby flat, and she moved to sell their Remuera home but discovered it was in Julian's name (so was most of their other property). When it came to property Julian fought unscrupulously. She considered letting him have it all, but her lawyers argued that at least half of everything belonged to her by right. She thought about it and decided to fight; many years of her life had been invested in getting Julian where he was now. He refused, however, to split their assets equally. And the legal wrangling continued. He offered to buy her out at much less than she was entitled to. 'Meorees don't need as much as us to live on!' he wounded her over the phone. 'Get stuffed!' she replied.

At every opportunity she took the girls to Ahipara, and when they returned to the city she sought out the new relatives whose addresses Nanny had given them. (With Grace, she was compiling a family tree — she also used the libraries and archives.) Whenever she visited her city relatives she was confronted by the stark realities of what over a century of colonialism had done to a people. It filled her with a rage she found difficult to control, but also with admiration for her people's dogged determination to survive, and to survive as Maori. Stuff integration and assimilation! She joined the activists, studied Maori language with Nanny, helped wherever possible with money — the only resource she had a lot of. She was often hurt by relatives and other Maori who insisted on treating her as a Pakeha. She felt more alive than ever before, nursing her intense rage against a society that had institutionalised racism against her and her children.

    . . . In one year I've come a long way, with my girls, in establishing our new family in Aotearoa, in growing into our Maoriness. It's bloody scary but I'm starting to feel at home in my new skeleton. The girls are much better at it than I am.

    Julian continues his attack, through his lawyers, to get custody of the kids. He's not content just having George. (My son's refusal to be with us burns like a self-renewing wound in my heart. But I'm still hoping that one day he'll see and understand what I'm trying to do.)

I know Julian has private detectives following me. He's after an easy divorce, with him winning everything in the pot. I'm sure he'll even jack up my being caught in bed with some hired stud. (To protect my interests, my lawyers are having him followed. Ola, it's bloody awful what we stoop to, to save ourselves when love/fondness has turned to hatred.) Poor conniving Julian, he's so typical of our monocultural, male, puritanical Pakeha upbringing . . .

Next year Shona's going to board at Queen Elizabeth School. She's got cousins there, and she wants to go. Julian's agreed to it — he thinks that'll keep Shona away from me. However, I had to agree to George going to King's College the year after next. King's College is poor Julian's dream of the school he should've gone to . . .

We're going to Ahipara next week to spend our first Christmas with our whanau . . .

Mark is a highly skilled carpenter so, when Dad refused to let us pay for a firm to renovate his house, Mark and I moved in and started renovations. Gill's second letter, dated 10 December 1976, didn't arrive until the first week of January 1977, while we were repainting the sitting room. I read it over lunch and for the next few days worried about her.

It was a short letter, only two pages long.

Julian and his lawyers were proving unshakeable in their pursuit, she wrote. She was wary of every man who showed an interest in her, suspecting them to be plants to entice her into a costly adultery and victory for Julian. Poor Julian didn't know that her lawyers were keeping a detailed record of his daily life. There were no women as yet, money and power and an immaculate puritanism were Julian's bedmates. He'd never been unfaithful to her but needed to be to seen with attractive women — and many women were attracted by his wealth.

Their divorce was still a stand-off. Julian had agreed, however, to a substantial monthly income for her and the kids. They'd sold the Remuera house too, and she'd used her share of the proceeds to set up a trust fund for her children and Nanny Mataao. As she'd helped in Julian's business ventures, she'd made sure she had at least a fifteen per cent shareholding in them, under her name. Most of the income from them was now going into the trust fund.

Shona was loving school, her Maori was now better than hers and Karin's. She visited the school often and was helping with their fundraising despite her having to work with 'the Maori upper middle class who were just as pretentious, conservative and status conscious as their Pakeha equivalent'.

Because Karin was with her, the poor kid was having to be her confessor and listen to her worries and problems. Karin was bypassing childhood straight into a wise middle age. She was now a wizard at karate.

Together they'd composed this poster for their front door: TAHA MAORI IS THE WAY YOU ARE NOW ENTERING. WE ARE DISCIPLES OF MATAAO AORANGI AND BRUCE LEE.

George was a lost cause. He visited them rarely. During the school holidays though, the girls talked to him on the phone almost every day, and their father took them out together once a week. She was relieved the girls weren't showing any animosity towards Julian, but was hurt (and sometimes angered) by George's coldness towards her.

Otherwise all was well. 1976 had zipped by in her intense participation in the life of the Aorangi: hui, tangi, weddings, visits to help here and there, going to Nanny whenever she was needed, taking part in protest meetings and a land march, and completing the family tree.

Life was full. She loved even the pain.

Her third letter, received at the end of November 1977 but written over a period of a month (Gill dated each section), exuded the rich feeling of being on top of things. The only disturbing chord was Julian's machinations. Three times he had the girls for weekends and refused, until a court order was issued, to let them return to her. His lawyers had filed writs that she was 'an immoral, incompetent parent'. After dirty court fights, during which they even used her participation in protests and being a Maori to try and discredit her, she got her daughters back. And each time, the girls became more vocal about disliking their father.

Otherwise her life was 'one hundred and one per cent' successful. She was now a fully accepted member of the Whanau Aorangi, Nanny's confidante and student and messenger, provider of money when needed, family historian and genealogist, marae dishwasher and cook and cleaner, good party singer but still a clumsy dancer and Maori speaker.

Her sex-life was almost non-existent. Not that men weren't interested; she was fairly lean again. But she preferred celibacy and the fullness of her life.

The girls were expert at restoring her confidence, saving her from embarassing situations, taking their fair share of the housework, correcting her Maori, and massaging her to sleep whenever she was tense.

She visited Shona often and was still helping with school activities, but some of the teachers and parents on the school committee were what her cousin Grace called 'house niggers', devoted to Pakehafying their people.

It seemed that the kotuku had made it to the summit of Taranaki, and I was happy for her.

During early 1978, the problems that Mark and I had pretended didn't exist surfaced. For instance, I was drinking heavily at parties and arguing with people, and picked on Mark when he tried to restrain my inexplicable anger. I'd shout at him at home, trying to get him to react, take a stand, but he never did. He was gentle, placid Mark — infuriatingly so. After each of my verbal flagellations, he forgave me readily, and that infuriated me more. To avoid 'our problems' we travelled more to the other Island countries, supposedly for Mark to find out how he (and Grandpa's Piles) could help. He insisted that we live in those countries as average tourists. For a while I tolerated the frugality, and then, with a septic foot in Avarua, I exploded and against his wishes packed my bags and shifted to the Rarotongan, the most expensive hotel in the Cook Islands. Mark followed but said nothing about what I'd done — which angered me. From then on we lived in expensive accommodation wherever we went, and Mark found himself going out alone on his humanitarian surveys, while I enjoyed the pools, bars and the attention of the men.

One night in the Solomons, in our hotel room that was feverish with heat — no air-conditioning — Mark was writing his diary after a barely edible dinner of fish and I was fuming and pretending to be reading. I heard myself asking, 'Why do you have to do this?' He looked puzzled. 'Why do you have to assume responsibility for the poor in the world? Why don't you be like your grandpa and continue enjoying your grand larceny? After all, America is founded on that!' He turned to his diary. 'Fuck you!' I said, and burst into tears.

So, preoccupied with my own problems, I forgot Gill.

I don't suffer from migraines often, but as I walked through the hot crowded Savalalo Market I felt one coming on, so I hurried to the fish section, bought a string of gatala (Mark's favourite), which the vendor wrapped in newspaper, and drove home.

The migraine was a punching fist of pain behind my forehead. I thumped the fish down on the kitchen bench. The fish burst out of the newspaper. I ran the cold tap, splashed water on my face and massaged my forehead with my fingers, but the pain remained fierce. Pulling the string of fish out of its newspaper wrapping, I dropped it into the sink and started washing it under the running water. I looked for a knife. My eyes caught the newspaper. I continued washing the fish, dreading the thought of having to gut them. Again I glanced at the newspaper. Then back to the fish. The migraine was stilled. Back to the newspaper. To the photo. To the two photos. Gill. Karin. Faces. My frantic hands smoothed out the wrinkled page and came away sticky with slime, but I didn't notice.

'RB BREWERIES MANAGER'S WIFE AND DAUGHTER DIE IN VAN ACCIDENT.'

Mark was holding me and whispering, 'It's okay, okay,' as I slapped at the newspaper.

The newspaper was about a month old. I sat beside Mark as he rang Auckland. Julian's secretary confirmed that Mrs Brakes and her younger daughter, Karin, had died in a motor accident just outside Kaitaia. Apart from that she had no other details. He explained to her who we were and why we wanted to speak to Julian. Mr Brakes was not in Auckland, and she didn't know where he was, she said. I took the phone from Mark and, after pleading with her to give us Julian's contact number, which she refused, I called her a heartless bitch and slammed the phone down.

Mark rang Shona's school and explained to the principal why we wanted to talk to Shona. Sorry, she said, but Shona's father had asked that his daughter be protected from all inquiries, especially from the media. I explained to her who I was and why I needed to talk to Shona. She said that Shona had collapsed on being told about her mother's and sister's death and was now recovering in a home. 'Which home?' I asked. She didn't know — and she wasn't lying, but she was sure that Shona was receiving the best medical treatment available; after all, Mr Brakes was a wealthy man. 'Are you Maori?' I heard myself asking her, for no logical reason at all. 'Yes, Te Arawa,' she replied.

Shona was in the home for most of 1978, Grace said. Suffering from what she was told later was a 'nervous breakdown'. In her will Gill had stipulated that if anything happened to her, Nanny and Grace were to be her daughters' legal guardians, but Julian and 'his football team of lawyers' kept them entangled in a legal war for all of 1978, and Shona had to stay in the home. It took Grace, Patu and some of the whanau most of that time to find the home. ('Boy, when the Pakeha want to bury someone or something,' said Grace, 'they really know know to do it! Fighting that bastard Julian is to fight the whole of Pakehadom, they even use *their* law against you. Not a new technique. Most of our land was stolen *legally* through Acts of Parliament!') Grace didn't want a continuation of the legal war, so she got Patu and his son Johnny, a Vietnam veteran, to break into the home and bring Shona north. When the police questioned them they pretended blissful ignorance. Julian threatened them through his private detectives; Grace threatened him right back with slander. When the detectives persisted, Julian received an anonymous phone call telling him he'd 'lose his knackers' if he continued, and would he like the press to learn his daughter had been kidnapped?

Shona was hidden at one of their tapu places in the hills, guarded by Johnny and treated by a skilled tohunga from Nanny Teremoana's tribe in the Waikato. Grace went to see her often, but only at night because their house was under surveillance.

Shona recovered quickly and the day before they took her back to school, Nanny spent the night with her at Ringahina. Next afternoon, Shona appeared at the school hostel. Questioned by Julian, the police and her teachers about her disappearance, she pleaded amnesia and threatened another nervous breakdown. So they left her alone.

When I asked Grace about the accident, she said it had occurred on Cousin Wiremu's farm, just outside Kaitaia. Gill and Karin had taken Nanny Whaiora, Mataao's cousin, back there. A fine day, road conditions good.

It happened as they were turning back onto the main road, on their way back, so Grace found out almost two hours later when Wiremu, after rushing Gill and Karin to hospital, came to tell them.

When they got to the hospital both were dead.

Later Wiremu took her, Patu and Johnny to the scene of the accident. The van, crushed in, was lying upside down, ten or fifteen feet below one side of the road. It looked as if it had slid off the edge after stalling and rolling back.

The police described it as a 'freak accident', but an accident all the same. The press were more interested in the victims being Julian Brakes's wife and daughter. Their stories focused almost exclusively on that. Some dwelled on Gill's separation from Julian.

At least Julian didn't oppose the tangi at the marae for Gill and Karin.

They were buried beside Reverend Aorangi and Nanny Teremoana, at Ahipara, by their family church.

After the burial, Nanny deteriorated, becoming what she was now, within a year. She believed she had been responsible for the atua taking them away. The atua were punishing her for not having loved Roimata, her only sister. (The details of their relationship she never revealed to Grace or to Gill.)

For as long as she lived, Grace would not forget Gill's and her children's arrival at 'The Mansion'.

Grace and Nanny were on the verandah. About 10 a.m., very hot and muggy. Nanny was weaving a kete, Grace was reading Alistair Campbell's *Mine Eyes Dazzle* and loving the poems. She sensed Nanny stopping her work. She looked over. Nanny was watching the yellow van that was driving up their driveway. Three people in it. Pakeha. Female.

Nanny got up and shuffled to the steps.

The van stopped. The driver, a largish Pakeha woman with a floppy sunhat, a light green dress and sandshoes, stepped out. Then two girls. In sunhats. They looked so frightened.

The children crowded into the woman's sides. Shielding them with her arms, the woman brought them forward. They were as pale as unsunned fish. 'Are you lost?' Grace called. The woman shook her head. Grace noticed that Nanny was trembling. 'Anything wrong?' Grace asked her in Maori.

Nanny beckoned to them. One — two — three frightened steps forward. 'Come!' Nanny said to them.

'I'm — I'm Gill — Smythe,' the woman said. 'At least — that was my maiden name. These are my daughters. I don't want to be rude, but is this the residence of Miss Ma-ta-ao Aorangi?'

'It is her,' Nanny whispered in Maori. 'It is Roimata!' Grace caught her as she started falling. The woman rushed over and helped her put Nanny in her chair.

'Is she all right?' the woman asked.

Before Grace could say anything, Nanny started wailing. She reached up and, arms grasped around the woman's waist, held onto her, crying, 'Beloved, beloved, Roimata!'

The woman looked at Grace for help.

'Yes, she is Nanny Mataao, Roimata's sister,' Grace told her.

The woman embraced Nanny and wept.

'Come,' Grace called to the children.

The younger one stepped forward. 'I'm Karin,' she said. 'This is Shona, my sister.'

'Welcome home,' Grace said. 'I'm your aunt, Auntie Grace.'

Just as the orange sun's edge began dipping into the western horizon, Shona left the rocks and walked past us into Ringahina. I sat up to follow her but Grace said no.

A while later, the sun half sunk in the horizon, we tried to look unconcerned as we entered Ringahina.

Shona was starting the fire for our dinner. The food to be cooked was already on a serving dish beside her. She didn't look at us. We prepared the lilos and sleeping bags while Shona cooked.

As the night fell we ate in silence. Grace lit our Coleman lamp and the sandflies started suiciding against the hot glass, while a playful breeze kicked at the ridges and sent little sandslides down toward us.

After dinner we took the dirty dishes down to the water and Shona and I washed them while Grace held up the Coleman so we could see what we were doing. The tide was coming in, sucking at our legs and swallowing the sand from under our feet.

Shona lay between us on the lilos. We waited for her, as we looked up into the stars and I imagined them whispering conspiratorially to one another. Plotting what? To take over Earth?

'The letters have told me much that I didn't understand before,'

Shona started. 'Specially about what took place between my mother and *that* man. He's a prick, isn't he?'

'But he's still your father,' Grace interrupted.

'A prick and a redneck, and he's my father — so I've got to work out something between him and me (and George, my poor brother).' She reached out and held my hand. 'But I'm okay now, I know that. I'm well, thanks to Nanny and Auntie and everyone . . .' She explained that when Julian came to her school and told her about *the accident* — that was how he and her teachers would refer to it — she switched off, like a light, click! — out. That was the most accurate description for what happened. And how long she'd switched off she'd never know, for that state has no memory. But in the darkness, which she wasn't scared of, Nanny, Grace and many of the whanau watched over her as she *grew*. Yes, she felt as if she was a plant growing, and she was sometimes out of herself marvelling at her rapid growth. Alien voices kept intruding into the miracle of her growing, threatening voices that told her she was being stupid growing so quickly because the faster she grew the quicker she'd reach her death. 'Stop!' they instructed her, but she fought them off. The buggers were just envious, she decided, because what was wrong with dying early? Only the body died; she would be out of it searching for another creature in which to live. This time she was going to be reborn as a dolphin and retrace Kupe's route back to Hawaiki and Gill and Karin.

Sometimes — and she dreaded it — she found herself in the nun's spotlessly white cell she'd seen in a film, snared between its padded walls that sucked up her protests, licked their chops after each mouthful, and demanded more. Bloody cannibals!

Twice Julian broke into her growing and, with large round globules of tears in his eyes, pleaded with her to stop her senseless growing and get well and come home to George, who was missing her, 'Bugger off!' she told him the second time, and he didn't return.

She recalled a tui — a fat lump of a bird with one good eye and its ruffled necktie of white feathers — pecking at her eardrum: tuck! tuck! tuck! tuck! She sat up in her bed and didn't understand why she was in *that* room, in that bright morning, with french windows opening out to rolling lawns and oak trees and flower gardens — another imported English park at the expense of indigenous forest. ('As migrants/explorers/conquerors/settlers we take our baggage of visions, ways of seeing and doing things, and impose them on what we see as disorder, wilderness, the uncivilised,' Grace said. 'The Pakeha saw Aotearoa as one thriving paddock fattening cows, sheep and themselves. We Maori were seen as part of the wild flora and fauna that had to be *cleared*!')

Awake, Shona pinched her arm to make sure she was real and really in that room; gasped when she saw she was attached, through a tube in

106

her arm, to a bottle of clear liquid hanging from a stand by her bed. Where was she? What was that tube?

The door swung open. In strutted a gaunt, middle-aged nurse in a white uniform, who rushed over to her. 'So we're awake at last, eh luv?' the nurse asked, feeling Shona's forehead. 'Normal temperature, that's good.' She smelled of chocolate. Shona demanded to know where she was and what was wrong with her. The nurse took two tablets out of a bottle and saying, 'This'll relax you, luv,' got her to swallow them. 'Good, good, Doctor Gravet'll be pleased.'

Soon after that, Shona was glad to be back in the fertile dark, growing to Nanny's applause. 'We'll head north soon,' Nanny whispered. But the nurse (and later, Doctor Gravet, a pink, bald-headed man with splotches of freckles over his head and a fussy voice that demanded obedience) insisted on bringing her back to that bed, that room that stank of chocolate, to their timetable of pills, injections, temperature-taking, questions and more questions about how she felt, was feeling, seeing, being, remembering, without telling her why they were doing it.

As the breeze whispered through the stars and over the dunes, and brushed the corners of our hearing, Shona described the battle over her attention between Nanny (and the forces of growing) and Doctor Gravet (and the voices of threatening sanity), clicking out of the sanctuary of fertile darkness into the hygienic light of Nurse Franklin and back again, continuously, until she awoke one morning and *knew* she was in the north, near Ahipara, clothed in sunshine that felt like fresh green leaves. She could feel herself melting into the spirit of the land, into the flow and sweep of the hills and the amniotic darkness of the cave inhabited by her ancestors, and her new guardians, Grace, Johnny and Tohunga Paki.

They helped her accept Gill's and Karin's deaths as a new beginning, for them and for her.

She was well enough now to describe the experience openly, unafraid of 'clicking out' again, and able to see her father for who he really was and try to understand him.

We slept well that night, woke to a misty drizzle, and after a quick breakfast, loaded our things onto the pick-up.

This time Grace let Shona drive, and did she drive! But Grace was no longer afraid of her speed — Shona was in control of her life. Starting with our Maori and English versions of 'Twinkle, twinkle, nosy star', we sang Ninety Mile Beach away, stopping occasionally to pick wild flowers (and three illegal kitfuls of toheroa). We arrived two hours later at their family church in the mellow shade of pohutukawa, and in the small urupa in the churchyard laid our flowers on Gill's and Karin's graves. The light rain started again, cool, forgiving.

The kotuku had dared to search for the summit of Taranaki and had found it. Gill was home, I thought, as the rain washed over us. She and Karin lived on in Shona and the mythology of the Whanau Aorangi as woven by their new keeper, Matiu Moses Aorangi, saved from the winter by the Grace of the atua.

'Thank you,' I said to Shona and Grace. They looked puzzled. 'For bringing me north to Nanny and into your home.' Grace wound her arm around my shoulders.

I was less afraid of returning home to Mark and our marriage. 'Give it another go,' Grace said to me.

'Yeah, Auntie, give it another go,' echoed Shona.

Rain, rain, don't go away,
please stay with me another day.
Rain, rain, don't go away,
please return home with me to stay.

23

The house is hushed. You're not upset as you'd expected, you're not angry as you'd wanted to be, but you're excited, that is the description for it. You returned from New Zealand about a month ago, determined to make your marriage come alive again (and it was), but now this revelation.

Mark won't be back from Savai'i until tomorrow afternoon, so you have time to contemplate the radical possibilities and questions raised by the four letters and annual financial statements sent to Mark by a Mr Thomas Trood Hoode of the Los Angeles accounting firm of Hoode, Mullins and Coldham. You'd discovered them this morning in Mark's desk while you were cleaning it.

And those possibilities are:

(1) There are no Grandpa's Piles. Mark's large income is from substantial investments he'd made through Hoode, Mullins and Coldham before he'd joined the Peace Corps. So if there were Piles, they were Mark's, not Grandpa's. But where (and how?) had Mark made his initial capital? In Canada where he'd gone to evade the Vietnam draft? But the Canadian episode could be a lie too. You ponder these questions and recall Mark telling you about a close friend who, at the height of the flower power euphoria in San Francisco, had made a fortune smuggling marijuana and one haul of cocaine from Colombia and selling it to the flower children. Strangely, you *prefer* that possibility as the initial source of Mark's investments.

(2) There are no austere, conscious-ridden parents doing penance for Grandpa's sins, on a spartan dairy farm in the cold depths of Iowa. Mr Hoode's letters/statements refer to large monthly transfers from Mark's account to a Mr and Mrs J. E. Stripter of Carson, LA, obviously Mark's parents, who were now, according to Hoode, 'enjoying a very comfortable retirement' thanks to Mark. 'Should I tell them where you are living?' Hoode asks Mark. Why is Mark keeping his whereabouts a secret from his parents?

(3) His name wasn't an alias, but what about everything else he'd told you he was/is? And why had he done it? (He loves you, you're sure of that.) We are partly 'fictions' of our own creating, vanity, of our fear of being

109

exposed as not being the people we project. But why had Mark projected to you the particular mythology that Hoode's accounting has exposed?

(4) How do you reconcile the honest, unassuming, hard-working, considerate Mark you've always known with this other Mark, the self-mythologiser, confidence trickster who, you have to admit, intrigues and fascinates you?

For a long, inventive while you debate whether you should confront him with what you know. Nor can you decide if he'd planted Hoode's correspondence for you to discover. With the *new* Mark — or, more correctly, this *new side* of Mark — everything is unpredictable. And this Mark excites you immensely with his possibilities. You'd grown bored — and your relationship was dying in that boredom — with the old Mark.

You decide not to reveal to him that you know. You will explore the new Mark. Your passionate exploration should draw out of him the rich possibilities that Hoode's correspondence promises, such surprises should sustain your marriage and transform it into a love that will feed you magnificently until you die.

You are an infinite trembling, anticipating the stranger who is capable of grand larceny, and with whom you will be 'unfaithful' to the husband you're bored with.

24

'You don't like New York, do you?' I ask.

Pita shakes his head and strolls over to the row of windows that open out across the summer skyline of Manhattan. 'How can people live in this?' he says in Samoan. (He is fluent in English but will speak it only if he has to.) He and I and Mark have spent nearly a month travelling through America. New York is our last stop before we return home.

'Apart from New York, have you enjoyed our trip?' I ask in English.

'It has been worthwhile,' he explains. (In our relationship I've nearly always been the child and he the parent.)

'But you didn't really want to come.'

'You wanted me to come.'

'Yes,' I admit. 'I needed you to come with us.' He is seventeen and precociously wise; blond and blue-eyed, but he is Samoan through to the marrow of his bones. He even prefers Pita to his registered name, Peter.

'I'm glad I came,' he eases my guilt. 'I've learnt a lot.'

'You always do,' I try to bait him. He ignores it. The light glows on his body; the noble savage outlined against the most modern backdrop in the world. 'Why do you always talk down to me?'

'I'm sorry.' He turns his face away and leaves me dangling in my foolishness.

I've left most of his upbringing to Aunt Fusi, my grandparents, father and the people of our village. During schooldays he lives with Aunt Fusi and me in Apia; every other instant he spends in Sapepe with my grandparents — he insists on it, and even my father had to give way. Already Lagona, my grandfather, has taught him everything he knows about our aiga, village, the fa'a Samoa and fishing (which is Lagona's special gift). And Pita is loved by everyone in Sapepe. (I envy him that too because I'm still a stranger to most Sapepeans.) Mark, whom I married when Pita was about nine, describes him as 'The Noble Savage as Einstein'.

'. . . It was good visiting Mark's friends in the many places we went to,' he is saying.

'But you haven't said whether you like them.'

'I liked them — I liked them very much.'

'But what was wrong?'

He hesitates, then says, 'They are so alone.'

'Perhaps Americans *want* to live that way.'

'Why?' he confronts me.

Lost for reasons, I say, 'Well, Americans are individualistic, they don't want to rely on the group. It all depends on your upbringing.'

'And this is what it leads to?' He gestures at the city. Manhattan is a steel-hided huddle of anger trying to reach up to the gods but not succeeding. 'Each window is a spyhole into a cage, each cage is stuck on to another cage, yet each is separate, alone . . .' His manner of speaking is my grandfather's: slow, lucid, like the testimony of an Old Testament prophet. 'Heaps and heaps of people, yet cut off from one another. They are rooted not in earth but in cold steel . . .' I love him (or should I say, I *need* him) more than anyone else, yet I envy all that he is, and am terrified of his beauty. 'You love it here, don't you?' he asks.

'New York?'

'Yes.'

I can never lie to him. 'Yes, I love it, even its violence and decadence. Do you find that strange?'

'In one way, yes. In another, no, because I too feel a fascination with it.'

I go and stand beside him.

For a long, quiet time we watch (and flow in) the dazzling light that seems to be brimming up out of the city's roots and filling each structure and the sky with a teeth-like whiteness.

Manhattan, born out of the soul of the exile and the refugee, you are a magnificent beast, so different from everything that I have experienced. You devour us, you feed us, you poison us, you will not free us.

Manhattan, one day my son will match you. One day he will forgive you and love even your sins.

'It's over, isn't it?' Pita breaks into my song.

'What?' I look up at him. 'You mean between Mark and me?'

'Yes.'

'Yes, it's over,' I admit at last (to myself), and there is no guilt anymore. 'We came to America to give it one last try.' I see tears in Pita's eyes. 'Mark understands,' I try to console him. 'It's best this way for both of us.' I put my arm around him. 'Pita, love between two people *can* die.'

'One day I'll understand it all,' he sighs. 'Everything.'

'How?'

'Through the wisdom of our people . . .'

'And through physics!' I joke, pushing my elbow gently into his ribs.

*

PITA TAVITA MONROE, Son of Olamaiileoti Farou Monroe/Browne (first husband)/Stripter (second husband)/Fischer (third husband), great-grandson of le Afioga a Lagona Fiapese of the Aiga Sa-Lagona of Sapepe, only heir of unknown father who was/is probably an atua and physicist! (Ha! Ha!)*

Though Pita jokes about it in the above, his father could've been a god *and* a physicist. I can't be sure because Pita was conceived in between my first and second husbands during a frightening five weeks of the most painful loneliness I've ever tried to defeat, in what now seems to have been a gluttonous gaggle of men. It was as if I'd wanted to self-destruct in faceless flesh.

On finding that I was pregnant my loneliness vanished — just like that. He (Pita) had risen up out of my emptiness to occupy it wholly, aptly, and I sang with joy.

I've never been ashamed of his illegitimacy. Not an ounce of guilt. Just a defiant pride in his conception and birth and then in him. And not once has he revealed any shame or concern about the circumstances of his birth.

Pita's quest to understand the physical laws of the universe and reality is to try and find his origins. That is not important to me, though. Every time he's with me I'm astounded that I'm his mother, and I have to touch him to convince myself that he exists, that he's not a mythical creature out of some fanciful science fiction saga.

> *Pita, Pita, physics-eater,*
> *how beautiful your wisdom grows.*
>
> *Pita, Pita, physics-eater,*
> *please help your poor mother grow.*

---

* Written in English by my son in one of his exercise books.

113

25

Once again I've had to spend weeks struggling to write the following *honestly*.

On rereading what I've written, I'm again gripped by the fear of being 'exposed' if what I've written ever becomes public. The art of writing keeps leading me through and out of my accepted self into new areas of freedom and self. Now I know why such art is considered dangerous by many people and societies. It threatens, it challenges, it subverts who and what we are at any given time; it takes us into heresy, the new, the unexplored — and who wants to be challenged, subverted? Who wants to give up habit, the status quo, the familiar self for the unknown? Who wants to court public condemnation, ridicule, persecution?

It's too late now for me to retreat into my familiar shell and limits. The act of writing — the recording of my life (what I remember and *how* I remember it) — keeps leading me on, with a new, exhilarating courage. It is determining who I am becoming; it is inventing and discovering me.

Summer, Tourist Season.
Blue District, Times Square, NY.
The Present.

You're disguised as a man, in blue jeans, golf cap, casual jacket and sports shirt, nerves steadied by two stiff vodkas and Mark's reassurances that all tourists tour the porno district; your American tour would be incomplete without it.

Ravenous rock music. You're in a telephone-booth-like compartment gazing out through a small sliding window at a circular arena and stage on which naked women, in high-heeled shoes, strut, dance, shimmy and display themselves for the two dimes you slipped into the door slot to get into the booth. Women, slim, tall, fat, black, white, brown, all manner of shape, size, movement. Dry tightness in your throat, belly; a fire burning up through the skin of your face. You're shocked at your own unexpected fascination.

Around the arena, arms and hands are reaching up out of the booths at the uninhibited parade of women, who are clutching fistfuls of dollar notes. A dollar a feel, you realise as the women pull the dollar notes out of the eager hands, open their legs and move up to the hands.

A dollar in your right hand, your arm stretching out towards the slim woman who's sleek with sweat. The gaunt face, mouth a purple slit, eyes as smooth as river pebbles, looks down at you, smiles a knowing smile. She pulls the dollar out of your grip. Twirls round, her back to you. You gasp, knowing what she's going to do. Her lean flanks and back are beaded with sweat, each bead glittering as she wriggles to the music's beat and backs towards you, with her arse protruding provocatively. Arse groove tufted with hair. Red slit centering on you. Nearer. Nearer. You hesitate. Then your hand, your fingers, are in there groping, caressing the moistness. A dollar a feel, a grope. *A grope a day keeps Sigmund Freud away*.

The woman dances away.

You back out of the booth. Ashamed? Disgusted with yourself? Your feminist sisters will condemn you for this.

You find yourself walking alongside shop after glowing shop of adult books.

Mark steers you into one of the shops. Four walls of magazines, comics, novels, playing cards, sexual aids; a whole neat kingdom of pornography. Any combination and variation of sex, a whole gymnastic orgy (sometimes of impossible positions and hilarity). The imagination's the limit! Total enslavement and humiliation of women. Even cruelty: masochism, sadism, men bursting murderous sperm while they strangle their partners. Animalism. Voyeurism. Fetishism. All the darkness's -isms.

A short while later you find yourself in the aisle between rows of video machines. 'Put some dimes in and have a look,' Mark instructs you.

Someone taps you on the shoulder. You wheel. A slender youth confronts you with an outstretched hand. 'Please?' he asks. His eyes roll drunkenly; he can barely hold himself up. 'Please?'

Mark tries to pull you away. You shove a dollar into the youth's hand and brush past him, knowing you won't forget the wild, broken gleam in his eyes. Not ever.

Times Square: a buck a life, a buck for any life. That's what your civilised self tells you, but you *want* to see and taste it all, want to *feed* (that's the word) on the degradation, the violence, the filth, the decadence. And you're high on watching yourself feeding on your rapacious guilt. Suddenly you're not afraid of yourself anymore (well, not now, anyway).

Voyeurs all on the ship of guilt,
observing one another.

Inside the cab we daren't touch each other. We huddle in our corners trying not to show our pain.

Pita isn't in the apartment.

No warmth. No gentleness. We grapple and fight like wild sea beasts caught in a thick fluid silence, choking on the unattainable orgasm promised by Times Square.

We try everything but I can't come. Mark's exhausted. I use a dildo on myself, like a scalpel searching for the pain's source. Get free. Free. But I can't break free. Can't.

'I'm sorry.'

'For what?'

'For using you.'

'I used you too.'

'There's nothing left now, eh?'

'No.'

'It was good while it lasted.'

'Yes.'

Mark, you were so kind, so generous. You expected little of me. All you wanted was to be with me. And I used you — your wealth, your tolerance. I thought I could learn to love you. I was wrong. But it was good some of the time, even the fights, quarrels and cruelties.

26

THE PACIFIC FOUNDATION

Dear Ola,

As you can see from the fancy letterhead, I'm now a 'respectable bureaucrat' in charge of a foundation I've established to help Pacific Island countries and help bribe my conscience. By the way, Dad died last October and Mom followed him a few weeks later. Their ashes were scattered over the centre of their failed dairy farm, which protected them effectively from Grandpa's Piles. I miss them very much. I miss you and Pita too.

It's been a hectic, difficult time for me since I last saw you. Grandpa's Piles have a very determined, cunning and loyal army of bodyguards in the form of Nathan, Trust, James and Blythe — a law firm. And an endless gauntlet of conniving, competing company presidents, directors, managers and boards of directors who treat me as if I'm a charming but potentially dangerous idiot who accidentally inherited Grandpa's Piles. There are also vigilantly hungry charities and philanthropies (both genuine and ungenuine) that Grandpa's lucrative Piles have kept alive for years.

I never dreamt I'd be letting myself into the wars when I decided to redirect Grandpa's Piles towards some of Fanon's wretched of the earth. (Pardon the exaggeration.) The bloody monster, once Grandpa created it, just used him (and others after him) to grow bigger, hungrier, greedier, becoming an ever-expanding empire and a law unto itself. It scares the shit out of me. I'm sure that's why Mom and Dad ran away from it. (It, of course, changed me by determining my parents' life.) My battles to get my way have forced me to be suspicious and ruthless. But enough of that self-pity.

Poor Grandpa. Why he bequeathed his Piles to poor Mom, his one and only live heir, I'll never know. He'd destroyed his own children and other heirs with unlimited expense accounts. Now I've got it, or has it got me? This sounds like something out of a bad novel by the mediocre John O'Hara. Which reminds me, I don't even have time now to read American fiction, my favourite passion.

Ola, I've decided to bequeath some of Grandpa's Piles to those who'll enjoy it or who need it to test their moral courage.

For example, I've set up a trust fund for you and Pita (you're my only aiga left). The proceeds from the fund should be enough to satisfy your extravagant tastes, and be a difficult enough challenge to your courage to resist wasteful consumption. Or be consumed by it.

If Pita still wants to come to MIT, the trust will pay for everything. He deserves it, he's a oncer. If he wants to, he can stay with me any time (and perhaps help me ride the Piles).

You can't turn the trust fund down. It's been set up in such a way that if you don't want the profits from it you'll have to decide where the money goes. I hope you don't mind accepting some of the responsibility for Grandpa's Piles.

Give my alofa to Finau, Penina, Pita and your aiga.

Samoa and you remain anchors in my life.

Alofa tele atu,
Mark

P.S. I've also transferred the ownership of our property in Samoa to you.

Is the above another of Mark's fabrications?

27

Dearest Carl,

It's about 9 p.m. and we've just spent the whole day travelling up from Jerusalem. We're staying in a small motel in Kfar Blum kibbutz, and Dad is asleep in the next room. He's really enjoying our trip. He's healthier than he's been for a long time, so alive and energetic I feel I'm the aged parent and he's the spritely, adventurous daughter.

We left Jerusalem at 9 a.m. today, after Gideon, our liaison officer, and Oren, our driver, traced our route for us on a road map: up the Jordan Valley, round the Sea of Galilee, up the Golan Heights, and then here.

You start descending sharply as soon as you leave Jerusalem. You feel as if you're in an aircraft, your ears pop. And soon you're in Bedouin country, which has little vegetation and is sparsely populated. Then round a swift bend, Oren slowed down and pointed up a hillside to our left. Pegged out like a ragged army camp were tents and other shelters belonging to a small band of Bedouins; nothing out of Hollywood and *The Desert Song*!

'. . . To farm this land, rescue it from the desert, we have to get the Bedouins to settle down in one place,' Gideon was saying. 'They've refused, they're a proud people.'

'Do we have to fence in everyone?' I asked without thinking. Gideon just grinned. Poor Dad pretended he hadn't heard.

Oren switched on the car radio. In Israel it's a national habit to switch on to the news every hour in case there's a military emergency or alert. Growing up here, you develop inbuilt sensors to warn you of any sign of danger. Without them you're exposed to death. What's it like living permanently on the sword's edge? What does it do to people? Can war become a normal part of everyday life? Like the air you breathe? Only the hope that one day peace will rescue you from the edge keeps you going.

Gideon and Oren whispered to each other in Hebrew. 'What's wrong?' I asked.

'An eight-year-old boy has been kidnapped in Tel Aviv, a ransom has been demanded, and a full-scale search is on,' Gideon explained. I knew without asking that the child was Jewish. From then on, on the hour, like everyone else in Israel, we were to follow the saga of the kidnapping.

As you know, darling, every well-brought-up Samoan is raised on the heroic Joshua and how, with holy golden horns, he and his brave warriors blew down the mighty walls of Jericho. Well, as we sped down the desolate slopes towards the dark green expanse that is the oasis of Jericho, those magnificent horns trumpeted again in my Hollywood-riddled head: TRALALALA! But instead of a golden victory, Dad and I found ourselves in a hearse-slow Oldsmobile nosing its way through a wretched maze of roofless adobe huts and buildings. The sprawling refugee camp was a creature that had been picked clean of its flesh and voice.

'It was a Palestinian refugee camp until the last war,' Gideon explained. 'They fled when the war began.'

I glanced at Dad and sensed he was empty of Joshua's victorious song. 'This is the first I have seen,' he murmured in Samoan. His first refugee camp was passing through his eyes and into his heart.

We later passed through other deserted refugee camps on the northern outskirts of the oasis, and as I write this, I can still hear their staring silence as they await the children of peace to return and turn them into laughter-filled playgrounds.

The oasis is vibrantly green with tropical life: plantations of bananas, date palms, watermelons, papaya and citrus, ablaze with flowers and the scent of jasmine.

Oren stopped our car at a small roadside shop. Dad hurried out and, doing a dance on the footpath, called to me, 'It's just like Samoa!' I steered him into the shop where we bought ice-cold orange juice. 'Beautiful,' Dad kept sighing as he drank his juice.

'The sap of Israel,' I joked with Gideon and Oren, and got stuck into my long glass of orange juice.

The desert of the Jordan Valley is blooming again; highly scientific and profitable agriculture, the most modern in the world, so I've read. Dad kept saying in Samoan, 'It's just as I've been told: God's people are reclaiming the desert.'

Dad and I are learning to cherish every bit of vegetation here. Samoa is green all year round and the vegetation is wild and luxuriant, and we take that for granted. (I suppose that's why we have no qualms about cutting down trees.) Here it's so arid, it's hard to believe anything can be grown. So a gum tree, a sabra, a cypress, a pine, any shrub or tree, is precious, especially when you see it silhouetted against the barren hills and burning sky. It's proof that, with care and irrigation, the hostile desert can be made to yield green fingers.

As we headed further north, the military became more visible: soldiers on leave hitching rides home; army patrols sweeping along the dirt road immediately on the Israeli side of the barbed-wire border fence; the area from the highway to the fence and beyond to the Jordan River had been cleared of vegetation. We had to stop at army checkpoints, and Gideon had to show his official pass. Even now, I shiver with sharp fright whenever our car is stopped and the lead soldier moves with measured pace up to our driver's door, his sub-machine-gun half pointing at the ground, his forefinger on the trigger. Every time I have to undergo this, I keep deathly still; one wrong move by me and the finger might panic and press down. Dad enjoys it. Bless his bloodthirsty warrior ancestry!

Anyway, as yet we hadn't sighted the mythical Jordan River — the invisible presence in the ravine to our right. Gideon kept locating it for us, and Oren looked amused. Beyond the ravine were the plains of Jordan, a green tidal wave that rolled up into hills and mountains and haze.

'There!' said Oren, stopping the car.

And there it was — down a slope and across a narrow strip of land, glistening like a wet eel, between shrub-covered banks; a lazy weave of water that was about five metres wide.

'That's it?' Dad asked in Samoan. (I couldn't believe it was that small either. It was certainly not the Amazon of our Bible-filled childhood.)

Dad started chuckling. We laughed as we drove on. We kept crossing creek-size stretches that were the famous Jordan River. 'It *should* be bigger,' Dad whispered to me.

'It remains large in *my* mind,' I said. Fact can rarely cut down to size the epic grandeur of our childhood mythologies. We see what we believe, or should I say, we see what we want to believe, or, put another way, we see what we were brought up to believe in the way we were taught to see. Hell, I'm starting to talk like Pita!

We stopped for petrol at a gas station (with a small café) at the southern tip of the Sea of Galilee. The café was crowded with soldiers but there was little noise. We bought cold drinks and sat at a table facing the sea. 'That's the Sea of Galilee?' Dad kept asking me in Samoan. I assured him it was. He sipped his drink like an impatient child. The sea looked swollen and dark blue. 'Our Saviour walked over *that* water,' he said. And I remembered Pasolini's film, *The Gospel According to Saint Matthew*, and the unforgettable sequence of Jesus walking fearlessly towards His disciples' boat, challenging the depths, His robes shining like armour plating, defeating mass and gravity with His faith, under a black sky, with the hungry waves sucking at His feet, ready to swallow Him up the moment He lost His courage.

'May I have an ice cream?' Dad asked.

The blonde waitress was an American. She handed me the ice creams and, as I made my way back to our table, some of the soldiers said shalom. Most of them were about Pita's age. That's what I'll always remember of the Israeli soldier: his composed quietness which masks an impregnable resolve at once fascinating and admirable but also frightening in one so young. He is the smiling, baby-faced warrior/killer/saviour/conqueror, handsomely efficient, walking the terror of the Void, with his simple faith.

Half an hour after we left the gas station, our powerful Oldsmobile found it difficult conquering the steep back road up to the Golan Heights. No sign of settlements, just steep hillsides and terraces covered with sun-burnt grass and thistles with sparkling purple flowers, and fluttering heat-waves. Then half-buried bunkers, a notice about minefields, long stretches of rolled barbed wire, steel spikes and posts. No need to ask if battles had raged here in 1967 when the Israelis took the Heights from the Syrians. Hand-to-hand fighting; each Syrian bunker and centre of resistance had to be taken, up the cruel inclines, the ravines and hollows. The cost had been high. I explained it all to Dad.

'Brave, very brave!' he congratulated Gideon and Oren. 'Malo tau!' (It was the first time he'd spoken to them directly.) He reached over the front seat and gripped their shoulders.

As we crossed the wide fertile plateau that is the Heights, Gideon explained that Israel had established a series of kibbutzim in the area and was turning the land into productive farms. Dad plagued him with ques-tions about crops, yields, population, etc. I was glad to let them answer his questions and lead him wherever he wanted to go. He was now with King David's warriors; the Philistines had been routed.

Occasionally we passed clusters of gutted military buildings and huts; bullets and fire had scarred their walls, and they were disintegrating quickly, giving way to weeds and undergrowth.

Carl, it's late and I'm feeling tired. Dad's coughing. I'll go and see how he is.

We came here for Dad's sake. Now I'm not sure it wasn't really for my benefit. Was it to get away from you and the bitter quarrels that now punctuate our marriage like exclamation marks?

I miss you, Carl. At night I concentrate so hard on imagining you're here that you almost materialise in my bed, in my arms, in me. But it's again of the flesh. (I'm starting to talk like Dad!) I don't seem to be able to love anyone outside myself. I've tried with you, darling. Really tried. Have I been expecting too much of others? To see the Jordan River as the magnificent Amazon when it's really a small, muddy, sometimes stagnant stream?

Perhaps through Israel, I'll learn to love, for the first time. To break free of my narcissism.

Promise that you will wait until I return home. Please?

Alofa tele atu.
Shalom.
Ola

28

I remember one winter night after lights out in our dormitory at boarding school. I remember saying to Gill in the next bed (and a vocal atheist), 'Jesus walked on water.'

'Bullshit!' she hissed.

'Bullshit to you!' I replied.

'No one can walk on water. It's scientifically impossible!'

'Jesus had invisible wings which kept him above the water,' someone called from the darkest end of the dormitory. A chorus of giggling and sniggering erupted.

'Fuck you without wings!' I called back.

'Yeah, you keep out of this!' Gill came to my aid.

When things quietened down again, Gill whispered, 'Ola, you weren't serious, were you?'

'About what?'

'You know, about Jesus walking on water.'

'I was. I am.'

'Hell, you can't go through life believing that!'

'Why not?'

'Ola, you just can't.'

'I'm going to try.'

29

Gideon tells us that in order to survive, Israel has to control the Sea of Galilee, the Dead Sea and the sources of the Jordan.

We are sixty-five per cent water. (Better than lettuce, which is almost all water.)

Our brains are eighty per cent water.

We are more water than blood. So our water-ties to one another are more important than our blood-ties!

We carry within us the seas out of which we came.

30

I was to observe my father grow old as senior clerk in Thurroughs Company Limited. He had risen to his highest level, the Thurroughs children rose to theirs as managers, and my father did not resent it. (I'm convinced of that now.) I tried to make him see the injustice in it, but he refused to; he was content with what he was/had: his modest position and salary and home (without debts); his respected deaconship at the Protestant Church, where I attended Sunday school and became, to my father's delight, a star pupil and later a Bible class teacher and a daughter admired by the other parents; his richly placid marriage to Penina and the four children (three boys and a girl) they were to have. Within the colonial system he accepted the level of his life, and refused to be steered by me into rebelling against that condition. In anger I would point out that *Mister* Thurroughs represented everything that was dictating his servitude. 'Thurroughs is my friend and can't be what he isn't, and he's been good to *us!*' he would reply.

He was, so to speak poetically, a Mr Thurroughs in brown skin. He epitomised loyalty to employer, God, family and country. He was a supremely kind and loving parent who endured with grace, accepting gladly the limits of his condition and being content within them.

On retirement he received a gold watch at a farewell feast put on by the firm, but no pension. So for a few years, when I returned from New Zealand, I supported our family from my meagre earnings as a teacher. To keep him happy I borrowed money from Thurroughs Co. Ltd (without his knowledge) and built and stocked a small store for him to run. He enjoyed running it and ran it well enough to provide comfortably for us. When I encouraged him to expand the business, he said, 'It's big enough for us.' Once again he was limiting his condition, not because he was afraid of risk but because he was content living within those limits.

If he could've cut his ties to our village and the fa'a Samoa, he would have. He raised me on what he admired: the Papalagi way, Thurroughs's way. I was to speak English, get a degree, be the virtuous English lady and marry a successful Papalagi (or, if I had to have second best, a wealthy part-European). I will never understand fully why he was like this.

Perhaps he saw early in his life that the quickest way to succeed in colonial Samoa was to acquire English and Papalagi ways. (He was correct there.) But that wasn't the explanation really. For even after Samoa became independent and it became advantageous to be Samoan, he continued to model his children's lives on the Papalagi, or his interpretation of that way. I think he didn't want any other alternative. And he wasn't a mimic man. He *chose* the Papalagi way, for most of his life.

It is painful for me to remember that during my university days I condemned him (to myself) as an Uncle Tom. So unjust and cruel a judgment.

We see others through our selves, and because we don't know our selves well, we see through a distorted lens. (An attempt at wisdom!)

FOOTPRINTS

We can't ever rewalk
the exact footprints we make
in the stories of our lives.
But we'll hear again our footsteps,
like the psalms our parents
sang us, the hour our stories end.

Perhaps out of our footprints
our children will nurse
wiser lullabies.

126

31

Some of us pretend we don't exist beneath the navel. Or, if we do exist there, it's an open invitation to Satan, madness and anarchy.

Some of us exist *only* beneath the navel; our lives revolve round our demanding genitals.

It's difficult for anyone to achieve a liveable balance between the two regions. And of course it depends on how old you are. For instance, as a frisky teenager I kept tripping over my forbidden lower region, it kept getting me into trouble. In my old age when my lower depths dry up, as it were, I'll probably think only of higher things (such as heaven and admission to that region).

I've tried to make my navel (and moa) my sacred centre. I vibrate out from that centre in an ever-widening spiral.

As a university student I was very keen on anthropology. (I still try and read everything that is published about the Pacific.) For almost four years I struggled to understand Levi-Strauss's structuralism, but eventually gave up in shameful disgust at my inability to do so.

Last year, at a noisy government cocktail party in Apia, I met a distinguished French professor of anthropology (who shall remain anonymous because libel can be expensive). On discovering I was a Levi-Strauss fan, he tried seducing me by simplifying Levi-Strauss's ideas to suit my simple mind and offering me, between his numerous whiskies, his hotel room for more lectures about that 'great man', whom he described, in his quaint accent, as 'the brightest man living in France today'. Raw or cooked, I asked the professor, who had twitchy eyes, a twitchy nose, twitchy little hands, and Batman's middle-aged smell. He was nonplussed. So I turned down his free bedroom lectures politely.

Which reminds me. The three or four professors I'd met outside normal lectures had been middle-aged, unwise, but graciously randy. The most gracious (and therefore the most randy) was a professor of literature (whose name and nationality will remain unmentioned). As soon as he knew W. B. Yeats was one of my loves, he proceeded to show me that he understood Yeats's poetry inside out, but I sensed he had no feeling for it, and resisted his randiness. (I must admit it was difficult because he was bronzely handsome in a decadent, boozy Dylan Thomas sort of way.)

He switched from Yeats and tried the starchy T. S. Eliot on me. No, too dry, I resisted. The professor wasn't too subtle and immediately sledge-hammered me with Bill Shakespeare. 'No, Bill's too flowery and melodramatic and big!' I resisted. 'Don't you like them big?' he leered. 'Not *that* big!' I replied. 'How about e. e. cummings then?' 'I can't stand faulty typewriters and the absence of capital letters,' I countered. 'Robbie Burns?' A pleasurable twitch shot through my centre. (There had been a time when that earthy Scot had appealed to my G-spot.)

How about Robert Graves / Robert Lowell / Robert Duncan / Robert Creely / Robert Frost? He recited all the Robert poets (including R. L. Stevenson, whose poetry I find insipid) that he knew. I declined the Roberts, though I frequently experience a muscular fire in my centre whenever I read Lowell's confessions.

The professor's graciousness was turning into nasty self-pity, predictably male. 'You don't like Papalagi poets then, especially the big ones,' he accused me. (Poor Dylan Thomas, he'd turn in his alcoholic grave if he knew how badly his decadent look-alike was behaving.) 'I go for quality not size or skin colour,' I cut him graciously.

Black Americans then / Africans / Polynesians / West Indians / Indians, etc. 'Name a few,' I requested. Leroi Jones aka Imamu Amiri Baraka / Ishmael Reed / Don L. Lee / Wole Soyinka / Alistair Campbell / Oswald Mtshali / Hone Tuwhare / Edward Braithwaite / Derek Walcott. I was tempted (being partial to permanently suntanned people) but resisted their beautiful anger. So the sorely pressed professor lost his cool. 'You like them female then!' he accused me. 'For instance?' I smiled. He hurled their names at me: Sylvia Plath / Anne Sexton / Adrienne Rich / Fleur Adcock / Nikki Giovanni . . . and suddenly, embarrassingly, he didn't know any more poetesses (what a name!), so I hurled twenty poetesses back. He looked so vulnerable in his angry, ungracious defeat, I was tempted to hold his well-groomed hand, lead him home and console him. (After all, that Dylan Thomas look-alike *did* know a lot about poets and poetry, a passion with me.)

'Don't be so fickle, lassie!' Robbie Burns licked my left (and more susceptible) earlobe, and stopped me from taking poetic pity on the cuddly professor of literature.

Next morning he sent me a graciously worded note of apology (inviting me to dinner).

In my gracious reply turning down his gracious invitation, I wrote, in my most graciously aristocratic handwriting, 'Last night you should have tried the selflessly gracious Japanese poets on my uncivilised centre. At the moment, I'm into compact poets who resemble Bruce Lee.'

128

What if Pita becomes a university professor? That question woke me up.

(Poor Pita!) I rushed into his room and, shaking him awake, ordered, 'Promise me you'll never become a university professor. Promise me!'

'Don't be so bloody silly, Ola!' He shook off my grip, turned his back to me and went back to sleep.

32

Kibbutz Mavo Hamma was built on the most strategic military position on the Golan Heights, at a spectacular point overlooking the sheer drop down to the plains of Northern Galilee.

Low, prefabricated buildings, houses and huts. Between them were concrete air-raid shelters. Few trees anywhere but the flower gardens around the houses wore brilliant colours. The breeze was heavy with the smell of ploughed earth, silage and fertiliser. Into the heavens streamed heatwaves like colonies of moths; the heat buzzed in my ears.

A sturdily built man with sparse brown hair and neatly cropped beard greeted us outside the dining hall. Scottish accent. (Later he would tell us he had come, as a volunteer, from Scotland in 1972 and had stayed to marry an Israeli. A sociologist from the cold become farmer and frontiersman.)

It was only a short distance from the dining room to the edge where we stood on the narrow platform (formerly a Syrian artillery site) and looked down at the flowing plains and sea which divide the Golan Heights from the ranges to the east. A checkerboard of green fields, kibbutzim and moshavs, and acres and acres of fish ponds (a surprise for me). 'Down there we were at the mercy of the Syrian guns,' Gideon said.

'Very true,' Dad said. Gideon and Oren took him over to the very edge and showed him where the guns had been placed; told him how far their range had been, and so forth. I could see my father memorising every detail for his friends back home; the rich tales he was going to tell them about the merciless Syrians and the victorious Israelites storming the Heights. Every time I looked down I trembled with fear, so I moved back from the edge onto more solid ground.

After a brief tour of the kibbutz factory, where they manufactured soil meters, we were shown the children's house.

Spacious and cool, noisy. Our host's wife was the chief supervisor, a beauty who seemed to have come straight out of the sabra myth: jet-black hair, deeply tanned skin, not an ounce of fat. Four children ganged round her legs, demanding attention. I sat down with them, and two of them rushed into my arms, talking in Hebrew. I told them I couldn't speak Hebrew, and they broke into English.

My father and the others went off to see the rest of the kibbutz. The supervisors quietened their energetic wards and got me to tell them about Samoa. On a globe I showed them where the Pacific Ocean was, but I discovered there was no Samoa in that ocean, so I chalked it in, described its size, climate and people. The children grew bored and restless. I saw the guitar on the shelf, got it, tuned it — my audience was attentive again, and started singing them a lullaby my Aunt Fusi used to sing to me when I was a child:

Sua maia le tai e,
Sua maia le tai e,
Le faiga figota, le faiga lili e,
Fai mai le lo'omatua
e le fia ai se faisua
e tausia ai lona soifua . . .

As I sang and held their hushed attention, the song took me out of myself back to my islands, and I had to consciously block out the homesickness and memories of Pita as a child and Carl (especially Carl) and another disintegrating marriage.

When I finished, they clapped and cheered. The little girl beside me reached up and kissed me on the cheek. She smelled of sun. I held her tightly.

'Thank you,' our host's wife said.

I sang them more songs from my childhood.

'Mavo Hamma is like a house perched on the perilous edge of the sea, always in danger of annihilation, one flood tide could sweep it away forever, but it's here, and there is hope,' my father said in Samoan as we drove away from the kibbutz, with the children waving goodbye to us.

'It must take a special type of person to want to live here,' I said.

'Is something wrong?' he asked. I shook my head, leaned back in my seat and closed my eyes.

Gideon explained that only four per cent of the population live in kibbutzim, but their contribution to the nation was enormous. Since 1948 they had provided many of Israel's leaders, especially for the armed forces and government; fearless settlers reclaiming the marginal lands under enemy fire, proving that socialism could work and work democratically. 'For hundreds of years we were stereotyped as physical weaklings, scholars and miserly capitalists who despised manual work. That's why, I think, our pioneers, who *were* scholars and professional people, went into farming and based their kibbutzim on agriculture solely.'

'Don't forget the profit motive!' joked Oren.

As my father asked questions about the kibbutz and their personal lives, we discovered that they had been raised on kibbutzim but had later left, finding the life too confining. 'You either like it or you don't, you either fit in or you don't. Some people are made for it,' Gideon claimed.

'I'm afraid Ola wasn't,' my father laughed. 'Not tough enough.'

'Too decadent and in love with material possessions; too individualistic and capitalistic; too selfish and spoilt!' I itemised. And when they laughed I laughed with them.

As our car sped down from the Heights and we withdrew into ourselves, I could think only of Carl and our marriage. I imagined us living in a kibbutz, and concluded that he was too much of an aggressive loner and manipulator and accumulator of wealth to fit in. 'A stupid idea!' he'd say if I ever suggested it. 'Honey, you and I love too much the good things of this life.'

No pioneering socialism for us.

33

Hot Easter Sunday morning. Pastor Viliamu is in the pulpit sermonising forcefully that, though Christ was dead, crucified by the Jews, He was to rise again.

A little girl, with long pigtails and a frilly white dress and who has been sitting attentively beside her grandfather, jumps to her feet on the pew and asks, 'When is He coming again?' And catches Pastor Viliamu with his rigid left hand in mid-air and a word, like a fish bone, caught in his mouth. The congregation rivet her with their surprised silence. Her embarrassed grandfather shushes her and cradles her against his side. 'But I want to know!' she insists loud enough for everyone to hear.

Speaking directly to her, Pastor Viliamu says, 'The Jews killed our Saviour but He conquered death and rose again on the third day . . .'

On their way home after the service, she tries to figure out which day was to be the third day. 'It's to be Wednesday, isn't it?' she asks her grandfather. 'He's returning on Wednesday.' She skips on ahead.

Such a clever and beautiful child, but a pity her father is raising her the papalagi way, he thinks.

'Are there Jews in Samoa?'

'Not that I know of.'

'That's good. Jews are bad people; they crucified Jesus.'

I keep looking for the racist stereotype of the dark, hook-nosed Shylock Jew.

But see blond, blue-eyed Jews,

flat-nosed, bulbous-nosed Jews,

Samoan-looking Jews,

white Jews, black Jews, multi-coloured Jews.

I keep looking for Jeffrey Hunter as Jesus,

Charlton Heston as Moses,

Orson Welles as King Saul.

It's a Cecil B. de Mille Production. And I'm just a cheap film extra in a cast of thousands. Maybe they'll offer me the role of Moshe Dayan's black eye-patch?

'Freud *had* something.'

   'What?'

   'Cancer of the mouth, which killed him.'

   Wordsworth was bloody wrong when he said, 'The child is the father of the man.'

   Woman is father/mother of the child and the man, who then turns and rapes her.

   Feminists can do without men; they can masturbate.

   I'm a feminist so I masturbate (often) but also fuck (frequently if I like the man).

   I masturbate so I exist.

   I fuck so I am.

34

In the mythologies of most cultures the gods of death are usually fero-cious female cannibals who grind their incestuous young to death in their obsidian-teethed 'man-stranglers'. Witness also the other euphemisms for cunt: snatch, trap, slit, sin-pot, thing, crack, hole, quim, cavern, etc., etc.

Remember too the taboos associated with menstruating.

Women of the world, unite! Throw off your euphemisms!

I believe in free love.

There's no such creature. All love costs.

If you mean free love as described by the matriarch Margaret Mead in her *Coming of Age in Samoa*, then I've again not met one genuine free lover, not even in Samoa. Mead lied, was misled, wanted to believe in the romantic myth of a South Seas paradise. And became famous because of it.

> All love (including sex) costs!
> All love (excluding sex) costs!
> All sex (including love) costs!
> All sex (excluding love) costs!

35

Noon. The Sea of Galilee was the colour of molten lead, languid, ponderous, and I imagined it a pregnant woman caressing her fullness and sighing, though I must admit I was as sick as a dog during my only pregnancy.

We got out of the car and strolled to the Ein Gev restaurant, with my father between Gideon and Oren. The Three Musketeers, I thought. A large air-conditioned bus was parked in front of the restaurant, and the restaurant's verandah was full of tourists eating at long tables. A fish pond lay immediately below the wooden verandah, and some of the tourists were tossing bits of bread into the dance of catfish and carp.

We sat down at a table in the dining room and ordered beer. (My father insisted on beer — which surprised me.) We couldn't escape the strong odour of oil-fried fish; and every time the kitchen doors opened, the loud sizzling invaded the dining room. 'I'm really hungry,' my father said.

Our mugs of cold beer arrived and he raised his and said, 'Manuia!' to Gideon and Oren, who clinked mugs with his. (I was being left out of the musketeers' circle.)

'Shalom!' Gideon said.

I watched my father sucking back his beer. He almost gagged but, when he saw his warrior companions draining theirs, he continued drinking, thumped his mug down onto the table, with a forced 'Ahh', wiped the froth off his mouth with the back of his hand and exclaimed, 'Manaia! Beautiful!' (His first beer ever and he'd handled it like a veteran.) 'More?' he asked his fit mates, who nodded.

Soon there were three more mugs. My father avoided looking at me. I sipped my beer — and it was good, ice-tingling cold unclutching my insides — and was relieved my father was only sipping his second beer.

I don't know how they got to it, but my father was soon telling them he was seventy-five.

'You don't look it, sir,' Gideon said.

'No,' I added. 'He looks as if he's just my older brother.'

'You don't look a day over fifty-five, sir,' said Oren, ignoring my intrusion, so I retreated into my beer.

Soon, prompted by my *young* father's enthusiastic questions, Gideon and Oren were giving him an enthusiastic description of fish farming in Israel. I observed the tourists on the verandah.

In the middle of each table was a miniature British flag. British Christians? They seemed self-conscious and restricted, and their sunburnt faces and yellow pallor made them look so foreign in a country of earth-brown people.

Oren and the short, rotund waiter who came to serve us were obviously friends. 'What edible food do you have today?' Oren asked him.

'Fish!' The waiter looked comical in his black bow tie, white shirt and black trousers, and with only short bristly hair on his temples.

'Always fish!' countered Oren.

'What do you expect? This is the Sea of Galilee!' Turning to us, he said, 'It's excellent fish bred (and fed) in our very own fish ponds. Crisply fried, it's very tasty.' He nodded towards the verandah. We looked. The British tourists were picking through plates of whole fish.

'I'm a Christian and a tourist so I'll have fish,' I declared.

'So will I,' my father said.

'And you being Jewish tourists, what are you having?' the waiter confronted Gideon and Oren.

'Kosher, boneless fish,' Oren replied.

'Same here,' chorused Gideon.

Bowing his shiny bald head towards them, the waiter clicked his heels, wheeled like a soldier and, as he marched off towards the kitchen, declared, 'And up you too, Kosher-wise!'

My father and his musketeers laughed.

While waiting for our food I talked with Oren. It was difficult to tell how old he was because he was so trim and fit, with grey-streaked hair, hollow cheeks and bronze skin (like Jeff Chandler's). During our trip, as I'd observed the cool way he handled our car and smoked his cigarettes, I'd transported him to Texas and a cowboy film in which, dressed in the tight black-leather outfit of a Hollywood gunfighter, he'd galloped across the prairie, calm and collected, oblivious to the villainous bullets whizzing past him.

He told me his parents had come from Turkey, and he'd been born in the Jewish Quarter of Jerusalem. Later they'd fled to Warsaw, and when he was twelve they'd returned to Israel. (I wanted to ask if he'd been in the Warsaw ghetto uprising, but didn't.) He'd fought in the wars of 1956, 1967 and 1973; had lived with his family first in New York then Buenos Aires, working as the Israeli embassy chauffeur, and enjoying both cities immensely.

'Are you expert at checking cars for booby traps?' I asked.

'A little bit,' he chuckled.

'Do you carry a gun when you take official visitors around?'

'Sometimes.' No further information. So I had to return to his family.

He was now witnessing his children repeating his military experience: his eldest, a son, was halfway through his three-year compulsory military training, and the next year his daughter was starting hers. 'Though I'm sad about them, I look forward to training with my unit, my friends, every July. At least for a month I'm away from my family, job and boredom.' War and fear of war and preparing for it had become part of the air he breathed, and he confessed he didn't suffer the nerve-sapping anxiety and tension that accompanied that condition. However, he feared for his family.

His face was nearly always set in a mask of inscrutability, empty of surprise. He wasn't going to be surprised even by the worst that life could offer. It was his duty to protect his family (and country) and, whether he liked it or not, he had to accept it. His controlled response to laughter and violence, his stillness and alert scrutiny, spoke of two thousand years of witnessing and suffering horrific inhumanity and injustice. But this time there was to be no meek turning of the other cheek. I sensed that both he and Gideon had killed, but when I tried to imagine them doing it I couldn't.

After eating our meal of fried fish and a salad of avocado, tomatoes, olives and lettuce, and cleaning it down with more beer (my father was tipsy), we headed for Capurnium, where Saint Peter is said to have lived.

About thirty minutes out of Ein Gev, my father, his mouth slightly open, his head on my shoulder, was fast asleep. 'He's having a wonderful time, thanks to you,' I said to Gideon and Oren. 'He's enjoying it so much, he drank his first beer, today.' They didn't believe me. 'Yes, it's true. He's been a staunch fundamentalist Christian all his life, never letting go, never allowing himself the Devil's pleasures, Satan's drink.'

They laughed with me as my father slept on.

As we approached the Capurnium archaeological site at the end of a road lined by magnificent gum trees, Gideon reminded me circuitously that he and Oren were not Christians. 'My knowledge of the New Testament is very sketchy so I don't know much about the Christian holy places,' he apologised. (I didn't believe him.) 'But I have a good guidebook here.' He got it out of the glove compartment and flicked through it. 'Here, here's Capurnium.' He pointed to the relevant section and handed me the book. (The warrior was again being the diplomat.)

Oren parked our car under some gum trees. My father stirred and woke up. (I wasn't going to mention the beer.) I explained to him that, according to the guidebook, archaeological evidence had been found at Capurnium to suggest that Saint Peter had lived there; a Catholic priest, in the 1920s, had devoted his life to digging up and reassembling the archaeological puzzle that was the Capurnium synagogue.

As soon as my father rolled out of the car, he broke out of his weariness and strode through the sun. Oren stayed in the car and listened to the radio.

It didn't take long to see the whole site, as it is only about a hundred metres across: a compact network of meagre homes, buildings and streets dominated by the half-assembled synagogue. I'm not much for ruins but my father kept murmuring in astonishment, 'To think that Peter was born and raised here. Just think of it, Ola.'

'Just like the village you were born and raised in,' I tested him.

Shaking his head, he said, 'No, our village isn't important. This is. One of our Lord's disciples lived here.' I retreated into the shade of some palms and sat on the low wall there. My father and Gideon joined me, and in silence we watched the other visitors.

A group of twelve middle-aged Japanese men, with impressive cameras and led by a Japanese guide, seemed more interested in the ruins as a stage set for photographing themselves singly, in small groups, and then as a stolid team in two severe rows on the synagogue's front steps. As they shifted away, we started back to our car.

Although the noticeboard stated clearly that the house directly in front of it was *probably* where Peter had lived, the squat, bespectacled guide was saying, 'And as we know, this *is* where our beloved Saint Peter was born and where he grew up.' No iota of doubt in his faith. At most of the Christian holy places we were to visit I would witness this dogmatic (and infuriating) Christian certainty; no one else, not even the archaeologists, were correct.

'They still haven't found him,' my father told me when I got back to our car. 'The kidnapped boy.'

'The Prime Minister is to be interviewed about it on TV tonight,' Oren added. He switched off the radio. 'The kidnappers have sent instructions about how the ransom is to be handed over to them.' He started the car.

We were again snared in the violent reality of Israel. We drove on in silence. Through the gaps in the humming line of gums I could see the sea swaying to the sun's incessant throbbing, and I wished we could be sure — as certain as that Christian guide had been about Saint Peter's home — that the kidnapped boy would be rescued, but I knew that with terrorism we can be certain only of the inevitable violence, the commitment to dying for the cause.

The image of a dead boy floating in the Sea of Galilee clogged my head. I pushed it out but a little of its dreaded presence lingered.

36

There is no doubt *whatsoever* there is a God, our God. There is no doubt *whatsoever* that Jesus, our Saviour, was His Son. There is no doubt *whatsoever* that Jesus died for *our* sins to save the world. Is that clear, Ola?

(No reply.)

So from now on you will *not* question Reverend Jeffries or me or any of your elders, understand?

(No reply.)

You're just a little girl. It is a sin to question the Holy Book.

(No reply.)

37

Four days without exercise, too much rich food and drink, you're heavy and stiff, aching joints and muscles, but that will go as soon as your shoes pound the pavement, treading on your squat shadow, stretching, through the settlement under low cypresses and pines, into the heady odour of eucalyptus mingled with humus. A couple working in their flower garden. You wave, they wave back. Relax, flow, try to be. Blond kid on a bike swerves away from you. WOWW! he calls. WOWW! Sun still a relentless fireball over the western hills. Breathe in — out. Lock into the rhythm. Flow.

You head for the front entrance and the open road. Around you are orderly fields of green peppers. Footsteps behind you, coming fast. Gideon. 'Ola, you shouldn't run out of the kibbutz — it's not safe. There's a running track over there.' Behind a dense barrier of trees. You follow him, admiring his easy stride. He's pulling ahead down the path through the trees and onto the track.

A 400-metre dirt track. With small grandstand. No one else. Still too hot in the day. Brace for the challenge. Your shoes into the dry surface — crunch-crunch-crunch. Not too fast, don't force it. You're level with Gideon. You can take him, run him off his feet. 'Ten kilometres,' you tell him.

'Not me!' he laughs. Ten kilometres to endure, break through, be. You surge ahead, your whole being flowing to the rhythm, ignoring the heat.

One round. Two. Three. You're sinking, relaxing into your self, becoming self-contained, caught in the currents of self. Time slows down. Your shadow on the track is a huge black bird carrying you effortlessly.

'You have a gift for running because you *want* to run, you *need* to run,' Mrs Rashly, your high school physed instructor, told you. (Suck in hard, you smell again her ripe apple scent — sweet, trusting.)

Your gift to run where? Away from what? Running for the sake of it?

You run to keep your weight down.

To look trim.

To keep fit.

To expend nervous tension.

141

Work out your anxieties (and shit, there're a lot of those), your sexual kinks.

You're not being fashionable.

You run because you need to, you *have* to, you have a gift for it.

You hate competitive running, you compete against yourself, against the pain and through it.

And when you run clear beyond self and the pain you feel as if you're becoming part of everything, that your every cell is merging with the light/the heat/the sky.

Sometimes you imagine you're so part of everything you'll never be able to assume your natural bodily form again, that you're permanently free in the amniotic fluid that is the unity-that-is-all.

And you've run the whole planet over: LA, New York, Philadelphia, Chicago, London, Kassel, Frankfurt, Corfu, Bombay, Tokyo, Nagoya, Yokohama, Hiroshima, Hong Kong, Singapore, most New Zealand towns, in most of the islands of the Pacific, even in places you won't ever remember. You're a Permanent Runner more accurately than a Permanent Traveller.

Does a deer know it is running? Does it feel like you when it is running? What about a dog, a bear, a rat? Do they know they're running? Do they enjoy it? Experience the free joy of it? The withdrawal into self and the healing magic of muscle and speed?

'That's enough!' someone you know is calling at the centre of your head. You're imagining it. But again the voice, the instruction. Your father moves into your view on the track. 'That's enough, Ola!' You come to rest.

'I gave up after five kilometres,' laughs Gideon.

A heavy cooling skin of wetness is tightening around you like a slow squeeze. Rivulets of sweat. Your smell encases you. You're back into your natural form.

'You're no longer young,' your father tells you, drying your face with a towel; you're the little daughter being fussed over.

> Back
> to flesh
> to bone
> to age
> to weight and mass
> to earth
> Wired
> Tied

As you walk back to the hotel between your father and Gideon, you remember that Mrs Rashly had died during your second year at university. (What had she looked like?) Had died of a stroke? You can't remember. But you can still smell (in the depths of your head) her apple scent.

Running towards your death (and through it?).

38

Why do I now talk more and more to myself (and in writing)? Getting more neurotic, more cut off from others? Valuing my solitude more? And why in the form of these stupid notes riddled with smart-alecky, self-defensive wind / bluster / glib rationalisations / *Reader's Digest* psychology / *Time* magazine wisdom / etc? I should've been a Lenny Bruce, the frenetically self-destructive spokesperson of my tame generation; one genuine belly laugh a day keeps the Devil / the CIA / your psychiatrist / your priest / your father-in-law / blackheads / cellulite / the Income Tax Department / and flab away.

The greatest comedian I've known was a classmate at boarding school: Lucille McClay. Pinkie, we nicknamed her after her favourite colour for underwear. Descendant of a long line of Scottish dissenters, rebellious Presbyterians, and a great-grandmother who, in Pinkie's inimitable description, fucked her melodiously merry way from the stinking bowels of Glasgow into the puritanical middle-class kitchens of London and into indentured slavery in pagan New Zealand and an almost celibate marriage with barely enough fucking to squeeze out Pinkie's grandmother, who, in turn, disintegrated under an insatiable railway worker, into fifteen pugnacious children (one of whom was Pinkie's father) and eighty grandchildren (mainly teachers, nurses, clerks, and spineless).

Stumpy, freckle-faced, with pounamu-green eyes, pudding-basin haircut, mouth like a Jersey cow's ever-shitting arsehole (her description), chest as flat as the Canterbury Plains (again her description), short muscular arms (made for squeezing a boy to death) and small, delicate hands (pianist's fingers to tune virgin thingumajigs into steaming volcanoes), solidly broad hips and flanks and thighs thick enough to strangle any living creature to death. Pinkie, the unsuppressible (do you mean irrepressible?), the always-moving, darting here and there, absorbing everything, as if time was running out (like the steam of a horse's piss on a winter's day).

In the weekends, when our house mistress was elsewhere or asleep, Pinkie entertained us with the most fabulously varied repertoire of dirty jokes ever amassed or created by one single, fertile teenage mind. She would've been dux if our school had judged that dubious honour

144

according to the number and originality of dirty jokes a student conjured up.

We loved her forbidden gift, revelling in the guiltiness, dirtiness of it, in the rich, abandoned, poetic, downright filthy language she used. She could string together the most taboo (and most overused) words and imagery in English (Taranaki English) and make them whole and healthy again; forbidden poems which struck hidden chords in our primeval selves and brought encores of laughter bursting out of our depths.

My strictly censored mind has always been a sieve when it comes to retaining dirty jokes (or any jokes for that matter), so I can't reconstruct any of Pinkie's creations. She was a genius at alliteration though.

Right now let me imagine our English teacher, Miss Flavell, asking Pinkie what alliteration is.

'I can't define it, Miss Flavell, but I can give you an example of it.'

'Go ahead, Miss McClay.'

Blossoming to her full height, all five feet of her, Pinkie recites, 'The frightened foal flies fleetingly out of the full-bellied frightened mare's fluttery.'

Or, 'The barbaric baron bared his bold bic to the bored barren princess (bless her bland bravery), who bared her blonde bickus back at him.'

The year after she finished the fifth form and left school, she married a farmer (a shotgun job so typical of pre-1970 New Zealand), and went to live on his farm, which was buried in the shadow of Mount Taranaki. For five years she had a child every year (one died after a few months), then a series of nervous breakdowns that crescendoed to the perfect stereotyped suicide: razor-slit wrists in a hot bath.

Had she left a suicide note, this may have been it:

'Ya see, mate, I couldn't get the frigging cows and the dogs and those bleeding hills (as empty as a dead pig's bladder) and that bald-headed mountain (which reminds me of a fat mongrel's fart) to listen to my stupid jokes anymore.

They'd heard them all before, and my bloody brain couldn' come up with any more pearls, and my timing was all fucking wrong! Poor Jim, my husband, wouldn' allow my jokes to heal his door-wide hernia. My kids, the greedy bleeding lot of them, had had enough too. Ya understand, mate, I didn' exist anymore, not for them. And what good is a comic without an original joke or an audience, eh?

So, my High-an'-Mighty Mountain, I want to end it in your shadow 'cause I've got only myself for an audience and I'm sick to death of that audience. But before I go here's one last desperate try: Mrs Cow-Cocky Comic invited the compassionate crunt to caress her crunchy crotch into crunteous caramel.'

EPITAPH

Once there was a milkmaid called Pinkie
who could humour her cows
until they pissed themselves silly.
One day she discovered her cows weren't listening
so she strangled herself with her pink undies.

39

'They're not mean and miserly, are they?'
  'Who?'
  'The Jews.'
  'What do you think?'
  'They're . . . they're kind and generous . . .'
  'Like us Samoans?'
  'Yes.'
  'And they bleed too, just like us.'

Saturday 14 June. At breakfast Oren informs us that the search for the kidnapped boy is now being concentrated on a certain district of Tel Aviv. 'We will catch them,' he adds.

Banyas is a large freshwater spring at the foot of the northern range which separates Israel from Syria and Jordan. It is one of the three sources of the Jordan River. Mount Hermon is the highest peak in the range and its snow provides the water for Banyas and the Jordan. Gideon explains this to us as we drive to the spring.

'Mount Hermon is referred to in one of our famous love songs,' my father tells him. 'The composer compares his love to "the dew from Mount Hermon".'

This poetic image is dispelled, however, as Gideon describes Mount Hermon's military importance, and most crucial of all, its importance as the source of the water that keeps Israel alive. Prompted by my father's questions, he relates how Israeli forces recaptured the mountain at a brutal price.

It is a cool crisp morning, the sky is clear as far as I can see. I wish I was out on the road, which is winding through rows of cypresses, in my running gear and running and running to the morning's eager pulse, my pores absorbing the coolness, my breath weaving through my head and blowing out the tiredness, freeing me of who I am. Running. Running. Not giving in.

The spring flows out of a break in the sloping cliff face and forms a fast stream which is sea-green in colour. I can see that from the road where we park our car.

At the park entrance is an Israeli Army post. A machine-gun, with three soldiers, is mounted on the flat roof of the building opposite the park entrance, and as we go through the park there are more soldiers.

The bold beating of skin drums echoes down from the top of the stream. Inside I start dancing to the rhythm. I sense it in my father too; an automatic response to the primeval beat which weaves the world together.

The circular pool at the head of the stream (and out of which the spring bubbles vigorously) is full of Arab boys laughing and splashing one another. On the bank are two boys, drums clutched between their legs, their hands beating out the intricate rhythm that blends with the skip and swirl of the stream. We come up to them but they refuse to acknowledge our presence.

Squatting at the pool's edge, I thrust my hand into the water. It is bone-cutting cold. I shake my hand dry, sensing that the Arabs are noting our every move.

Further up, the head of the spring is surrounded by massive rocks and boulders. We pick our way through them towards what appears to be a cave with a tangle of small trees and boulders at its mouth. Three nuns in blue habits are entering the cave.

'That's where the Syrians had their military post,' Oren says, pointing up at the cliff top. The area looks burnt and scarred by fire. 'One of their tanks crashed down from there. It was found here' — he indicates the low hollow in front of us — 'a week after the war ended. The bodies of the crew were still in it.' For me the air of Banyas shivers threateningly.

'Shalom,' Gideon greets the nuns as they emerge from the cave.

'Hello,' one of them replies in New Zealand English. Their eggshell whiteness says they are from a winter country.

We find that the cave is only a shallow indentation in the cliff. I turn and look down over the pool and stream and park. Many other visitors have arrived and are swimming in the stream or picnicking under the trees. The stream continues humming to the boys' drum-beat. It is difficult to believe that this has been the scene of a battle, of rivulets of young blood veining the brilliant water, of anguished cries and the tearing sound of guns, of death's drum-beat.

None of the Arabs greets us — they seem too preoccupied with their water games — as we return down the slope. I glance at the two drummers and catch one of them scrutinising me. He looks away quickly, his hands continuing their dance on the skin of his drum.

The drummers' bodies, hair and shorts are bejewelled with drops of water that glitter and make the boys look as if they are burning with a flameless fire, flesh transformed into eternity.

Their rhythm, their drum-beat, is the rhythm of the stream and the trees and the wind and sky and the dancing inside me, a rhythm defying and denying war and death.

41

'WITTGENSTEIN WAS AN INTELLECTUAL WANKER!'
  'No, he was an aphorist!'*

I met a Hans Wittgenstein in Kassel, Germany, five years ago. He was a butcher. The Grimm Brothers lived in Kassel too. Must be a meaning somewhere in that.

---

* Graffiti on a Ponsonby wall, Auckland City.

42

There is a cold spot for the Jew in the hearts of most non-Jews. We begin to acquire that fatal spot in our childhoods. For instance, Pita, I was brought up in a Christianity which preached (and still preaches) that the Jews crucified our Saviour, that the Pharisees were vicious, power-hungry hypocrites. One of our Samoan sayings is: 'You are like a Pharisee', meaning, 'You are a heartless hypocrite'.

From the Papalagi and his education we have inherited such attitudes as: Never trust a Jew; Jews are greedy and miserly. From Shakespeare we've inherited Shylock and his murderous pound of flesh. From Dickens we've inherited Fagan — mean, cruel, rapacious.

Anti-Semitism became (and remains) part of our way of life in Samoa, even though we're thousands of miles away from the Holy Land and Europe and most of us have never met a Jew.

As Samoans brought up on Christianity we hold the Holy Land in great reverence and awe, yet in our hearts there's a cold spot for the Jew, who had hooked, out of the Void and Chaos, the Jehovah we now worship . . .*

. . . Many of the great modern physicists were/are Jewish. I guess I'm not racist, because I don't see them as Jews but as very brainy physicists who are helping me crack open my mysteries . . .

By the way, Ola, the Void is not empty. It is alive and we and our planet are only a tiny part of it. And the Chaos you referred to in your letter originated out of the Big Bang which gave birth/and is giving birth to our universe. But I don't want to bore you with the physics B/S I'm learning here . . .†

---

* An extract from a letter Ola sent Pita while she was in Israel.
† An extract from Pita's reply to Ola's Israel letter.

43

In the late afternoon, after we checked into the hotel on the Kfar Blum kibbutz, I took my father to his room and started unpacking his suitcase. 'I'm tired,' he yawned. I told him to shower and sleep for a couple of hours before we had dinner with Ben Steiner, the kibbutz secretary, and his family in the kibbutz dining hall. 'Are you enjoying our trip?' he asked. I nodded. 'I am too, I'm learning a lot,' he confessed. 'Are you *sure* you're enjoying it?'

'Yes, Dad,' I replied in English. I started hanging up his clothes. 'Okay,' I turned to him. 'I'm enjoying our trip — I too am learning much from it, especially about myself, but things — things aren't well between Carl and me.' (It is unusual in Samoa for fathers and daughters to discuss personal problems.)

'Why haven't you told me before?'

'I didn't want to worry you. I didn't want to admit I was failing again . . .'

'Failing in what?'

'This is my third marriage, Dad!'

'I know that. I also know Carl wouldn't do anything to hurt you . . .'

'Neither did the others, but those marriages failed too.'

'It wasn't your fault.'

'And it wasn't theirs? So whose fault was it?' I sat down on the bed. He turned and looked out the window. 'I don't know why I ever married Matthew. (You didn't know him.) Mark I thought I loved. Now I know I needed his money, because I was a pampered oreo.' He looked at me. 'An oreo is someone who's brown on the outside but white inside,' I explained.

'You're not like that.'

'Are you sure? Really sure?' My question hung in the room.

He started for the bathroom. 'I'll shower now,' he muttered. He was running away from it again, and I let him. 'By the way,' he called, 'you can stop loving someone — and it's not your fault; it's natural.'

I hurried to my room, stripped off my clothes and stepped under the shower. While the fast cool jet of water massaged my head and shoulders, I caressed my breasts and belly, inciting sexual desire to blot out other emotions and thoughts, and then masturbated to a long whimpering orgasm.

After that I slept easily, and woke at 6.30 p.m. to find the world was still blind with sunshine. I remembered the days were long because it was the dry season. Here the sun took a slow death.

My father was already dressed and waiting when I went to fetch him. I was surprised he was wearing a lavalava for the first time on our trip.

We mentioned nothing about the lavalava and what had happened that afternoon as we walked to the hotel lounge and Gideon, who, after his rest, was looking exuberantly handsome in khaki trousers, a red shirt and sandals.

'Oren's gone to visit some friends for the night,' he told us.

I expected Ben Steiner, our host, to be a large presence befitting the prosperous size of Kfar Blum, but the smiling man who marched across the lounge to us was barely five feet tall. He was portly, with a large head and large hands and feet. When he introduced himself I recognised his New York accent immediately.

We drank and talked. He, with his wife, and twenty other couples from America had founded Kfar Blum about thirty years before. I liked his sense of irony, a gift I later discovered was prevalent among Israel's pioneers, an irony rich with well-told anecdotes and allegories, humour and boundless optimism. This allowed the acceptance of the world as a puzzle of irreconcilable contradictions, and for them to view their achievements as diminutive chords, mere eye blinks, when measured up against the world's pain and magnificence. Underlying this was a solid pragmatism. 'To survive the malaria swamps, the enemy raids, and reclaim the land, we *had* to be practical. Kfar Blum is now a 700-member community and a large enterprise of farms and factories. To keep it viable, we have to be practical. To stay alive, we have to be tinkers, tailors, soldiers, candlestick-makers,' Ben Steiner explained.

'But it hasn't meant relinquishing your sense of humour,' Gideon interjected.

'No, nor your eye, which is always awake to your foibles and pretensions,' laughed Ben.

During this my father maintained an observing silence, which he later nursed as we strolled through the neat settlement to the dining hall. Gideon and I covered up by trying to match Ben's effervescent conversation as we waited in the courtyard for Ben's family. The warm evening nestled down over us and the families joining the food queues, and the courtyard becoming noisy with children.

As soon as we sat down at the table in the centre of the dining hall I felt secure. I was back in my boarding-school days. Around us other families were getting their children settled. Though there were about three hundred people, the noise was muted and controlled: communal living imposes its natural limits on noise and extravagant behaviour; people learn without being told that you have to share the space according to an agreed to pattern of living; even solitude and privacy are communal property. I also knew that the food would be wholesome and served in generous helpings. Life was good and rewarding if lived simply and in pursuit of moderation. Hard work, thrift, dedication, equal sharing, cleanliness, fair play and patriotism were the supreme virtues. To each according to need and effort. Unbridled consumerism was a sin.

When I caught my father observing me I smiled at him, recognising that his life had been lived according to such values. I reached out and touched his hand.

Ruth, Ben's wife, and their son and daughter-in-law came and, after Ben introduced them to us, we joined the food line and were served roast chicken, cabbage and corn, roast potatoes and thick gravy, and vegetable salad.

As soon as we sat down at our table my father clasped his hands on the table, closed his eyes and bowed his head. There was an awkward pause. Then we followed his example. Again to my surprise, he said grace in Samoan.

'I am very hungry,' he told the others.

'I am too,' Ben helped him. Our two elders dug into their food; we joined them.

My father ate as if his existence depended on devoting his total attention to his food. When he was almost finished I heaped half of mine on to his plate.

The others talked as they ate, pretending they were unaware of the battle my father was waging with himself.

We cleared the table and, while we had coffee, talked about the kibbutz.

Ruth was the community matriarch and teacher. Silver-haired, constrained energy, tense nerves harnessed tightly. She was a vital strand of Kfar Blum, of its heartbeat, which she had shaped over thirty years of struggle. I envied her purpose and dedication which had given direction and meaning to her life.

Susan, the Steiners' daughter-in-law, was in her late twenties. She was an American, slim and attractive, with straight blonde hair down to her shoulders; she wore a casual white shirt knotted at her waist, and hip-tight white jean shorts. Her suntanned skin glowed. For a long while she observed and listened, then, when I asked her, she described how she came to be in Kfar Blum.

She had always wanted to go on to Australia. (Why? She didn't know.) In the 1960s, on her way to her mythical Australia, she had stopped off in Kfar Blum. But alas she had fallen in love with a handsome sabra (namely the ugly guy sitting next to her!) and had married him. 'So much for my dream of visiting the land of the kangaroos,' she laughed. I found myself envying her too.

'What do you do?' I heard my father asking Susan's husband, whose name I was not to remember.

'I'm an environmental control officer,' he replied and, with an impish glint in his eyes, added, 'We try to make sure Israel's natural environment doesn't get ruined, even by war.' Up to then he had maintained his silent reserve. Now as he laughed he reminded me of his father.

'What do you do when you have to fight as a soldier?' my father pursued him.

'Oh, that! I try not to kill the trees, the water, the rocks, the birds,' he countered. Susan nudged him. 'The height of man's obscenity is of course the neutron bomb, which is being designed to kill people but not harm property. Very human. Very obscene!'

We were still trying to control our mirth as we left the dining hall and sat in the murmuring gloom of the courtyard.

Above us the millions of stars were laughing too.

'Tell us about some of the places you've been to,' Susan asked. I waited for my father to speak.

'This is my first trip abroad,' he told them. 'But Ola, she has travelled widely; she's what I would call the Permanent Traveller.'

His description, I had to admit to myself, was accurate, painfully so. 'Yes, I'm permanently in motion, a pelagic Samoan,' I tried joking.

'How did you find America?' asked Susan.

Within a short time I was immersed in a detailed account of my three visits to Susan's homeland and, to my astonishment, I sensed they were enjoying my tale.

Among us, only my father hadn't lived abroad. In exile our hearts had yearned (sometimes with an awful pain) for the sight, smell, feel and taste of home, for our childhoods in the lands of our birth. I knew the pain well, for I had lived abroad for thirteen years.

Exiles become hopeless romantics: they construct ideal images of home, mirages of hope to grasp on to. For two thousand years the scattered Jews must have yearned for Jerusalem. When they had returned they had found desert and ruins, but they had transformed that into the green dreams of their exile.

As the night deepened and the chorus of cicadas sang to the blood's pulsing, I described Samoa with a love I had never displayed publicly before.

Later, in the dark as we strolled back to the hotel, my father said, 'I have never heard you talk like that before. You are still able to pray.'

155

'Are you sure?' I asked.

Gideon said goodnight and went off to his room while we sat on the verandah. We were cauled in the cicadas' chorus, the heat was lifting and a cool breeze — more a gentle presence than a current — rubbed its soothing fingers across my face. In the heaven's belly was a dull thirsty glow.

'You were correct. I *am* a permanent traveller,' I said.

'I was only joking.'

'Perhaps that's why none of my marriages have worked out.'

'I did *not* mean what I said at dinner!'

So in silence we sat, for a long while, and I sensed he was thinking of Samoa. I visualised Pita, dressed in his favourite T-shirt with the slogan WHAT THE HELL IS QUANTUM MECHANICS?, studying at his desk in his room at university, his brow knitted in imitation of Einstein as he pondered the true nature of reality. Pita knew, without any doubt, where he was going, what he wanted to find and be. Carl was probably at Aggie's Hotel, dining with overseas clients, striking more lucrative deals. He too was deadly clear about where he was and where he wanted to go.

'In my heart there is a cold spot for the Jew,' my father's confession came out of the dark silence. 'I've found that out, since we've been here.'

'But is it going away?'

'Yes, I hope it is.' He paused and said, 'Your mother would have loved this journey.' For a moment I thought he was referring to Penina. 'She was very beautiful, very understanding.' I marvelled at the permanence of his love for my long-dead mother, a kind of love I had not found in my relationship with any other man, and was still searching for.

44

Miss Bristol, Miss Bristol,*
in your pink polka-dot dress,
read me the story of Chicken-Licken
and how he held up the sky.
Please, Miss Bristol.

Miss Bristol, Miss Bristol,
with your strange Palagi smell,
fire-white hair and sea-blue eyes,
John, he pull my hair,
he kick my muli.

Miss Bristol, Miss Bristol,
if my mother had lived
I would have wanted her
to be like you.
Miss Bristol, please hold me.

Miss Bristol, Miss Bristol,
you happened in my life so long
long ago but you are still with me,
a beautiful nursery rhyme
on my tongue.

---

* Miss Bristol was my first teacher at school. She was a Pakeha New Zealander.

45

It is as if I am again being carried in my mother's dying womb. But there is to be no Caesarian rescue.

I	I
I was	I was
I was never	I was not
I was never born	I was not born
I wasn't born	
I was never born	

46

Into the wind and up the highway we sped through rich orchards and
wheat fields, then swinging wide to our right we shot along the western
side of the Mount of Beatitudes, shaded by sprawling gum trees, the car
tyres crunching over the carpet of leaves that covered the road.

Dutifully (and for Gideon's benefit) I opened the guidebook, read, and
told my father that this was the setting for the Sermon on the Mount.

I was surprised when Oren said he was coming with us.

The air was swooning with the heady odour of eucalyptus. No one
about.

Through a narrow iron gate we entered the compound of lush gardens
and shrubs which contained a Sisters' seminary and a church. In the deep
shade of the gums, the earth was dank and black like Samoa's.

'It's a Catholic church,' Oren said.

'Why Catholic?' my father asked. Oren shrugged his shoulders as if
to say, that had been a decision between the rival Christian sects.

'Erected over the spot where Christ is believed to have delivered His
revolutionary sermon,' I said.

'Revolutionary?' my father challenged.

'Yes, because He extolled the virtues of meekness and poverty, and
frightened the establishment by declaring that the last will be first and the
first shall be last, and the poor shall inherit the earth!'

'That's your *educated* interpretation,' he retaliated in Samoan. I
stopped myself from arguing with him and hurried down through the
gardens and steps to the church, filling my head with a Che Guevara
Jesus, His long hair and beard wild with revolutionary fervour.

I nearly turned back when I saw the British tourists (who'd lunched
at Ein Gev) and two nuns on the verandah. 'Join us,' one of the nuns
called. 'We're going to hold a service.'

'Thank you,' my father replied, brushing past me with his
musketeers.

They filed into the church. I stood on the verandah.

In an easy swoop the Mount rolled down to the Sea of Galilee, which
rose up mercury-grey into cloud and the land on the other side. Ideal setting for the stereotyped Hollywood epic of Jesus' life. My tough Che

gave way to the well-manicured, painted Jeffrey Hunter, who suited the modern, varnished church.

'. . . Let us pray,' the leader of the tour group declared as I entered the church. Everyone bowed their heads. I sat at the back behind the Three Musketeers.

The furnishings were simple, and the dome sparkled with glitter. I tried to relax in the coolness of the building and the smell of incense.

As the leader prayed, I observed Gideon and Oren. Though their eyes were shut, I sensed they were scrutinising every detail of the Christian service. As Jews, how were they seeing it?

The man's prayer was the familiar litany I'd grown up with. I tried to identify with the pilgrims' fundamentalist faith in a world and life that had meaning because there was a God.

Everyone sat up on the Amen. The leader stood up, clasped his hands across his paunch, and I recognised in his studied manner the pastors and deacons I'd known in my youth; all the stern, boring Sundays of prayers, sermons and well-worn Bible readings. 'Brothers and sisters,' he began, 'as you know, this' — and he pointed with his clasped hands, like a diviner's rod, at his feet — 'is where our beloved Saviour stood and spoke to the sinful multitudes . . .' I glanced at my father. His face radiated a believing light and I cursed my inability to believe, the loss of my childhood.

I headed for the door.

The sun was a fierce flail as I left the shade of the gardens and hurried to our car.

All the way to Kfar Blum I hugged my corner of the car and refused to talk to my father.

A few nights later my dreams would be haunted by fanatical pilgrims flagellating their naked bodies with wicked, masochistic whips as they retraced Christ's pilgrimage to the leafless tree, their lacerations brimming with a crimson holiness, a mad wisdom; then, through that frightening imagery, rising up to the surface like the bedrock of a river, would emerge that triumphant symbol of Yad Vashem: the child's shoe in the memorial pillar, my father's gift to me, and from it would emanate a wondrous, healing light.

47

'Ageing is a disease like any other disease. We once believed it was a natural process, an inevitability. Now we know better. And when we find a cure for it, we'll be able to live forever.'

'What if I don't want to live forever?'

'Shit, you're crazy if you don't want to!'*

'Aunt Fusi, please don't go away.'

'I won't, Ola, I'll be well again soon. Anyway, even if I did go away, I'd wait for you in God's House.'

'Where's that?'

'In Heaven, Ola, in Heaven.'

'What if you found yourself in Hell? Do I have to come there?'†

SOME PET HATES

Housework: used throughout our male-dominated planet as a means of enslaving us (women). I was fortunate my father and Aunt Fusi never let me do much housework — a very un-Samoan way of raising a child/girl. Washing dishes I detest most of all — every time I do it I feel as if I'm washing myself down the plughole.

Cooking: once again, my father and Aunt Fusi let others do this while I stuck to my studies. Again, I grew up to be a very un-Samoan female, who even manages to burn water. I never had the touch/inclination/call it what you will for this 'art form'. (Love good cooking though.) Again, a weapon for enslaving us.

Funerals: was brought up to be very Samoan in this, i.e., to feel guilty if I don't contribute to and participate in funerals of friends/relatives/ acquaintances, etc. — one's alofa for the one being funeralised should be displayed publicly in kind/money/tears/eulogies, etc. Too long/too expen-

---

* A university conversation with Gill, my atheist friend, who was a wizard in science.

† Aunt Fusi didn't die. She recovered quickly from her bout of flu. I was ten, I think, at the time.

sive/too demanding on my acting ability. *We should ban dying!* my grand-mother once pronounced when she had to contribute her most prized pig to a relative's funeral. In Samoa don't turn on your radio between 7 and 8 a.m.; that's when the funeral notices are broadcast. As long as you don't hear so-and-so's funeral is on, you don't have to feel guilty about not con-tributing to or participating in her/his final send-off. And later, when an especially vindictive relative hints at why you didn't attend so-and-so's 'beautiful farewell', you can honestly say sorry but you hadn't known about it. Better still, un-Samoanise your conscience so even if you hear the funeral notice you can just contribute fifty seconds of silence (in your bathroom) and leave it at that. That way it's easier on your nerves and savings. But be prepared to be branded by your relatives as a 'miserly Papalagi' even if you're not one genetically.

Dogs: apart from Durango I wasn't raised on 'pets'. Most of us are kind only to animals/creatures/plants we can eat. Consequently I can't love our neighbour's dogs, not only because you can't eat them but they insist on shitting on our driveway and lawns. (They tell me dogs behave like their owners, but I've not yet found human shit on our property. I'll give our neighbour, a loquacious WHO adviser from India, the benefit of the doubt.)

Aunt Fusi's habit of swilling the first mouthful of her tea and beer before swallowing them. Odd, but she doesn't do it with other drinks.

Pita thunderously cracking the joints of his fingers and toes, or, like a Houdini, trimming his toenails with his teeth. (Bloody unhygienic these teenage boys.)

Dad when annoyed, looking through me as if through a toilet seat. I've wanted him to look through me as if through a *lifejacket* but he never has.

My inability to stop using the adjectives 'shitty', 'bloody' and 'fuckin' — a habit contracted at boarding school.

My inability to prevent the white bird of ageing from walking across my skin and leaving its footprints there.

48

I had two brothers, Ola. They died before you were born. Strange that we're in the heart of Israel, sitting by a swimming pool crowded with magnificently built kibbutzim (is that the correct word?) and their energetic children, on a hot Sunday morning thousands of miles away from our village, and I should think of Va'a and Pese — those were their names. Strange how after all these years of keeping them to myself I should now want to bequeath them to you. All I know is that it *is* important that I offer them to you as part of your heritage.

As you well know, my father was a strict taskmaster, a matai whose children (and other descendants) *had* to be better than any other children. And he was hard on his eldest son, Va'a. As soon as Va'a could carry a yoke and a bushknife, he was made our father's constant apprentice in all spheres of work. By the time he was fifteen he was doing the work of a man: he did most of the work on the plantation, the heavy cooking, the fishing, and even had to care for us. (And we were a heavy burden, especially Pese, who was born mentally retarded.) Va'a never complained — not to me anyway. He even sacrificed his schooling for me — cutting copra to pay my fees at Maluafou later, and doing the chores at home while Pese and I attended the pastor's school.

I can see him now: short, slightly built but strong, light brown hair, with our mother's eyes and mouth, composed and calm. (Oren reminds me of him.) Someone who became a man before he was a child. I can see him waking at dawn, dressing in his tattered working lavalava and then hurrying through our coconut plantation, gathering nuts to feed the pigs with, then, in the kitchen fale, boiling the kettle to make koko, and cooking a fa'alifu. If the tide was right, he'd go fishing with shanghai and steel rod and return with a string of fish and cook them over charcoal. At midmorning into the plantation to plant more crops. Day in, day out, except Sunday, when he had only the umu to make. Relentlessly without complaint (like our mother, come to think of it now). The ideal son of a matai, living according to one of the basic ideals of our fa'a Samoa: the way to leadership is through service.

You know what, Ola? As I acquired more and more education at the pastor's school (and my parents planned to send me to Apia for more schooling) I began to look down on my brother. It wasn't only that he wasn't as educated as me. I also wanted him to be like other boys, to rebel — if only occasionally — against his condition, his role of ideal son. (I was jealous of him.) So just before I left for Apia, I tried to get him to rebel, to at least get angry publicly at something . . . It was a Sunday afternoon and we were reading the Bible. 'Here, you read,' I gave Va'a the Bible. He hesitated. 'Yes, Va'a, let's hear you read,' our father called. And Va'a tried and it came out brokenly. 'That's terrible!' I criticised. 'Pese can read better than that!' I wanted him to hit me, yell at me, 'And whose fault is that? I've slaved to get you where you can read properly, so eat shit!' (Or something like that.) But he just smiled and said, 'I'm not bright enough to learn properly.' I despised him then and made up my mind not to remain in the village and be like him. His life was servitude to ritual and habit, mindless service to his elders.

Two years after I started attending Maluafou School, Va'a had a wife and one child, who joined him in his ritual of exemplary service. Just over a year later, he was dead . . . I felt nothing, Ola. Not sorrow. (Maybe relief.) Nothing, Ola! And he was my brother, my flesh and blood. (I've had to live with that.) He died, so I later worked out, of a bleeding ulcer. When I learned what caused ulcers, I couldn't hold back the guilt, though I tried very hard to do so. Worry, tension, anxiety, holding it all in, that's what killed him. Yes, Va'a, my magnificently strong brother — and if he were here now I'd get on my knees and beg for his forgiveness — died *inside*, while on the outside he appeared to be in tune with his fate, his role of the loyal uncomplaining son . . . My poor brother.

You would've liked him, Ola, even though you don't have ulcers and you refuse to accept things and people as they are. You're like him in one way: you persist; once you decide on a course of action, you persist, you suffer but you persist tenaciously and, like Va'a, you never betray your kin, you serve them without complaint (well, not too much, anyway) even though many of them are mean, vicious, liars and bludgers . . . You may well ask: how can I be like him when I never knew him? But perhaps through me (and the guilt I feel about him) he has transmitted some of his qualities to you. And, Ola, please don't bother me with your arguments about cultural determinism, heredity, etc. All I know is that you are like him. I'm sure if you ask Pita, he'll be able to explain in your educated terms what I'm trying to tell you. And it's more than upbringing and genes and what's that other thing Pita talks about a lot? Yes, DNA. It's more than that too. (Now I'm sounding like Pita and you. I should never listen to that boy when he insists on trying to educate me in physics and what's that other thing? Yes, mole-molecular biology, whatever that is! At least Pita still believes in God, though I daren't ask him to define what he means by God.)

164

I can't resurrect Va'a and ask him for his forgiveness. His wife remarried not long after Va'a died and took their son to her new husband's village. I don't know what's happened to the boy, so I can't pay my debt to Va'a through his son. I've had to live with it all this time; it's been a bleeding ulcer in my centre.

Similarly I've had to live with Pese, our mentally handicapped brother.

Pese was two years older than me. And when I was strong enough my parents expected me to look after him.

Deep down we were ashamed of Pese. He was proof to others that there was something wrong with our aiga; he was incomplete, consequently we were incomplete, deformed. His deformity was also a sign of God's displeasure with us — or so other people said.

As soon as I was able to dress myself, I had to dress Pese; as soon as I could feed myself, I had to feed Pese; as soon as I could wash and clean myself, I had to do the same for Pese, and so it went on as I grew up. He became my second self. I possessed two mouths, four eyes, two noses, four legs, and even two anuses to wipe clean. But one brain, mine. He was with me almost twenty-four hours every day.

To make my job easier I trained him to play a game with me; he had to imitate everything I did. (Even the way I used the toilet.) And he did try, he *really* did; and though he spilled and dribbled his food, didn't use things as well as I did, and took twice as long to perform what I did, he tried with all his concentration. And he never got angry or vindictive. He just didn't know how to be malicious. Everyone claimed that though Pese had been born without part of his brain, he had also been born without hate or anger. I refused to see this, because, to me then, he was an inescapable burden, my second self but a burden, a distorted image of myself, slower, clumsier, dumber. Wherever I went, everyone expected Pese to be with me; my identity was incomplete without him and his constant mimicking of everything I did and was.

He cost me many friends who, because Pese was strange, considered me strange. (Others accepted him and cared for him and through him became my firm friends.) At first I was reluctant to protect him from the jokes, pranks and ridicule. But when I realised they were attacking me (by attacking my second self), I defended him (and myself) and sometimes got beaten up for it. Pese eventually developed an ingenious defence: he would roll his eyes, moan and groan as if he was insane, bare his teeth and growl like a tiger, and our tormentors would scatter, believing he was insane enough to rip them apart. After each success Pese would laugh victoriously.

At times he provided comic relief for us. For instance, whenever I read aloud, he would open his Bible and read aloud in my voice but in his unintelligible language. If I merely mouthed the words, he would do the same, to everyone's amusement. Often in church I had to restrain him from imitating our pastor. Once when our father didn't like what the pastor was preaching, he stopped me from stopping Pese, who got up and mimicked the melodramatic gestures and voice of our pastor. The church quivered with suppressed laughter and our pastor had to shorten his sermon.

When I attended pastor's school, the pastor had to accept Pese too. Pese had his own slate and Bible; he was promoted when I was; he sat exams with me and when I won prizes, he received them with me in front of the congregation.

When I became interested in girls, he did too. But the girls stayed clear of us because of Pese. I tried all sorts of ruses to escape from him so I could be with a girl I'd arranged to meet but he always found me. As I've said, he was truly my second self, as close to me as my own smell and shadow. So as a young man I didn't have much of a love life. (And neither did Pese.)

I didn't know then — or want to know — how fortunate I was.

Pese, my second self, died unexpectedly. One sunny morning I woke up to find he wasn't breathing anymore. (He was twenty, I was eighteen.) God had granted my secret wish to be free of my burden. Just like that! I had *wished* him away. But it wasn't to be that easy. God has many ways of punishing us. The day after Pese was buried, I *missed* him. The loss was an excrutiating physical pain. It was as if my extra legs, eyes, head, stomach and heart had been torn away but I could still feel them. Yes, Ola, I could still feel my brother trying to complete me. Without him I was incomplete. Do you understand, Ola? In dying and taking his physical presence away from me, he had only entered another dimension but he was still with me, he *had* to be with me to complete me.

Eventually I learned to live with the pain. I felt that he was with me everywhere I went, imitating me. Even when I was with a woman. Uncanny?

It wasn't until I fell in love with your mother that Pese's presence eased away. She provided my completion. When she died, Pese returned to comfort me whenever I couldn't conjure up her presence.

Last night when I couldn't sleep he came and sat with me and, in our twin way, echoed all that I said and thought. I fell asleep with him beside me. This morning when you woke me, I realised what I've missed. It was in you, Ola, in your search to be more: I've been missing my brother's wise love, his lack of malice, the unconditional trust he put in me as his anchor, his protector. He had given me his life to care for and I had *willed* him away.

At that time I thought he needed me, but it was the other way around.

I needed him. He was fashioned, by our wise God, without those qualities that make us hurtful and evil. For that I needed him always.

In my old age, Ola, I'm fortunate that he still returns whenever I need him. To be my confessor and protector. And I now find myself imitating him. Is that a sign I'm learning some of his trust and wisdom? Or is it a sign I'm getting senile?

Who knows, Ola? Now that I've placed him in your reality, he may visit you and you can learn from him. I know he's been with Pita since Pita was born; he's told me. The instant Pita left your womb and entered our world, Pese visited him. Why do you think Pita is so intelligent and wise? Why do you think he understands those complicated sciences and is searching for other ways of understanding who and what we are?

My grandson is very lucky. He has an uncle he never knew in real life but who has chosen to complete him, protect him . . . One day soon, Ola, you must tell Pita about Pese.

I've been fortunate to have had (and still have) two such forgiving brothers . . .

What about my parents, you ask. Yes, that's another story for another pause during our pilgrimage through this unreasonably hot Holy Land. (I wonder if Hell gets this hot?) Right now I'll leave you to continue frying your hard skin in this hard sun. I'm off to the hotel's air-conditioning and more sleep, seeing there are no Christian services in this non-Christian kibbutz that I can attend.

49

So in the course of a conversation, during which he did most of the conversing, I've acquired two new uncles and the guilt (his) that goes with them. Two heroic and tragic figures (he had prescribed them that stature) who still visit him (he's certainly not going senile) and who he hopes will visit me. Why he decided to pass them to me to be part of my pantheon of mythical beings, my Dead, I'll never fathom. I don't know if I should be glad or curse him for doing it. Not that I'm ever ungrateful to be saddled with more relatives, dead or alive or in between.

Va'a and Pese (Boat and Song, in English), like Laurel and Hardy, Abbott and Costello, Tom and Jerry. What am I supposed to do with them? How can I relax and get a tan if I've got two invisible uncles sitting on either side of me, waiting for me to say, 'Hi, how are you? Please forgive my dad, he didn't mean to betray you, be the selfish bugger that he was when you knew him!' They don't understand Kiwi English anyway, from a niece they never knew would be born out of death.

'Okay, youse jokers, please leave me alone for now. I just wanna get a simple suntan, a cool swim then I'll be better armed to cope with ya. Okay? Your loving brother has just gone back to his cool hotel room. I'm sure he'd love to see ya. So please follow him, wake him up, he'd love to talk to ya about old times. Okay? Right now I wanna head that's absolutely empty of regrets or guilt or anything. Give us a break, okay? I love all my relatives — ya heard what my old man said about me being loyal to all our relatives! And good Christian Samoan uncles aren't supposed to sit beside their bikinied niece ogling her tan. Ya know that! So go wake up your brother.'

I enjoyed constructing conversations with my (dead) uncles, in various English slangs, and giving them shape, voices, smells, personalities, futures (yes, even those now that they were alive in me and Pita).

My skin started stinging from the heat. I went to swim.

> *Inside us the Dead*
> *like sweet-honeyed tamarind pods*
> *that will burst in tomorrow's sun . . .*

Inside me the Dead
woven into my flesh
like the music of bone flutes . . .

As I approached the water, those lines, by a Samoan poet, echoed in
my head; apt description of how I felt about my Dead.

Arching my body, I dived. The water's coolness drove the heat out
of me. Caught in the grip of water, I was on my own, free even of my
uncles. Leisurely and avoiding the other swimmers, I swam to the shallow
end of the pool.

A few metres away, standing in the water, a father was teaching his
young son to jump into the pool. The giggling boy kept taking mincing
steps to the pool's edge, hesitating, then retreating. 'C'mon,' his father
coaxed. 'Don't be afraid.' The boy whooped in delight, minced forward
again, then retreated. I remembered how I'd taught Pita. Pita had teased
me too, pretending he was afraid, withdrawing, giggling, arms clasped
around his chest, then prancing forward. I had grabbed him and pulled
him into the water. 'Ola, Ola!' he had shrieked (he never calls me Mum
or Mother), dog-paddling furiously while I had laughed and then
embraced him.

With that memory came a cutting homesickness. Pita had started that
journey every child makes away from his mother and towards his own
life, hopefully carrying his Dead (his mother among them) without hating
them.

I pushed myself forward and sprinted towards the deep end. Chock!
Chock! Chock! my arms chopped into the water. My son was leaving me,
in his place I had received two uncles who weren't going to let me forget
my father's guilt and the shallowness of my life. It wasn't a fair and just
swap. It wasn't.

I pulled myself out of the pool, rushed up to my towel and started
drying myself roughly.

Stopped. I was being stupid. A creature shuffled behind me. I
wheeled. A small deer was edging its way along under the row of young
cypresses that bordered the pool area. It stopped and peered at me. Its
hide was the sheen of new steel, the colour of early evening.

I turned and surveyed the pool, the swimmers and sunbathers. In
affluent societies hair dyes, face-lifts, wigs and toupees, severe diets and
other ways of disguising age are a way of life. Here, no one appeared self-
conscious about flab, wrinkles, grey hair, sagging bellies and chins, vari-
cose veins and the other ravages of age. Kfar Blum was a pioneer venture
that had succeeded, become comfortable and middle-aged. The socialist
radical, the defiant rebel, the youthful experiment in utopia had fallen into
prosperous ways. 'For our community to grow, become more dynamic,

we need young married couples,' Ben had confessed to us at dinner the previous night.

I was fortunate to have a son (who loved me) and a father (who had given me two new uncles). So lucky. What other Dead was my clever dad going to give me during our pilgrimage? I was going to give him some of my Dead and Not-yet-Dead. A fair swap.

50

Miss Susan Sharon Willersey, known to all her students as Crocodile Willersey, was our house mistress for the five years I was at boarding school. I recall, from reading a brief history of our school, that she had been born in 1908 in a small Waikato farming town and at the age of ten had enrolled at our preparatory school; had then survived (brilliantly) our high school; had attended university and graduated MA (Honours in Latin); and had returned to our school to teach and be a dormitory mistress. A few years later she was put in charge of Beyle House, our house.

So when I started in 1953, Crocodile was in her fit mid-forties, already a school institution more myth than bone, more goddess than human (and she tended to behave that way).

Certain stories concerning the derivation of her illustrious nickname prevailed (and were added to) during my time at school.

One story, in line with the motto of our school (Perseverance is the Way to Knowledge), had it that Miss Willersey's first students called her Crocodile because she was a model of perseverance and fortitude, which they believed were the moral virtues of a crocodile.

Another story claimed that because Miss Willersey was a devout Anglican, possessing spiritual purity beyond blemish (is that correct?), an Anglican missionary who had visited our school after spending twenty invigorating years in the Dark Continent (his description) had described Miss Willersey in our school assembly as a saint with the courage and purity and powers of the African crocodile (which was sacred to many tribes). Proof of her steadfastness and purity, so this story went, was her kind refusal to marry the widowed missionary because, as she reasoned (and he was extremely understanding), she was already married to her church, to her school and students, and to her profession.

The most unkind story attributed her nickname to her appearance: Miss Willersey looked and behaved like a crocodile — she was long, long-teethed, long-eared, long-fingered, long-arsed, long-everythinged. Others argued she had skin like crocodile hide, and that her behaviour was slippery, always suspicious, decisively cruel and sadistic and unforgiving, like a crocodile's.

As a new third former and a naive Samoan who had been reared to

obey her elders without question, I refused to believe the unfavourable
stories about Miss Willersey's nickname. Miss Willersey was always kind
and helpful (though distant, as was her manner with all of us) to me in our
house and during her Latin classes. Because I was in the top third form
I had to take Latin, though I was really struggling with another foreign
language, English (and New Zealand English at that). We felt (and liked
it) that she treated her 'Island girls' (there were six of us) in a specially
protective way. 'You must always be proud of your race,' she kept
reminding us. (She made it a point to slow down her English when
speaking to us so we could understand her.)

During her Latin classes I didn't suffer her verbal and physical (the
swift ruler) chastisements, though I was a dumb, bumbling student. Not
for several months anyway.

However, in November during that magical third form year, I had to
accept the negative interpretations of Miss Willersey's nickname.

I can't remember what aspect of Latin we were revising orally in class
that summer day. All I remember well were: Croc's mounting anger as
student after student (even her brightest) kept making errors; my loudly
beating heart as her questioning came closer and closer to me; the stale
smell of woollen cardigans and shoes; Croc's long physique stretching
longer, more threateningly; and some of my classmates snivelling into
their handkerchiefs as Croc lacerated them verbally for errors (sins) committed.

'Life!' she called coldly, looking at her feet. Silence. I didn't realise
she was calling me. 'Life!' she repeated, this time her eyes boring into me.
(I was almost wetting my pants, and this was contrary to Miss Willersey's
constant exhortation to us: ladies learn early how to control their
bladders.) I wanted desperately to say, 'Yes, Miss Willersey?' but found
I couldn't, I was scared.

'Life?' She was now advancing towards me, filling me with her frightening lengthening. 'You *are* called Life, aren't you, Monroe? That *is* your
nickname?'

Nodding my head, I muttered, 'Yes — yes.' A squeaking. My heart
was struggling like a trapped bird in my throat. 'Yes, yes, Miss
Willersey.'

'And your name is Life, isn't?'

'Yes.' I was almost in tears. (Leaking everywhere, I was!)

'What does Ola mean, exactly?'

'Life, Miss Willersey.'

'But Ola is not a noun, is it?' she asked. Utterly confused, leaking
every which way and thoroughly shit-scared, I just shook my head. 'Ola
doesn't mean Life; it is a verb, it means "to live", "to grow", doesn't it?'
I nodded furiously.

'Don't you even know your own language, young lady?' I bowed my head (in shame); my trembling hands were clutching the desk top. 'Speak up, young lady.'

'No, Miss Willersey.' I swallowed back my tears.

'Now, Miss Life, or should I say, Miss To-Live, let's see if you know Latin a little better than you know your own language!' Measuredly, she marched back to the front of our class. Shit, shit, shit! I cursed myself (and my fear) silently. Her footsteps stopped. Silence. She was turning to face me. Save me someone!

'Excuse me, Miss Willersey,' the saving voice intruded.

'Yes, what is it?'

'I think I heard someone knocking on the door, Miss Willersey.' It was Gill, the ever-aware, always courageous Gill. The room sighed. Miss Willersey had lost the initiative. 'Shall I go and see who it is, Miss Willersey?' Gill asked, standing up and gazing unwaveringly at the teacher. We all focused on her. A collective defiance and courage. For a faltering moment I thought she wasn't going to give in.

Then she looked away from Gill and said, 'Well, all right, and be quick about it!'

'You all right, Miss To-Live?' Gill asked me after class when my friends crowded around me in the corridor.

'Yes,' I thanked her.

'Croc's a bloody bitch!' someone said.

'Yeah!' the others echoed.

So for the remainder of my third form year and most of my fourth form year I looked on Miss Susan Sharon Willersey as the crocodile, to be wary of, to pretend good behaviour with, to watch all the time in case she struck out at me. Not that she ever again treated me unreasonably in class, despite my getting dumber and dumber in Latin (and less and less afraid of her).

In those two years, Gill topped our class in Latin, with little effort and in clever defiance of Crocodile. Gill also helped me get the magical fifty per cent I needed to pass and stay out of Crocodile's wrath.

Winter was almost over, the days were getting warmer, our swimming pool was filled and the more adventurous (foolhardy?) used it regularly. Gill and I (and the rest of Miss Rashly's cross-country team) began to rise before light and run the four miles through the school farm. Some mornings, on our sweaty way back, we would meet a silent Crocodile in grey woollen skirt and thick sweater and boots, striding briskly through the cold.

'Morning, girls!' she would greet us.

'Morning, Miss Willersey!' we would reply.

'Exercise, regular exercise, that's the way, girls!'

In our fourth form dormitory my bed was nearest the main door that opened out onto the lounge, opposite which was the front door to Crocodile's apartment, forbidden domain unless we were summoned to it to be questioned (and punished) for a misdemeanor, or invited to it for hot cocoa and biscuits (prefects were the usual invitees). Because it was forbidden territory we were curious about what went on in there: how Croc lived, what she looked like without her formidably thick make-up and stern outfits, and so on. As a Samoan I wasn't familiar with how Papalagi (and especially Crocodile) lived out their private lives. I tried but I couldn't picture Miss Willersey in her apartment in her bed or in her bath in nothing else (not even in her skin) but in her make-up, immaculately coiffured hair and severe suit. (I couldn't even imagine her using the toilet! Pardon the indiscretion, which is unbecoming of one of Miss Willersey's girls!)

The self-styled realists and sophisticates among us — and they were mainly seniors who had to pretend to such status — whispered involved and terribly upsetting (exciting) tales about Crocodile's men (and lack of men), who visited (and didn't visit) her in the dead of night. We, the gullible juniors, inexperienced in the ways of men and sex, found these lurid tales erotically exciting (upsetting) but never admitted it. We all feigned disgust and disbelief. And quite frankly I couldn't imagine Miss Willersey (in her virgin skin) with a man (in his experienced skin) in her bed in the wildly lustful embrace of *knowing each other* (our Methodist Bible class teacher's description of the act of fucking). No, I really tried but couldn't put Crocodile into that forbidden but feverishly exciting position. At the time I *did* believe in Miss Willersey's strict moral standards concerning the relationship between the sexes. (I was a virgin, and that's what Miss Willersey and my other elders wanted me to retain and give to the man I married.)

One sophisticate, the precociously pretentious and overweight daughter of a Wellington surgeon and one of Crocodile's pet prefects, suggested that Croc's nightly visitors weren't men. That immediately put more disgustingly exciting possibilities into our wantonly frustrated (and virgin) imaginations.

'Who then?' an innocent junior asked.

'What then?' another junior asked.

'Impossible! Bloody filthy!' the wise Gill countered.

'It happens!' the fat sophisticate argued.

'How do you know?' someone asked.

'I just know, that's all!'

'Because your mother is a lesbian!' Gill, the honest, socked it to her. We had to break up the fight between Gill and the sophisticate.

174

'Bugger her!' Gill swore as we led her out of the locker room. 'She sucks up to Miss Willersey and then says Crock's a les!'

'What's — what's a les . . . lesbian?' I forced myself to ask Gill at prep that evening. She looked surprised, concluded with a shrug that I didn't really know, printed something on a piece of paper and, after handing it to me, watched me read it.

A FEMALE WHO IS ATTRACTED TO OTHER FEMALES!

'What do you mean?' I whispered. (We weren't allowed to talk during prep.)

She wrote on the paper: 'You Islanders are supposed to know a lot more about sex than us poor Pakehas. A les is a female who does it with other females. Savvy?'

'Up you too,' I wrote back. We started giggling.

'Gill, stand up!' the prefect on duty called.

'Oh, shit,' Gill whispered under her breath.

'Were you talking?'

'Life just wanted me to spell a word for her,' Gill replied.

'What word?'

'Les-,' Gill started to say. My heart nearly stopped. 'Life wanted to know how to spell Lesley.' Relief.

'Well, spell it out aloud for all of us.' And Gill did so, crisply, all the time behind her back giving the prefect the up-you sign.

After this incident, I found myself observing the Crocodile's domain more closely for unusual sounds, voices, visitors, and though I refused to think of the possibility of her being a lesbian, I tried to discern a pattern in her female visitors (students included), but no pattern emerged. Also, there were no unusual sounds. (Croc didn't even sing in the bath!)

Some creature, almost human, was trapped in the centre of my head, sobbing, mourning an enormous loss. It was wrapping its pain around my dreaming and I struggled to break away from its tentacles. I couldn't. I woke to find myself awake (and relieved I wasn't strangling in the weeping) in the dark of our dormitory. Everyone else was fast asleep.

Then I knew it was Miss Willersey. I knew it and tried not to panic, not give in to the feeling I wasn't going to be able to cope. I wrapped the blankets around my head. It was none of my business. But I couldn't escape.

I found myself standing with my ear to Miss Willersey's door. Shivering. Her light was on, I could tell from the slit of light under the door. The sobbing was more audible but it sounded muffled, as if she was crying into a pillow or cushion. Uncontrolled. Emerging from the depths of a fathomless grief. Drawing me into its depths.

My hand opened the door before I could stop it. Warily I peered into the light. My eyes adjusted quickly to the glare. The neat and orderly arrangement of furniture, wall pictures, ornaments and bookcases came into focus.

Miss Willersey was enthroned in an armchair against the far wall, unaware of my presence, unaware of where she was and who she was, having relinquished in her grief all that was the Crocodile. She was dressed in a shabby dressing gown, brown slippers, hair in wild disarray, tears melting away her make-up in streaks down her face, her long-fingered hands clasped to her mouth trying to block the sound.

Shutting the door behind me quietly, I edged closer to her, hoping she would see me and order me out of her room and then I wouldn't have to cope with the new, vulnerable Miss Willersey.

All around us (and in me) her grief was like the incessant buzzing of a swarm of bees, around and around, spiralling up out of the hollow hive of her being and weaving round and round in my head, driving me towards her and her sorrow, which had gone beyond her courage to measure and bear.

And I moved into her measure and, lost for whatever else to do, wrapped my arms around her head, and immediately her arms were around me tightly and my body was the cushion for her grief.

At once she became my comfort, the mother I'd never had but always yearned for, and I cried silently into her pain. Mother and daughter, daughter and mother. A revelation I hoped would hold true for as long as I was to know her.

Her weeping eased. Her arms relaxed around me. She turned her face away. 'Please,' she murmured. I looked away. Got the box of tissues on the table and put it in her shaking hands. Tearing out a handful of tissues, she wiped her eyes and face.

I started to leave. 'It's Ola, isn't it?' she asked, face still turned away. In her voice was a gentleness I had never heard before.

'Yes.'

'Thank you. I'm . . . I'm sorry you've had to see me like this.' She was ripping out more tissues.

'Is there anything else I can do?' I asked.

'No, thank you.' She started straightening her dressing gown and hair. The Crocodile was returning. I walked to the door. 'Ola!' she stopped me. I didn't look back at her. 'This is our secret. Please don't tell the others.'

'I won't, Miss Willersey. Good night.'

'Good night, Ola.'

I shut the door behind me quietly. And on *our* secret.

Next morning there was a short article in the newspaper about her mother's death in Hamilton, in an old people's home. Miss Willersey left on the bus for Hamilton that afternoon.

'The Croc's mother's crocked,' some girls joked at our table at dinner that evening.

Yes, Crocodile Willersey remained married to her school and students until she died in 1982. By becoming a school tradition and a mythical being in the memories of her students (generations of them), she has lived on, and we will bequeath her to our children.

Miss Susan Sharon Willersey, the Crocodile, I will always think of you with alofa. (And forgive me — I've forgotten nearly all the Latin you taught me!) By the way, you were wrong about the meaning of Ola; it can also be a noun, Life.

51

'Thank you for giving me the Crocodile (whom I didn't ask for).'

'How do you find her?'

'A miserable way to be a person.'

'Is it a fair exchange?'

'For what?'

'For Va'a and Pese.'

'So that's why you've unleashed the Crocodile on me.'

'As I've said, she's got *long* teeth. Would you like more of my Dead (and Not-yet Dead)?'

'No, thank you. Not tonight anyway. It's enough to have to sleep with Miss Susan Sharon Willersey tonight.'

'Good night, Dad. Tomorrow night I'll tell you about some of my other Not-so-Dead.'

52

Tel Hai is a memorial cemetery set among tall pines and thriving gardens on a windswept hilltop. The central memorial stone is the Lion of Judea. My father and I wander through the cemetery. Like the other memorials in Israel, Tel Hai is used to teach history to the young, especially the history of Israeli resistance to oppression; to inspire courage, self-sacrifice, pride and national unity. Nearby are camps used for youth rallies and training.

We stop under the whispering trees and look down and across the valley dreaming in the early afternoon sun. 'When I described my walk through Yad Vashem I forgot to tell you something else I saw,' my father says. 'The mention of youth camps brought it back to me.' He turns and we continue walking between rows of pruned roses. 'There's a glass display case in Yad Vashem with the framed photograph of a man called Eichmann. You know about him?' I nod. 'What did he do?'

'He had thousands of Jews executed in the Camps.'

'That explains it. As I was passing, I noticed a group milling in front of his photograph. When the boys — young they were, about ten years old — thought no one was looking, some of them poked their tongues at Eichmann. Others shook their clenched fists. Now it's obvious to me that those boys had been taught their history well.'

I tried to justify the children's hostile reaction by telling him that one of the monstrous stereotypes of the Jew — foisted on him by his tormentors over two thousands years — is that of a masochist who enjoys and needs suffering to find salvation, who deliberately seeks martyrdom in order to find happiness. The clenched fists of those boys were a revolt against that stereotype. 'The Israelis won't be intimidated,' I argue. 'Rebellion has been a major feature of their history.'

My father ponders and then asks, 'But when does just rebellion become intimidation, a blind nationalistic fervour? When does the just victor — if there is such a creature — become the conquering oppressor?'

'What about the Palestinians?' I whisper to myself.

'What did you say?'

'Nothing. Just a puzzle.'

'What puzzle?'

'The same you've just put to me.'

You can't win, I think as we stroll back to the front gate and our car.

In the shallow ditch near the gate is a scatter of thistles with their purple and deep blue blooms. Kneeling down, I pluck one and examine it, gazing into its ever-shifting, sparkling depths. In those depths I see Eichmann's haunted face: the dead eyes, the bland violence of the civil servant. A garden of arms rises up in front of it, clenched fists shaking, shaking defiantly.

Heil! Heil!

Always the reminders of war, but I'm starting not to see them. They're becoming part of my reality, to be taken for granted. Given time I can adjust to anything, live with anything, accept anything.

Even Eichmann?

53

Fano Paulo, Leifiifi Intermediate School
Mata Reupena, Leifiifi Intermediate School
Brenda Jones, Leifiifi Intermediate School
Melisa Fusiaiga, Accelerate School
Olamaiileoti Monroe, Leifiifi Intermediate School
Mago Logovai, Accelerate School
Tesema Tuivailoa, Marist Brothers' School
Sinapati Mutia, Accelerate School
Salote Pelu, Accelerate School

This is the government scholarship group I went to New Zealand with at the beginning of 1953. About 250 students sat the qualifying exam, we were selected, I came fifth in the exam. Just before Christmas Day our names were announced over 2AP, the national radio station. My father, Aunt Fusi and countless other relatives wept, for to be a scholarshipper was to be envied and admired nationally. 'Ola's specialness is coming true!' Aunt Fusi exclaimed that Sunday when our relatives gathered in Apia at our house for to'ona'i. My grandparents came from Sapepe.

I felt very special. For my father, whose plans I was starting to fulfil. And for God, who, everyone at church told me, was taking special care of me. Reverend Jeffries even praised me from the pulpit.

I also felt vindictively special in relation to my father's employers, the Thurrough family. None of their children had ever won a scholarship.

My guess is that between 1945, when the scholarship scheme started, and this year (1983), over fifty per cent of our scholarshippers have remained abroad, refusing to return home to serve their bonds.

None of my group failed, and we returned to pursue 'successful careers'. It wouldn't be immodest to claim that our group has been the most successful ever sent, on taxpayers' money, to study abroad.

Here are brief profiles of our group:

FANO PAULO was the youngest of the three sons of Pastor Paulo, who, at that time, was the most influential elder in the LMS Church, and one in an illustrious family line of pastors that began when the missionaries converted the first Paulo in 1839. Seventy-year-old Pastor Paulo wanted Fano to start a new family tradition in law. At that time most parents wanted their children to be pastors, doctors, lawyers or teachers, in that order, not really for the money but for the status. Making profits was considered by strict Christians as usury, unbecoming of a true Christian aristocrat and gentleman.

Fano did moderately well at high school; did exceptionally well at law in Wellington; he married Elisa, another scholarship student, and they returned home in 1964. For nine years they lived in a comfortable and inexpensive government house at Mulinu'u while he developed into the most tenacious prosecutor in the Attorney-General's Office. Five years after establishing a lucrative practice (the first Samoan to do so) they shifted into an ultra-modern house, with a huge mortgage, up on the slopes of Vailima. His beautiful daughter is now studying law at Canterbury University (on a government scholarship) and his exceptionally handsome son is in the sixth form (and expected to gain a scholarship) at Samoa College, the élite high school where Elisa has taught English since they returned.

For every Samoan who aspires to the modern middle-class life, the Paulos are their model, the dream to follow.

MATA REUPENA eventually got her medical degree at Otago University after three extra years of tragic love affairs and a child, which her village parents adopted. She's now Doctor Mata Downright, married to an Australian engineer, and in charge of our National Community Health Unit. (We were never close; we see each other as rivals.)

BRENDA JONES, eldest daughter of one of our wealthiest merchant families, completed her nursing training in minimum time, scrupulously avoiding affairs of the heart, returned as a sister to our National Hospital and within a year, on her parents' instructions (she obeyed them always, poor Brenda) married Paul Frankz, heir to another merchant family, had five children in quick succession while she tolerated her husband's countless infidelities, discovered she had VD and left him for good to become matron at the hospital. She's now forty-five, a shapely spinster respected (and ogled) by the doctors and patients and without financial worries because of the hefty trust account set up for her by her frugal parents. She and I have remained close friends. She envies what she claims is my talent for 'owning' men and doing what I like with them; I envy her honest naivety, and dedication to helping others.

MELISA FUSIAIGA, champion shotputter and discus thrower at high school, conscientious plodder who had to sit School Certificate twice, eventually made it to Teachers' Training College, where she blossomed into the fervent leader of the Student Christian Movement and preached fiery sermons on Auckland's street corners. On qualifying as a teacher, she surprised us by converting to the Seventh Day Adventist Church. She returned home not to teach school but to be a missionary, who soon established records in converting people to her faith. At the age of thirty-five she married a seventy-year-old widower (the most powerful elder in her church) and surprised us again by having two sons, after which her husband died (of a heart attack, I heard) and she replaced him in the church council. We're not close but I admire her immensely. Once, two years ago, we met in the post office. She held my arm and said, 'Ola, I will remain astounded by your energy, your love of life, your refusal to be less. Stay as you are, always!' I've not been able to crack that loving puzzle.

MAGO LOGOVAI, when our group first left for New Zealand, was considered by the Education Department officials to be the most brilliant of us. He proved it at high school, where he topped his classes, was hero-worshipped by his juniors (and the girls at the neighbouring high school — and for a time by me and the other girls in our group) for his feats in rugby, cricket, tennis and swimming. (He captained his school in all these sports.)

He started a degree in accounting but, because he channelled his brilliance and enormous appetites into alcohol, women and the billiard saloons, failed his course that year and his scholarship was terminated by our government. Once he was back in Samoa he again became a brilliant sportsman and a 'promising' civil servant, whose directors insisted would one day realise his brilliance. One day he realised he was married and his wife (a portly teacher) was expecting their third child, and for two years he tried to forget that in gallons of brilliant alcohol which exploded in a drunken car crash on Christmas Eve. Almost a year later, he was wheeled home, paralysed from the waist down. He became a teetotaller and devout church deacon who remained a 'promising' civil servant. His brilliance is being fulfilled though by his nine children: for instance, his eldest daughter is a doctor, and his eldest son is a university lecturer and a national rugby representative.

I had a crush on Mago at high school. Every time I think of him now, I see the student god. Nailed to a wheelchair.

TESEMA TUIVAILOA, known to us affectionately as TT, is our country's High Commissioner to New Zealand. Like Mago, TT dropped out of university and the electronics degree he was doing. But, unlike Mago, TT fell madly in love. He married and had to go to work to support his wife and their baby. Two years later, when he was in a position to resume his studies, he discovered his heart wasn't in it — it was still with his frisky wife, Mata claims.

Up to their return to Samoa and his work in Foreign Affairs, TT had been faithful to his wife. (He was so trusting and naive, Mata claims.)

Then he went to London to train as a diplomat. That was in the 1960s, when the Beatles and the 'new morality' were erupting into vogue. TT returned with the latest fashions in clothes, and not to his wife and sons but to a soon mushrooming (mostly secret) harem, of married and single, local and expatriate women.

His precarious love life did not affect his diplomatic career adversely. In fact it enhanced it, Mata claims. TT is one gigantic success with the female 'diplomats' wherever he goes on diplomatic missions.

Last year he returned from New Zealand, supposedly for a holiday. To our surprise he married (secretly) the daughter of one of our prominent doctors. (She looks and behaves just like his first wife at her age, Mata claims.)

We have always known that Mata has had a thing for TT, as it were. That's why she follows the details of his life avidly (and viciously) and insists on reporting them to us.

SINAPATI MUTIA, we have always called Sinbad the Pirate, and true to his nickname he became a vicious pirate.

When we first went to New Zealand, we felt sorry for him. He was illegitimate, puny and shy. But we soon had to be wary of him. You name the sport, the competition, and he'd try his utmost to humiliate you. To him everything was (and is) a battle. If he can't win, he'll wait and plan and pay you back. We learned to respect him when he drove himself to qualify as a dentist in minimum time, while we partied and failed some units and had to borrow money from him.

Sinbad the Pirate is now a Member of Parliament who is conniving unscrupulously to be Prime Minister — a driven pirate who uses any means to win in business and politics. (He even wears extra-thick shoes to increase his height.) It is rumoured that he spent about a hundred thousand dollars to buy his three-hundred-vote electorate in the last general elections; much of the money is said to have come from the sale of smuggled goods.

Fano reckons Sinbad is going to spend the rest of his life trying to beat his non-existent father and add length and thickness to his small prick in an unwinnable contest.

SALOTE PELU was my favourite out of our group. She passed away about three years ago; a superb nursing sister who diagnosed too late that she had breast cancer.

Every time I think of her I have to choke back the tears. She was the least tainted/corrupted of us, the least changed by the whole élite scholarship experience, the one who remained the most Samoan.

54

It took us a fast forty-five minutes to reach Hazor, which had been the most important city in the area in ancient times. Now it was a massive archaeological excavation, showing that human settlement had begun there at least five thousand years before. (I was getting tired of inspecting ruins and historical sites, but my father's enthusiasm for them was increasing.)

We left our car and Oren at the gate beside the office and walked up to the mound, with my father leaning his weight on Gideon's shoulder.

We couldn't escape the afternoon sun. The few stunted trees didn't provide any shade. The only shelter — a narrow open shed with two benches — was occupied by a middle-aged man and two women, hatted, their skins purple-red with sunburn. American tourists, I thought. On the sides of the deep ravines on three sides of the mound, the hills and fields were vibrating and fluttering with angry heat waves. My eyes hurt in the glare and wept as we inspected the ruins of houses, temples and the dry moat. My father asked Gideon a list of questions about Hazor. Gideon replied patiently and in detail. Drenched with sweat, I felt unreal in the midst of their conversation about something I wasn't interested in. (We were inspecting an ancient cemetery and I wasn't feeling any affinity to the Dead there.)

Hazor's source of water was a man-made crater about fifty metres across and thirty-eight metres deep. My father insisted on exploring it, so, trying to hide my impatience, I descended with them down the hundred and fifty steps (my father counted them aloud) the ancient Hazorians (my coinage) had sculpted into one wall.

It grew cooler as we descended.

At the bottom, a narrower cave slanted down to our left. We followed the steps into it and found it a cool relief from the heat. Its fecund smell of mud, wet limestone and water was also refreshing. I lowered my left foot into the still pond and, holding it there, let the crisp coolness flow up into me.

'Must've been very difficult work digging down to this water,' my father remarked.

'Yes, considering they had only stone implements and a crude technology to do it with,' Gideon said. I didn't care about technology right then; I just wanted the coolness of the water in the heart of Hazor.

Opposite the mound, on the other side of the highway in the property of a kibbutz, was the Hazor Museum, which was surrounded by neat lawns and a border of gum trees. The modern two-storeyed building reminded me of an air-raid shelter raised above the ground. The bottom floor was all glass and contained the lobby and office. I followed the others to it. The front glass wall was pockmarked with a line of ragged bullet holes. 'The last war,' Oren said.

I was glad when we entered the lobby and were out of the sun.

A wizened old man with prominent ears and an almost bald head, rimless glasses, well-worn checkered shirt and khaki trousers got up from behind his desk. (There was no one else there.) Gideon spoke to him in Hebrew. The old man relaxed. He shuffled to us, smiling. We shook hands. His grip was powerful, his hand hard and rough.

'Before you go upstairs to see our collection, I should tell you a little about our museum,' he said, displaying an ill-fitting set of false teeth. (I couldn't identify his thick accent.) 'The Hazor Museum is owned by the government; it doesn't belong to our kibbutz, and it's not run by a professional archaeologist or curator.' A faint laugh. 'As you can see, I'm just a humble farmer. Humble and old, but I try my best.' He paused, his shoulders heaving with suppressed mirth. 'Our museum houses the artifacts from the Hazor mound. The display has been arranged to give you the whole history of ancient Hazor. Strategically, Hazor was important because it was located at the bottleneck of two valleys. Whoever commanded Hazor controlled this whole area and the trade which moved up and down the valleys. So far our archaeologists have found twenty-one distinct levels of civilisation at Hazor, a whole history of construction, prosperity and power, then brutal conquest and destruction, followed by reconstruction, rebirth, power. A story we're all familiar with, worldwide.' Paused. 'So you see, the cycle of war is not new to Israel. Measured up against the five thousand years that was Hazor, the forty-year history of modern Israel is like the blinking of an eye and a youthful eye at that. My eyes are old, they blink too slowly.' He paused again; we were enjoying his delightful self-mockery. 'As you can see,' he continued, pointing to the bullet holes in the glass, 'life in our area hasn't changed much, we continue to fight one another. Some people wanted us to replace that bullet-riddled glass. I asked them why. This is a museum, isn't it? This is a museum about Hazor and its wars. So why not preserve the modern wars of Hazor too? These beautiful holes!' He chortled wickedly. 'They couldn't defeat such logic and agreed to leave this sad glass alone, a true reflection of our times.' He laughed and we laughed with him. 'Against Hazor's old age we should be humble. We're inspired to resist, to survive, to struggle.' His eyes shone with a mischievous wisdom. 'Of course, like all mortals since time immemorial, we too want to be remembered as somebodies. Our vanity is only too human.' He dried the laughter at the corners of his eyes with his handkerchief and asked if we had any questions. Perhaps we would have questions after we viewed the collection, we told him. He nodded and, remembering, said, 'And if you too want to be remembered at Hazor by this young museum, please sign this.' He opened and pushed the visitors book over the desk to us.

My father signed it with a grand flourish. I did too. I mean, who wants to be forgotten by such a wise curator and his young ward known as the Hazor Museum?

An hour later as we were leaving, he shook our hands, saying, 'Come again. Who knows? I'll probably still be here.' There was the brightness of a patient eternity in his smiling eyes.

'For me he'll always be here, as the Keeper of Hazor,' my father remarked as we returned to our car.

Forgiving us our vanity even before we reveal it, I completed his statement in my thoughts.

Wise Keeper of a Cemetery with a Heart of Cool Water.

55

I am who I am plus my husband, my son, my father, my aiga, my other
circumstances, and this sentence about who I am and the feeling I *should*
be more.

      Tonight I'm haunted by all the things
      I should've done, by all the choices
      I should've made, by all the people
      I should've loved, by all the voices
      I should've listened to
      Tonight I want to empty myself
      of all that I am
      and let the night flood in to fill me

56

As soon as the Blooms came into the Steiners' sitting room where we were enjoying Ruth's home-made ice cream, and Mrs Bloom was introduced and we shook hands, I sensed she was considering me a threat to her being the centre of attention.

The splendidly bronze, well-groomed Blooms made the room feel smaller, shabbier, apologetic. He was patricianly tall, with a clean-cut profile, neat wave of white hair and moustache, which made him look like Douglas Fairbanks Jnr in *The Pirate*. She was short and having weight problems, which she was trying to hide in her voluminous dress. She wore long earrings, heavy make-up, and a face-lift. Affluent middle-class Americans going 'fake rustic socialist'. And so incongruous in the fairly spartan lifestyle of the kibbutz. I was glad I hadn't put on any make-up and was dressed in khaki shorts and a plain T-shirt.

My father, Gideon and I ate our ice cream slowly and said little, leaving poor Ben to react, with inane questions and remarks, to the Blooms' almost non-stop description of their Israeli tour. Ruth sat opposite us in an armchair, trying to appear interested.

'. . . Herb and I are amateur archaeologists. We signed up for this dig, back in LA. Thirty of us amateurs. Yeah. With Professor Mike Speicus,' she was saying.

'Yeah, we had been on two previous digs, in Egypt and the Sudan. This time we thought we should come to Israel and do a dig here. After all, we are Jewish!' he continued their story. They laughed at his last remark.

'Herb gave himself four weeks' vacation (from his law firm) so that we could come here and help dig up our Jewish roots, eh.' She was now shrieking with laughter. 'Dig it, Ben?' The fat on her neck and arms wobbled.

'Excuse me,' my father interrupted, 'what is a dig?'

'We're from Samoa,' I apologised for him.

'Don't worry about it. Our motto is: If you don't know, ask,' she replied. 'Okay, Herb darling, you explain.' And he was off into a patronising description of archaeology and what digs were.

'. . . Whew, it was back-breaking work in the sun,' she brought the topic back to themselves. 'Tough sleeping in spartan barracks on hard beds. (They *were* hard, weren't they, darling?) Eating a hell of a basic diet (and sand). Mind you, it was good for my weight . . .' As far as I was concerned, she was *still* fat.

'But it was worth it,' he took over from her. 'Good for the body and the soul. And I certainly needed the exercise.'

'Yes, darling, you *were* getting flabby. Israel's good for cutting down on calories and for bolstering one's spiritual values and rediscovering one's roots.'

'Did you find anything valuable?' Ruth asked.

'Yeah, we did, right on the last day. You tell it, honey.'

Sweeping back his mane with his hands, he said, 'Well, Sue and I made the only valuable find out of our whole party, and right on the last day . . .' He went on to describe, blow by laborious blow, how they had done it and what the artifacts were.

Just as he was finishing that episode, she started telling us anecdotes about the 'extra-curricular activities' (her phrase) of the diggers. 'Isn't that right, darling? Professor Speicus had this young thing, a student of his at UCLA. Boy, did they forget they were in the Holy Land and do some pretty hectic night digging of their own! But then every archaeologist to his own tastes in digs, eh!' She laughed shrilly, her crimped hair flashing like coils of copper.

'He had good taste there, I must say,' Herb joined her, winking at me.

'. . . And there was this poor innocent couple, the Franksters,' she was saying. 'From Alabama, real country like Billy Graham and Charlie Pride. Didn't know what hit them when they caught an eyeful of Prof Speicus and his student excavating!'

'Poor Tom nearly had a coronary right there, and poor — what was her name?'

'Janice,' she replied.

'Yeah, poor green Janice had to give him mouth-to-mouth resuscitation. Reverend Falwell would've loved it!'

'They were a real ache in the posterior,' she laughed.

Then they turned their cruel attention to the other couples in their party.

I visualised her hair dye being rinsed out to reveal healthy streaks of grey, her heavy make-up flaking away to bare the wise grace of age, her manicured hands becoming thick and strong, her neurotic dieting giving way to abundant muscle, as she accepted her age and limitations and strengths.

'We've never been to Samoa,' she was saying. 'Is it a good place for a vacation?'

190

'It is as good a place as any other,' my father replied. 'Depends on what you're looking for.'

'If it's like Tahiti, it'll be another tropical paradise. Isn't that right, darling?' she said, and Herb was off again, this time focusing on the supposedly easy virtues of Tahitian women.

'More ice cream anybody?' Ruth rescued us. Gideon, Dad, Ben and I said yes. Predictably the Blooms refused on grounds of calories.

'Are there any of us in your country?' she asked. I didn't understand. 'Jews,' she added.

'I don't know,' I replied.

'Probably are,' said Herb. 'Hardly any corner of the globe where you won't find us. We're pretty tough, eh Ben!'

It was again the diplomatic Gideon who made the first move. 'I'm sorry but I have to show our guests,' meaning us, 'around this area, this afternoon,' he apologised to the Steiners.

'Yes, I want to look at the fish farming here,' my father said, standing up.

Herb Bloom began talking about fish farming but Ben said, 'I'll just see our guests out.' He shepherded us out on to the verandah. 'I'm sorry about that,' he apologised as soon as we were out of the Blooms' hearing. 'They're friends from way back. They chose the American way, we chose the kibbutz and home-made ice cream. And they *do* contribute a lot of money to Israel. Giving money salves your conscience — and you don't have to risk your life.'

'Watch it!' I said. 'You're getting cynical in your old age.' I kissed him on the cheek.

With me in the middle, Gideon, my father and I linked arms and marched back to the hotel.

'Pretty monstrous,' Gideon said.

'What?'

'Those people.'

'Oh, them,' laughed my father. 'You can *dig* them up anywhere, even in Samoa, eh Ola.'

'What's a dig?' I mimicked his question to the Blooms.

'Spiritual or archaeological?' Gideon echoed.

'Both!' I laughed.

'As long as you don't get a heart attack pursuing Professor Speicus's *other* style of digging!' my father improved on the joke.

Oblivious to the heat and whoever was observing us, we laughed as we marched.

With their arms around me, they lifted me off my feet and I marched in the air.

Goodbye, Mrs Bloom, I welcome losing you.

During our last evening in the kibbutz, as the darkness hatched its brood of mellow silence over the plains and encircling hills and mountains, Ruth came to say goodbye. We asked her to take us for a walk around the kibbutz.

The kibbutzim and moshavs on the Golan Heights were afire with lights that were like breathing pores in the landscape's flesh.

'Hear the guns?' Ruth whispered. We stopped and listened. 'Hear them? In Lebanon?' she asked, pointing at the mountains ahead. My father and I concentrated more intently. Still nothing. 'Listen to the swish and thud,' she indicated. We tried again. A long swishing sound then a trembling thud, barely audible. Since 1948, Ruth had lived with the guns and bombing and she could hear them through her skin, recognise them in the quivering of the air and earth. A sixth sense.

Again I looked up at the lights of the settlements on the hills: they pulsated; they looked as if one flash of wind could extinguish them. Candles on a birthday cake.

From beyond them, in Lebanon and the infinite darkness, arose the almost inaudible swish and thud, swish and thud.

In Samoa elders are not supposed to show affection for women and children publicly. My father was of that tradition. So for me it was a surprise to see him embracing Ruth, kissing her on the cheek, and saying, 'Thank you. We have learned much.'

Holding on to his outstretched arms, she said, 'It was good having you here with us.'

After I said goodbye to her, I wound my arm around my father as we stood on the hotel verandah and watched Ruth walking off into the darkness. Just before she disappeared beyond the light, she turned and waving called, 'Shalom!'

'Shalom!' my father called back.

57

'Ola, what would you like me to send you?'

'I don't know.'

'I'll send you a dragon. I'll put it in an envelope, put a two-cent stamp on it, and mail it.'

'That'll be great!'

58

Aunt Fusi heard the squealing coming from the hibiscus hedge in front of their house. She hurried out. A white piglet was entangled in the hedge. 'Where are you from?' she coaxed it as she reached in and tried to catch it. The piglet kept squealing as it retreated deeper into the thick web of branches and leaves. 'Don't go away,' she crooned but the animal wasn't having any of that. Because of her size Aunt Fusi couldn't penetrate further into the hedge. 'All right, piggy, don't go away.' She stepped back out of the hedge and looked at the house. 'Ola, Ola? Where are you?' she called. No sign of anyone.

A girl burst out of the house and sprinted towards her. She was about nine, wore her hair in a long pigtail, and was dressed only in shorts. 'Here, Fusi,' she replied. Aunt Fusi stretched to her full, threatening size. The girl stopped a few safe paces away.

'It's a little pig, isn't it?' The girl ignored Aunt Fusi's threat and ran past her to the hedge.

'Don't frighten it!'

'I won't.' The girl thrust her head and shoulders into the hedge. The piglet started squealing again.

'Careful!' Aunt Fusi cautioned her.

'Piggy, piggy, don't run away,' the girl whispered as she crept forward. The piglet panted, saliva dripping out of its mouth.

'Ola, is it all right?'

'Yes,' Ola replied, patting the piglet's snout and getting a grip around it with both hands. 'Now, piggy-piggy-piggy.'

'Watch out, it might run away!'

'Shhh!' Ola dismissed her. 'Your voice is scaring it.' She embraced the animal and, cradling it in her arms like a baby, backed out of the hedge. 'Piggy-piggy-piggy, it's all right. You're safe. Fusi and I love you and will take good care of you.'

'I don't *love* pigs and especially pigs which aren't ours!' Aunt Fusi said.

'I do. And I want to keep this as a pet.'

'It's not ours!'

'Well, if no one claims it in the next few days, I'm going to keep it.'

'What's your father going to say?'

Caressing the piglet's head, Ola said, 'Piggy-piggy-piggy, I'm going to ask Finau if I can keep you. Is that all right, piggy?'

'But you can't have pigs as pets!'

'Why not?'

'Pigs are dirty animals. They live in mud and make messes everywhere!'

'Dogs make messes too. All you've got to do is train them properly. Isn't that right, piggy-piggy-piggy?'

'But you can't have it in the house. That's final!' said Aunt Fusi, knowing that Finau, her brother and Ola's father, was again going to give in to his only daughter's demand.

'Here, you hold it, Fusi,' Ola said. Aunt Fusi backed away. 'Pigs don't bite.'

'But they're dirty creatures!'

'I'll wash it every day with soap and water. Eh, piggy-piggy-piggy.'

As they strolled back to the house Aunt Fusi wished the piglet hadn't got tangled in *their* hedge. Why not the neighbours'? (They *deserved* pigs as house pets.) However, being a staunch Christian, she supposed that, like the sacrificial ram God had sent to Abraham as a substitute for Isaac, God might have sent the piglet (and it was white, the colour of holiness) to their aiga (and Ola) for a special purpose. And Ola, the child born out of death, had a special talent for loving abandoned creatures. At least that was Aunt Fusi's rationalisation for having once again allowed Ola to have her way.

Ola, Fa'atupu and Meleane, her village cousins who were living with them, got an empty wooden crate, covered the bottom of it with scrap paper, and placed the piglet in it with a discarded corned-beef tin full of water. 'You take it to the kitchen fale,' Aunt Fusi instructed them. 'And don't ever bring it into the house.'

So while Aunt Fusi sewed in the house the three girls crooned the piglet to sleep and then debated on a name for it.

'Pinkie!' Fa'atupu argued, saying the animal was pink so it should have the English name.

'Toemaua!' Meleane reasoned that the piglet had been lost and found again. Secretly she wanted an English name for it but she couldn't think of any.

Remembering her favourite story, as told to her class by Miss Bristol the first year she was at school, Ola wanted the name Licken, as in Chicken Licken.

'It's a pig!' laughed Fa'atupu.

'Not a chicken!' Meleane added.

'How about Billy then?' Ola suggested. 'As in Billy Goats Gruff.' (Her

195

second favourite story, as told by Miss Bristol.)

'A goat?' scoffed Fa'atupu.

'A billy goat?' Meleane added.

'Billy's a very common English name for people!'

And so the heated exchange continued. 'Stop that arguing!' Aunt Fusi ordered them from the house.

'We'll ask Fusi,' Ola decided and rushed towards the house before her cousins could stop her. Fa'atupu and Meleane followed her.

'You tell Fusi your names!' Ola instructed them when they sat down on the floor beside Aunt Fusi, who was hand-stitching a shirt for Finau.

'Go ahead, tell me,' Fusi encouraged them. They did. 'But the piglet doesn't belong to you three yet,' she reminded them.

'I'm sure it will,' Ola pronounced. 'And we should call it Billy.'

'That's a good name,' Aunt Fusi mused. 'But it was the name of an outlaw, Billy the Kid.' Aunt Fusi was addicted to western films. 'He was left-handed and could outdraw anyone. He killed twenty-one gunfighters who tried to outdraw him . . .'

'See, I told you Billy was a good name!' Ola said to her cousins.

'It's obvious you can't agree on a name,' Aunt Fusi said.

'You decide then,' Ola interjected, sure Aunt Fusi would choose hers.

Aunt Fusi lowered her sewing into her lap and pondered, while they watched her. 'There's an excellent serial at the Tivoli,' she spoke more to herself. 'It's called *The Durango Kid*. Very exciting . . .'

'That's right, Fusi!' Ola tried to hurry her.

'. . . Has this villain with a wooden leg, a black eye patch, a rattle and a dangerous horse . . .'

'Yes!' Ola interrupted again.

Aunt Fusi blinked and was back in the difficult present of having to decide between her three wards. 'Why don't we leave it to Finau?' she tried to get out of it.

'No, *you* decide!' Ola said. 'We let Fusi decide, agreed?' she asked the other two, who nodded reluctantly, and once again put Aunt Fusi back into the predicament she thought she had just extricated herself from.

Shutting her eyes, Aunt Fusi pondered again. 'How about Piki?'

'No!' the girls chorused.

'How about Moli?'

'No!' they chorused.

And so she recited any name that came into her head, turning the pursuit of a name into a delightful, rhythmic game. 'Your turn,' she instructed Ola.

'How about Solo?' Ola began.

'No!' the others chanted.

'How about Polo?'

'No!' This time they clapped as well.

'How about Desoto?'

'No!' Clap.

And so it went. Then it was Fa'atupu's turn. This time not only did the other girls chant 'No!' and clap but they danced round Aunt Fusi in time to the beat of the questions and the clapping, while Aunt Fusi clapped and chanted.

Immediately after Meleane's recital, they cheered and laughed.

'We still haven't got a name,' Ola reminded them.

'Why don't we call it Durango?' Aunt Fusi suggested. 'Is it male or female?'

'Male,' replied Ola.

'How do you know?' asked Meleane.

'I've looked.'

'So call it the Durango Kid — he's a very tough hero,' Aunt Fusi said.

'All right.' Ola pranced around Aunt Fusi and chanted the name Durango Kid. Her cousins joined her.

That was how the Durango Kid came to the aiga of Finau Lagona. He would become known in the neighbourhood as Durango.

Finau ruled that Durango was not allowed in the house, and they weren't to expect help from anyone else in their aiga in taking care of their pet. Immediately the three girls argued about who was to feed Durango that evening. So after lotu, the patient Finau, with their agreement, wrote out a roster of weekly duties; each girl was to have a day and then a weekend looking after Durango. They weren't to neglect any of their duties, he emphasised.

As yet Durango was too young to eat solids, so Finau brought home a baby's bottle which they filled with warm diluted condensed milk and fed to Durango. Each night he was washed and towelled dry with rags Aunt Fusi provided, and then wrapped up and sung to sleep. If he wasn't asleep before their evening lotu, the children brought him in his box and left him just under the back steps. Sometimes he would squeal and one of the children had to take him back to the kitchen fale.

When he could walk properly Ola made him a harness out of twisted rags. They fitted this around his shoulders and front legs, tied a leash plaited out of fau to it, and led him around with it.

Every day after school, after doing their chores, they trained him to follow them around without the leash. After he mastered that, they taught him to stop, lie down, get up, follow, nudge them with his snout and beg for food or affection.

Durango grew quickly with all the food they gave him: meal scraps and leftovers, succulent copra, fruit, banana skins and even the sweets and biscuits they were given. He used his intelligence to get whatever he wanted from the children. His personality reflected that of Ola: self-centred, stubborn and impetuous. Their aiga, with the exception of Aunt Fusi, doted on him. Nothing was too good for His Majesty the Durango Kid.

At first, the children in the neighbourhood and school teased them about having a pig for a pet, a pig on a leash. The girls hid their annoyance well. Some of the boys danced past their hedge and, squealing like pigs, called, 'Durango? Durango? How's your durango?' and laughed wildly.

However, as the stories of Durango's intelligence and wit spread, the other children became curious and sought ways of befriending Ola and her cousins so they could be invited to meet His Majesty. The clever Ola always agreed, but at a price. Durango loved fruit, bread and food like that, she informed them.

'Ice cream?' one wealthy girl asked.

'Why not?' Ola replied. The girl turned up that afternoon with two large ice-cream cones. Gave one to Ola and the other to Durango, who gulped it down in one crunch.

One afternoon they panicked when they got home and he was gone from their property. They found him foraging in a ditch not far away. At Ola's instigation they spent until nightfall leading him around their boundary hedge, slapping him hard on the shoulders every time he strayed over the boundary. Two more sessions of this and he learned not to go over the edge ('and into someone's umu!' Ola frightened him).

'Where's the cooked taro I had in the safe?' Aunt Fusi asked the girls one afternoon. They remained silent. 'And the leftover bread, where's that?' Ola was the first to rush off to the kitchen fale on the pretext of helping the older women there.

'That pig is starting to eat us out of house and home,' Aunt Fusi complained to Finau when he came home from work.

'It's a large pig,' Finau replied.

'And it's getting hungrier!' From the house they could see Ola riding it around the kitchen fale while the others watched. 'See what I mean?' Aunt Fusi added. 'And it's digging up everything.' The ground around the kitchen fale had been rooted up. 'And the smell!'

That Saturday Finau brought some timber and, helped by the other men of their aiga, built a large sty and a rectangular wooden fence around that sty, behind the kitchen fale. 'He's not going to like that,' Ola said to Finau.

'He's going to live in *that* area. That's final. He's getting bigger and bigger and taking over *our* area!'

'Can't we take him out occasionally?'

'Twice a week when you're around to stop him from digging up the ground.'

It was a regular happening now for many of the neighbourhood children to gather at Durango's pen and feed him whatever food they had brought. Sometimes Ola allowed the smaller ones to ride Durango. The other children were also granted the *privilege* of washing him down every evening with coconut fibre and buckets of water, and cleaning out his sty and pen while Ola and her cousins supervised them. At this time Ola was told by one of her teachers that pigs should eat fresh grass to balance their diet. She got a bushknife and a coconut-frond basket and went with her cousins to the nearby swamp and cut some elephant grass. It was difficult, itchy work. The pleasure though of watching Durango enjoying the grass with a wild chomping was adequate reward for the muddy itchiness. They also didn't have to cut grass after this; there were always willing volunteers among the other children.

At first Ola thought Durango was ill, just lying there in his sty indifferent to the food she was offering him. Head resting on the ground, he just peered up at her. 'What's wrong?' she asked, caressing his head. He flicked his ears. When she saw the blood stains on the ground beside him, she tried to get him to roll over. She pushed. He wouldn't budge. 'Come on, Durango. What's wrong?'

Then she noticed the two neat slits.

'Why did it have to be done?' she demanded of Aunt Fusi, who continued ironing. 'Why?'

'Your father got a man to come this morning and do it,' Aunt Fusi replied. 'Every male pig has to have it done, otherwise . . .'

'Otherwise what?'

'You don't talk to me like that!' Aunt Fusi glared at her. 'You forget who you're talking to!'

'But why?' Ola persisted, this time politely.

'Otherwise it would go wild and become uncontrollable. It's nothing unusual.'

It took Durango about a week to recover and be his usually demanding self. Ola, Fa'atupu and Meleane never told any of the other children that Durango had been castrated. It was something shameful, a topic unsuitable for children.

Three or so months later, the girls told Finau that the pig needed a larger sty. Dutifully Finau brought home more timber and that weekend enlarged Durango's sty and pen.

'Why are we having two saka tonight?' Aunt Fusi asked the women who were doing the cooking. They looked at one another and away from her. 'Well, why?' On the open fire were two large kerosene tins — one was full of taro, the other of green bananas. 'Are we having more people tonight?'

'One is for . . .' one woman mumbled.

'Louder!' Aunt Fusi demanded.

'One's for the animal,' the woman admitted.

'He's a big animal,' another apologised.

'And what else is His Majesty having tonight?' Aunt Fusi asked.

'Nothing else,' someone else lied. Aunt Fusi glared at her. 'Well, not *much* else.'

'What? Come on, what not-much-else?'

'Only some diluted milk to soak his bananas in,' Ola said from behind her.

Aunt Fusi wheeled swiftly. 'Do you know something? That — that pig (and he's a pig, not a human being) — is getting better food than most of us!' Ola gazed at the ground. 'Ola, that creature is a *pig*. Do you understand? He may be your pet but he is still a pig! One day you'll learn the difference!' Aunt Fusi stamped off towards the house.

'You've got us in trouble again,' Ola castigated Durango. He rubbed the side of his face against the second rung of the fence. 'You're not a human being. You understand? You're a pig, an animal.'

After school, Ola and her cousins and a few other friends went to the cemetery and got a basketful of frangipani blossoms, which they sewed into long lei when they got home. Afterwards, they swept out Durango's sty and pen while he slept, got some fresh grass and spread it over the ground, changed his water and cooked a saka of breadfruit. By that time the other children had arrived with their presents: crunchy green banana skins, pieces of juicy sugar cane, fresh vi and mangoes and papaya, cooked taro and other food scraps. The scrumptious smell enticed Durango out of his sleep and drove him almost into a frenzy as he danced along the fence, sniffing at the children and chomping his jaws.

'It's all right. Be patient!' Ola kept telling him.

Fa'atupu, Meleane and two other girls took the lei and wound them around his neck. When he discovered he couldn't get at them, he rushed to the fence again.

Ola tossed him a ripe papaya. Durango's mighty jaws started grinding it. Fa'atupu tossed him a vi. He made short work of that. One by one the children threw him a gift.

'Happy birthday to you, happy birthday to you,' sang Ola. The others joined in.

He was a year old. (Or so Ola had guessed.)

Gluttonous though he was, he could manage only about half his birthday presents. He then retreated into his sty and was asleep within a few minutes.

'Pigs get birthday parties in Samoa, though we don't celebrate people's birthdays,' Aunt Fusi informed Finau that evening.

'The children were only playing,' he excused them.

'Only the Durango Kid gets a *Palagi* birthday party in Samoa,' she said. 'They're going to kill him with too much food. Soon he'll be too fat to walk.'

'It's *their* pig,' Finau said. But when Aunt Fusi wasn't there, he explained to the girls that too much food was bad for Durango. Give him less food and get him to exercise, he told them and then felt stupid — Durango wasn't a human being.

So they exercised Durango by walking him around the boundary every afternoon except Sundays, when not even humans were supposed to exercise. And when he tried to con them with his soulful eyes, they gave him only half his usual meal. This seemed to steady his weight.

They were just finishing their evening meal when Aunt Fusi said off-handedly, 'A man came to look at Durango this morning.' They waited. She wasn't hurrying.

'Well?' Ola asked.

'To see if he was for sale,' Aunt Fusi said. The girls cringed. 'He needed a large pig to take to an important funeral and heard we had one.'

'No!' Ola said.

'Don't worry, I told him our Durango *wasn't* a pig — not to us anyway,' laughed Aunt Fusi. 'The man looked at His Majesty and said how handsome he was.'

'You won't ever let it happen, will you, Finau?' Ola pleaded.

'Let what happen?' he asked.

'Durango to be sold.'

'It's your pig,' he decided. 'It'll be up to you.'

'We'll never sell him!' vowed Ola.

'No, never!' echoed Fa'atupu and Meleane.

For Durango's second birthday, Ola wrote a poem in English at school during their English lesson. She was too shy to show it to her teacher or to Fa'atupu and Meleane, but when she was alone with Finau she told him about it.

'Read it aloud to me,' he encouraged her.

'It's not very good,' she said. Then she read:

> *Durango he is my pet,*
> *Durango he is my brother*
> *like no other.*

'Very good! Your English is getting better than mine.'

59

'You don't remember much about him, do you, Dad?'

'Who?'

'His Majesty the Durango Kid.'

'Ah, the pig.'

'Yes, Durango *was* a pig.'

'I'm sorry. I wasn't thinking . . .'

'He *was* a pig and that's how I should've thought of him then but I didn't. It would've saved me all that misery.

> *Durango he is my pet,*
> *Durango he is my brother*
> *like no other.*

'You still remember that?'

'I'm not senile yet and the Durango Kid was more than a pig to me too.'

'As I sink more into middle age, I remember more about him. He was magnificent, wasn't he?'

'Yes.'

'It was through his death I first experienced what death and loss can be. God sent him to me for a purpose. Aunt Fusi was right . . . Dad, after all these years have you forgiven Fusi?'

'I don't want to talk about it.'

60

'A man has come to stay with us,' Aunt Fusi told her wards when they came home from school not long after Durango's second birthday. She motioned her head towards the kitchen fale. A dark spindly man with grey hair and his ribs showing was sitting on the tuai, scraping coconuts into a tanoa and tossing some of the bits to Durango, who was at the fence.

'What's his name?' asked Ola.

'Esau. He's a good person. And he needs a home,' she said.

'It's all right, Fusi,' Ola reassured her. 'We'll like him. I'm sure Finau will too.'

Ola led her cousins towards Durango. 'Is he a relative?' Meleane asked.

'No, he's Fusi's husband,' Ola replied. They stopped at a safe distance so he couldn't hear them.

'Husband?' Fa'atupu refused to believe. 'Fusi's never had a husband before.'

'And they're not married,' Meleane emphasised.

'Most people don't get married in church,' Ola pointed out. 'They just decide to be husband and wife and live together.'

Durango came up and sniffed around their legs. They fussed around with him while they scrutinised the man. 'He's got a lot of sores,' whispered Fa'atupu.

'And he's older than Finau . . .' added Meleane.

'Shhh! He'll hear you!' hissed Ola.

'Here, give the pig some of this coconut!' the man called.

Ola nudged Meleane, who whispered, 'You get it.' So Ola had to go and get the coconut shell full of scraped coconut.

They fed the coconut to Durango in small handfuls. 'All his sores have healed,' whispered Ola.

'But he's still ugly,' Fa'atupu insisted.

'He is still Fusi's husband,' Ola argued. 'And we love her, don't we?' The other two nodded.

The other members of their aiga, apart from Finau, arrived home from work and, though they were surprised to see the man, said nothing about him to Aunt Fusi. Some of the women wished he was younger and better looking. 'Like Durango, the other stray, whom Aunt Fusi rescued from the hedge,' someone described him. For Esau was obviously a stray. His presence *felt* impermanent. When he talked with them as they prepared the evening meal, his voice, gestures and mannerisms seemed wistfully remote, as if he was of no value to himself.

They kept away from Finau when he came home, spent a few minutes watching Durango being washed and then went into the house, where Aunt Fusi was waiting. Nothing unusual happened.

The girls showered outside and went in to get dressed. Finau was writing something at his desk. Aunt Fusi got them their clothes and combed their hair. 'Finau said it's all right,' she whispered to Ola.

When their aiga gathered for lotu that evening, Esau insisted on sitting against the back wall with the other men and women. As was their practice, Aunt Fusi and the girls sat at the front while Finau sat against the left-hand wall and conducted the lotu.

'Sir, come to the front,' Finau invited Esau, indicating the place beside Aunt Fusi. Esau declined politely. 'That is your seat, sir,' Finau insisted.

Head bowed, Esau stood up and shuffled to the front, saying, 'Tulou, tulou,' and sat down beside Aunt Fusi.

Finau recited the first line of the hymn. Aunt Fusi started singing. The others joined in. Ola looked at Esau. He seemed so alone, so she nudged his knee with her elbow and, turning her hymn book to the appropriate page, extended the book to him. He smiled and, holding the other end of the hymn book, sang with her.

Usually only Finau, Aunt Fusi and the girls ate first, with the girls sharing Aunt Fusi's foodmat, while the rest of the aiga served them. That night the girls got a separate foodmat, and Aunt Fusi shared Esau's. Now instead of Finau and Aunt Fusi talking freely throughout the meal while the others maintained a respectful silence, Finau tried to draw the reserved Esau into a conversation, and ignored the others. Important routines and relationships had been altered within their aiga. Ola understood and accepted those changes, but Fa'atupu and Meleane became more resentful when they had to shift out of Aunt Fusi's bedroom and sleep with Ola in the sitting room. 'Fusi doesn't love us anymore,' Meleane said as they lay in their net.

'That's not true,' Ola said. 'And don't ever say that again!'

'I can say whatever I like!' Meleane threatened.

'Go to sleep now!' Finau called to them from his bedroom.

Ola clutched Meleane's arm and whispered into her ear, 'If you ever say that again about Fusi, I'll — I'll slap your mouth!'

Ola couldn't sleep for a long time, frightened of the possibility of being *without* Aunt Fusi, the only mother she had ever known.

Esau fitted quietly into their aiga. While the girls went to school and the other adults went to their jobs, he stayed home (with Aunt Fusi) and took care of the chickens and Durango, grew vegetables and other crops, did repairs around the house, and kept their compound clean and tidy. He said little and most of the time they forgot he was there.

Ola and Aunt Fusi were alone in the house. They could hear Esau cutting the grass by the front hedge with his bushknife. Fa'atupu and Meleane were in the village for the weekend. 'Did you have a husband before?' Ola asked. She was lying on her stomach with her head on Fusi's knee while Aunt Fusi searched for utu in her hair. The light caressing feel of Aunt Fusi's hands foraging in her hair was relaxing.

'I did, twice. A long time ago in Sapepe. I eloped with the first one to his aiga, in our village, and Lagona came and got us to come and live in our aiga. We quarrelled a lot. Finau and my other brothers didn't like him for that. Finally Finau beat him up badly for hitting me one day and he left and never returned. I didn't mind really. The second one was from Lefaga. He came in a concert party that performed in our village. He was the mandolin player. Very good at it, he was.' She chuckled. 'I eloped with him, after the concert, to his village. Once again Lagona came and persuaded his aiga to let us come and live with him. We did. We were quite happy together. No children though.' She paused. 'He must have got fed up with me. One day a women's concert party from Falealili performed in our village and he eloped with one of the women. That happened after Finau had started working in Apia. Lagona sent me to Apia to look after him. When he married your mother — and she was a beautiful lady I got on well with — I stayed on to serve them. Lagona sent other relatives to help. Then God took your mother away — and I'm sure she's in God's House now waiting for us — and I've had you and Finau to take care of . . . Hold still, Ola. Now here's a big utu!'

'Let me see.' Ola looked up. Aunt Fusi opened her thumb and middle finger. Under her thumb-nail wriggled a fat utu.

'You should wash your hair more thoroughly,' Aunt Fusi cautioned. She crunched the utu between her front teeth and spat it out.

'Where's Esau from?' Ola distracted her.

'From many places,' Aunt Fusi said. 'He was born in Falealupo, Savai'i, a long way from here. His aiga neglected him, I think. As a boy he came to Upolu with a malaga from his village and didn't go back. Stayed here in Vaimoso with some relatives. He didn't go to school; did all their work at home. He's a good carpenter; learned it from a New Zealand carpenter who was here. He doesn't like working for other people though, so he eventually left and went to Pago Pago. Spent a few years there. (He hasn't told me much about what he did there.) He even lived in Manu'a, the oldest part of Samoa, and home of the Tuimanu'a. He knows a lot about the religion we had before the Light came; learned it while he was in Manu'a. But he doesn't talk about that much because it's about the Time of Darkness. I don't encourage him to discuss it; it's all pagan, better forgotten. We're Christian now.'

'He's old, isn't he?'

'If sixty is old, then he's old,' Aunt Fusi laughed. 'I'm forty-one so I must be young. Am I?'

'Yes.'

'And beautiful?'

'Yes — and large!' laughed Ola.

Aunt Fusi slapped her head playfully. 'The utu in your hair are going to suck out your blood and brains!'

Aunt Fusi then described how she had met Esau in the market, where he was selling Chinese cabbages. This had surprised her, as he was the only Samoan, among Chinese vendors, willing to sell vegetables publicly. So she bought vegetables from him every time she went shopping. She noticed that he was reserving his best vegetables for her and at a cheaper price. They talked longer — she did most of the talking, telling him about her aiga and her bright niece, Ola, and even about His Majesty Durango. 'I discovered he was living in Lepea with some friends. They were letting him use some of their land for his garden.' She paused and Ola sensed she was figuring out how she was going to say what she wanted to say next. 'I still haven't worked out why I asked him to come and live here with me,' she admitted.

Ola waited. When Aunt Fusi was slow to continue, Ola asked, 'Was it because he needed someone to look after him?'

Aunt Fusi's eyes brightened. 'Yes. That must've been part of the reason.'

'Like you've been looking after me because I don't have a mother?' Ola asked. 'Like we adopted Durango because he was a stray?' Ola rolled on to her back and gazed up into Aunt Fusi's face.

'You always know the reasons, don't you, Ola?'

'I like Esau very much.'

'Because of me or because he's a good person?'

'Both!'

'Here, sit up,' Aunt Fusi said. Ola sat up with her back to her. Aunt Fusi got the comb and, with long gentle strokes, started combing Ola's hair. 'Your father doesn't like Esau,' Aunt Fusi remarked.

'Yes, he does!'

'I hope I don't have to choose between them,' Aunt Fusi whispered.

61

Dearest Pita,

Tonight I'm lying on my Tel Aviv hotel bed, tired from travelling all day, trying to sort out my thoughts about what I've experienced here, so that I can explain them to you in the orderly, meaningful way you insist things should be described. (I'm trying to *see* according to the new physics.) Every time I write to you I feel like a student trying to explain something, with my teacher looking on critically, ready to correct my grammatical errors.

Your grandfather is growing *younger* every day. And enjoying our pilgrimage. We came here so he could see the Holy Land, but our journey is turning into a rediscovery of our relationship, of daughter and father seen in the experiencing of Israel. He's revealing to me the world of his early life in the village and when I was a child, and I'm telling him about my life abroad and my disastrous marriages. Its been very refreshing — though at times painful.

The highway to Haifa weaves placidly through prosperous farmland, which reminded me of the lush farms around Paris and Kassel (which Carl and I visited nearly two years ago), and made me want to stop the car, jump out and, rolling lazily in the golden grass, breathe in the sweet aromas of the orchards and gardens. I realised, as were were travelling through that countryside, that we do *see* through our cultures and art; I was looking at the scenery through Renoir's paintings.

Anyway, Haifa is Israel's only port and one of its main industrial cities, polluted, dirty, noisy, argumentative, bursting with vibrant life, bulwark of trade unionism. (Much of that description I gleaned from Gideon as our car climbed Mount Carmel, the city's centre.)

As our car wove and curved, gathering speed, I started feeling dizzy, and hoped we would reach the top before I embarrassed everyone with an unpretty bout of vomiting. Oren, bless him, must have noticed (in the rear-view mirror) my predicament and sped faster, swung left along the ridge and stopped. Quickly I opened my door and got out.

'All right?' your grandfather asked me in Samoan. He held my elbow and steered me across the road. We stood at the steel fence and looked down at the inner city and harbour. My nausea vanished as I gripped the steel railing.

The air above the city was brown and grey with industrial smog. The wharf complex, factories and buildings around the harbour looked forbidding, harder than Haifa's orange earth. Directly below us was the star-shaped Bahai Centre — a starfish lost in the massiveness of a coral reef. A new, almost luminous building shone like bone. The waters of the harbour disappeared into the swirling haze (that is the curtain dividing Israel from the Arab countries).

Your grandfather's face was beaded with sweat, but he seemed oblivious to the heat. After days of the intense Israeli sun, he was almost black, and he didn't mind. (And you know how, like most Samoans, he has avoided being *black*.) 'I'm almost as black as you now!' I tested him out, raising my left arm and comparing it to his.

Chuckling, he said, 'You're still not as healthy. Plus mine is permanent.'

I scratched his skin with the nail of my forefinger. 'You're right there,' I laughed. 'It *is* permanent!'

A large tourist bus stopped about fifty metres away from us. We watched its gaggle of passengers spill out and, flocking to the fence, immediately start photographing the panoramic view with their insatiable cameras. Your grandfather looked amused. 'Tourism is one of our major industries,' Gideon said.

(Every time I see tourists armed with cameras I wonder what kind of reality they are seeing through those instruments; what is it like looking at everything in terms of setting up a shot?)

I returned to gaze at the immensity of the harbour and sky, and let it draw my imagination into its being, tantalising it, peopling it with a rich imagery.

'How do you do?' the distinctly British female voice intruded into my daydreaming from over my right shoulder.

'How do you do,' your grandfather replied. I looked.

There she was. All five fragile feet of her, in what was once a white artist's smock. About sixty-five. Smiling. Hunched shoulders, austere face sucked in around penetratingly sea-green eyes which made me feel uncomfortable (and slightly resentful).

Her right hand was clutching a thick roll of what turned out to be watercolour paintings. 'Would you care to look at my paintings?' she asked. Unrolling them she held one up to your grandfather (who was looking at me for help).

'We have to leave now,' I heard myself apologising. Haifa Harbour was the colour of her eyes.

'They're cheap,' she said, smiling. I found myself edging back off the footpath. 'They're good — I painted them myself.'

'No thank you,' I heard Gideon saying to her. Your grandfather and I were now halfway across the road.

'We should've bought one,' your grandfather said in Samoan as we drove past her. 'She needs the money.' I couldn't look at her but I felt her eyes on me.

Why was I upset? Because I refused to believe anyone in Israel would beg, and especially anyone who was British. On arriving at that illogical conclusion, I felt more ridiculous; I mean, why shouldn't a British Israeli not be capable of begging? It was the way she'd done it, using art and a façade of respectability as a cover. Typically colonial, I thought, and immediately regretted thinking that. Had she been begging? What if she was a genuine artist trying to live off her art?

I couldn't banish her so I picked at the puzzle she had become.

Then they filed, with their tattered glory, into my mind: the wretched Arab in the Temple Mount; the puppet-like drunks of the New York Bowery (quaint in tourist posters and literature but grotesquely sad in real life); the woman swathed in thick scarves asleep in a Broadway theatre doorway, all her possessions in one plastic bag; three nodding, inward-centred drug addicts on the edge of Harlem; the deranged skeletal man raving silently as he chased his frantic shadow round and round a Central Park footpath; the spaced-out man, in a white suit, pink carnation in the buttonhole, standing in the middle of Berkeley, gazing into nothingness, while people streamed by ignoring his fear and pain; the incessant waves of beggars in Bombay as insistent and meticulous as the sleek crows of that city . . .

And without fully comprehending her meaning, I wished that we had bought one of her paintings.

But it was too late.

Pita, I'll always view Haifa in that woman's vulnerable light. She stands at the summit of Mount Carmel surveying the city, the harbour and sky, with her roll of paintings like a magic wand in her hand, the wind's lazy murmur is her unmistakably British accent, the harbour waters the sea-green accusation of her eyes.

Something strange is happening to me, Pita. I'm beginning to feel (and see) a close affinity to everything, even objects. 'Everything is intelligent,' said Pythagoras. I can't recall where I first discovered that revelation, but for the past few days it's been playing itself, like a prayer wheel, through my head. I can't rid myself of it; I don't seem to want to though it's kept me awake at night.

Do objects have a consciousness? For instance, does that door (into my hotel room)? What is a door? If it is 'intelligent', does it know itself?

Last night I sat in the cool of my hotel room verandah, gazing up into the stars swirling in the dark and letting those questions sing in my head. Eventually I went back into my room, sat at the desk, and tried to answer them. After numerous rewrites this is what I arrived at about the door:

> *A door is the presence*
> *of opening*
> *and shutting, the feel*
> *of swinging*
> *inwards and outwards,*
> *a pulling back*
> *or a pushing forward,*
> *the expectation of visitors*
> *(and departures),*
> *the hoarding*
> *of secrets and privacy*
> *a locking in*
> *a locking out,*
> *the return*
> *the escape, the possibility*
> *of all that.*
> *A door contemplates all*
> *its possibilities*
> *and knows*
> *it is all*
> *other doors.*

After the door (and please don't laugh at your poor mother's attempts to understand) I contemplated the stone I had picked up in Tiberias on the shores of Galilee, and wrote this (again after numerous revisions):

> *The round solid grasp of a hand*
> *this black stone, worn smooth*
> *by the water's touch, wears*
> *a quiet morning skin.*
>
> *It is a still eye*
> *gazing in on itself, measuring*
> *its weight and aptness.*
>
> *It will replicate itself*
> *stone upon stone dovetailed*
> *together like hands knowing*

themselves a quiet morning
curling inwards on the earth's secrets.
'Everything is intelligent,' said Pythagoras.

Perhaps I am a poet, eh son? No harm in a failed schoolteacher, with a BA in Anthropology — minus Levi-Strauss, who wasn't in vogue in the late 1950s — dreaming, is there?

I think I'm learning to *see* more, to discern the unity, the consciousness that binds everything, and know I'm an inseparable part of it, not *apart* from it, trying to measure it, dominate it, conquer it, subjugate it. It is a humbling revelation and, as you well know, your beloved mother is not a humble person (usually).

I've just reread this disjointed 'epistle' and I hope you can make heads and tails of it. Don't be too cruel to it; it's worth five out of ten for fairly correct grammar. I seemed to have climbed Mount Carmel to find a disturbing British angel, then descended to experience a door and a stone. Bloody strange. But wonderful. *Perhaps I'm a poet and don't know it!* (Corny, but it rhymes.)

All my alofa,
Ola

62

For their first two days in Tel Aviv she didn't go on the tiring sightseeing excursions her father made with Gideon and Oren. She would get up late, swim in the hotel pool, shop for presents for people back home, lunch alone, sleep again, wake up and study the English translation of an anthology of modern Israeli poetry Gideon had given her. She didn't even go on her usual evening run. So when Daniel drove in from Jerusalem on the third day and told them they were going that night to a party at a poet's home, she was well rested and eager for it.

'But we would be intruding,' her father said.

'The party's for you.'

'For us?' she asked.

'They want to meet you. They've never met Samoans. (They didn't know where Samoa was until I showed them on a map.) And you like poetry, Ola. Here's your chance to meet some of our poets and writers.'

Though it was about 8 p.m., it was still broad daylight and the heat was fierce and clinging when they parked in front of the large two-storeyed house in a long street of similar houses, in one of the city's oldest suburbs. The colour of the house had been toned down by age and weather, and the footpath was covered with bone-dry leaves that crackled under their shoes.

Daniel opened the front door and told them to go in.

The house smelt of fresh limes, and they could hear talking in the room at the end of the corridor. They followed Daniel.

Her father edged closer to her as Daniel rapped on the door, which swung open immediately. A woman with fiery red hair and a grey dress that set off her almost porcelain-white skin stepped out and Daniel moved into her tight embrace. They laughed and talked in Hebrew, then Daniel said, 'Racheli, I'd like you to meet Mr Finau Lagona and his daughter Ola from Western Samoa.'

'Delighted!' Racheli said, shaking Ola's hand. 'Welcome to my home!' In her manner was an unconditional invitation to be friends.

Racheli steered them into the sitting room and introduced them to the three people there: Shula Leib, a buxom peroxide blonde who was an anthropologist and a recent migrant from Brazil; Amnon Leibowitz, a chubby red-faced novelist who, in his tight shirt and tie, looked as if he was finding it difficult to breathe; and Avi Beni, an austere-looking man with powerful spectacles shielding his piercing eyes, short grey hair, open-neck shirt and sandals, and who Racheli described as 'our last poet from the desert'.

'Now that you've met the four most important intellectuals in Israel . . .' said Racheli.

'What about me?' joked Daniel.

'Sorry, the *five* most brilliant Israelis in Israel. Now that you've met us (and I hope like us enough to want to drink and eat with us in this terribly neurotic city), what can I get you to drink?' She pointed at the array of bottles on the table by the fireplace. 'We've been at war since 1947 and have learned to live frugally, as you can see!' She then named some of the different liquors and mixes they could have with them.

'Dad?' Ola asked her father, who was sitting ramrod straight beside her on the settee.

'Just a soft drink,' he replied.

'With some vodka in it, and I'll have a vodka and tonic, thank you,' Ola said.

'Avi, seeing you're now a teetotaller after a lifetime of debauchery and expert drinking, please mix our guests their drinks,' Racheli said. Avi bowed and went to get the drinks. Racheli told them to help themselves to the assortment of savouries, cheese, pickles, dips and crackers on the table around which they were sitting.

Ola relaxed as she sipped her ice-cold drink. She surveyed the room. Small metal and clay sculptures stood on the shelves above the fireplace; on the walls hung paintings, all originals. 'The work of Israeli artists,' Racheli informed her. A tense regretful pause.

'The artists are dead,' Daniel whispered to Ola. 'Killed in the wars.'

Shula, the anthropologist, handed her a tray of crackers and a dip. 'Go on, it's good. Won't make you as fat as me.'

'. . . I was in the Negev up to this morning,' Racheli was telling the others, 'fulfilling my duty (as a poet) to the motherland.'

'What? Chasing Egyptian tanks?' Avi interrupted. The others laughed.

'No, inspiring creativity and poetry in our schoolkids!' She went on to describe the three months she had spent touring schools, giving readings and holding writing workshops.

'And getting good pay for it!' laughed Avi.

'Poets have got to eat too,' she replied. 'We can't all be like you; we can't survive on goats' milk, locusts and honey!'

Another poet, Uri Damon, and his wife entered and sat down after being introduced. They were soon holding large mugs of beer that Avi

213

insisted on giving them. 'Apart from being a poet, Uri is our leading journalist, a sage and pundit. He writes some pretty good poems, so we can forgive him his very conservative political views,' Avi said.

A short while later David Goldin, a literature professor and novelist, arrived. 'David writes sad sagas about sad streets and sad migrants,' Amnon remarked.

'And who you put into your last novel as an egotistical and cowardly lieutenant who worships T. S. Eliot's poetry, which you class as "dry masturbation"!' countered David Goldin.

'Cheers!' Amnon laughed, raising his glass of beer.

'Amnon, why do you persist on wearing ties in the desert?' Racheli asked. She reached down and started undoing his tie.

'My humble father was a constipated rabbi,' Amnon said.

'Is that why you write such gloomy stories?' David remarked.

Racheli folded Amnon's tie and put it in his shirt pocket. 'Thank you, Angel of Mercy,' said Amnon, caressing her cheek.

Knowing that the conversation would eventually shift to focus on them, Ola quietly finished three drinks and was on her fourth one when Shula asked, 'How accurate is Margaret Mead's *Coming of Age in Samoa?*'

'That's a very heavy question,' Ola said.

'So here's a lighter one,' said Racheli. 'What does the word Samoa mean?' It was obvious that they were not expecting her father to reply.

'Some people say it means the Family of Moa, others say it means the Sacred Centre,' he said. He drank. They wanted him to continue. He didn't. He handed his glass to Avi, who started mixing him another vodka and lemonade.

'Moa means "chicken" or "centre",' Ola explained.

'Yes, Samoa could be called the Family of Chicken!' her father chuckled. 'Or the Sacred Centre. Your moa is this.' He pushed his hand into the top of his belly just below his ribcage. 'That is the centre of a human being.'

'Which meaning do you prefer?' Daniel asked.

'In my present mood I prefer the chicken. I like roast chicken. It is better than the moa of man today, which is emptiness!' Avi handed him his drink. He raised it, saying, 'Manuia!' Took a long sip. 'Beautiful!' he sighed. 'Good to fill the moa, the emptiness.' Ola noticed that the Israelis' attention was now centred on her father, on the wisdom he was revealing, a wisdom which was surprising her too. 'This person is an uneducated person,' he continued, looking at Racheli. 'I had little schooling; this is my first trip away from home. Ola can tell you more about our country and our way of life.'

'If I promise you all the vodka and lemonade you can drink, will you just keep talking about anything you may want to talk about?' Avi said.

'My daughter does not like me to drink a lot. You see, before we came here liquor had never touched my mouth . . .'

'But you're enjoying it now!' Ola remarked.

'Yes. It heals my aches and pains. Oils my creaky body.'

'Shalom!' called Racheli. They raised their glasses and drank. And then even Ola waited for him to continue.

At first he described the climate and geography of Samoa, the settling of it by Polynesians, the social and political organisation, the aiga, the nu'u, the itu, the nation. Ola was impressed with his clarity and detail.

'But those are merely the flesh. I will now give you the bones. You all know the biblical Genesis, but we also have ours.' He straightened up and Ola could feel the power surging up in him. Half closing his eyes, he recited in Samoan: *O Tagaloa le atua e nofo i le vanimonimo; ua na faia mea uma, ua na o ia e leai se Lagi, e leai se Nu'u* . . . Caught up in his power, Ola found herself translating aloud each of his lines: *Tagaloa builder of lands is His name; He created every thing; the Rock grew where He stood. And He said to the Rock, 'Split asunder,' and Papa-ta'oto was born, then Papa-sosolo, then Papa-lau-a'au* . . . Their voices blended; father and daughter weaving their lives together in the primeval song of creation. Ola remembered her grandfather describing the gift of the true orator and poet: 'The orator must empty himself of all that he is and let the Word, the gift, fill him, speak through him.' Now for the first time in her life, she was seeing it in her father.

And as he sang she became his timeless song, immersed completely in his current.

She surfaced when they applauded. 'Thank you!' cried Racheli.

'It was beautiful, beautiful!' Shula whispered, dabbing her eyes. Ola glanced at her father. Why hadn't he ever shown her this source of wisdom before?

'That solo — poetry — was part of our biology before Christianity came,' he told them, with his head bowed. 'We now refer to that time as the Time of Darkness before the Light. One hundred and fifty years of Christianity has erased that Genesis. Most of my generation and our children and their children don't know a single line from it. (We know *your* Genesis, as recorded in the Bible.) Before I came here I considered our ancient religion and beliefs as superstition, as Darkness. This person you see before you is considered an ideal Christian.' It was difficult for him to go on. 'To think that we gave up thousands of years of knowledge about ourselves, our world, our planet. To give up a whole way of seeing,' he murmured. 'The loss, the loss, it is immense. It is the size of God's wisdom . . .'

'Dad?' Ola tried to console him.

'. . . Once all was a circle, a sacred circle, a unity of tree, bird, earth, fire, air, water, man, rock, atua, aitu. All was blessed with mana. Together, dreaming, giving meaning to one another,' he confessed more to himself than to the others. Then looking at them he said, 'The Holy Land has helped me to see myself and what I've become. And through that see my beginnings and my country in a new way.' He now caught Ola in his eyes. 'I now know, yes, this person knows, that he is what he has lost.'

'No,' she whispered.

'Yes, I am merely a Christian. But perhaps that is enough.' He asked Avi for another drink.

Racheli asked, 'Are you sure you aren't my father?'

'Wrong colour!' he quipped.

'But you weave songs like him. He built this house. He was a carpenter (and a poet) from Russia. To him the world was peopled by only artists and carpenters. People who were neither, weren't real to him. Would you like to see his house? He's dead of course and I'm housekeeping for him.' She stood up and extended her hand to him. He held it and stood up. 'Ola, your father is a very handsome man. I could fall in love with him.' She pulled her up too. 'Come, let me show you the shell I live in.' At the door she turned and told the others, 'And while we're away don't eat all my food and drink all my liquor. I'm a poor writer too!'

'Shylock!' someone called.

'Wrong sex!' she countered.

As she led them into her study next door she said, 'We're of a generation. I've known nearly all of them since I was at university. We're the remaining few.'

Her study was surprisingly small and without books. With a wooden desk at the far wall beneath the only window, a hard wooden chair, some pencils and ballpoint pens in a cup, and a black lamp on the desk, a neat stack of plain paper, and bare floor and grey walls. 'Like a cell, isn't it?' she introduced her study. 'It's enough for me. I fit it well.' She walked and stood in the centre of it. Yes, the room fitted her like a second skin, thought Ola. 'It has all I want and need: my Dead, my spirits, all the poems I'm going to catch . . . You like it?' They nodded. 'My father died in here in that simple chair, which he made. I found him that evening. He had been rereading my first collection of poems. He was seventy-eight.'

'May I sit?' he asked.

'Of course.' She pulled out the chair. He fitted himself into it. 'Perfect fit, isn't it, Ola?' Racheli said.

'Yes,' Ola joked.

'I try it out almost every day. I'm only just starting to fit it,' Racheli explained.

216

The smell of limes disappeared when they went upstairs. 'I can't stand Tel Aviv but I can't live in any other house. It's worse if I try living outside Israel.'

She opened the bedroom door. 'My son's room. Yes, he's here.' She beckoned them in.

On the bed that stood against the far wall was a teenager who was sitting in a yoga pose and staring unblinkingly into the dead TV screen above the head of his bed. A pale youth with her red hair and mouth. 'Paul's into yoga, as his American father would say. Right now he's into himself and we shouldn't disturb him. Eh, Paul?' she called. No movement from her son. 'Erik, my other son, lives with his father in New York.' They withdrew from the room.

'I tried to live in America but failed. My house, my Dead, my spirits kept pulling me back.'

'We too have our Dead. We too are rooted to a particular place and die if we live away from it for too long,' Finau told her.

'I won't show you my bedroom, it's a mess!' Racheli said.

They went into what was her father's bedroom. 'My father was almost totally self-taught,' she said. One wall of the room was stacked to the ceiling with neat piles of books. Half the room, to the skeletal bed made of boards, was filled nearly up to the light bulb with cartons of magazines and books.

Ola's father moved around the boxes. 'He respected learning,' he murmured.

'He kept complaining about the money he spent on his books, but he kept on buying them. And before he died he repeatedly told me not to forget to burn them after he died,' Racheli said.

'Why haven't you carried out his wish?' asked Ola.

'I come in here once a week and dust and clean and read. And for that day he's with me again,' replied Racheli. Ola watched Racheli scrutinising Finau as he shuffled among the stacks. 'Your father fits right into this room,' Racheli whispered.

'But you can't have him,' Ola said. 'I need him!'

'You're very lucky!' laughed Racheli. 'I was lucky too.' Touching Ola's hand, Racheli added, 'But we have also been unfortunate to have such men as our fathers.'

'Unfortunate?'

'Yes, because no other men in our lives can measure up to them.'

For a moment Ola looked into Racheli's eyes, hesitated, then said, 'I need another drink.'

They re-entered the sitting room and were immediately in the middle of a passionate debate. 'Our country's most important achievement since 1947 has been the revival and development of modern Hebrew,' Amnon was saying. His shirt was plastered to his body. 'Isn't that right?' he appealed to Racheli.

Racheli ignored him as she got drinks for Ola and her father.

'Our two famous novelists have been at it since you left the room,' Daniel said to her. 'And they're going to bore our guests!'

'So I'd better explain to our guests what it's all about,' she offered. 'Hebrew was dormant for two thousand years. The rabbis kept it alive and it wasn't until 1947 that it was revived as our national language. Since then we've succeeded in teaching it to our migrants from every corner of the world . . .'

'We've used it to try and rediscover and redefine what Jewishness is,' Amnon interrupted. 'To shape our national character and personality; to cope with the modern sciences . . .'

'To develop a modern literature and make a living for hopeless people like Amnon and David!' Racheli took control of the conversation again.

Soon after this David started a heated argument about what a Jew was. Again Amnon was his main opponent, with the others encouraging them. The argument developed into an even more heated debate about Menachim Begin's establishment of settlements on the West Bank.

'Get two Jews together,' Racheli whispered to Ola, 'and you'll get an argument. We fight all the time among ourselves.'

'But there is strong unity,' Ola's father said. 'I can tell.'

Ola drank more and more as she listened. Here were some of Israel's most sensitive interpreters, questioning their nation's existence and their individual existences within it. An ancient, untiring debate. Israel existed because they questioned her existence; God existed because they questioned His existence; they existed because they questioned their purpose for living; they questioned even their talents as artists. The questions were permanent, not the answers, and wrestling constantly with the questions enabled them to find hope and meaning in their lives. She envied them, and when she detected a deep-rooted anxiety and despair in their struggle, felt a painful affinity to them. They had been fighting for Israel since 1948. They walked the tightrope above the abyss of despair. And each day they doubted their ability and strength to maintain their balance on the rope. Doubted even the meaning and value of their struggle. You grow old, you grow tired, you despair, but you keep on going. You don't want the struggle to be your children's legacy, but you will doubt their worthiness (as Israelis and Jews and human beings) if they don't have that legacy to live out, endure.

She finished her drink. Avi got her another one and sat down beside her. 'All that arguing must be boring you to tears,' he said.

'It's fascinating,' she said, grateful he had saved her from her self-pity.

'Some of us try, through seances, to communicate with our relatives and friends killed in the wars,' Uri confessed.

An extraordinary confession, unconnected to the kidnapping yet inextricably tied to it in a profoundly mystical way, Ola thought. She glanced at her father. He had withdrawn into himself, curled around his vodka warmth.

She tried focusing on everything and everybody in the room. She concentrated on Racheli, but Racheli began melting into her alabaster whiteness and the greyness of her dress. She turned to Shula. Shula too began losing her bodily form, becoming vapour. Ola shut her eyes, afraid of what was happening. When she looked at Avi he was a mere outline, a spirit, a presence. She reached out but couldn't reach him. She looked at the others. All spirits, presences, vapours. *The loss, the loss, it is immense!* her father's chant echoed in her head, and she held onto it to save herself from disappearing too. The chant would save her and resurrect the others.

Rising slowly to her unsteady, frightened feet, she chanted, *O Tagaloa, the Supreme God, lived in the Void; He made all things; only He, there was no Sky, no Land* . . . She was the vessel through which the spirit was singing and recreating the world, giving it life and form. *Tagaloa, builder of lands is His name; He created everything; the Rock grew where He stood. And He said* . . . She was singing over the abyss, balancing on death's edge, conquering it.

And when she opened her eyes everything was being reborn, becoming matter and form and colour and sound and movement.

Across the room she saw her father standing up to welcome and rejoice in her magic. Tagaloa, Supreme God, Creator. Cradled in his arms was a sleeping child, the kidnapped boy.

And around her the world was whole again. Circled. Healed. Magical.

63

'You were very drunk last night, Ola. Daniel and I had to carry you back.'

'It was the spirit filling me, working through me. You had a lot of it too!'

'But I took it better than you.'

'Thank you for last night, Dad.'

'I didn't put the party on.'

'Not that. Thank you for teaching me *our* Genesis.'

'It won't save the kidnapped boy.'

'But I can use it to try and save myself.'

'You sing it quite ably.'

'Who taught it to you?'

'My father's father. Last night was the first time I've recited it since he died almost sixty-five years ago.'

64

I keep expecting rain
I don't mind the fiercely crisp
Israeli heat but I need rain
    I am *used* to rain
    Now I even dream of it at night
    Slow mellow, cool rain washing over
my head down my face and all over
me unclenching my pores
    Rain
    Samoan rain
    Like a gentle lover melting
into me and me into his melting
    Rain

65

Dearest Pita,

You'll remember that Jorge Luis Borges, the Argentinian writer who is now very old and blind, is one of my favourite authors. Well, as I continued to ponder the 'intelligence' of objects — this time a favourite kitchen knife I have in Samoa — Borges came into it naturally, unobtrusively. Many of Borges's stories are profound allegories about duelling knives and gauchos.

So while your teenage grandfather and his musketeers, Daniel and Oren, were out last night sampling Tel Aviv's night life, I wrote this. It came easily; a joyous surprise to a non-poet like me! I think it's what is called 'prose poetry'.

KNIFE

This knife on the kitchen
table,
    black wooden handle with
two shiny eyes of rivets,
    single-
edged and curving to a metaphysical
point on which angels can't perch,
    is caught in its breathing
shadow,
    a quiet legend of itself
open to the hanging light in
    Borges's dreaming.

This knife smiles a slow quiver
    of teethlight savouring
        the blood's rich message.

Whose blood? Gauchos duelling
    in grimy saloons lost in
    the myths of the pampas.

This knife hones its alertness on
the expectation of hunting/stab-
bing/slashing/cutting,
on crouch-
ing deadstill like its victims.

It fits
the assassin's grip, the dueller's
mad courage, which will grant
it shape and ferocity.
Or is it the reverse? asks Borges.

It's more than its
shadow and smile, more than
the legend of light
in Borges's blindness, more than
the last quiver of the blood, more than
the expectation of victims and
the dueller's triumph.

This knife is
more than Borges's allegories.
It is
itself.
It is
a simple kitchen knife.

Am I making sense, son? For the first time I think I'm making sense to myself. (Who knows, maybe by the end of this pilgrimage I may become not too bad a poet.) At least contemplating the intelligence of objects is less harrowing than trying to control the demands of the flesh. (I'm still biblical.) Israel's heat must be drying up all the Freud in me. Or is it the first major omen of approaching menopause?

By the way, the Israeli girls of your age are quite stunning. Black-eyed. Black-haired. Olive-skinned. Fit. Trim. Efficient. Orderly. Committed. And I'm sure, very unpuritanical. Just your type. You'd love them. Haven't seen any of them in skirts yet. They are trousered in military trousers all the trousered time. But still very sexy!

Luv ya, kid,
Shalom and alofa,
Ola

66

When I was about ten, Lagona Fiapese, my father's father, told us of a famous taulaaitu who caught a ferocious white shark, the most courageous of all creatures, and, after taming it, released it again. On the last day of each month he'd stand on the beach and, using a magic chant, call the shark to come to him. The creature would steer through the treacherous reef passage into the bay, swim right up to the shallows, and was willing even to die crawling over the sand to him. He'd lift it in his gifted arms and walk it back into the healing water.

'What was his magic chant?' I asked the father of my father.

'We remember the story and the shark, but the chant has been lost,' he replied.

'If we found the chant again, we'd be able to call the white shark back,' I suggested.

'That taulaaitu lived before the Papalagi came, in the time of magic and mana; now it is Christianity and science,' he said.

I didn't understand my father's father then, and I'm not sure I understand him now.

67

'Snow, I've never touched snow,' you hear your father telling Oren. You're once again cocooned in the air-conditioned safety of your car. You're on your way to Bethlehem. It's desert out there in the 9 a.m. world. Rock. Dust. Heat. And he thinks of snow.

'I have,' says Oren. Silence.

Where?' your father asks.

'On Mount Hermon,' is all Oren says. War, soldiers, dying in the snow.

You look out at rugged, broken hills and ravines, burning. No sign of snow anywhere . . . *I'm dreaming of a white Christmas, just like the ones I used to know* . . . awful sentimental corn, Bing Crosby, you push him out of your head.

Snow without winter. Cotton snow on the first Christmas tree you remember your father bringing home. (You were about seven.) An artificial pine tree about three feet high, with imitation leaves and detachable branches you screwed into the trunk. You and Aunt Fusi helped him assemble and decorate it, copying a coloured photo: a real pine tree reaching almost to the ceiling, festooned with shimmering tinsel and strings of electric lights and paper lanterns and stockings and cut-outs of angels, and with artificial snow along its branches and underneath it. All radiating a dazzling holy light. A huge fire is blazing in the fireplace and three blond children (a girl in the centre) in their pyjamas kneeling in front of it, gazing spellbound up at their tree. Everything is hushed with the expectation of Santa Claus . . .*Silent night, holy night, all is calm, all is bright* . . .

Your Christmas tree paled beside such American magnificence, but it was *your* tree and the only Christmas tree in your envious neighbourhood. It was topped with a red star cut out of cardboard and pasted over with glitter, festooned with tinsel, and with cotton-snow-laden branches and snow radiating out from its base. A tree that your family enjoyed for about six Christmases before it was replaced by larger more expensive artificial trees with heavier loads of cotton snow and crowned with strings of electric lights that blinked and changed colours like a heart beating.

Even now, as you recapture that tree and the little girl who was mesmerised by it, the trembling happiness of that time weaves through you again, light and soft like cotton snow, and the biblical verses about Jesus' birth, which Aunt Fusi and your father and your Sunday school teachers made you memorise, return and you don't resist them: *Now when Jesus was born in Bethlehem of Judea in the days of Herod the King, behold there came wise men from the east to Jerusalem . . .*

It's desert out there, harsh, forbidding.

> *A cold coming we had of it,*
> *Just the worst time of the year*
> *For a journey, and such a long journey . . .*

T. S. Eliot's is a more accurate description of the Magi's journey, but the happy lilt in you, revived by memories of your first Christmas tree and cotton snow, can't be dispelled.

> *Now as I was young and easy under the apple boughs*
> *About the lilting house and happy as the grass was green,*
> *The night above the dingle starry,*
> *Time let me hail and climb*
> *Golden in the heydays of his eyes,*
> *And honoured . . .*

Dylan Thomas sings through you again and you let his song caress every part of you.

> *Oh as I was young and easy in the mercy of his means,*
> *Time held me green and dying*
> *Though I sang in my chains like the sea.*

'We're there!' your father disrupts your dreaming. 'Bethlehem.' In that one utterance you can feel all his expectations of the birth of the one great person in his life. He is at the centre of his mythology. You look at him. In his eyes are caught the details of the city; he's sucking them in, sifting through them, searching, comparing the reality to his mythology. *We see what we believe*, you're convinced of that. You remember that Bethlehem was recaptured recently from the Arabs: its population is predominantly Arab and Christian. (Goodwill towards all men?) It's a flourishing tourist centre, and everywhere are signs in English (and Arabic) peddling hamburgers and french fries . . . *I'm dreaming of a white Christmas* . . . you shut that commercialised reality out, switch it off like a radio. A modern city and nowhere in sight are the stable and manger. Over two thousand years of reverence, worship, orthodoxy. And you're no longer that little Christmas girl constructing your artificial Christmas tree. You touch his hand. He smiles and then continues to drink in the city.

'Dad, I've never touched snow either,' you lie to him. You're travelling fast up a narrow street walled in by buildings and fences. You think you're in an animal's burrow.

'It's just water anyway,' Oren jokes. 'It melts at your touch.' He stops the car in front of an arched gate in a high brick wall and opposite a jewellery shop. 'The Church of the Nativity,' Oren motions with his head at the gate. 'I'll get a guide to show you through it.' He goes into the jewellery shop.

Your father stands in front of the gate. You're behind him and you think he's shaped like the key that fits that gate. 'Ola,' he whispers, his back still turned to you, 'He was born in there!' You detect a tinge of sadness in his voice. Had it been a birth or a death?

A moment later a paunchy man in a tartan shirt and black tie, crew-cut hair (slick with oil) and well-clipped moustache emerges from the shop and hurries to you. There is no one else in sight.

He introduces himself. Your father shakes his hand. 'I am a Christian too,' he says. 'I will show you His birthplace.'

'We're from Samoa,' your father says.

'In the Pacific, the South Pacific!' your guide exclaims. 'Polynesia. When I was a sailor, many years ago, I went through your region. Never visited your country though. What a pleasant surprise! The South Pacific!' You can feel your father warming to him. 'Follow me, please,' your guide says.

You go through the gate into the courtyard of the church. It's all cream-coloured stone exuding the rising heat of the mid-morning sun. You can't see anyone else, anywhere.

You enter the church, the high-roofed Basilica. There's no one there either. Just that haunting silence the Japanese call 'a long slender silence', mournful yet slightly ominous, the silence you've always associated with the thick rainforests of Samoa. Your guide's voice, as he describes the history of the Basilica and what is in it, is now at the edge of your hearing. Just you and the silence awaiting the child's return to the manger, restoring to it its true meaning now lost in this respectable splendour of marble, stone, wood, incense, gold, reverence, silk, icons, the rows of pink Bethlehem pillars and the glittering eight-sided altar.

> . . . The Darkness drops again; but now I know
> That twenty centuries of stony sleep
> Were vexed to nightmare by a rocking cradle,
> And what rough beast, its hour come round at last,
> Slouches towards Bethlehem to be born?

Your father shuffles up to the altar. You are afraid for him (for no reason at all). He is the centre. He has come to be reborn.

Curved steps descend to the Grotto. You follow your father down. The cool of the place envelopes you. Your father's neck glows. What's going through his mind? Bugger Yeats, he can have his Antichrist back, free of charge! But you can't shake off the slender silence and the chill of his 'Second Coming', which became part of you ever since you first read it at high school. Is your father seeing past all this stone and marble? Where is everybody?

'The stable and manger,' your guide informs you. 'Go in.' He indicates the Grotto.

Four candles in the low cave-like structure give it an easy, shifting glow. The white marble floor is veined and stained with streaks of red and black, and focuses on the silver star that overlies the spot of Jesus' birth. You count the points of the star. Fourteen. Why fourteen? On the back wall hang icons which are black and brown with age; incense lamps dangle from the roof. You forget your father as you contemplate the structure and its meaning, as you try to give birth to the Christmas child you once were. You wake to him when he sits down cross-legged in front of the Grotto, bends forward slightly, and starts praying. The verses of your childhood return:

When they saw the star, they rejoiced with exceeding great joy . . .

You sit down beside your father and stare at the silver star and the circular hole at its centre, the entrance down into the miracle, into the Void, the earth's core, the gods, the galaxies, what Yeats called 'the abyss of yourself'. You concentrate on your stillness, on your moa, centre, and the prayer of silence your father is creating. And you drift up, suspended above time, becoming a welcomed part of the smell of burning incense and candles and age and stone, and the sadness which holds it all together. You drift. Drift . . .

'It is all right,' you hear your father call you. 'It is all right.' He anchors you again to your body. You blink and look at him. Tears in his eyes. You want him to tell you why, but you're too scared to ask him. 'I talked to Him about taking care of Penina and our aiga,' he says. 'And . . .' You wait. He turns away. 'And I asked Him to help you,' he says at last.

Before you can say anything to him, he leans to one side and, using his hands, pushes himself up to his unsteady feet. 'Getting old,' he mutters. He reaches down, clutches your hand and pulls you up. 'Thank you for bringing me here, to our Lord's place of birth,' he says. 'Now I can die contented.' He shuffles away before you can speak.

You have to hurry to catch up to him and the guide. Where is everybody else?

'Is it usually *this* quiet?' you ask your guide.

'No, but it's been a very poor tourist season. Very poor.' His breath smells of sherbet; his shirt is streaked with sweat.

For about thirty minutes your guide shows you the other parts of the church, giving you a detailed history of everything. You feign an avid interest because your father has withdrawn into himself, walking tenderly as if renewing his connection to the earth.

'It's very hot, you must be thirsty,' your guide says. 'There's a shop outside. Let me invite you for coffee.' He takes out a white handkerchief and starts drying his face. Immediately you know he is the owner of the shop, the jewellery shop, and you're now to pay for his services as your guide. You can't refuse his offer; after all, you've come in a government limousine and should therefore be of means, and you *are* Christians. 'There are also cold fruit juices if you prefer,' he adds. You glance at your father.

'What else can we do?' he says in Samoan. 'We're back in the real world, and you can afford it!'

It is a stunningly prosperous shop. A treasure house: black shelf after black shelf, display case after display case, of jewellery made of gold, silver, diamonds and other precious stones; rows of varnished carvings of biblical scenes. You, dear pilgrim, on leaving Christ's *humble* birthplace, have to encounter this treasure house and come to terms with it.

No other customers.

'Coffee, madam?' a handsome young salesman asks you.

'Coffee, sir?' another handsome young salesman asks your father. (They look like brothers, and like Rudolph Valentino.)

'No thanks,' you mutter.

'Yes please,' your father replies. (He's really enjoying your predicament.)

'A fruit juice then?' your salesman asks you. You shake your head, edge away and start examining the jewellery in the nearest glass case. You resent being trapped; it would be unchristian not to repay your guide, who's now ensconced in a comfortable leather chair by the front door, sipping his coffee and smiling at you, knowing (and probably enjoying it) that he's got you.

You find a shelf of Yemenite jewellery which you like. The pieces are made of silver and semi-precious stones; the most striking is a blue-green stone that glows like the sea within the lagoon on a bright day. You want the bracelets as presents for Penina and some of your friends. Taking your father's sleeve, you tug him over to look at them. 'Beautiful!' he says, and immediately the two salesmen are opening the glass lid and taking out the padded containers and placing them before you. Rings, bracelets, necklaces, pendants. You sense what your father is going to do, and you feel more at ease. He's been a merchant, a trader, most of his life.

Soon he's got them showing him piece after piece. He appraises each one, gets them to describe how it was made, and so on. Occasionally he asks for your opinion, which you give as a nod or a wave of your regal hand. He finds fault with each one.

You move to the next display. The salesmen work hard to please your father. They unpack even their most expensive Yemenite jewellery and bring out more from the back room. Your guide, the owner, is now hovering like a protective hen over his salesmen, adding the enticing remark here, the admiring silence there, while you and your father discuss the merits of this piece and that.

The salesmen are impressed with your father's expert scrutiny. They take him from expensive to madly expensive to exorbitantly expensive to millionaire's row. You revel in his performance and the way he's making them pay for what you *have* to buy.

You're now in the kingdom of gold. Glass cases full of it. His eyes drink in the golden glow. He becomes more persuasive; he even quotes the latest gold prices, refers to King Solomon's mines, identifies most of the motifs in the pieces.

'Here, Ola, let's see how this looks on you.' He puts a large ring on your finger. 'Not too bad.' On your ears he puts the earrings that go with the ring and, around your haughty neck, the necklace. You turn slowly so he can view them. 'Beautiful!' he tells everyone. 'Isn't that right?' he asks. Their praise is immediate and enthusiastic. You bow slightly.

Oren is now beside the front door, drinking orange juice. 'How old is your wife?' your father calls to him.

'Not too old,' laughs Oren.

'Not too old for this?' He holds up your left arm to show him the gold bracelet he has put around your wrist. Oren backs away. 'Come over here!' your father instructs him. He does so. 'What about these rings?' your father asks, holding up your left hand and the four rings he then puts on your fingers. Oren grins and shakes his head. 'Oren, my friend, you don't have to wear them; the gift is for your beautiful wife.' Laughing softly, Oren retreats to his orange drink.

'I like this.' You take the ring off your middle finger. It has a bird motif with one red eye.

'That shall be for Oren's wife,' your father says.

'Would you like to look at anything else, sir?' the owner asks. He is sweating profusely.

232

'You've been very helpful, thank you. We will now choose what else we want to buy,' your father says.

The owner hustles his salesman to the other side, where they start tidying the shelves. You look around the shop, at the disorder your father has caused. Most of the display cases are open, their contents lying on the counters.

'What can we afford?' your father asks in Samoan.

'We've got enough, Rockefeller!' You almost laugh, wanting to hug him. You've never seen this side of him, impish, daring, the actor and confidence man. Or is it a new side he has just discovered and is enjoying as he watches it perfect itself? *Was it for birth or death you came to Bethlehem?*

'Are you sure we've got enough?'

'Yes! It's only money, anyway.'

'For this?' He takes the bird ring off your finger. You nod. 'And this?' He takes the lightest gold necklace off your neck. You nod.

As he leads you to the Yemenite jewellery, you think: had he seen and accepted his death, in the manger? Was that why he had wept? Is that why he now acts like someone living beyond death, beyond the abyss of himself, challenging the gods?

'Choose,' he invites you. You pick two bracelets, a ring and a necklace.

'I hope, sir, you can afford all those!'

'It's only money!' he mimics you. 'Anything else you want?' You shake your head and swallow your laughter.

He raises his hand. The salesmen scurry over; the owner follows. Your father gives them his purchases. You withdraw to the other side, pretending to be interested in the wares there. You hear him ordering gift cards for each present: Oren's wife, Penina, his daughters and you.

While they are wrapping the gifts according to his precise instructions, the owner asks him, 'Are you a minister, sir?'

'If you mean a politician, no. I have a *small* business.'

'Oh,' replies the owner, impressed. 'And the young lady?'

'My daughter. She's a . . . a . . .' You await his identification. 'She's a poet.' Somehow you don't think that odd. Not even as a joke. 'She also works as my personal secretary.' He is preparing them for your signing of the traveller's cheques, which, a short while later, you do with a lot of flourish.

You laugh freely as you drive away from the Church of the Nativity down the narrow street that had earlier reminded you of a burrow.

'I was good, wasn't I?' your father exclaims in Samoan.

'Very good!'

'Never thought I had it in me.'

'Neither did I. Dad, that was a splendid performance.'

'Just think: if I'd discovered my talent as a boy, I would now be a millionaire.'

'You are a millionaire.' And you laugh some more, while he chortles on and off, on and off.

'Oren, here's a small gift for your wife.' He reaches over the front seat. Oren pushes the packet away. 'The gift is *not* for you; you can't refuse it. It's for your wife, so just give it to her and tell her it's from a Samoan millionaire! And for my daughter, the poet, a small token of my gratitude for bringing me to this land which is fast turning me into a pagan!'

He hands you a package. Inside are the earrings, the ring and the necklace he made you model.

'You didn't get anything for yourself,' you remind him.

'Don't worry about me.'

When you arrive at the hotel he hurries you through the lobby, up in the lift and into his room.

'Sit!' he says. He pulls his left hand out of his pocket and flashes it once past your face. You don't understand. He flashes it again.

'No, can't be!' you cry, half-rising out of the chair.

'Yes!' he laughs, nodding his head. He pulls the diamond-studded gold ring off his third finger and, holding it between his thumb and forefinger, brings it almost up to your nose. It glistens tauntingly. 'I did it. And I enjoyed doing it!' He pauses and you look at him through the circle of the ring. The gold gleam of the ring is like a halo around his face. 'I've never stolen anything before; I've always lived within the laws of both God and man.' His eyes are like the centre of the silver star, deciphering the Void, giving it meaning. 'And I feel no remorse.'

'I'm glad,' you interrupt.

'And I'm not going to be caught either. Even if they notice the ring is missing they won't report it to the police.'

'Why not?'

'Because our friend, the guide and merchant barbarian who now owns the holy places everywhere, won't want the public to know I'm a cleverer merchant than he is.'

'You can't be sure of that.'

'I'm dead sure. He won't want to admit his defeat to me. Let's go and celebrate,' he declares. 'Have a thick steak, wine, the lot!'

'You're acquiring very extravagant tastes. Don't forget, you're supposed to be a frugal, law-abiding, timid Christian pilgrim . . .'

'And you're the spendthrift, fun-loving decadent pagan!' He puts on his new ring and holds his hand up to the light. He sighs as he admires his daring. He is like you were, as the Christmas child, captivated by the light of that first Christmas tree he brought home.

> *. . . and so we continued*
> *And arrived at evening, not a moment too soon*
> *Finding the place; it was (you may say) satisfactory.*

Yesterday in Bethlehem of Judea you met your father returning; it *was* satisfactory.

68

Shall I leave him there at his new beginning, possessed by his mischievous gaiety, in that air-conditioned seventeenth-storey room (indistinguishable from most hotel rooms), suspended (with me) in a country threatened always by war, or shall I let my tale unfold and take him (and me) to Golgotha and the fourteen Stations of the Cross and the return to Samoa?

Does any tale ever end?

A storyteller *lies* imaginatively, and the more deliberate she is about it, the more her tale is art and not life. But the deliberateness is what makes us more than what we are, giving us design, shape, purpose. Otherwise, what is there to protect us from the terror of existing without meaning?

This morning when I entered my study I realised for the first time how frugal and solidly concrete it is. A simple wooden bed, foam mattress and pillow; a small wooden table, chair, and reading lamp; no books or bookshelves. Bare of decoration, not even a mat on the floor. A cell much like Racheli's study in Tel Aviv. Not a deliberate austerity on my part. But as I've stripped decoration and unnecessary baggage/possessions/ etc. from myself, so I must've condensed my immediate surroundings (this room, this house that is my second skin) to their most honest essentials.

Why has it taken me this long — what a waste of years — to arrive at this truth? A poem/song/tale we can reshape/revise constantly until we arrive at a shape we deem most fit, most true. Why couldn't I have done that with my life?

Because art is not life.

THINGS TO BUY AND DO

1. Meat — 1.5 kg fillet, 2 kg mince, 1.5 kg sausages, 500 g salami (bloody expensive but Carl won't do without it)
2. 2 kg butter
3. 2 doz eggs — BP's
4. Vegies — carrots/cabbage/potatoes/beans
5. Milk
6. White T-shirt for Pita — Ah Tong's
7. Wine? 2 doz beer
8. Get Carl's shoes repaired
9. Lunch with Josh at Nelson's today — 1 p.m.
10. Ring Dad re Sunday's alofa for faifeau (too much)
11. Pay telephone/electricity accounts

Bugger. What a life — trivia!!!
Don't forget you're on a diet. Your arse is dropping too quickly.

70

He was still asleep when she had a light breakfast, got a taxi and went to the Israel Museum. However, when she got out in front of the museum, she decided she'd seen enough historical displays to last her a lifetime and wandered into what she discovered was a garden of modern sculptures. (Designed by Naguchi, she read on a placard.) A collection by some of the world's most influential sculptors, the massive pieces were poems and songs caught at their most apt revisions and locked into the shrubs and trees of the garden.

As she strolled, she realised she was walking over a surface of pebbles, like the paepae of a fale, crackling and giving way under her sandals. The sculptures had been placed in such a way as to hold themselves, the trees, paths and pebble floor together in a self-contained unit. She recognised the Henry Moore woman: a reclining black earth mother whose weight and presence the earth couldn't escape — or want to escape. She lingered in the statue's cool shadow, and for that while she was free of herself, her father and their pilgrimage; she was puny bone and flesh in the immensity of that goddess, and glad of it. Up the goddess's vagina she'd crawl and lie warm and safe in her womb. Never to be reborn.

She surfaced to the crunching of approaching feet, and hurried to the waist-high stone wall that bordered the garden and overlooked the city. Measured up against such art and achievement, she had no talent, no ability to become more; it was also too late; we are what we have lost or left unfulfilled.

For a long time she gazed down across Jerusalem's hills and valleys, letting the slow haze fondle and measure her pain like the diagnostic hands of a gifted taulasea. For a long time.

Later, as she left the garden, she thought, how would I describe this city? She would ponder this question for weeks and, one afternoon in the stillness of her house, which was shaded by a giant monkey-pod that reminded her of Henry Moore's earth mother, she would compose this answer (after many revisions):

Jerusalem is a radiant light which you inhale through your pores and which illuminates your being with a phosphorescent joy.

71

At the start of affairs, I nearly always warn my lovers not to fall in love with me. 'But why not?' some of them joke.

Most of them eventually declare they're in love with me. (Some of them are resentful about it.) They then demand that the affair continue indefinitely or permanently. At that stage I usually end it. I don't like being treated as property, or as the idealised object of what they say is love. Most objectionable is to be treated, by them, as mother confessor/sex machine more expert than their wives and other women.

I don't like one-night stands either, because AIDS and herpes, price of the new sexual freedom, aren't exactly enticing, and the sex is mainly unsatisfactory. But I've indulged in such liaisons (what a description!) primarily out of loneliness or boredom — nothing better to do, so why not? Or out of irresistible curiosity (he looks interesting) or sexual frustration (I've never been one for prolonged celibacy).

The Shrine of the Book, permanent home of the Dead Sea Scrolls, is ultra-modern in design but reflects the cave and location where the scrolls were found. It is made up of a large black dome and a white slab-like structure.

There was a scatter of visitors in front of the shrine, mainly English she guessed from their accents. For a still moment she watched the sunlight flowing like waves of electricity over the black surface of the dome, and thought of Samoa's sea at noon; then as she walked to the front entrance, she noticed that the slab, because it was bone-white, was reflecting all the light.

The easy coolness enveloped her as soon as she entered the shrine. She stood and observed the immense circular cave, walled around by temperature-controlled glass cases in which the precious scrolls were displayed. She recalled having read, in a tourist brochure, that the contrasting dome and slab depicted the theme of the eternal struggle between good and evil, between the Sons of the Light and the Sons of Darkness as told in the scrolls.

She started moving around the display. To her right, shuffling like a wooden puppet, was a thin old woman in a shabby brown suit and propped up by a carved walking stick. She heard the woman's ragged breathing and moved away from her, wanting no reminder of pain.

Methodically, she scrutinised each faded scroll; her sandals scraped audibly over the thick carpet. Across the circle were a young couple, arms around each other, whispering and giggling.

Soon she imagined the dome above her opening out, like a flower, into the infinity of space, a slow unfolding, a reaching out, searching for size, shape, a meaning to it all, out there in the cold light of God's head. She dared not look up; she held on to the steel railing in front of the display cases, afraid of being sucked up into the infinite void. The cold railing seemed to force her fingers to wrap themselves more tightly around the steel. She shut her eyes.

When her fear passed, she walked to the centre of the circle, to the rocket-shaped sculpture which pointed up at the eye of the dome.

She planted her feet, and allowed herself to become the centre of the mellow light and the scrolls: some of humankind's first worded gropings towards understanding God and the cosmos. She tingled to the dance of the circle, she began swaying to the rhythm which holds everything in an unbreakable circle, a unity-in-all.

She imagined she was in a spaceship adrift in outer space in a remote and future time in a science fiction novel called *The Shrine of the Book* and, around her helpless spaceship, the Sons of the Light and the Sons of Darkness were amassing their awesome armadas for their final confrontation, and she wouldn't be able to stop them.

'Our universe is left-handed,' Pita had told them once.

'Does that mean God is left-handed too?' his grandfather had asked.

'I'll have to think about that one,' Pita had replied in all seriousness.

73

If I was asked to say what I enjoy most, at this stage of my life, I'd say:

Ice-cold Vailima after an exhausting run, sucked down long and slow to the quiver of gullet and the applause of the thirsty belly, with your nerve ends tingling, in the company of friends you can relax with because there's no need to be anyone else but yourself;

Getting stuck into extra-hot chicken curry and roti, thick dhal soup, tamarind chutney, with your gluttonous scalp brimming with cool sweat; or into palusami and taro straight out of the umu, devouring the rich flavours of coconut milk and taro leaf mixed with the aromas of banana leaf/breadfruit leaf wrapping — a food as long as your childhood Sundays; or into an assortment of sushi of shrimp/octopus/sea eggs/and fish dipped in soy sauce and hot wasabi; or into sizzling teppenyaki grilled beef/pork/and vegetables; or into a heap of fresh oysters/mussels/toheroa/ tuatua/kina/tugane/faisua/paua with all the thick sea power and flavours seeping into your being; or into a brashly reckless novel which explores your greedy tastes, risking all; or into a bubbling arrogant chop suey of poems wild with the earth's sap and vices and which send exquisite shivers down your spine;

Having your legs apart, and being eaten by an uninhibited mouth and a strong expert tongue, your juice, like raw egg white, flowing down your thighs, and your brain a raucous choir trying to burst out through the top of your skull; or a long, lingering Sunday afternoon in your quiet house, the two of you reading lurid porn while you side-fuck to the wet clutch, pump and pull of the waves in Fagali'i Bay;

Floating almost dead still in a deep river pool shaded by tamanu trees that suck up the worries in your head, the coldness of water becoming you completely and you becoming the river, which catches the surprised reflection of the trees;

Sinking into yourself in your canvas chair as you look out at the evening swallowing up the bay, and the air smells of mangrove mud and coral — the odour of the birth sac bursting; or standing on the back verandah sipping ice-cold beer and watching (astounded) the sun pulling up the mountains of the Vaimauga; or sitting cross-legged in your head, combing the day's problems out of your hair, and humming a lullaby Aunt Fusi crooned into you as a child . . .

All that (and more).

The return now is always to what is, what is real, what my senses and imagination can touch, feel, grasp, enjoy, suffer. The rest is senseless duty, all in the head, and masochistic guilt.

Long live the Belly-Button.

74

'Tomorrow we'll visit the Garden of Gethsemane and the Via Dolorosa,' he declared at dinner. She glanced at him but he looked away, picked up his knife and fork and started eating, forgetting to say grace. 'Our trip has been very beneficial but it has to end.' For at least two days he had avoided retracing Christ's final suffering, and she hadn't asked him why, because he obviously didn't want to discuss it.

They ate in silence.

He wanted to play cards so they went to his room after dinner.

'They never had a chance, did they?' he asked halfway through their first game of Suipi. She looked at him. 'The Jews,' he said. She waited for him to explain; he didn't do so for two games.

While she shuffled the pack of cards for their third game he went and changed into a lavalava and orange T-shirt which Oren had bought him.

'Good, isn't it?' he said, pointing at the front of his T-shirt.

On it was a black and white photograph of Charlton Heston as the white-bearded Moses, and the bold caption: MOSES WAS BORN IN HOLLYWOOD.

'Vanity, all is vanity!' she laughed. 'Are you going to wear it at home?'

'Yes, and my friends are going to be jealous!'

'You've changed, Dad.'

'Yes, I'm enlarging my limits.'

As they played he kept running his hand over the caption and smiling to himself. She remembered how, throughout her childhood and youth, she'd been immersed in the stories of Judas Iscariot and his betrayal of Christ and his deserving suicide, in Pontius Pilate trying Jesus and then allowing the Jews to judge their heroic victim.

'What does Matthew say about the Jews at Jesus' trial?' she asked.

No pause in his game, the quote came automatically: '*Then answered all the people and said, His blood be on us and on our children.* By writing that, Matthew attributed to the Jewish people, for all time, a collective guilt for Christ's crucifixion. John goes further and identifies the Jews with the powers of evil: *Ye are of your father the Devil, and your will is to do your father's desires.*' Looking up at her, he added, 'Matthew and John were *not* Jews. And up to our trip here, I believed them.' He continued

244

playing. 'The Jews never had a chance. Everywhere they went, especially within Christendom, they were treated as Judas. And when Christianity spread to our islands, we did the same.' When she paused in her play, he said, 'Go on, play!' She misplayed and he whooped and took another suipi.

'Would it have been preferable if Christ hadn't allowed the prophecy of His martyrdom to come true?' she asked. He didn't respond. 'Would it have been better if Jesus had stopped Judas from betraying Him, and letting Himself be tried and crucified to overcome Death and prove He was God's only Son?'

'Won again!' he said, counting his score.

'Would it have been better?'

'I don't know anymore.' He started gathering up his cards. 'It's all in the cards anyway.'

'Christ committed suicide,' she challenged. 'He murdered Judas by letting Judas fulfil the prophecy. It was a deliberate act on Jesus' part . . .'

'It's very late,' he whispered.

'And by letting the Jewish people, His people, condemn Him in order to fulfil the prophecy, He allowed them to suffer the Holocaust!'

'As Pita would say, Ola, don't lay the heavy on me, not tonight anyway.'

'Do you want to sleep now?'

'No!' was his quick reply. 'I'm not tired.' She realised he didn't want to be left alone to contemplate the new questions challenging the basis of his life. She started shuffling the cards for another game. 'No,' he said. 'Just tell me another story of your Dead.'

75

Most of us (unfortunately) never discover the passions, obsessions and talents which we possess. The fortunate (among us) sometimes discover them accidentally.

Though Iosua was physically very thickset, with a large head and exceptionally large hands and feet, he was most inconspicuous in class, withdrawn, offering mumbled replies when I asked him questions; he always sat at the back, the true plodder who had studied extra hard to come from the village primary school to Samoa College and who, after two tries at School Certificate, qualified for the sixth form; a solid citizen who would have maintained his inconspicuousness if I hadn't introduced *Hamlet* (the play, that is) to his class.

I've never been one for Shakespeare: my high school teachers had ruined him for me, and I've always found the language of the plays extremely difficult. But for that fateful year, *Hamlet* was the set play for the University Entrance exam, and I *had* to teach it. Just imagine: *Hamlet* in the sweltering tropics in a language foreign to students who know little of Europe and castles in Denmark! So I decided I'd just try and teach them enough about the play to get them through the exam. For me also, the always intellectual, perpetually self-questioning Hamlet was a slightly ridiculous, sometimes silly, self-indulgent adolescent constantly picking at his deformed navel, unable to break out of the cerebral. ('Mental masturbator!' a friend once described him. 'Masochistic voyeur' was another description.)

Most of the students groaned (not too audibly though) when, one humid sweaty afternoon, I announced we were going to study *Hamlet*, starting the next day. I gave out copies of the play and told them to read them. I described the plot briefly, and tried to get them interested by announcing that Laurence Olivier, 'the greatest of all Shakespearean actors', had recorded the play and we would listen to that performance.

The next morning at the start of the period, I put on the first of the long-playing records. The students settled down quickly. I withdrew to the back and, pretending to be following my script and listening to the record, sank into the fuzzy, pleasant world of daydreams. (My usual escape from the boredom of teaching!) The rhythmic flow of the perform-

246

ance, of poetry and sound effects, the attentive silence of the students became a barely audible tide surging dully at the edge of my hearing. Throughout the years since then I've kept remembering the faint but annoying smell of fresh cow-shit wafting in from the paddocks only a short distance away. Why has that memory persisted? It's extraneous to this tale. Life is not art, I must remember that. Chaos is more usual than order, the Principle of Uncertainty is built into the cosmos, Pita would say. The smell of fresh cow-shit was there and had nothing to do with *Hamlet*, but it happened. It wasn't an evil omen, the Apparition come to Elsinore Castle! The fact of it was that I was in the belly of a mellow day-dream while my poor, bored students were trying to cope with the golden prince, who was trying to cope with his golden navel. The smell of cow-shit intruded, a coincidence.

I surfaced when the bell rang to end the period. The students started packing their books. One of them turned off the record-player. 'You may leave!' I told the class.

Three boys passed me as I walked up to my desk at the front of the classroom. '. . . *Not so, my Lord; I am too much in the sun.*' For a moment I couldn't believe I'd heard it: it was an almost perfect imitation of Olivier, so English and perfect an utterance couldn't have come from any of my students. I recognised Iosua as the middle of the three. No, he would be the last one capable of such mimicry!

Next day I walked into a noisy English class, put on the next record, and the students quietened down at once. As I went to sit at the back, I saw the sentence in red chalk on the black blackboard: I AM TOO MUCH IN THE SUN — HAMLET. I didn't say anything about it to the class.

Once, during the next thirty or so minutes of usual daydreaming, I noticed the girl next to me nodding to sleep. I coughed. She woke up and smiled. Just beyond her, Iosua was upright with intense attention, his eyes riveted on his script, his lips mouthing the text in time with the actors. At least one of them was excited by the prince's ordeal, I thought, and then returned to my daydreaming.

Fifteen minutes before the end of our period the next day, I stopped the record and asked them if they wanted me to explain anything. No requests. (Inwardly I was relieved because, as yet, I hadn't prepared any detailed explanations.)

'Well, can anyone quote any lines from the play?' (I had to fill in ten minutes, but what a stupid request to make, I thought.) For a short while, there were no offers. Then a thick but timid arm began to rise at the back just under the red sentence, the quotation, on the blackboard. I was reminded of a frightened sunflower, in the morning, unfolding and rising (compelled by its nature) to know the sunlight. 'Yes?' I asked the now-upright arm. It was Iosua, eyes still focused on his desk top, the top of this thickly haired head pointing at me. Some girls giggled. 'Yes, Iosua,' I encouraged him.

'I say something from the play?' (Atrocious English!) More giggling. His friends were squirming with him, praying he wasn't going to make a fool of himself.

'Go ahead. You don't have to stand up,' I said. With his head lowered, his face hidden from me, he spoke into his desk top, almost inaudibly. 'A bit louder,' I said. He raised his head slightly and spoke into the back of the student in front of him. 'Very good!' I said, even though I hadn't heard him clearly. He raised his face towards me at last. I remembered a calf being born, breaking out of the slickly wet caul, stretching its limbs, testing them hesitantly, afraid at first, then gaining confidence with each unimpeded stretch.

> . . . O, that this too too solid flesh would melt
> Thaw, and resolve itself into a dew.
> Or that the everlasting had not fix'd . . .

At first it was broken, barely intelligible. A ripple of mirth fluttered through the class.

'That was very good,' I congratulated him, realising that he had just committed a very courageous act: his peers frowned upon any student who paraded his knowledge or ability in front of a teacher; it wasn't Samoan, it was blatantly Papalagi to 'show off' one's individual talents. 'Do you know any more?' I asked. He shook his head.

That evening while I was drinking with friends at the RSA Club, I thought of him and how he had tried so hard to rise above his insignificance, his timidity and fear. For him the lines had been more than memorised ones, they had been a magical fish-hook fishing him out of the boundaries of himself. I envied his growing courage.

The class stopped laughing when I entered the room. I sensed they were trying to hide something from me. I glanced at Iosua. He looked embarrassed. I put on the next record. BUT BREAK MY HEART, FOR I MUST HOLD MY TONGUE — HAMLET was scrawled, in bold yellow chalk, across the top of the front blackboard. 'At least one person in this class knows *her* Hamlet!' I joked. Some of them laughed. They tried not to look at Iosua.

Before the end of the period, I tried it out again. He offered to recite. This time none of us laughed. It was an uncanny and astounding performance. Sitting intensely still in his chair, his eyes slits of concentration, his hands gripping the edge of the desk, he cast the miraculous net of his voice over us, trapping us.

His accent was still noticeably Samoan, yet it was a spell-binding mimicry of the record. This time the Ghost:

> *Ay, that incestuous, that adulterate beast,*
> *With witchcraft of his wits, with traitorous gifts —*
> *O wicked wit and gifts that have the power*
> *So to seduce! — won to his shameful lust*
> *The will of my most virtuous queen . . .*

As he recited, I thought: what God was speaking through him? What gift was pulling him above his mediocrity? We clapped when he finished. 'Go on, Hamlet!' someone called. He looked at me. I nodded.

> *. . . Let not the royal bed of Denmark be*
> *A couch for luxury and damned incest*
> *But howsomever thou pursuest this act,*
> *Taint not thy mind, nor let . . .*

I sensed the committed quality of obsession. This wasn't simply a performance: Iosua was discovering his gift for Hamlet, the gift that made him exceptional. How else could you explain his facility to absorb, so easily, uncannily, the record and fury of the prince's tale?

Some students whistled, we clapped, he bowed his head once and smiled and was the usual Iosua again, released by the god. 'He knows all of Hamlet's lines!' Mamafa, one of his friends, said.

'Not possible!' a girl challenged.

'Ask him!'

He was soon reciting whole chunks from Hamlet's soliloquies, almost flawlessly. The more he recited, the more confidently he assumed Olivier's voice and delivery. And through his performance and obvious love of Hamlet, I too was, for the first time in my life, falling in love with the play.

That week at the staff common room I asked about him. His other teachers agreed he wasn't very bright, but worked hard, obeyed his teachers, caused no problems whatsoever, would make a good clerk or civil servant, maybe even a dedicated primary schoolteacher. So I kept Iosua's gift to myself.

On Monday morning, I could hear him reciting as I approached the classroom. I entered quietly. He was standing in front of the class. He stopped when he noticed me. I nodded. He continued. I sat down quietly.

He was magnificent. A hypnotic energy emanated from him. He *was* Hamlet, and possessed. Though he did not act, his voice, his presence, performed it all. Such intensity was not of us: it was a terrible beauty.

249

Later, as the class was leaving, I asked him, 'Do you remember other plays as well?'

He shook his head. 'Just *Hamlet?*' He nodded. 'Why?'

'I don't know,' he mumbled. 'Hamlet was a great hero.' He was again empty of the god.

Could I have stopped Hamlet from possessing him totally, then? (Or was it the reverse, was he taking possession of Hamlet?) Without Hamlet he would probably have been safe, secure, protected from, unaware of his only gift. (I'm getting carried away again. I'm sure that at that time all I cared about was his miraculous transformation and gift, and about encouraging him to use it. It wasn't until later that I became aware of the danger.) In our next English lessons, I got other students to read the other roles to his Hamlet.

'Do you understand what you're reciting?' I asked him after the other students had gone.

'A little,' he replied. He looked up at me. In his eyes was a brilliant dazzle: he was high, high on Hamlet.

A day later a science teacher asked me if I was teaching *Hamlet* to the sixth form. That explains it, he laughed when I said yes.

'What?' I asked.

'Our sixth form now has a *real* Hamlet. They even get him to perform in my class. He signs all his assignments, Hamlet.'

'I'm sure he's just joking.'

'I hope he is,' he said.

In the staff common room some teachers started joking about our college acquiring 'a very gifted Hamlet who isn't particularly good at anything else.' 'Fatally flawed!' one of them quipped. They laughed. I was annoyed but said nothing.

I began to fear for him.

'Where is Iosua?' I asked at our next English period. Nobody seemed to know. I started the record.

'He has gone home,' Mamafa said. 'He's not well.' I tried to ignore the suppressed wave of laughter which surged through the class.

During that period while *Hamlet* played on, as it were, I couldn't escape my deepening anxiety about Iosua. At the end of the period Mamafa waited until the other students had left and then told me, 'He is not well. He is afraid.'

'Of what?'

'Of him — Hamlet.'

'But why?'

'He says, Hamlet won't leave him alone.' Mamafa paused and added, 'Miss Monroe, you must help him. The students and teachers are starting to poke fun at him!'

'I'll try,' I promised, though I was heavy with a feeling of help-lessness.

'It is as if he is two people. Every time he is Hamlet, which is happening more and more often, he finds it difficult to be himself again . . . What is happening to him?'

'Tell him to come and see me.'

I hardly slept that night, refusing to admit to myself that I had been responsible for Iosua's discovery of his gift, obsession, madness. How was I going to help him? I had to confront that too.

He was away from school for over a week, but Mamafa assured me he was well. My anxiety lessened. The day after we finished studying *Hamlet*, the students having completed their notes about the play, and I had told them we were moving into a study of modern poetry, he returned.

While the others were settling down, I asked him if he was all right. He grinned and took his usual seat at the back.

And for a couple of weeks, while we struggled through some modern poetry, he was again his usual withdrawn self, empty of the gift, offering little to our understanding of the poetry and understanding little of it. He even massacred a poem I got him to read aloud to the class. Further proof of his dull normality. I was elated he was safe, but I sensed in the class a feeling of disappointment that Hamlet had left us and we were again mired in our uninspired, boring normality without vision or daring, trapped in our perpetually deadening sanity. Better a plodding, normal Iosua though than an insane Hamlet, I persuaded myself. (I wasn't going to be responsible for a kid going crackers.)

Once again we forgot him in his inconspicuousness.

WITHOUT HIM I AM NOBODY in red chalk on the front black-board when I walked into my classroom before school started. Momentarily I was puzzled. A Jesus freak, I concluded. Lines from a hymn. I rubbed it off, sat down at my desk, and started working.

Next morning the same lines appeared in exactly the same place. A very persistent Jesus freak! Again, I erased it.

WITHOUT
WITHOUT THE
WITHOUT THE PRINCE
WITHOUT THE PRINCE I
WITHOUT THE PRINCE I AM
WITHOUT THE PRINCE I AM NOBODY

Good poem, I thought when I saw it, the following morning. I erased it, and before I left school that day wrote in the same place:

YOU ARE NOT NOBODY
YOU ARE A POET

AND DON'T KNOW IT
I went straight to my classroom the next morning.
MISS MONROE
LOVES THE PRINCE
BUT THE PRINCE WENT MAD
Annoyed. Puzzled. My anxiety jabbing at me again, I found myself rubbing that off quickly, unwilling and afraid to explore the extraordinary.

'Have any of you poets in this class been writing their brilliant verse on my blackboard?' I asked my sixth form that afternoon. They looked puzzled.

The next morning — and I still remember the persistent light rain sweeping across the classroom windows — I immediately identified, with erupting fear, my mysterious poet when I read this on the blackboard:

TO
TO BE
TO BE OR
TO BE OR NOT
TO BE OR NOT TO
TO BE OR NOT TO BE

I didn't see him that day because I didn't have his class. My fear, tinged with guilt, became disturbingly persistent. At the same time I experienced an irrepressible curiosity to go more into that terrible beauty and discover where he was at. Was he still possessed? Beyond the ordinary, touched by the gods? So before going home that day I wrote:

THAT
THAT IS
THAT IS THE
THAT IS THE QUESTION

His reply was simple (and really put the shits up me!).

THE CHOICE IS NOT TO BE

I kept imagining him using all sorts of violent methods to commit suicide, as I waited for his class to appear. My other classes passed in a frantic daze and frequent trips to the toilet to relieve my fear. I could've hugged him to death when he came as his usual normal self and grinned at me as he sat down. During the lesson I persuaded myself that my fears were unfounded.

I stayed after school in my small office to do some marking, and forgot about him quickly as I attacked the stack of assignments. At four o'clock I shut the last exercise book and discovered I was uncomfortably sticky with sweat, and thought of a long cold shower. I looked into the classroom. He was at the blackboard writing. His huge arm danced across its surface, leaving these words behind:

252

MISS MONROE,
THE PRINCE IS NOT TO BE

With intense fascination I observed him, knowing he was unaware of my presence.

Turning dramatically to face his audience of empty desks, he began his performance. The light from the upper louvres was like gold on his face; his eyes blazed with a holy fire, his rhythm and movement were flowing and sure and poetic, as he was transformed into Hamlet contemplating the beauty of the abyss, fascinated by it, vulnerable to it, tempting it. I tried not to watch but even my guilt tasted brilliantly sweet as I witnessed that magnificent hero making love to his self-indulgent fascination with madness and death, risking all.

> *. . . To die, to sleep —*
> *No more; and by a sleep to say we end*
> *The heartache and the thousand natural shocks*
> *That flesh is heir to. 'Tis a consummation*
> *Devoutly to be wished.*
> *To die, to sleep;*
> *To sleep, perchance to dream . . .*

Suddenly I wanted him to see me and stop (and thus stop me from enjoying his tragic dance), but he continued advancing over the abyss, fingering his own contemplation of his death, picking at it, tempting himself, dancing step by step closer to the eye of the abyss.

I moved forward. Too late. Still unaware of me, he swung towards the front door and, still caught in Hamlet's voice, swept out. *Exit.*

Through my tears, I watched him stride, his head held high, his whole body in command of the world, across the lushly green school grounds, descending to the main road. Away, diminishing in size with each brave step, with the palms, flame trees and the sky applauding. Hamlet, Prince. Conqueror of the Abyss.

He didn't return to school ever.

Mamafa told me that Iosua had been sent by his parents to live with relatives in New Zealand and attend school there. That salved my conscience: I didn't even check the truth of Mamafa's information — I didn't want to face the possibility that Iosua was insane and in a hospital. I wanted to live with a sane Iosua, a diligent student, in a prosperous New Zealand.

Good art would have me leave him, in my tale, suspended in a suspenseful bout of heroic madness, with the awed reader applauding his courage, but, alas, life is more tragic (and dreadful) than that.

Six or so years later, when I was holidaying in New Zealand, I visited relatives in Porirua and was waiting at the crowded station for a train into Wellington when someone tapped me lightly on the shoulder. I ignored it, thinking it was someone trying to pick me up. A more insistent tap. I turned sharply and cringed immediately. He was huge, a bulging-all-over Michelin Man with that unmistakable grin and a little girl sleeping in his arms. He nodded. Automatically I shook his hand and kissed him on the cheek.

'It is you, isn't it?' he asked hesitantly in Samoan.

'Yes. Are you well?' I replied in Samoan.

Nodding his head, he said, 'Yes, I am well. And you, Miss Monroe?' He was my student again, even the voice, the respect.

'I am well, thank you. Is that your daughter?' I caressed the girl's back.

'Yes. I have two other children.' In his awkward, almost inarticulate way he told me he was a foreman in a factory which manufactured mattresses, and lived with his wife, children and five other relatives in a low-rent state house. Then wistfully, as if it was too painful to say it, he admitted, 'I had a bit of illness.'

'Yes, I remember,' I joked.

His eyes lit up. 'It didn't last long,' he chuckled. 'I've been well ever since.'

'That's good.' I heard myself say, with the heroic image of him marching over the school fields caught in the heart of my head. Hamlet, I yearned to say to him. The magic word could free him once again.

'Are you still teaching?'

'No.' I was suddenly lost for anything else to say. The train was pulling into the platform and passengers were surging towards it.

'Would you like to visit our home?' he invited me.

'Thank you, but I have to go back into Wellington. I'm returning to Samoa tomorrow.' The lie was automatic, final, I didn't want to see what had become of Hamlet in the suburbs. I bent forward and kissed his daughter on the cheek. 'Goodbye!'

'Here,' he said, sheathing money in my coat pocket. 'Please!' he pleaded when I tried to return it to him.

'Goodbye!' I started hurrying to the open door of the carriage.

'Goodbye. May you have a safe journey!' he called.

The train started moving. I looked back and waved. In the milling crowd, his size, his shape, his aloneness made him look so apart, distinct. He waved slowly as if he was waving a heavy flag. I recalled how, in my class, he had first raised his timid arm and had volunteered to quote from *Hamlet*. I tried to push the memory out of my heart but couldn't.

Iosua
Hamlet
Prince for a dazzling day
But better that one passionate day
than never at all

76

Don't forget crabs move sideways in order to go forward. There are also many kinds of crabs and they have different styles of moving sideways.

Standing still, at times, *is* going forward (and is very healing). The secret now is to learn *how* to stand still and *be*.

77

I met Carl at a cocktail party at the Paulos', friends from my scholarship days. (Before that I'd seen him at other parties.) He was the eldest son and heir to Fischer Co. Ltd, import and export merchants, which, after Carl returned from New Zealand as an accountant, he'd expanded into other businesses.

He'd attended boarding school in Wellington and then university where, in the idiom of pre-Pill New Zealand, he got a girl 'into trouble' and married her.

A year after they returned to Samoa, another woman was in trouble. (Carl believes in contraception but leaves it to his partners.) He legitimised that heir by divorcing his wife and marrying his new heir's mother. When we met he was still maintaining two households, openly. The two spouses were jealous of each other and threatened constantly to leave him, but didn't because his wealth was the umbilical cord they couldn't feed without.

I parked in front of the Paulos'. The sun was disappearing over Mount Vaea. I went to the verandah, nodded to Carl and the other guests, and hurried into the lounge and three quick vodka-tonics and that floating feeling which would cushion me against the tide of inane conversations, petty jealousies and gossip.

Holding a fresh drink, I began moving from group to group, mainly of my generation and who now controlled our unfortunate country. Mainly New Zealand-educated (and ex-scholarship) and in the civil service or politics or business or in all three. Mainly children of pastors and civil servants who'd supported the colonial administration against the independence movement. Mostly with matai titles, though the first scholarship group which had returned home had demanded the abolition of the matai system. We spoke in a mixture of Samoan and English, inclining more towards English and fully English when we had to include non-Samoans in our often arrogant conversations. For instance, right then, within range of my wandering right ear, I heard: 'Agagafi ga ou alu ai ou ke fa'akau in Morris Hedstrom's. O le kaugaka ia! (Boy, the cost of living is impossible!) O le Malo legei ua kakau oga throw away . . .' My left ear, which is usually shy, was being invaded by: 'The new clothes i

BP o le magagaia ia. From America. Kele ia o ofu mo children . . .' My lucid eyes were sucking in: 'Politics is a matter of fa'aukauka, judgment, good sense. Look at Veli, la ua Palemia ae le'i alu i se a'oga. Take Mo'opaepae, our Migisika o Eleele, he's never been to school . . .'

We pursue the philosophy of Aiafu, Eaters-of-Others'-Sweat, over-indulging in everything. We were into flab, high blood pressure, gout and diabetes.

We didn't look out of place among the expatriates there, mainly diplomats and UNO 'experts and advisers'. Samoa has one of the highest ratios of foreign experts in the world. Every type of expert you need to claim you're 'developing'. Development is the new gospel.

I was getting drunk faster than usual, so I looked for an anchor. Elisa waved me over to her group by the french doors that opened out on to the back verandah, which dropped down to the ravine. As the dark pressed down on the bush-thick hills, the cicadas cried louder and louder.

Elisa whispered hello, kissed my cheek and hurried off. When my left ear caught the sound of the man who was centering the group's attention on his pretentious person, I muttered 'Shit!' No wonder Elisa had run away. Conducting his usual monologue was Doctor Pilchards, so nick-named by us but known on his birth certificate as Pilitati Masikeke, literally Pilchards Biscuitcake. He insisted that we address him as Doctor after his PhD in Sociology. He'd taken nine years to complete his doc-torate, on a scholarship that he'd kept lengthening by conning the scholar-ship donors.

'Hi, Life!' he interrupted his monologue.

'Hi, Doc!' I replied. Only my close friends call me Life, but the doctor was expert at appearing to be *real* friends with everyone, especially when he wanted something from them.

'. . . And then I was asked by the President of FAO to present my views about agricultural development in our small country. As you know, I'm chairman of our national committee promoting agricultural exports,' he continued. Beside him was his adoring wife, Dorothy, 'a Kiwi blonde from the high sheep country', the doctor described her. Next to her was Fa'atatau, wife of a genuine doctor but medical, who usually maintained a frightened silence and drank only Coke but, at one party, angered by her loquacious husband, had downed numerous gins and then performed a violent striptease, shouting, 'Ufa-komo! Ufa-komo!' Next to her floated Elsie James, scrunched-up spouse of a New Zealand engineer, who, when allowed to speak insisted on whingeing about everything and everyone, and whose middle-class obsession with material possessions and status had become more obsessive in the lush tropics. She complained inces-santly about having little money, but when she went abroad spent thou-sands on herself. Slotted into the space beside Elsie, like an inevitable accusation, was Ana Tuai, a favourite friend who could have been a better lawyer than her dull husband but had become trapped in the role of house-wife with five demanding children, and who now believed it was too late to free herself from that death. Beautiful and tragic Ana, I thought as I watched her maintaining the mask of the attentive housewife, as she listened to Doctor Pilchards and repeated, 'Is that so? Is that so?'

'. . . Did you know I had to save our Treasury from bankruptcy brought on by bad management?' Doctor Pilchards was saying. 'Well, I did. As you know, I have a BCom. Did it in the minimum time . . .' Poor Doctor Pilchards was his own worst enemy. He *was* handsome and attrac-tive to women; most of his academic qualifications were genuine; he *was* bright and worked quite hard and he had a pretty wife and beautiful children. '. . . Which reminds me,' he was saying, 'of the time I was in Noumea as head of our government delegation and I was asked by the other leaders to speak on their behalf . . .' Like me, Doctor Pilchards was a product of the Government Scholarship Scheme but, unlike me, he'd enjoyed a privileged upbringing in a pastor family whose congregation had kept it in fat comfort.

As the doctor bragged on — and he was never loud — our group drifted away, one by one. I was going to be marooned with the good doctor and his wife, who believed everything he said. After all, he believed his lies — call them what you like — after he created them, like a novelist who creates his own characters and truths. He even believed the life history he'd fed us about his wife, that she had an MA in Mathematics, was the only daughter of a South Island sheep 'baron' who owned a twenty-thousand-acre sheep station, a Rolls, a Jaguar, and twelve super-intelligent sheep dogs; a daughter who'd sacrificed that wealth to marry him, a poor Samoan. Dorothy *was* bright, she *was* pretty, and the doctor didn't need to exaggerate her into myth.

'And how are you, Life?' he asked when nearly everyone else had fled.

'Okay.'

'That's great, great!'

I pretended someone was beckoning me. I waved back. 'Excuse me, Doctor, but I've got to go.' And hurried off.

'Poor bastard, brag, all is brag,' I sighed into the fresh vodka-tonic Elisa handed me on the cool verandah.

'Sorry about that,' she laughed.

After Elisa went off to look after her other guests, I moved around unobtrusively. 'Stop drinking now,' I kept ordering myself, but my glass kept filling itself, it seemed. The liquor couldn't unclog my phlegmed-up throat, especially when I had to listen to: 'Dear, ga ou fai aku fo'i ia ke oe, don't buy that rubbish at Ah Mau's, go to Nelson's. So stop crying —

it's your own bloody fault . . .' And: '. . . The trouble with you Palagis is you're still acting like colonisers. Why don't you leave us alone and go back to your nobody jobs and to carrying your own suitcases?' (Another 'romantic revolutionary' who lived just like the Palagi he wanted out of his colony.) And: '. . . We had to appoint Lepeki but had to fiddle it a little, fa'akaukau i rules a le PSC. Nobody'll be able to fai se appeal. Ua makua'i mau ma clear mea uma . . .' And even more depressing: '. . . And, you know Johnny, my little sixteen-year-old boy, fell out of the car and cracked two of his front teeth and we had to rush him to the hospital. Geez, I've got nothing against locals but it's bloody hopeless up there. Johnny had to roll around in pain for nearly an hour before a doctor bothered to see him and even then he prescribed only aspirin. This bloody place is giving me the creeps . . .' ('Go back to Australia then,' I said in my foggy head.) And slightly more interesting: 'Did you hear about Miles and his housegirl? Well, ga alu loa le ko'alua i Giu Sila, pipi'i loa le kama o Miles i laga keige faigaluega. Must say, e ese le magaia o si keige. From Siumu — pei a se afafige o le koeaiga fo'i lea o Peko. Ia, ka'ilo pe koe fia soso le kakou kama i loga ko'alua Palagi. You know, the girls of the Malo Pipo are quite something — ga oga mau lava le koe mafai oga mamulu ese! For life . . .!'

I pushed through the crowd around the bar and, thrusting my empty glass at Fano, mumbled, 'Give me some more alofa on the rocks.'

Fano starting mixing my drink. 'Slow down, Ola,' he whispered. 'We don't want to have to listen to you rage, not tonight. Things are better than you think. We're just suffering from middle-age flab . . .'

'A whole generation?' I interjected.

'Yeah, and there's bugger all we can do to change it.' He handed me my drink. 'Take it easy, Ola. Just keep sipping your cool, sweet fa'a Samoa on the rocks. Consume, Ola. Enjoy. We all have the right to be obese!'

Others were demanding refills so I moved away from the bar.

At first, on our return from New Zealand, many of us had suffered a lacerating guilt but, as we'd eased into the corrupting comfort and 'respectability', we'd learned to live with that guilt and our betrayal of former ideals and principles.

The darkness was now bursting up from the depths of the ravine and licking the verandah railing that I was holding on to. The cicadas had stopped crying.

'Why are you sad?' his voice eased over my shoulder.

'I'm not!'

'Sorry!' Carl started to move off again.

'Stay — if you like, if you get me another vodka-tonic.'

I refused to look at him when he handed me my drink. I swam in the darkness below/ahead. 'Do you believe in aitu?' I asked.

A surprised hesitation and he said, 'No.'

'Why not?'

'My German half won't let me.'

'Bullshit! What about the Great Fatherland's aitu?'

'Who?'

'Hitler, No-balls Himmler, Eichmann.'

'Never thought about it that way . . .'

'You don't do much thinking, do you?'

'Lady, I didn't come here to be abused!'

'Why did you then?'

He hesitated again. 'Because I want to marry you!' I glanced at him. 'Got you, eh!' And he started laughing.

'Up you too!' I said, turned and stumbled through the crowded house and into my car.

'Do you have to drink so much?' Pita said when I rolled into his room.

'Bugger you then!' I snapped and hurried to the kitchen in the hope of finding Aunt Fusi.

She was at the sink washing dishes but didn't bother turning around. 'Bugger you too!' I shot at her back, but my bullet flicked off it like a rain-drop off a duck's unforgiving back.

'Go to bed!' Aunt Fusi's call chased me down the hallway.

'Fuck you all!' I shouted into the dumb, callous house.

At dawn I woke and found myself in a sleeping lavalava and tucked safely into my bed. Across the room, sleeping in the armchair, with her large face aglow in the dawn light, was Fusi. I fell asleep again, secure that she was there to bandage the wounds and massage away my fears. Aunt Fusi. Mother of my life.

A wordless, smiling Carl, arms outstretched, kept floating in and out of my dreaming. A good omen? No, for within two weeks of the cocktail party and my dining out with him twice, Carl's parents and wives (and their relatives and friends) and my friends (and relatives and enemies) had turned us into the centre of another juicy town scandal.

'I hear your wives are laying into me,' I told Carl the next time he rang. After I'd said it, I regretted it.

'What . . . what . . . what have . . . they been saying?' he stuttered. Whenever I got assertive, he tended to stutter.

'Don't worry. I don't give a damn anyway.'

Another lengthy pause. 'Ola, please . . . please don't ever lie to me. The best have tried to con me!'

'I wasn't; they're saying some pretty nasty things about me.'

'Like what?'

I grasped for the usual vicious stories that riddled such scandals, and said, 'Well, that I'm after your money . . .'

'And you believe it?'

'You don't have to attack me too!'

'Sorry,' he apologised. 'I'll talk to them about it.'

'Please don't. If you do they'll think there's truth in the rumours that we're sleeping together. Let's just ignore the whole thing.'

'Where do we go from here?'

'Wherever *you* want it to go, Carl. I'm fond of you so, if you feel the same about me, why don't we see where that'll take us?'

'Are you sure, Ola?' He always scratched his nose with his right thumb when he was nervous, and I visualised him doing that then as he held the receiver.

'I'm sure.' I *was* definite about it.

'Would you like to meet me in Japan? I'm going there on business the week after next.'

I'd always wanted to visit Japan, Land of Kabuke / Noh / Toyota / Kurosawa / and Kenzaburo Oe, one of my favourite novelists. 'I could go to Auckland just before that and then on to Japan,' I said.

'What are going to be *your* reasons for travelling?'

'Oh, to get away from you — end this scandalous affair. Or, to visit a very sick relative!' I laughed. 'Then on to Tokyo — no one has to know about that leg of my healing.'

After he'd stopped laughing he asked, 'Are you sure, Ola?'

'Yes, I'm more sure than sure. And if they find out about it, they'll really have something to be scandalised about.'

'You're really something, aren't you?' I realised he never swore. Not one single swear word in the time I'd known him. What that's got to do with this story, I don't know.

That night, five minutes before midnight, when evil aitu are supposed to haunt us, Carl's legal wife, Sharon, used the telephone to wake me from my celibate bed and haunt me, in an aitu-like voice, with, 'Bitch, you leave my husband alone or I'll get my aiga to fa'alauakau you and bite off your adulterous ear. Ua e fa'alogo mai, bitch? Go *thing* some other poor sod ma ave aga kupe!'

'Please return to your foul grave,' I whispered back in my Queen Elizabeth II accent.

She started choking (I hoped) on her anger and shouted, in her squeaky Kiwi accent, 'Komo!' thus betraying our feminist cause: we women shouldn't use (and thereby degrade) our central organ as a term of vile abuse.

'Stiff cock to you!' I whispered in my Grace Kelly voice, trying to correct her male chauvinist abuse.

'Ufa!' she shouted. Now that was neutral — both sexes have arses.

'Same to you!' I whispered in my Germaine Greer voice, complimenting the absence of sexism in her last remark.

'I'll come and cut off your . . . !'

'Balls?' I interjected in my Meryl Streep accent from *The French Lieutenant's Woman.*

'Fuck you! Fuck you!'

'Yeah, I'm in need of one right now,' I whispered back. I shut off her haunting by putting the receiver down.

Esther, Carl's illegal wife, tried haunting me through a letter I received two days later. She pleaded she had two teenage children who needed an ample income to continue enjoying the high standard of living and education they were accustomed to. Carl, their loving/concerned father, had more than enough money to support her children (and her) and his *other* wife (and her three spoilt children) and, if I played it unselfishly, me (and my bright son, Pita — she even knew his name). We women had to protect ourselves and our children and the years we'd invested in our husbands' careers and businesses. She was full of admiration for me, for my university education, my frank and open life style, and my success in having raised myself up out of my *humble* origins. She just wanted to remind me that it was unfair of me to want Carl to myself. (Carl had made that clear to her, and she loved Carl more for having been honest with her.) I was being inconsiderate, especially when my previous husband, the wealthy American Peace Corps volunteer, had left me so well provided for. It was heartless of me to make *our* Carl believe that I loved him and only him. Be reasonable, she argued and she would ensure that our Carl never found out about my present and past string of lovers. She ended: 'Please think of Sharon and her children and me and mine but, even more importantly, of your future with our Carl, whom we all love and should be willing to share, fairly.'

Esther the Feather, as I so nicknamed her, was offering polygamy, a contented harem in three separate households, to protect her investment. With more thought, I sympathised with her. There were/are millions of middle-aged women fighting for lucrative divorce settlements as just compensation for lives that had gone into pissed/shat-in napkins, screaming/demanding kids and insensitive husbands, into a whole existence of being fed upon. And for all I knew about Carl at that time, he might be capable of loving us all genuinely. Look at the Muslims! Remember our pre-Christian ancestors! Love at first sight and forever is a myth, good for the marriage/family industry. You can fall out of love and grow into love and loving more than one lover. But I wasn't going to reply to Esther, not in writing through the mail, or in any of my feminist accents.

*

263

Whatever else came out of our Japanese visit, the following *attempts* at poems came out of it. I wrote them a few months after our return and, like most of my other attempts, I've not shown them to anyone:

MY MOTHER DANCES

Through the shadows cast by the moon tonight
the memory of my mother dances
like the flame-red carp I watched
in the black waters of the lake
of the Golden Pavilion in Kyoto.
Such burning grace.

Though I'm ill with my future
and want to confess it to her,
I won't. Not tonight.
For my mother dances
in the Golden Pavilion
of my heart.

How she can dance.
Even the moon is spellbound
with her grace.

THE TREE

The ancient Zen temple in Kamakura.
A pine tree older than the temple
is the unblinking eye of the courtyard.
Its wisdom is rooted deeply.
Long wooden crutches prop up
its lower limbs.
Straw bandages bind its wounds.
I stand in its shade.
The tree is weeping.
I wear this summer morning
that will end.

HIROSHIMA

You made me see
that all paths lead
to the healing song of the heart
such a song which can make
the thousand paper cranes

festooning your limbs
open their magical wings
and soar up through the black rain
and the fireball
defiantly to discover clear skies

Hiroshima
heal me

It began guardedly as soon as Carl's business hosts, representatives of Tamura Enterprises, left us in our luxurious suite in a hotel in the heart of Tokyo.

'They know you're not my wife; they've met Sharon. But the Japanese are very efficient and discreet arrangers of everything,' Carl said.

'I'm never going to feel comfortable bowing,' I said.

'Just shake their hands and, from then on, the handshake will replace the bowing, in your case anyway.'

I went over to the windows, which were alight with bright summer sun, and looked out at the grey haze covering the city. When he touched my elbow I turned and moved into his arms and our first kiss, long and gentle, none of the aggression that I'd expected of him, no frantic urgency. His was the fragrance of fresh lemon mellowed with cologne. I'll always remember that.

We lingered in our explorations, kissing/caressing/fondling/savouring every discovery, with my senses more alive than I cared to remember. It was as if the jaded years had been shed and I was rediscovering (and taken with the blazing wonder of it) the feel/shape/sound/smell/taste/flow and magic of a man's body.

'Carl! Carl!' I murmured.

We slept and when we woke it was night. I sensed he was feeling awkward too. I got under the sheets. 'Thank you. I needed that badly. It's been a long time.'

'And any man would've done?'

'I'm sorry. I didn't mean it that way.'

'What did you mean then?'

'It was beautiful because it was you.' I put my arms around him.

'I'm all right!' he said. 'Let's start anew — as if we've not known other lovers.'

'Yes,' I replied, dismissing the feeling of inadequacy I'd discerned in his declaration. 'Yes, let's.'

'Don't ever tell me anything about the others.'

'Who?' I found myself pushing him.

'You know.'

'Men?'

'Yes.' He embraced me. 'Promise me.'

'I promise.'

Soon we were a fierce tangle of heat/weaving and singing bone/flesh/ mouths and . . .

Something brushes against your forehead — a dream of butterflies? the flick of a feather? Carl's fingers? And your eyes are open, catching the light filtering through the blue curtained windows. For a moment, panic, where are you? Glance at the man beside you. Carl. Your breath quickens, dry twitches in your belly, as you examine his sleeping face, and the memories of the night flood your inner eye. Your fingers touch and brush over the side of his neck — he's real, not a night lover who'd come to captivate you and then fled at the first light. No. He's there. In sleep, vulnerable to everything — you could even cut open the veins pulsating in his neck and drain out the blood into your thirsty mouth, into your overwhelming need for him to be you, in you.

You dress in your running gear, sighing repeatedly at the unbelievable reality of being with him, of your not waking to a deadness in your heart and just another lover with his disappointing odour, physical disintegration, mushrooming paunch and snoring. You keep glancing at him — he's still there and he's still the lover you shaped/discovered in the night. Marvellous, the joy of it.

On consulting the receptionist about jogging routes, you choose the four-block one that includes the central park and the Emperor's Palace. You run out into a Sunday that's already hotter and more humid than Samoa, but you're oblivious to the heat because you are singing still with your rediscovery of *love* — yes, and you're not scared anymore of calling it that, singing with the wonder of it, tasting it in the morning air and the silence of the empty streets, hugely singing, and Tokyo, its metal-skinned buildings/streets/parks, is a welcoming creature around you, embracing you and you transmitting your joy into it, flying as your pores/heart breathe in the day and Carl and more Carl, the smell/taste/heat/beauty of him, you and the unity around you fuse in a oneness that you believe will never alter or in the altering will not leave you once again stranded on an island without meaning, knowing that this is more than you've expected ever, more, much more, and you remember Gill and your heady promise that one day you'll *be* more, like Jesus walking the down-sucking waves, and you open out and summer pours in to fill you, and you run and run, sieve to the word's pain/joy/beauty. Fly, bird of the dawn, you hear Aunt

Fusi whispering in your head. Fly . . .

You become aware of the thick wetness of sweat over you, and then of your clothes drenched through with it, and around you Tokyo is withdrawing from you, the unity breaking, you hear your feet pounding on the path, more traffic and people and you're different from them, more conspicuous because you're larger than them — you'll always feel a giant among the Japanese, a big-footed, clumsy meat-eating giant. You're weaving through the park now, over lawns under rows and rows of cypresses and pines that have been trimmed to look alike, through their still shadows, with pain now vibrating through your lower back and down your legs, and unconsciously, you begin to sense — and you're frightened at first — that the trees are reading your every thought, and you try and shrug it off but can't. It grips you tighter and you run faster, but the trees seem endless, their rows pulling you into their slender sadness — that's the only way you can describe it, a sadness as deep as you've experienced in the mountains of Upolu and the lava fields of Savai'i, the sadness that lies behind everything, waiting because it *knows* it is the end (and the beginning) of everything. In the distractions that clutter up your life you don't want to hear that silence, that humming chord that weaves us to all things. You slow to a walk, weighed down by the inevitable honesty of it. You stop and turn, sweeping your eyes around the rows of trees, focusing on each one, with a dizzy hum filling your ears. What are the trees saying? Again the tangle of dark green sadness. The trees are dying. The signs are there: limbs sagging, leaves drooping/falling, trunks scarred and burned by the acid air. You continue running, your body is now a dose of pain. Your eyes sting in the poisoned air. Ahead, caught in the gap at the end of the path, is the walled palace, and in your inner eye you see the moat around it and the Emperor, a zoologist, suited and tied even in the height of summer, watering his garden of chrysanthemums as lucidly brilliant as Van Gogh suns. You push against the weight and drag of your body. You run faster. The air stings your nostrils and throat. Carl!

The bed is a sea of blankets and tangled sheets. You strip off your wet clothes that feel like animal skins still ripe with blood, and thrust your head into the ocean, searching for Carl.

'Hold me!' you cry. 'Hold me!' The dying trees hum in your head.

Months later, in a letter to Gill in New Zealand, you'll write: '. . . In Tokyo, in love with Carl (and love), I ran through a park, searching for the Sun God but found only cypresses and pines suffocating in the polluted air, and a wizened zoologist watering his chrysanthemums that reminded me of the searing pain that must've cut through Van Gogh's brain as the knife had sliced through his ear. I imagined Van Gogh mixing his paints with the blood from that wound and then painting those enraged suns through which I now *see* all other suns and the things they luminate . . .'

I've found that if you show an unhesitating appreciation of other people's national foods and cooking they'll allow you (sometimes unreservedly) into their hearts, or into whatever organ they consider the seat of their deepest affections. Don't forget, the heart isn't the universal home of those feelings. For instance, we Samoans consider that location to be the space between your heart and lungs; the moa, or centre of your belly, is where the self resides, and your liver, not your entrails, is for courage. I've been fortunate that I can eat anything and everything that is food.

Carl told me that Tadao Tamura-san, the venerable president of Tamura Enterprises Ltd, was taking us out for dinner. Tamura-san had visited Samoa a few times and they'd established profitable business connections. 'Quite a guy!' was Carl's description of our host, but I still thought I'd meet the stereotyped Japanese businessman — inscrutable, annoyingly polite and reticent, and a teetotaller.

As we came out of the lift into the hotel lobby, a chunky man with gold-rimmed spectacles and in a white suit, striped tie, and shoes that snared your reflection hurried — more a fast shuffle than a walk — to us.

'Tamura-san, I'd like you to meet Ola,' Carl introduced me.

I started to bow but Tamura-san reached out and, shaking my hand firmly, said, 'You are very beautiful, Ola-san. Very beautiful.' I sensed Carl enjoying my surprised discomfort. 'I hope you like Japanese food, Ola-san. I know that Carl enjoys only very safe Japanese cuisine such as tempura (which originated in Korea) and fillet steak (which originated with General MacArthur).' Carl started laughing. 'I'm still hoping, and all of us humble Japanese never give up hope of converting barbarians to our civilised diet, that Carl will learn.'

'I'll eat anything,' I said, still disoriented by his not playing to the stereotype. 'I'll eat anything *you* recommend, Tamura-san.' And bowed. He guffawed — that wasn't Japanese either.

'Please don't ask for whale meat,' he whispered as we walked through the front doors of the hotel.

'Why not?' I asked, thinking he was joking.

'I'm an executive member of the Anti-Whaling Association here in Tokyo. I hope you like other seafood (and sea-life) though, because that's what we finless, webless Japanese eat mostly. Unashamedly, we eat just about everything that moves in the ocean.' Holding my elbow he said, 'Come, the restaurant is just around the corner.' He didn't mispronounce his 'l's and 'r's either, not like my favourite Japanese actor, Toshiro Mifune.

As soon as we were seated in the private room on cushions on the floor, with our legs stretched down and across the shallow pit under our table, Tamura-san said, 'I've taken the liberty of pre-ordering our meal for tonight — I hope you don't mind. And Ola-san, like Carl, you must take whatever I say, especially under the influence of whisky, with a few — what is the English expression? — yes, with more than a few grains of salt.' As he chuckled I noted his numerous gold teeth. A waitress knelt beside him, placed a container of whisky and a bucket of ice on the table and backed out again. 'They know my vices well,' he said. We declined his offer of whisky and asked for sake. 'Bless the Scottish — this is the only worthwhile thing they invented. And tonight, it's all for me!'

Sipping his first drink, he continued his highly original lesson about his people as viewed through what they insisted on 'masticating and disposing into their unfortunate stomachs and then through their equally unlucky alimentary canals'. More lucid insights emerged as the whisky heated up his imagination. 'Unfortunately or fortunately, depending on your values and preferences, I was born into a peasant family rich in poverty and unquenchable ambitions (much like Japan itself), and had to survive with endless optimism (and endless hard work) and an over-imaginative tongue and brain. Into a small village in the remote mountains, famous only for its primitive pottery and our gift to make anything — yes, even our mistakes and failures — *taste* good . . .' His conversation was quickly dispelling my stereotype of the Japanese tycoon.

'. . . As you know, my unimportant country has always been poor in natural resources, so the sea had to be our main source of food — and we learned to eat just about everything in it. We also learned how to make whatever was edible on land worth eating. And to make it more palatable we learned how to present it. Out of poverty we produced food as art. (Or so our tourist brochures say.)'

Right then our meal began arriving, served first by two sushi chefs and then two waitresses. Tamura-san traced the history of each dish and its variations from district to district, season to season: sushi — fresh and cooled sea-egg yellow on rice balls wrapped in seaweed; sashimi — raw tuna dipped in soya sauce and wasabi; a variety of pickles; barbecued eel; miso soup — central to the arrangement; bowls of steamed rice; and endless sake heated and served in small cups. Tamura-san kept apologising for tainting our meal with 'the foreign blood of the Scottish'. 'Eat! Eat!' he encouraged us. I noticed he wasn't eating very much. I turned his conversation back to his life.

'Out of eight sons I was the only one who survived. My father, like his father and his father, was a potter, and like him I was illiterate, and we were exploited by our landlords, treated like beasts of burden. The war was a disaster for mankind but a liberation for me and many peasant

269

sons of my generation. I was drafted into the Emperor's army, a reluctant recruit whose ignorant parents were proud of serving (and even dying for) the Sun God. In the army I learned to read and write at an insatiable pace, it was as if I'd discovered the rope that would pull me up to the Sun God's face. I hid that appetite well, behind the obedient, stupid mask of the loyal peasant, and just read everything. And as the war neared, I also perfected my unpatriotic motto: 'Learn not to get killed while you learn'. I'm very un-Japanese in that I've always admitted to being a coward, though I never betrayed the Emperor and my family's honour; never ran away in battle, but I didn't expose myself to any unnecessary danger either. Whenever our suicidally brave officers tried to whip up our suicidally patriotic fervour I told myself, "Tamura, what's your wealthy Emperor ever done for you and your family?"

'Our Sun God has always been too far away for an ignorant peasant like me. Emperor-worship was for our noble classes, who enriched themselves in the Emperor's service and in his golden name imposed a mass culture throughout our country, a culture centred on the Emperor and the aristocracy. Smaller cultures, like mine, were swept away. Now the Sun God has become faceless technology, money, television — all the ills of the societies we borrowed them from.'

A few minutes later he was describing how he'd been captured and imprisoned in a British prison camp in Malaya. He'd not wanted to escape, no sir! In that camp he was safe from patriotism, self-sacrifice and possible death, and in there he found a language he loved (apart from Japanese, that is) — English. He worked his way into the prison library and the friendship of Wilson-san in charge of that library, which very few people used. During the four years, Wilson-san taught him English and Shakespeare and Tennyson, which he loved; Rudyard Kipling, whose colonialistic attitudes he detested — though he admired Mowgli; G. K. Chesterton, who, he believed (but didn't tell Wilson-san) was happily insane; Robert Louis Stevenson — and he still reread *Treasure Island* as his favourite *philosophical* work; and most precious of all, Edgar Rice Burroughs, gifted author of the noble Tarzan epics, the *Four Just Men* and other great works which had inspired him to rise from ignorant pauper (Burroughs-san himself had been a pauper) to be a Tarzan of business.

He went on: 'One can love a people's literature but not the people. Our British wardens were arrogant and ignorant, they hid the latter under a humourless inscrutability and pretence at learning and civilisation. They didn't even fart openly or make appreciative noises while eating. In short, beings who considered it the height of civilised behaviour not to show any emotions. I could never understand their preoccupation with cats, cricket, sherry, class and inscrutable sex. And to think that our own aristocracy aped the English aristocracy! It wasn't just technology we

270

borrowed from the West . . . To the Queen of England!' he toasted.

He didn't like the English, he explained, but he owed them and Wilson-san a great debt. In the post-war development of his country, knowing English was a valuable asset. On his release from the army, he'd been hired as an executive trainee, by one of Japan's biggest corporations, because of his fluency in English, and, using his village's talent for making anything taste good, he'd climbed the executive ladder swiftly, earning a reputation for loyalty, dedication, hard work and ruthlessness. 'Briefly,' he said, 'they respected me because I was making them rich — sheer greed. I was a magician at making profits. And they feared me, like the apes feared their master Tarzan. To Burroughs-san!' he toasted. We downed our drinks again. 'Illitelate peasant flom nothing village go all the way to skysclaper penthouse office likee most Japanee business tycoon today,' he parodied his English and his life. 'Likee Nixon flom shabbee law office lies to White House lies — success stoly. To our unbeatable industrial miracle and Toyota City!' We downed our drinks. And he was silent, into himself. Carl and I looked at each other. Tamura-san's spectacles were misting over. I did a very un-Japanese thing: I reached over and grasped his right hand. 'Yes, you are very beautiful, Ola-san,' he whispered from a great distance. 'Forgive an old bachelor for getting drunk; he's so far away from his village and can't return there. My country — thanks to former peasant boys like me — is now so far away from the clay.' (This reference to the clay puzzled me until the afternoon before we left Japan.)

'Did you guess he's over eighty?' Carl asked as we took the lift up to our room. I shook my head and maintained the silence Tamura-san had bequeathed to me. 'What's the matter?' He hugged me to his side. I shook my head again. 'He gets morbid when he's had a lot to drink.' There it was, that annoying lack of understanding.

'It was a delicious meal.'

'Yes, Tamura-san is quite a gourmet!' I buried my face in his shoulder. He hadn't learnt anything from the old man. 'I liked that bit about being Tarzan; he *is* a Tarzan in business. Do you know how much he's worth?' I refused to reply.

The afternoon before we left Japan, almost two weeks later, Tamura-san sent me a gift, with his secretary, who looked more ancient than his boss and who knocked hesitantly on the door, shuffled in, bowed and extended the parcel to me with both hands. I invited him to sit down but he declined and waited while I opened the parcel.

In it was a small clay pot, which had been open-fired because its surface was splotched with burn marks. With it was a letter:

Please accept this unworthy gift from an inconsiderate old man who ruined your first dinner in Japan. And in gratitude for having been a patient and beautiful listener. Remain beautiful in spirit, Ola.

The pot is from my village and made by my great-great-grandfather and given to me by my mother after I returned from the war. It was not intended, by my dear mother, as an urn for my ashes. She had wanted me to bequeath it to my children, but I have never married.

Modern Japanese have no time for or appreciation of the clay out of which we came. Treasure it in a world that has gone to the dogs, I think the unlovable English would say. And leave it to your children.

'Please thank Tamura-san for me for the clay,' I said to his secretary, who shuffled backwards out of the room.

I never told Carl about the gift because I feared his reaction: 'It's not a very expensive pot, is it?' In Carl's value system he would've been wrong about the pot; it is ancient Bizan, worth thousands of dollars. For me (and I hope, for Pita who will inherit it) the gift is more precious than money, it is the clay.

Was that gift the secret that began the other secrets that piled up during our life together? But I forget that Carl had already made me promise to keep my former lovers to myself, and he knew, without my telling him, that I didn't want to hear about his wives. We'd placed a ban on large areas of our individual histories and experiences and, as our relationship lengthened, those areas enlarged too, without our mentioning it.

Because I'm a woman — surprise! — Carl and Tamura Enterprises, without consulting me, planned our itinerary according to the traditional male concept of woman: flower shows/tea ceremonies/museums/art galleries displaying traditional Japanese art — none of the disturbing modern for poor me, shopping and more shopping, etc. So, while Carl was busy with business negotiations and other exclusively male work (such as lunches and after-work drinking), Tamura Enterprises provided me with a 'liaison officer', one Mrs Mioko Yashimura, and a neatly typed itinerary for Tokyo that would've exhausted the tough Queen of England with its demanding boredom.

During our first day, which started at 8.30 a.m. sharp, when Carl delivered me into Mrs Yashimura's hands, and ended at 5.30 p.m. sharp when she delivered me to my hotel desk and got me my key, I stuck grimly to the grimly efficient Mrs Yashimura, who, politely but firmly, stuck to our programme, which accounted for every second of our day. We visited two department stores — more specifically the women's wear departments, where, as was expected of me, I expressed enthusiasm at the quality of the merchandise and, with Mrs Yashimura's expert advice, bought an expensive array of perfumes and toiletries 'for myself and my

272

daughters'. (Carl had three daughters which Tamura Enterprises knew about.) Our chauffeur took the parcels back to our company limousine. (I was flattered having a grey-uniformed/capped chauffeur. Watch it, girl, wealth corrupts the soul!) We then toured three art galleries, a museum, a Shinto shrine, and a Mikimoto pearl emporium. There were no shadows in the traditional paintings — the world and its fauna and flora are *afloat*, transient, the artist tries to snare the ever-changing approximation of what is; the gloomy museum smelled of fresh radish and incense; I recognised the striking gardens behind the Shinto shrine as the setting of a moving love scene in an early Kurosawa film — I've forgotten the title of it. Our tour was laced together by Mrs Yashimura's melodious, extremely knowledgeable and up-to-date commentary about *everything*. I tested her once: 'What are those trees?' The information clocked out like a computer: ginkgo trees, useless as firewood or building material, but beautiful/pleasing in shape, and home of millions of birds which had once fled the treeless city. 'There are a hundred and fifty ginkgo trees in this street, seventy-five on each side of the road.'

That night, while replenishing my exhausted spirit with real spirits (vodka on the rocks), I pleaded with Carl to let me decide what I wanted to see/do/be.

'Honey, they're being very generous and considerate hosts, and they've put a lot of thought and time into looking after you,' he insisted. He put his arms around me. 'We must never cause them to lose face or think we don't like what they're providing for us.'

I mixed another vodka.

Next morning I tried to look enthusiastic when he delivered me to Mrs Yashimura.

'Good morning, Mrs Fischer. How are you this morning?' she enthused, straight out of a *Teach Yourself English* book.

'I am fine, thank you, Mrs Yashimura,' I replied in kind.

That hectic morning it was a Buddhist temple — and I tingled at the touch, on my hands and bare feet, of its ancient wooden floors, a laboriously long tea ceremony with a group of Americans and a Japanese expert explaining it in an American accent, a store specialising in cloisonné jewellery — I bought a pocketful of rings/pendants/bracelets/ earrings; and lunch in an ancient restaurant famous for its noodles — the Emperor had dined there too.

Long wooden tables and benches, bare, pock-marked with age. Mrs Yashimura sandwiched us down between two men who smelled of radish and garlic. No one paid us any attention, so I believed. I was to learn later that the Japanese have the uncanny ability of not looking at you — it's bad manners — yet they see everything you do. Next time, try turning around fast when they least expect it and you'll catch their eager eyes sliding away from your exposed back, like hermit crabs retreating into their civilised shells.

The steaming noodles were served in seven small bowls that were piled up in front of me in the form of a pagoda. A large bowl filled with a light radish-soya sauce, and uncooked quail's eggs came with it. Mrs Yashimura showed me how to break the eggs and mix them into the sauce. A fan of the Japanese style of eating — fast, noisy and devoted to showing appreciation — I didn't care how my guide and the other customers were going to view *my* style.

Within seconds I was engrossed in the attack, hungry chopsticks into the noodles, shovelling them out into the sauce and then into my mouth, slurping and sucking back long and gasping. While I was unselfconsciously unnoodling the pagoda, as it were, Mrs Yashimura giggled — the first recognisably individual gesture she'd made while with me. I sucked louder, slurping in a long long long noodle, and her giggles became laughter, soft but still laughter. The other customers smiled and nodded their approval. I bowed.

'You expert noodle eater!' Mrs Yashimura congratulated me. Pleased with myself for having broken through her polite exterior, I ate my whole pagoda to her three storeys.

An hour later, belly round with noodles, we left the now-packed restaurant. Once outside, she was her businesslike self again. She started itemising our afternoon schedule. I moved against her hip and put my arm around her waist. Not a visible flinch but, as she recited our destinations, she edged away. I held on.

'Mioko?' I called her deliberately. She missed a step. 'Is there a park nearby?' She pretended she was puzzled. 'A park?' I repeated. She nodded and continued with her list. 'Well, let's go there. I'm tired and just want to rest a while. All right?'

'All right, Mrs Fischer.' She tried to restore her equilibrium and our mistress-servant relationship.

The lawn was soft under my back as I stretched out in the shade of the ginkgo trees. She sat down on the bench and arranged her knees to hold together, hands clutched on them, back to be ramrod straight, in the proper stance of the proper guide keeping watch over her unpredictable ward. She was even wearing nylon stockings, white shoes and a fawn blazer with the Tamura Enterprises monogram; her jet-black hair and make-up were straight out of a conservative, middle-class fashion magazine. One must not be different, call attention to oneself: it is the group that is important, the relationships, the *Wa*, in that group, to nurse/cultivate/keep in harmonious order. Kaput to individualism, the unexpected, diversity.

'Are you all right, Mrs Fischer?' she asked. Things weren't going to schedule, and schedules determined expectations, governed behaviour and the proper perimeters of conduct and order; detailed plans and schedules were essential for progress, order, development, and keeping at bay such evils as laziness, inefficiency, differences, starvation, poverty, vandalism, infidelity.

'I'm all right, Mioko,' I sighed as the clouds glided, like caressing hands, through my eyes into my drowsy head.

'Don't forget, Mrs Fischer, we are expected at four places this afternoon . . .'

'Mioko, relax. We're both tired. We'll rest and then walk back to the hotel.' It was a firm instruction, and she was lost for what to do. A carefully devised way to get the maximum benefit out of the day was being ruined, wasted; a whole untimetabled and therefore empty afternoon had to be survived. Before she could reassert her schedule I closed my eyes and pretended I was falling asleep. And I *did* fall into a sleep full of Pita and Fusi searching for sea-eggs on the reef and a dog barking to the mountains of Upolu crooning a Bob Dylan song — I can't remember the song.

Over the years I'd trained myself to take lunchtime naps lasting no longer than twenty minutes. This time it was ten minutes over schedule. I opened my eyes and caught Mioko still in her rigidly protective posture but fast asleep. (I let her sleep on. Whenever people approached I'd put my fingers to my lips, indicating silence, and they passed by quietly. (Bless the super-polite Japanese.)

When her eyes flicked open thirty minutes later, she was on her feet in a panic, looking at her watch, at me, at the day dying, her lips trying to find the correct formula to save our wasted afternoon. 'Nothing to worry about, Mioko,' I said.

'But Mrs Fischer . . .'

'But what? We've already been to those places we should've gone to. We flew there in our sleep!' I got up and she helped me brush the bits off my clothes and out of my hair. 'Shall we go?' She nodded.

On our way back, I held her elbow and insisted on dawdling so she'd dawdle too; she didn't seem to mind. I steered our conversation to her life. She provided me with enough information to keep me *out* of her life: she was forty-one years old — she looked only twenty-five, I complimented her; wife of a humble civil servant — I later found out he was third in charge at the Department of Finance; a BA graduate in Public Relations at Tokyo University with a Tokyo Prefecture Diploma in Professional Guiding; now in her third 'absorbing and rewarding' year with Tamura Enterprises; before that she'd been a humble housewife.

'Any children, Mioko?'

'Two, Mrs Fischer.' I waited. Nothing else.

'Boys? Girls? Ages?' I demanded.

'A boy, a girl: fourteen years and ten years.' Her eyes were lighting up.

'And?'

'Will have no more children. Japan is too crowded. We have a car but Tokyo is too crowded to use it often . . .'

'And their names?' I ignored the car.

'Masashi and Yoko.' And she was away, telling me about their schooling, grades and teachers. She wanted Masashi to be a scientist (any kind of scientist), and Yoko to get a good degree and go to traditional school and learn all the skills (such as flower arranging, the tea ceremony, cooking) that a good wife had to have. (Behind the ultra-modern face of Japan is the still enslaved, obedient and long-suffering wife.) At my prompting, the hot blazer came off and she unbuttoned her collar.

For the rest of the week, we ignored our schedule and didn't tell Carl or Tamura Enterprises. We also abandoned the chauffeured limo — I ordered the driver to have a good holiday — and we walked or used the underground. Visited a sushi bar — Mioko pretended shock — and ate our way from one end of the seafood displayed to the other, to the sweet accompaniment of gallons of ice-cold beer for me and lemonade for my 'shocked' companion. Invaded the Ginza, once notorious for Sodom and Gomorrah and other lucrative vices, but now flashy neon and glitter, bars, discos and well-controlled prostitution.

We didn't meet any Yakusa but I introduced Mioko to pub crawling, which I told her was an ancient Polynesian custom. Keen on pursuing Polynesian-ness, she became a devout student, drinking one gin and lemonade to my every three vodkas, as we 'crawled' from one bar to another. Three loquacious hours later I was buzzing, giggly, and liquid with alcohol, while Mioko, my novice apprentice, was as sober as a Palagi judge. And not a hair out of place.

I was disappointed no men had tried to pick us up, and asked, 'Where are they?'

Mioko understood and replied, 'Too early. All men at work. They come home — too tired for anything!' And giggled.

On our last Tokyo day, I suggested that we visit a Turkish bath (which I'd read somewhere was one of novelist Kenzaburo Oe's favourite recreations). 'NO!' she yelped.

'I know it's for men only, but . . .'

'NO!' she barked, sharp and clear and cold, so Dylan Thomas would have described it. So we went to the 11 a.m. session of *Superman II* and loved it, munching popcorn, and she chortled while I cheered.

For lunch she said, 'Ola, you must eat at my most best restaurant.'

'Yes, please!' I was intrigued.

We turned the corner. 'There!' she pointed. A McDonald's packed with lunchers.

'You're kidding!'

'No, I am not kidding. McDonald's and Kentucky Fried Chicken now most popular restaurants in Tokyo — and perhaps all Japan.'

We gorged double-burgers, large french fries, large Cokes. 'Good? Good?' she kept asking.

'Delicious!' I sang.

'Meat is good for growth. My children, they are taller than me and husband. I feed them much New Zealand lamb and American steak, though they are very dear. Also potatoes and butter. Meat eaters grow big and tall. Our national average height has gone up by two inches since the war.' I got another double-burger and we halved it. 'Ola, are all women in your country as . . . ?' She was looking for the polite word.

'As *massive* as me?' I helped her. She nodded. 'I'm just average. Small in fact.' (Liar, my inner voice accused me.)

'Polynesians are always big,' she sighed.

We wandered for another hour or so, talking about our families; mine now had three daughters in it. When we were thirsty again I steered her into another bar and persuaded her to have 'one last farewell drink'; that one led her to trying my other favourite drinks: pina colada, black russian, margarita, and campari and soda. God, her capacity was incredible — must be beginner's luck!

'Very expensive,' she kept apologising.

'It's only money. With the compliments of Fischer Enterprises!'

On our way back to the hotel, she put her arm around me.

She insisted on coming up in the lift. At my door, she said, 'Ola-san, thank you for the best job I've ever done. You are my most close friend.' We hugged. 'I love black russian!' she cried into my shoulder.

In every city Carl and I visited after that there was a Tamura Enterprises guide to look after us. None were women, now that Carl was with me. And after Tokyo's male-determined itinerary I wasn't going to suffer again.

In Nagoya, our first stop after Tokyo, they'd scheduled, at Carl's request, that we visit the Noritake factory, famous even in our insignificant Samoa for its cutlery and crockery. I hugged and kissed Carl when he insisted that we go there, but I refused to go. I'd seen a poster advertising the daily training sessions of Yukio Watanabe, world superheavyweight champion of sumo; they were being held in the grounds of a nearby Buddhist temple.

'What about that?' I confronted Carl, who looked at our guide, another clone (but male) of the proper Mrs Yashimura before I'd corrupted her.

277

He blinked a few times behind his silver-rimmed glasses, bowed and said: 'It is very good that the gracious Mrs Fischer is interested in our most ancient and venerable sport, or art, to be exact. Even our most high Emperor attends the championship, and is the patron of sumo.' (He was smooth-talking me like the Mikado.) 'But I have to inform, most humbly, that sumo is *not* for ladies, not while the champion is training.'

'Are you sure about that, sir?' I asked before Carl could lean on me again. The Mikado looked at Carl to save him. Carl looked away.

'Perhaps Mrs Fischer would like to learn about our famous tea ceremony?'

'Carl, I'll not be condescended to,' I said in Samoan, smiling all the time. 'Tell this gracious male chauvinist machine that it's sumo or I assassinate his gracious Emperor!' Carl was decisive and tough in business but he hated offending his hosts, anywhere. 'Right, you and the Mikado here go to the tea ceremony and I'll go wrestle the superstar of sumo.' I bowed to our guide and headed for the door.

They hurried after me.

Seated in the second row, Carl sulked, the Mikado stared at the ring as if he'd been struck blind by lightning, I enjoyed the spectacle. When the magnificent Yukio swayed like a battleship up the aisle and into the circle, I forgot my spoilt companions and clapped. During the next hour Yukio lifted and threw almost twenty opponents out of the ring, one after another, and I loved it.

'I knew we should've come to see him,' Carl said as we left the tent. I looked at him, he looked away.

I tapped his arm and said, 'You're a bit of a bullshitter, eh?' He hugged me. The Mikado pretended he wasn't witnessing our uncivilised show of affection in public.

Once Carl and I were back in our bedroom I threw off my skirt and blouse and, dressed only in bra and panties, I grunted and went into the half-squat sumo stance, hands on my knees. Lifted my left foot and stamped it down, then the other, and circled Carl, challenging him. He faced me, trying not to laugh. I rushed at him. We grappled. I grabbed round him and hitched my right hand under his belt; he lunged at mine — no belt, just my flimsy knickers, which ripped off as he tried to lift me. I locked my left arm round his neck and, with my right hand around his belt, lifted — UPPPP! He went up all right, but his weight pushed me backwards and flat on my bare arse and then on to my back. Before he could pin me, I locked my knees around his hips and rolled him over on to his back, and pinned his arms to the floor with my knees.

'That ain't sumo!' he insisted. 'Sumo is the way of fair play!'

'Give up!' I demanded. He nodded. I released his arms. He jerked up his belly, heaving me off, and then pinned me to the floor.

278

'I give up,' I laughed. He relaxed. I heaved him off and pinned him.

'That hurt!' he cried. There was a livid mark on his left shoulder where it had hit the bed. I lay against him and licked the hurt away; he put his arms around me.

Soon we were making love in the easy but powerful pace of sumo.

'I love you.'

'I love you, sumo-style.'

At dawn the next day, I woke up and scribbled:

In the grounds of the temple in Nagoya, in a marquee that glowed in the summer sun like a silkworm's cocoon, I fell in love with the emperor of sumo

He was more magnificent than Hirohito

> *bigger than Fuji*
> *swifter than the bullet train*
> *slicker than Tokyo/New York and Suva*
> *handsomer than Goliath and David slinged together*
> *braver than my father's wishes for me to be a preacher*
> *a better singer than Ali/Dylan/Elvis/and Zapata's sombrero*
> *gentler than a baby's bottom*
> *sexier than Richard Pryor/Mad Max/and Tina Turner*

as he strutted his heavy stuff as god/superstar/the Seven Samurai
> *and Godzilla*

I wanted to take him home to teach me his way
> *the way of sumo, sumo-do*

In Japanese, DO is way, as in JU-DO, KARATE-DO, JUJITSU-DO, ZEN-DO, SUMO-DO. My way is OLA-DO, the way of Life. And for an unbelievably intense while, Carl and I would live it out together, growing in alofa.

We flew back to Auckland and Carl left the next day for home. I stayed for a week in a Queen Street hotel, restless, missing him. Every day I rang him at his office; everything was normal, he kept reassuring me. However, when he said that Sharon and Esther hadn't mentioned my name once, I knew things were badly askew. When it came to gossip and scandals, Carl was the least observant of people.

So I rang Aunt Fusi, whose antenna for juicy stories picked up everything — a remarkable ability considering she rarely left home, and while in elaborate flight describing my 'exciting visit/holiday', I asked, 'And how are things in Apia?'

'They're sharpening their knives,' she confessed.

'Who? What?' I pretended.

'The wives of that man!'

'What man?' I continued lying.

Her long sigh whistled into my ear. 'Ola, I am *not* a child.'

Whenever Fusi played displeased mother with me I was gripped by a defensive guilt (and protest at being treated as a child) so I countered, 'And I'm not a child either!'

'And Pita knows about it too,' she really attacked me.

'How did he know about it?'

'You don't know much about your own son, do you?'

'Just stop there!' I ordered, sensed she was going to put the phone down and said, 'And don't you dare put the phone down!' Click! She put it down.

Half an hour later, when I'd calmed down, I rang her again and apologised my way back into her haughty affections. (Both Fusi and my dad were suckers for apologies.)

'Your father is very upset,' she raked her nails over my guilt. 'And you know he hasn't been well lately.' (God, she knew how to strangle me with my own guilt.)

'And Pita — how's he taking it?'

'He hasn't been eating much,' she began. ('The liar!' I thought to myself.)

'And?' I tried to hurry her.

'Threatening to go and live with Lagona and come to school by bus from there.'

'Bullshit!' I wanted to yell at her but said, 'You order him not to.'

'All right,' she sighed. 'But you've got problems, Ola.'

'I can take care of myself.'

'Why do you always get into . . . into messes like this?' She sensed I needed her advice and added, 'Just come home . . .'

'I love him, Fusi,' I heard my pitiful scared self confessing.

'It's not the first time, Ola.'

'This time I think it may — *will* last.'

'But he's got a wife and children. The complications . . .'

'Fusi, I thought it wouldn't go this far . . .'

'You never do — you've always had your way. Blame your father for that.'

'We were in Japan for the last two weeks,' I confessed.

'And a liar too. Blame not your father or me for that.'

So I told her all about it. Yes and sigh, yes and sigh, she encouraged my narration. Fusi is a romantic, hopelessly in love with love and stories of love and especially stories of love set in exotic places, and Japan *was* exotic, despite her prejudices against 'le au fitipupu'u', the gang of shorties, meaning the Japanese.

A final swooning sigh, the echo of a suppressed sob, when I ended. 'And what are we going to do about it?' I used my most vulnerable, daughterish tone.

'You come home, Ola. If *they* touch you I'll take a rope and hang them. And don't you ever show them you're scared of them. Hear me?'

'Yes, Fusi,' I replied, glad once again that I'd inherited her courage, reckless and suicidal, at times, though it was. Courage meant fighting to the bitter end and you did it for aiga, friends.

She and Pita were waiting for me at the airport and, in front of the crowd outside the customs area, she hugged me and whispered, 'Don't be afraid of anything.'

How I wanted to fling my arms around Pita and for him to reciprocate, but he just smiled, pecked me on the cheek, picked up my suitcase and ambled off to the car.

As he drove I kept looking at him, but he rambled on about his weekend in Sapepe — enough details to appear he was keen on telling me but not enough to show me that he loved me.

'A man called Carl Fischer rang for you this morning,' he said as if it was part of his story. I ignored it, Fusi ignored it, Pita continued his boring saga, but Carl was now sitting between us, unavoidably the centre of our relationship — at least for a time.

'And your father wants you to ring,' Fusi said when we got into the house. 'He rang yesterday — Pita answered the phone.'

In the privacy of my bedroom I clenched my fists and hugged my knees to my chest. Why, why were they coming at me at once, together? And wished I were back in Japan, in the idyllic eye of the storm, unaware of the storm, with Carl to myself.

'You've got to go out and confront it,' Fusi said at lunch as I picked at my food.

'Where's Pita?' I demanded. She didn't know. 'He despises me, doesn't he?'

'Are you stupid? He's your son!'

'But some children *do* hate their parents.'

She ignored me and said, 'Don't just sit around pitying yourself. Go out there and face it. You always get like this when you're in trouble.' Paused and, gripping my arm, added, 'Ring your father — he's a sucker for your stories; ring that man — I'm sure you've got him around your little toe; and show those stupid women you don't care about their lies. Attack.'

I dialled Dad's number and held the phone away from my ear, preparing for *his* attack, but he welcomed me home and was receptive to my enthusiastic description of my Auckland holiday 'with our generous and hospitable relatives who he'd helped pay to migrate to New Zealand'. 'And what have you been doing?' I ended my tale.

In his usual methodical style he filled me in on what he'd lived out ('survived', his description) while I'd been away. I retained little of it, but his familiar sound strengthened me again. Not once did he mention Carl or refer to the gossip. 'Take care of yourself — you know what I mean,' he ended.

And with Dad's support I was ready for the storm, or so I believed then.

Fusi noted my renewed courage, and placed the three invitations in front of me. She watched me opening them.

On Tuesday night, dinner at the Matelieses', First Secretary at the Australian High Commission, and a golfing friend of Carl's; on Thursday night dinner at the Sanderses', Carl's lawyer, who had a greedy finger in every business deal going; on Saturday evening a cocktail party at Aggie's Fale to be hosted by Aipunou So'otala, Minister of Lands, who, rumour claimed, had been bankrolled into power by Carl.

'I'm going,' I announced to Fusi.

'Good,' she said, one brave Amazon to another.

Carl rang that evening from his office. It was good, so good, just to hear him.

'Why are you putting me through the mill?' I asked.

'What mill?'

'Those parties.'

'I just want to be with you.'

'Couldn't you have arranged a less public way? Don't you realise we are living with other people, your loving spouses, for example?'

'I can handle them . . .'

'How?'

'I'll just order them to leave you alone.'

'God, Carl, you're out of this world. People are too afraid of you to interfere with your life so you think all's well with others and this awful town!'

'Please don't swear,' he said. 'I love you,' he added, 'and darling, please remember to stay away from those others.'

That night during my restless sleep, his remark picked at me.

I got out Tamura-san's gift, and while it glowed in the swimming light of my beside lamp, I observed it, letting the breathing clay absorb me into its sinews.

Ferocious dogs are the main hazard when you run through the villages, so before they were up, I ran from the bay through Fagali'i and Moata'a villages to Apia Park, and started attacking a fast six kilometres around the race track, with the brisk morning air hitting the bottom of my lungs. Dew covered the neat playing fields; pigs were already foraging in the ditches. I glanced up at the stands. An old man, wrapped in a stained sleeping sheet, was watching.

In a short while I was running effortlessly.

Later, as I ran off the track to return home, I waved to the old man. No movement.

I carried his memory as I ran back through the villages towards an egg-yellow sun just peeping over the eastern ranges. Met the first bus heading for town. The driver beeped his horn. I waved. No dogs still. Just a small boy leading his slow grandfather towards the toilets on the seashore. 'Ola!' the boy called. I waved and ran faster. People were stirring in the houses and fale.

I pumped the weights as I lay on my back on the bench on the verandah. Up, down, up, down. My muscles and bones threatening to break. Up, down, up.

'Mum, you're going to kill yourself!' Pita scolded me from his bedroom doorway.

'You're just jealous I'm fitter than you!' Up, down, up. 'Your generation are a lazy lot.' Up, down, up. He dismissed me with a shrug and disappeared into the kitchen for breakfast. Unhealthy beggar, lives on mountains of cornflakes. Won't heed my advice about a healthy diet. Up, down, up. My upper half and arms were going numb. Stop! My heart thundered against my shuddering ribs.

I crawled into the sitting room, lay on a towel and, with sweat pouring from my every pore, stared empty-eyed into the ceiling.

'We don't want to over-train for the war, do we?' Fusi said. She tossed me a clean towel.

The lazy murmur of the morning tide spread through me, massaging the aches and numbness out of my body. Scent of pua, faint but there like a persistent hope. I inhaled, and held it in my lungs.

That evening, after dressing, I steadied myself with two vodkas, paraded in front of Fusi, who said, 'Beautiful!', got an untidy wave from Pita, who was feeding at the dinner table and, as I got into the car, thought, 'Son, won't you ever love me?'

'Don't get sozzled!' Pita called, as if responding to my hope. I backed out of the garage.

Many of our rich (and aspiring rich), foreign diplomats and business people live in airy houses on the cool slopes of Vailima, above the heat, dust, stench and shabbiness of the town where they make their money, and pay no rates or accept any responsibility for the town's maintenance.

Mabel and John Matelies and their two red-haired children were from 'far but tough Toowoomba' (his description). They lived in a long narrow house surrounded by vigorous teuila at the edge of a forested ravine. I'd met them before at High Commission functions.

Five cars in the parking area, one was Carl's. No noise from the house. The lights from the sitting room turned me into a leprous yellow as I approached. A profusion of pot plants and hanging creepers lined both sides of the front door.

Carl refused to look at me as Mabel introduced me to their other guests. Sloan Thinsome was the Director of Agriculture; Melissa, his wife, was a nurse (and an ally of Sharon's). Both had been educated in New Zealand and spoke English like Kiwi cow-cockies; faithful pursuers of the Palagi middle-class dream, they rejected the fa'a Samoa, though their grandparents were from the village. Sera and Fala Auala (nick-named 'Road' by his friends), unpredictable and fiery Director of Education, believed the truth was whatever his ego decided, and talked incessantly of 'having ideals in a banana republic run by kept politicians'. His rapid rise, from raw graduate to director, wasn't because of his 'ideals' but his uncle who was a Minister. A wispy Australian — Jim Laxton, I think his name was — reminded me of the ghost of R. L. Stevenson, because of his droopy moustache and porcelain-white skin. Elisa and Fano kissed me on the cheek. The men were John Matelies's golfing partners.

While we waited for dinner, we chatted, drank, chatted, ate a seafood pâté and banana chips. I sat on one drink and said the right things. I recollect little of that chatter. No substance worth retaining, except that Road monopolised the discussion with his exaggerated gestures, chomping mouth, flashing eyes. I pitied his wife, who huddled around her glass of wine, not wanting to listen.

We were served by the servant who came and told Mabel that dinner was ready. But just as we were walking to the table, Road asked Carl, 'How was Japan? The geishas any good?'

Carl smiled and said, 'The food was terrific!' He took his seat at the table. I caught Melissa looking at me.

The food came straight out of Anglo-Saxon Australia: roast lamb, roast potatoes, roast pumpkin, roast parsnips, green peas, thick gravy and mint sauce. I chewed my way through it, not once showing I was hurting. Up fork, into smiling mouth you go juicy lamb, chew teeth, suck at the blood and pulp, swallow gullet. Again. Don't look at Carl. Mabel talked about her children, so did Sera, so did Melissa, so did Elisa. Gag your lie detector. Up fork, into chomping mouth lamb . . .

I declined the dessert of vanilla ice cream, green jelly and whipped cream.

During coffee, cheese and crackers — I had only the coffee — Road analysed why he thought the Japanese were so successful in business. He attributed it to their 'short legs, which forced them to take two steps to our one; short arses, which meant they didn't have to defecate as much as us and therefore eat more of the earth's resources; short arms, which meant they had to try twice as hard to reach as high as us — in short, because they were short, like Napoleon and General Giap, they worked harder to be big people.'

'Did Sharon go with you?' Melissa asked Carl.

'No, she was too busy with the children.'

'We could've looked after the kids,' she said.

A reassuring knee pressed against mine. Elisa nodded when I looked at her. I placed my hand on her knee. She squeezed it.

'They say the women are great over there,' our Aussie host said. The other men laughed.

'Yeah, Oriental sheilas are the most obedient!' laughed the pot-bellied Sloan. Melissa looked defensive.

'What's Melissa got to say about *that*?' Carl pursued her.

'They wouldn't be able to carry *his* belly!' she said. A joke but cruel and meant to be, and we tried to salvage Sloan by laughing.

And so the evening died (for me, that is) and I left shortly after.

Once in my car, I hugged the steering wheel and pressed my forehead against it. A short while later I drove to Mulinu'u, stopped by the beach and watched the sea rising and falling in the half-light, with the stars caught in it like pua petals.

Carl's car was parked on the road side outside our house. My headlights caught him waving to me to stop.

'You had to tell them, didn't you?' I shouted through the car window. 'Why did you? Did you have to brag to the boys about your latest fuck?'

'I didn't . . . didn't tell them!'

'You're a bloody liar too!' I drove into our driveway, rushed out, locked the iron gate and left him stranded in the night.

I didn't see Pita lying on the sitting room sofa as I rushed in and, pulling tissues out of the packet on the bookcase, started wiping my tears away.

'Are you okay?' he asked. I turned my back to him.

'I'm not sozzled, if that's what you're thinking.' I heard him move up and stand behind me.

'I'm sorry.'

'It's not you.' I felt him turn to leave. 'Pita?'

'Yes?' he asked. I couldn't plead. So when his arms came around my shoulders I turned and, wrapping my arms around him, cried into his warmth.

'Is it that man?' he asked as I sipped the coffee he'd made for me, and we sat down at the kitchen table. I nodded. 'Do you — you *like* him?'

'I think I love him.'

'You always suffer when you're in love, eh?'

'There are a lot of complications in this case.'

'But even if there weren't, you'd still suffer.'

285

'Is that what you've observed?'

He nodded and then, in the serious manner of my father and grandfather, said, in Samoan, 'It's because you *see* too clearly, even when you don't want to.'

'Too critically, you mean.'

'Lagona told me once that to see people and things in all their flaws and weaknesses and not forgive them is to not accept what is. One can never be happy that way . . . It's too complicated for me. I'm only good at maths and fishing.'

I reached over and held his hand. 'Thank you.'

'Why don't you come to Sapepe this weekend? You haven't been for months, and Lagona doesn't like that.'

'I'll see. Were you waiting up for me tonight?'

'Not really. I was just reading.'

'Liar!' I said. And we laughed.

For the next two days I refused to return Carl's calls, but I was determined to go to the Sanderses' dinner party. Fusi kept bolstering my courage with stories about Carl's spouses and their 'dirty' allies tearing me to pieces all over town. At night I couldn't sleep properly because of anger and attacks of cowardice that left me almost weeping. At dawn I'd stagger out of bed and run Apia Park — the old man was there on the stands — and return to a punishing hour of weights.

Three quick vodkas in my bedroom as I dressed stilled the quivering shrimps in my belly. 'Fa!' I called to Fusi and hurried into the garage before she could inspect me.

As I drove down the driveway into the evening light that seemed to be bursting from the roots of the trees, I looked back. Fusi was standing motionless on the balcony, like an indestructible stone god absorbing the light into her body.

The Sanderses' home is on a beach, in a narrow inlet sheltered from the sea by an uninhabited sandbar that's covered with palms.

Cars were lined on both sides of the road behind the house. I parked under some ironwood trees, got out, brushed my hands through my nervous hair, and started up the path through a garden of frangipani, avocado and teuila. I'd been to other parties at the Sanderses', and had enjoyed the extravagance and abundant informality.

Stanley Samuel Sanders, known to his friends as SSS, described their house as 'a cheap prefab'. It's not one but two prefabricated houses, with spacious verandahs and decks, which had travelled all the way from California to join in a sprawl facing the sunset.

I hesitated on the back porch. I could see through the windows that people were busy in the kitchen. Among them was Josh, SSS's wife.

'Doesn't Josh remind you of Dorothy Lamour?' SSS keeps asking everyone ever since they got married the month after SSS's wife had left for New Zealand with their children. Josh *did* look like Lamour (in *The Road to Burma*) and looked more and more like her, to us, as SSS promoted that likeness. SSS had a real talent for promoting and selling his 'realities'. Josh was his latest promotion. He wanted Dorothy Lamour as his wife, so he was selling Josh (to himself) and us as that.

Before I could open the screen door, SSS was there behind the screen. He had a way of materialising like Mandrake the Magician. SSS is short and trim, and never gains weight despite his notorious appetites for food/ drink/money/and women.

'God, it's good ta see ya, Ola!' He cultivated his Kiwi accent. He gripped my hand with both hands, kissed me on the cheek. 'You'll love the jokers here tonight. A beaut crowd.' He steered me into the kitchen and beckoned to Josh, who rushed over and embraced me. 'Don't worry aboud a thing, Ola. Josh and I are ya friends. We know what id's like surviving a divorce and the scandal that goes with id in this bloody town of ratbags and jealous bastards.'

'Yeah, Ola,' Josh whispered. 'We're your friends.'

'Gosh, Ola, ya look neat. A beaut, as always!' he said. 'I keep telling Josh to copy ya style — in everything.'

'Yeah, Ola. I always try to be like you,' Josh echoed. I put my arm around her.

I noticed SSS's new moustache, which made him look like a bantam-size Zapata, and said, 'That's neat!'

'Ya think so? Thanks, Ola.' He smoothed it down. 'Josh doesn't like it. But she's got no style like you, Ola.'

'She's more beautiful than Dorothy Lamour,' I said.

'Thank you, Ola. You're always so accurate and kind and generous. Get Ola her usual,' he said to Josh.

He led me to the lounge, which opened out to the front balcony and beach and inlet. 'We didn't invite *them*,' he whispered. 'Not even their miserable wives.' Josh pushed a large cold vodka and tonic into my hand.

'Thanks,' I said.

'Don' mention it. Don' forget we're your friends.' Even her accent was now American. She left to serve the others.

SSS led me to Elisa and the nearest group of women.

I couldn't see Carl anywhere. I relaxed as I drank.

The light of the setting sun was swimming through the palms on the sandbar and lighting up the whole house and everyone there. As I raised my glass to drink from it, the liquid was simmering fire. I drank it slowly and felt porous, dissolving into the light of the liquid, wanting to be part of it, the light drawing me out into the inlet, whose surface was rippling, like feathers, under the caressing flow of the breeze. The others talked,

I nodded but didn't hear what they were saying, as the breeze danced into my eyes and later enticed me out on to the front balcony and the world that was suffused with the golden dying of the sun.

For a moment I didn't realise someone was speaking to me. I surfaced. Found myself leaning against the balcony railing. 'How's Carl?' the blurred but threatening creature said. The inlet looked so peaceful. 'How's Carl?'

'Were you speaking to me?' I asked.

It nodded. I turned and focused. Sandra Ching, one of Sharon's relatives, whom I'd taught with at Samoa College. 'Yeah,' she mumbled. (Drunk, so early in the evening.) I edged away. 'I was talking to you.' She pursued me. 'You can't keep your paws off other people's husbands, can yar? Yar can't, can yar?' I glanced around. No one was watching. She moved towards me. I stepped back. Pretended to stumble against the railing. She reached forward to steady me. I pulled her. Jabbed my karate-tightened hand into her surprised diaphragm. Pufftt! Her glass shattered on the floor. I caught her as she collapsed. Held her up. Some people rushed over and took her from me.

'Had too much to drink,' I said. They carried her into the house. 'I hope she's okay,' I said to Josh and Elisa.

'She's becoming a bloody alcoholic,' Josh whispered.

'Too many children, too little income to support an extravagant lifestyle, and now a husband who's being investigated for misusing government funds. Poor Sandra,' said Elisa.

Josh got me another drink. I stood with Elisa and watched the light being swallowed up by the quick dark; the inlet waited and watched.

Someone switched on the balcony lights. SSS and two youths were on the lawn lighting the barbecues. 'Things okay, Ola?' he called. 'Sorry about Sandra. Bugger me days, but everyone's drinking me out of house . . .'

'Prefab!' I reminded him.

'Boy, ya're quick, Ola!' And laughed. 'Hi, Elisa! Fano making any money?'

'No, you're taking it all!' she replied.

'C'mon. There's enough for every lawyer in this poor town!' he laughed. 'Enough ta go round.'

Soon the strong smell of steak, sausages and chicken pieces sizzling on the barbecues was invading even the reefs of stars that had risen out of the darkness of the heavens. 'Smells great!' Elisa called to SSS.

'Yeah, bloody great,' he replied. Everyone believed SSS was the best barbecuer in the country: another reputation he'd promoted. 'Jus' the right sauces, temperature, charcoal — and coconut shells are the best — and the right touch.' He raised his mug of beer. We drank to him, and then watched, astounded, as he drained his beer in one tipping, burped and said, 'Nothing like good Kiwi piss, eh. Boy, nothing like it!' The smoke and smell of the barbecue swirled around us.

We retreated into the lounge.

Carl was talking to Fano and Road at the far side of the room, which was now packed with people who looked blurred in the thick cigarette smoke. I glanced at Elisa. She smiled.

'What the shit are we doing here?' I said.

'Correction,' she said. 'What is everyone doing here? And I'd better get you another drink before you get into one of your morbid moods again.'

For almost an hour we moved from group to group, but avoided Carl and Fano.

Dinner was served on two massive tables. Heaps of barbecued steak, chicken, sausages. Dishes of fish, ota, crabs, shrimps in coconut cream. Potato salad, vegetable salad. Pigeon (illegally caught). Palolo (out of season). Umu-cooked pork, taro and palusami. Heaps of sliced pineapple and watermelon. The usual bounty served up at élite parties.

Elisa and I weren't hungry. We got fresh drinks and sat on the cool balcony. 'Man, they can eat!' Elisa said in Samoan. I looked back into the dining room.

As usual the women were trying to appear ungreedy as they heaped food on to their plates. We watched as they locked themselves into the hefty soft chairs and settees, their mountainous plates in their solid laps, and started feeding. Muscles were sagging into rolls of flab; chins had multiplied into wobbly folds. As Josh moved among them, asking if they needed anything, I imagined her petiteness ballooning into a replica of the others, now that she was in the money and power.

Some women came and sat at a table not far from us. We didn't take much notice of them. Elisa suggested we eat some raw fish, so I went and got two small dishes of it, and fresh drinks.

'. . . Ese le sexy o Japanese food,' I heard coming from the women's table.

'Yeah, you can get hooked on sashimi and soy sauce.'

'Sa'o. And if you eat raw fe'e — and the Japs are good at that — you get strong and can last le po akoa.' Mounting mirth.

'Bloody bitches!' Elisa said.

'. . . Ese le fit o le kakou keine!' I recognised Agnes Neitz, Sharon's cousin.

'Aga fo'i e kamo'e every day,' Tina Helpford encouraged.

'And she lifts weights,' echoed Malaea Talanoa.

'Mea lega e happy ai le kokou kama . . .'

I got up. 'Don't!' Elisa said.

'I'm just going to get some food,' I said. I went to the tables.

They were watching. I heaped up my plate. I looked at them as I wove my way back between the tables. They pretended they hadn't been discussing me.

My shoe caught the leg of Agnes Neitz's chair, I stumbled and, as I caught the edge of the table, dumped my plate and its contents into Agnes's lap. 'Sorry, sorry!' I apologised. Elisa and Josh rushed to help clean up the mess.

'That was deliberate!' Agnes hissed, while smiling at me.

'Yes!' I hissed back, smiling. 'So what?'

'Fa'akali oe!' she threatened, smiling.

A short while later, Elisa, Josh and I were laughing about it in the kitchen.

'They dare not touch you,' Elisa said.

'No. Not with your black belt,' Josh added. The rumour in Apia was I had a black belt in karate. It was based on my having taken a few classes in karate, in New Zealand, and my addiction to physical fitness. I never corrected the rumour. Like SSS, I wanted to promote 'a reality' about myself that would make my foes think twice about committing violence on my delicate person.

Carl was waiting in the dark just beyond the edge of the back porch lights as I was leaving. He held my arm and, pulling me up against the ironwood tree, moved hard against me, burying his face in my neck and biting it. 'I've missed you,' he moaned.

'Slow down,' I protested. His embrace and biting were hurting. 'Stop!' He started pulling up the back of my dress. I clutched the hair at the back of his head and pulled back.

'No!' he objected. I pushed him away and held him at arm's length.

'Not only are you a liar, you're violent as well.' I wheeled and headed for my car. He stumbled after me.

'You . . . you-uu . . . can't . . . can't treat me like this!' he stuttered as I opened the car door.

'Why? Because you've always had your way in everything? Do you just strong-arm us when you feel like it?'

'Ola, I'm . . . I'm . . . !' I waited but he couldn't say it. I started getting into the car. He clutched my arm. I shrugged it off. He just stood there. 'Bug . . . bug . . . bugger you then!' I started laughing. He walked away. I held the back of his shirt; he stopped; I put my arms around him and, pressing myself against his back, kissed the back of his neck. 'What's funny?' he asked.

'You,' I whispered. 'You *can* swear; never thought you'd do it.'

290

'Don' . . . don't make fun of me.' Paused. I waited. 'Ola?'

'Yes?'

'I — I love you.'

A while later, after we'd driven away from the house and into the safety of some fau trees, we were making love in the car.

'Need a bigger car,' he whispered as we tried to fold into the cramped back seat.

'And mosquito repellant!'

'Going to have bites all over my arse,' he said.

'Did you come?' he asked as we drove back to his car at the Sanderses'.

'No,' I said, 'but it was good.' He seemed hurt. 'Don't worry,' I said. 'I'm not sold on *Cosmopolitan*'s twenty vaginal orgasms per session.' He didn't laugh.

That Friday, Elisa and Fano collected me for the Minister of Land's cocktail party. 'Are things all right?' Elisa asked me as Fano drove us to Aggie's Fale. I nodded.

'He's not worth it,' Fano said. 'And you don't look well.'

'You're just jealous,' I joked.

'What's going to happen?' asked Elisa.

'Whatever happens will happen,' I replied.

'And at Aipunou's parties *anything* can happen,' said Fano.

We parked by the sea in front of the hotel. 'Be careful,' Elisa cautioned me.

The Minister, Aipunou So'otala, and his wife, Epe, were at the fale entrance greeting their guests. We joined the queue; greeted and talked with the people we knew.

Aipunou and Epe were members of one of the first scholarship groups sent to New Zealand. They failed to qualify in anything but loving each other. They were shipped back to lowly clerical jobs, until Epe's uncle, after Independence, became a Cabinet Minister, and their promotion up the civil service ladder was rapid. She became the Minister's private secretary, and he the Assistant Registrar of the Lands and Titles Court. Overambition sometimes leads to disaster. Aipunou was promoted (quietly) out of the civil service for embezzling government funds, so rumour had it. With other mortals such a setback would have spelt permanent disaster. Not for Aipunou and Epe; they had hides as thick as dog's teeth.

He used his connections in their church to get hired as an English teacher in the church high school. He also made it known he was thinking of becoming a pastor. In the meantime Epe and her uncle, the Minister, continued promoting Aipunou as a possible Member of Parliament, within the Minister's political clique.

In the next elections Aipunou helped the Minister and SSS's clique get re-elected. Aipunou had learned early that everyone has a price. 'No honest idealist can get into Parliament on honesty alone. Voters vote for the right dollar value, and so do MPs,' he said publicly. And during election campaigns the fa'a Samoa is mountains of food/beer/money and more money/favours/ trucks/flattery/favours and more favours — all illegal but every candidate does it. Backed by SSS and his friends, Aipunou bought a ministerial portfolio in the next elections, and began 'eating' our lands to support the ostentatious lifestyle he and Epe believed they deserved.

'Our politicians are unique,' Fano whispered as we moved up the queue. 'They're the largest in the world.' As I re-examined our hosts' sizes and shapes, I agreed that the philosophy of aiafuing nearly gets you the following élite shape, physically and politically:

Both Aipunou and Epe are of this shape. (So is our Prime Minister.) Fat cancels out sexual differences.

Cuddlier than the Michelin Man or Yukio Watanabe, Super Heavyweight Champion of Sumo. But swiftly deadly.

Aipunou and Epe, like the many who consider themselves 'pure Samoans' (by blood, that is), detest us, Afakasi, the totolua (of two bloods), but have to hide it, unleashing it only through rumour-mongering during political campaigns, because it's unwise to be anti-Afakasi when our Head of State and over half of our MPs are part-Europeans behind their matai titles. It's also suicidal if you want financial backing from Afakasi like Carl.

It is unaristocratic in our culture to show, in public, that we dislike one another. So, though our hosts detested me, Aipunou gave me his multi-chinned smile and double handshake — more a caress, and Epe embraced me and kissed me on the cheek.

'Carl'll be glad to see you,' she whispered.

'And how is our lawyer?' Aipunou greeted Fano.

292

'Still trying to remain honest,' Fano said. Aipunou was still trying to win Fano's political support (and money).

'Still as beautiful as ever!' Epe was saying to Elisa, who, as we walked away from our abundant hosts, whispered, 'Toothless bitch!' I remembered Epe was minus three front teeth, which she refused to falsify, arguing that being 'a pure Samoan and poor' she didn't need to. (Too many unpaid debts was the real reason.)

Around the fale were the usual horde of cocktail circuiters: prominent civil servants (and young ones with connections), politicians (mainly those in power and their backers), business people (both local and foreign), foreign experts and representatives of foreign governments and agencies, a priest or pastor (or two). The composition rarely changed. The politicians changed when the government changed, but the same business people remained because they usually financed both sides in the elections. If they were caught financing only the losing side, the government quickly won them over through profitable contracts which they had to pay for (under the table). You can't afford permanent enemies (or friends). There are only permanent interests — MPs want to stay in power, businessmen want to continue profiteering (and controlling the MPs).

Carl was by the bar at the far side, with Sharon and her friends. 'Stay with me for a while?' I asked Elisa.

Doctor Pilchards and Dorothy waved to us from the crowded centre of the fale: it was obvious the others were avoiding them. Elisa waved back and steered me to Josh Sanders and some other friends. Fano went to get us drinks.

'We really enjoyed the other night,' Elisa said to Josh.

'The food was terrific,' I said.

'I'm glad you liked it. I'm a bloody hopeless cook . . .'

Esther, who was in a bright red dress and with a yellow flower over her ear, was talking animatedly with Father Tulotu, a white-haired French priest who'd been in Samoa for over forty years. When she saw me, she smiled. I nodded, she continued talking. Proof of what Carl had told me the day before: he'd *ordered* Esther and Sharon to leave me alone.

'Not too fast!' Fano cautioned me as I drained my first drink. 'You've lost a lot of weight.'

'You have too,' Josh echoed. 'You must be overdoing the running.'

Things were good between Carl and me, but I couldn't rid myself of the compulsion to train every morning. I couldn't eat or sleep properly, threatened by an inexplicable dread.

Three drinks or so later, I started my usual wandering but kept well away from Sharon and Esther. Occasionally I'd find Elisa beside me and feel protected. Occasionally I'd become starkly aware of male advances and move off. Occasionally I'd be among expert gossipers who dissected and added lurid embellishments to the latest scandals (and noted their skilful avoidance of the scandal featuring yours truly). Occasionally I'd be caught in the boring stream of small men weaving inflated tales about their self-importance. I found myself with two high-ranking widows, once the most powerful women in the land. They had survived the whole corrupting dance of power which, as an aphrodisiac, had gutted their husbands. Silently they drank and observed that celebration of ambition, greed, corruption, feeding. Just before I left them, the one who reminded me of the mother I'd created in my imagination, said, 'Ola, remember me to your father, tell him he shouldn't have refused me.' I wanted an explanation but she withdrew into the wise silence that bound them.

Most of the tables by the floodlit swimming pool were occupied. Some of my friends beckoned to me but I sat down on my own, closed my eyes and, clutching the edge of the table, tried to still my trembling.

'It's all right,' Elisa rescued me.

'If you want to be free of it, Ola, you'll have to leave Samoa,' Fano said. 'Otherwise you'll have to be happy with what we've become. And Carl is not the answer: he's right in it; he's what is, and you won't be able to change him.'

'But you and Elisa have survived,' I said.

'But for how much longer?' He stopped and we heard the avid silence of the people around, listening. 'Let's have some more alofa on the rocks! Waiter!' Fano called.

The drinking got heavier. Someone started singing; we all joined in. Many of the people in the fale came out, and Aipunou, whose only talent I admired was that of a song-maker, conducted the singing. With a few more whiskys, he picked soa to do the siva.

When it was Elisa's and my turn, we kicked off our shoes, whooped as we ran on to the edge of the pool, turned to face the audience, and danced.

I was free of the earth's gravity, hovering, swooping, diving and skimming across the waves of the world's pain, as free as on the morning Aunt Fusi and my grandmother had started teaching me the siva, years back, free to invent myself in the boundless freedom of the dance and the endless dreaming that is life, self-creating, self-delighting, self-inventing . . .

'Where were you last night?' he asked over the phone. (No greetings or preliminaries.)

'Here, in bed.' I was still nauseous from too much drinking. 10 a.m. on my watch.

'You weren't! Your rude house-girl kept telling me you hadn't come home . . . !'

'She's not my house-girl; she's my aunt.'

'I don't give a stuff! Why didn't you come to the hotel as we'd arranged?'

'I was too drunk and asked Fano and Elisa to bring me home.'

'Liar!' he shouted. I slammed the phone down. It rang again. I let it ring on, then picked it up.

'Carl, I've got a headache and don't feel well. I *was* home but too drunk to answer the phone. Fusi must've answered it.'

He was off. 'And did you have to dance like *that* in public?'

'Like what?'

'Like — like a . . . !'

'Say it!'

'Well, like a wanton woman!'

'I can dance in whatever way and wherever I choose.'

'And don't you care what I think?'

'No, I don't give a stuff! And you don't have to worry about my making you look *bad* in public; you don't *own* me, Carl.'

'And Fano — what about him?' I refused to be drawn into his sickness. 'What about him?' he repeated.

'Fano is like a brother to me,' I said. 'And, Carl, if you insist on that very sick line I'm going to end this conversation — and this relationship!'

'Ola, I love you so much, that's why I get so jealous and suspicious.'

'If it's assurances from me that you're better than any other man I've had an affair with, then I'll give them to you now.' I could hear him waiting. 'You're handsomer, more intelligent and considerate, and you're bigger, more virile and fuck better!'

'Are you feeling better now?' he asked.

I slammed the phone down. And then took it off the hook.

After taking a couple of Disprins, I got back into bed and, lying flat on my back, tried steadying the nausea, but it worsened. I staggered up and rushed to the bathroom. I thrust my head into the basin, choking and gagging as the thick blackness spewed out. Again. Again. As if my body wanted to reject all that I was.

'Fusi! Fusi!' I cried, the black bile dripping in sticky strings out of my mouth and nostrils.

'What's happened?' she asked. When she saw, she put her arms around me. 'It's all right. Just relax.' She patted my back and eased my vomiting.

'Look — it's black!'

'It's nothing, you've just got a bad stomach.'

Drenched with sweat, and cold to the quick of my bones, I hugged the basin, holding myself up out of the chasm I feared I was tumbling into. Again the bitter black surge.

'The toilet!' I said. Fusi helped me over and gave me a bowl. While I spewed into it, I shat the liquid blackness into the toilet. 'Fusi!' I kept pleading. 'Fusi!' She wiped my face with a wet facecloth.

A short while later, after she'd wiped me clean and wrapped a blanket around my shivering body, I was in bed again. 'What's happening to me?' I asked.

'Just an upset stomach,' she said.

Again the clogging heaviness and nausea. I struggled out of bed. Too late. The surge was out of my mouth and splattering red across the bedroom floor. 'It's blood, Fusi!' As I continued spewing, the clinging smell of it filled the room, and I imagined it invading the whole house, every cell of it.

'Pita!' Fusi called. 'Pita!' He ran in. 'Get Finau, quickly!'

Fusi cleaned me up again and put me into the bed in the spare room. We waited. I wept and shivered.

Dad and Pita came with a doctor, a cousin, who, while Dad sat holding my hand, examined me and said I had a bleeding ulcer. 'You've lost a lot of blood,' he said. 'Look.' He turned up the palms of my hands. Pale white, no redness left. 'You've got to be admitted to hospital. Let's hope the bleeding stops on its own.'

'If not?' Dad asked.

'We may have to operate. In the meantime you'll have to have a blood transfusion.'

It was Pita's blood.

And fortunately I didn't bleed again.

I spent nearly two weeks in hospital. Carl came twice. I refused to see him.

Dad and Fusi visited me every day but at different times. I was used to it and respected their undeclared war. Fusi brought me flasks of my favourite soups. Dad brought magazines and avoided being moralistic about my 'fast' lifestyle, which, I knew, he blamed for my ulcer. Penina and the grandchildren visited and distracted me from my worries with their gaiety and endless curiosity.

Then on Sunday afternoon, while a silk-like drizzle swirled across the windows and cooled the air in my room, the door opened.

Pita stepped back into the corridor. Into the doorway shuffled Lagona, my grandfather. (I hadn't visited him for three years.) So old now that he seemed ageless. Propped up by his walking stick; his frame bent permanently over it; grey, wizened head jutting forward as if he was searching for his future on the ground; unbuttoned white shirt revealing a body barked like the hide of an ancient aoa tree, on it the geography of a life lived long and simple; his legs like the strength of ancient ava roots.

Into the centre of the room he shuffled. Lagona, who refused — but had never said so — to visit me at my Fagali'i home, because it was too Palagi, a world away from Sapepe.

His eyesight was poor. His head circled, looking for me.

'I'm here,' I said. He smiled and shuffled over.

'Ah!' he sighed when he bumped into my bed. 'Ah!' he sighed as I embraced him and he kissed me and his familiar smell and warmth enveloped me as it had done in my childhood. 'Ah!' he sighed as he sat down in the chair that Pita brought him. Ah! My heart sighed as I held his hand, and his history and mana and alofa surged into me.

'Pita,' he called and patted the foot of my bed. Pita came and sat there. With the corner of his shirt he wiped the mucus out of his rheumy eyes — a gesture I was so familiar with. 'Let us pray,' he said, bowing his head. 'Father of the Heavens and Earth, it is with gratitude that we come to you today to thank you for saving all who are in this House of Maladies, for saving this *disobedient* daughter, a daughter who has strayed from Your path . . .' This was his way of reprimanding me. 'She was brought up by us in Your ways, the good ways, to honour You and her aiga, but, tempted by Satan and the sinful, pagan ways of foreigners, she has strayed. However, in Your wisdom You have chosen to save her again. The illness You have visited upon her is a painful but wise lesson. Let us hope she will heed Your wrath and return to You and her aiga and the true ways of true aristocrats . . .' His voice soothed my guilt.

Both Lagona and Pita looked at me when he finished praying. I tried to look repentant.

'And are you well now?' Lagona asked.

'Yes, I am well again.'

'Pita said you nearly bled to death,' he said. Pita looked away when I tried to make eye contact.

'Yes,' I admitted. 'I was very scared.' I then distracted him by asking, 'How did you come?'

'Pita came and got me in your car. It's a fast car. A beautiful car. Best car I've ever been in.' He chuckled, more to himself than to us, and added, 'Pita was too scared to drive as fast as I wanted him to.' He tapped Pita's knee, and they laughed together. 'Don't blame him; he's too young to want to die recklessly. Me, I'm up to my navel in the grave already.' Again they laughed. As soon as Pita had been able to run, carry a bush-knife and paddle, they'd been inseparable, and, unconsciously, they'd eased me out of their circle. I'd resented it but had said nothing. I had to accept that grandfathers don't raise girls. 'How fast were we going, Pita?'

'About seventy miles an hour.'

'Yes, that's it. I forgot. My brain's old.'

'How's our aiga?' I asked.

'They are well. But the young ones are lazier than ever. Would rather

eat tinned fish than go fishing. Pita's expert at fishing now. I taught him.'
I remembered how I'd yearned for him to teach me too when, in the
weekends, I'd watched them learning together; teach me how to fish,
clear land and plant crops, make an umu, plait sinnet — all the skills of
a man; and bless me too with the alofa he was giving Pita through his
teaching. But I was a girl/woman, and there is woman's work and man's
work, separate ways of being, to showing even alofa.

'Ola, you must stop drinking,' he drew me out of my thoughts. 'Drink
is poison to the body, which is God's house . . . You're never going to
drink, are you, Pita?'

'No, Lagona!' was his grandson's military reply.

'If I ever catch you doing it, I'll break this stick over your head,' he
said affectionately.

As their intimate banter continued I felt privileged to be listening in
on it, a witness to an alofa deeper than any I'd seen between other people.

'And tell your father to visit his aiga more often; they're forgetting
he exists. And tell him not to wear trousers when he comes.' They
laughed again.

That afternoon I floated in the stream of their healing laughter, an
ancient patriarch and a boy celebrating the joy that alofa can bring to our
lives.

'Put your trust in God again,' Lagona said. I caught my reflection in
the glowing pools of his eyes as he leant forward and we embraced.
'Everything changes in the Unity,' he said. 'We are sometimes left with
only one another.' He hesitated and added, 'And with God. We mustn't
forget Him. And, Ola, don't drive too fast. Even God's Road has an end!'
He laughed, and that wise, forgiving laughter will live with me always.

Two weeks after I left the hospital (to live with a recurring ulcer),
Carl shifted in with me. At his insistence (and on my father's advice and
with Fusi's consent and Pita's nonchalant silence) we got married in Pago
Pago three weeks later.

Lagona died in his sleep that June.

78

I've become a mere observer of other people's lives, an absorber of those lives to shape my own, perhaps to justify it.

As an observer I can't (fully) 'love' even those closest to me, for I analyse them too; analyse away my feelings about them.

My 'mind' won't let me accept people for who and what they are; I compare them always to their greater possibilities and find them lacking.

79

'Do you have to once again show my friends you don't like them?' Carl accused me as soon as we got into our bedroom. (We'd returned from a political fund-raising party at the Sanderses'.) I started undressing. 'You think you're so clean. Don't forget, your father was a clerk!'

'But he was honest,' I said. He gripped my arm. I pulled it away. 'Let's not fight. They're your friends, not mine . . . !'

'And you think they're dishonest?'

'That's putting it mildly. I'm not going to any more of your fund-raising.'

'If you think they're dishonest, why did you rub yourself up against a few of them tonight?'

'You're sick.'

I didn't see it. It wasn't the physical pain of the slap that shocked me. It was the act itself, for no one, not even my father, had ever hit me before, not like that, to hurt/violate/humiliate. For a few seconds I just grasped the side of my face. He recoiled to hit me again, my body reacted automatically to evade. He missed and stumbled past me. I drove my knee into his belly.

He stumbled against the wall, hugging his stomach. 'Bitch!'

'You ever hit me like that again — I'll *kill* you!'

Two days later, when he returned after sulking at his parents' home, we made up passionately. He reaffirmed his love and asked for my forgiveness.

There were to be many other quarrels. With each quarrel his jealousy and insecurity worsened and my cynical dismissal of it hardened, and I withdrew from his circle of friends. He went his way and I mine, and the secrets between us accumulated until there was little air left to breathe and enjoy together, and he turned to other women.

Dearest Carl,

This will be my last letter before we return home. It will probably get home after we do.

As you well know, I tend to see things in terms of well-organised stories, with a beginning, middle, climax and resolution. So to end our pilgrimage I had expected Dad to trace Christ's footsteps, along the Stations of the Cross, with the proper Christian awe, respect and sorrow, and arrive at a firmer faith. I had expected it even more after watching him change during our pilgrimage. True, some of the changes could be called pagan, e.g., his drinking of alcohol (and enjoying it), and his conning of the jewellery at Bethlehem (which I'll tell you about when I get home — it was brilliant), but not once have I felt that he had become less Christian. In fact, he is now more tolerant, more questioning. He even smiles and jokes more, and wears outrageous T-shirts.

Though I expected a novelistic ending to our pilgrimage, well-plotted stories are not life. I should have remembered that the most important change in Dad is his unpredictability, a quality that does not augur well for an exciting, well-contrived climax. (Pardon the Freudian slip in a word much overused by literary critics and teachers of literature. Right now though, I think I'm badly in need of one — a climax, that is.)

So the triumphant climax I had wanted wasn't to be. What did climax, as it were, was Dad becoming a dancer. Yes, a dancer.

He danced through the Via Dolorosa. True, he walked respectfully, viewed each station, even Calvary, with the appropriately solemn silence and prayer, but I sensed he was dancing inside, free of a great burden. I don't think he even saw the tasteless and ornate Hollywood façade of the stations. He seemed immune to that, protected from it by an impregnable armour of freedom.

Occasionally, to reassure me that he was still the Christian father I'd known, he'd say things such as: 'Just think of it, Ola, we are walking on Christ's final footsteps of pain and suffering.' Or, 'If only our family and friends were here to walk with us to His resurrection.' Or, 'His blood saved us, and He spilled it here on this road.' And, being his most dutiful daughter, I'd agree with him.

His quiet joy was infectious. I found I too didn't care anymore about the ugly Hollywood face of that Road. It wasn't important, Dad seemed to be saying. What was important was that he was *with* Christ, dancing with Him along the Road.

In the Holy Sepulchre Church, where Christ's body had lain in the tomb of Joseph of Arimathea, he knelt in the small anteroom and prayed. Before I knew it, I was kneeling beside him, feeling I was again capable of prayer. I forced myself not to though. (I mean, we can't have sceptics becoming blubbering Christians, can we?)

This afternoon when we got back to our hotel, he showered quickly, re-emerged from his room in his white tropical suit and the Gucci shoes I had bought him for his birthday three years before but which he had refused to wear, and invited Gideon, Oren, Daniel, Rani and me to dinner in the best Arab restaurant in Jerusalem. We ate stuffed pigeons and other dishes I'd never tasted before, and drank champagne, what now seems to have been gallons of it.

'It's time to go home now,' he said before he went off to bed.

I'm ready to come home too, Carl. I don't know what this whole trip has done to me. (I may never know.) But, as I've said, Dad's newfound joy is infectious. I've contracted some of it and now feel more tolerant of who I am and what other people are. I don't feel so compulsively that I need to be more.

Before I got up to write this letter, I tried catching you in my head but without success because certain lines kept intruding. They even forced me out of bed to write them down:

> *The night rents*
> *the house of my eyes.*

And uncannily I remembered reading many years ago, of a Japanese woman strangling her lover with his tie while they were making love, so he could achieve his final orgasm.

I'm leaving Israel with a father who has become a dancer. I don't know yet what that means; that description came to me just as I wrote it down just now, and I feel it is a true description.

I'm looking forward to coming home. Wait for me, Carl. Let's start again.

I know you've never had time for poetry but here's a short one I've written since we've been here. I hope you like it.*

---

* *I couldn't find the poem Ola attached to this letter.*

302

80

He's been found.
    Who?
    The kidnapped boy.
    And?
    Dead. Killed.

81

As we age and our brain cells die more quickly and new ones refuse to be born, we begin to forget who we are. But to my death I'll remember, as clear as a movie, how my father reacted to Gideon's announcement that the kidnapped boy had been killed: absolutely no visible sign of being upset, or pretence at being shocked.

'I'm sorry, very sorry,' he said. But he couldn't hide from me. My breakfast tasted like shit but, like him, I chewed and swallowed every morsel of it, and talked about what we were going to do that day.

'I'd like to visit the Wall once again,' he said to Gideon. 'Before we go I'll just go up to my room.'

I pretended I'd forgotten my handbag and followed him up and then into my room, where I stood at the door connecting our rooms and listened to what he was doing.

His bathroom door was opened and closed. A tap running.

Quietly I went into his room.

I could hear him brushing his teeth. On the small desk by his bed were three letters: one to Gideon, one to Oren, one to Daniel. Loud gargling and spitting into the basin. A thin strip of white paper folded in half. I opened it. PLEASE FORGIVE ME was scribbled on it. I folded it again and hurried back into my room.

When I heard him return to his bedroom I knocked and he called me in. His back was turned to me, and he was sheathing the strip of paper in his shirt pocket. Handing me the three letters, he asked me to give them to the people they were addressed to. He straightened his back and pulled back his shoulders as he examined his appearance in the full-length mirror on the door. 'Ready,' he said.

He marched past me out the door. I followed his smell of aftershave lotion and toothpaste.

On our way to the Wall through the alleyways, he talked with Gideon and Oren, while I was snared, like a puzzled fish, in the net of his message: *Please forgive me.*

As we emerged on to the square and the blinding noonday sun, I rubbed the glare out of my eyes. On the square, and thickening as we approached the Wall, was a large crowd of worshippers and pilgrims.

We stopped at the waist-high fence. 'I promised someone I'd place this at the Wall of the Temple,' my father declared. He pulled the message out of his shirt pocket. 'Is it all right?'

'Of course,' Gideon said. For an instant he looked at me.

I looked away. 'It'll be all right,' I said.

Around us swirled the sound of prayers.

We watched him weave a careful path through the crowd towards the Wall. For me, his movements slowed, as in a slow-motion film, while around him the world froze and focused on his swimming through the thick liquid light, a beautiful sea creature cruising to its lair in the reef. For a while he cruised the surface of the Wall, arms outstretched, hands and fingers exploring the rough, pitted stone surface, then he stopped, planted his feet firmly on the ground, took out his message, read it and pushed it into a joint between two of the stone blocks. Bowed his head. Prayed. While the hushed world watched, witnessed. He could not hide.

PLEASE FORGIVE ME.

'Thank you,' he said to Gideon and Oren, and we followed him back up the square in silence, his shadow unable to hide from the sun's honest eye.

Out of the mouth of the alleyway directly ahead of us snaked a dancing, clapping procession of Yemenite Jews, their drumming and the shrill ululating of the women shattering the grief and prayer of noon and restitching it in a new pattern of hope, joy.

In three weaving, swirling lines, hands held tightly shoulder-high, knees jerking up in time to the quick rhythm, women and girls leading.

We stepped aside while the procession danced by. The focus of the procession was a teenage boy, dressed in all his finery, with two old men on either side of him. These patriarchs, while they held the boy's hands, seemed to lose their age as they danced and held him up to the sun's blessing.

My father started clapping to the rhythm, and as the two patriarchs and the boy neared him, he jerked his body up and down to the dance. I too was reacting instinctively to the rhythm but I held back.

Smiling toothlessly, one of the patriarchs beckoned to my father who danced to him, his feet lifting up and down as if the ground was electrified. The patriarch grasped his outstretched left hand and pulled him into the body of the procession.

He laughed and danced.

It was to be the first and last time I was to ever see him dance in public, free of the father I'd known all my life. There, in the dance, he was a spirit free of the earth's grief, tied to the eternal history of patriarchs, locked into the blood of the boy at the centre of it all, at the beginning, his roots deep in the stone out of which we come.

And he was dancing past me, leaving me behind. I grabbed Gideon's and Oren's hands and, in a line, we danced into the procession and just behind my father.

Soon, as our lines snaked down towards the Wall and I allowed the dance to become sinewed in my veins, I too became part of the rhythm that held the earth, sky, air and sun together.

Before we veered away from the Wall, my father turned his face to me; it was alive with tears. But how he danced. Held up above the abyss by the magic of his ancient friends, the boy, and the song and the rhythm, his legs and knees stepping high. Dancing fearlessly over the tightrope. Dancing over the black down-sucking depths of the Galilee.

How he danced. Beyond forgiveness and grief.

> *My father danced at the Temple Wall.*
> *Please forgive me, he sang.*
> *He danced at the Wall*
> *and soothed the world's grief.*
> *He danced at the Wall*
> *and I sheltered in his shade.*

At my centre is that memory, that dance. Only death can wipe it away.

82

Time is everywhere linking everything. To alter it in one
place is to change the whole of it.
There is no time past or time future.
Only an ever-moving present.

Our va with others define us.
We can only be ourselves linked to everyone and everything
else in the Va, the Unity-that-is-All and now.

From the windows of the terminal building I gazed out at Tel Aviv airport. Everything glittered like the burnished armour of King David's
soldiers, an eternal memory from my Bible class childhood.

Twenty minutes later my father and I were in the airport bus heading
across the tarmac to our waiting plane and a rediscovery of Samoa, our
country, in the light of Israel. I looked back once more.

Daniel, Gideon and Oren were standing at the centre window, gazing
after us. They looked as if they were trapped in the heart of the shimmering pane of glass. That is how I will remember them for the rest of
my life: entombed in glass poised to shatter.

I waved but they were already too far away to see us.

83

Fusi told me Carl had left three days before we got back from Israel.

His lawyer, SSS Sanders, rang and told me 'his client' wanted a divorce. 'Be reasonable and I'll make sure you get your fair share,' Sanders said. I thought about it for a day and experienced no regrets that it was over. Nevertheless, to protect myself against any underhanded moves Sanders had in mind, I consulted Fano, who then acted on my behalf. I told Fano I wanted three years' worth of looking after.

Sanders (and Carl) agreed to the terms Fano put forward.

To this day Carl and I have not talked to each other, not a single word or gesture signifying we'd once known each other.

We can love, fall out of love (what an expression!), and not feel anything about it, nothing, as if it had never happened. But better that than falling out of love into hating each other, like so many couples I know.

I had a dream last night. A tall spindly man in a light blue suit, white shirt buttoned at the neck, Buster Keaton hat, with a featureless face of white talcum powder, marched up a series of temple steps and, raising a golden candelabra up to me, said, 'This is broken.' The centre candle holder had broken off; he was holding the broken piece in his left hand. 'Is there anyone here who can fix it?'

I stood gazing down into the unfathomable whiteness of his face, trying to recognise who it was, but I couldn't.

So corny and clichéd a dream, I had thought while I was having it.

Israel is with me still.
So is my father.

84

Old age and its physical ravages descended upon him quickly after our return from Israel.

First it was his eyes. (He'd never needed glasses). Penina told me about the appearance of the first cataract. When we asked him about it, he dismissed it as a minor ailment, an insult to his perfect health. Then the second cataract brimmed and spread, but he refused to discuss the problem. Penina rang me when she noticed he was bumping into things. Next morning, on the pretext that I'd come to collect some breadfruit from his garden, I called in and, after talking for a while, told him that he needed to see an eye specialist. He insisted the cataracts would disappear. Penina rang the next day to say that he'd sent for a taulasea who'd come and chanted incantations and treated his eyes with medicinal leaves — no improvement, however, so I talked to him over the phone. 'Soon you won't be able to read the Bible or your sermons in church,' I pandered to his vanity. He agreed to see the specialist.

The specialist recommended an operation, but Dad refused and compromised on spectacles, which he then didn't wear unless reminded by Penina or me. One of the few pleasures of his old age was reading, particularly the reading of westerns. His failing eyesight lessened that pleasure and in the evenings — if he didn't want to watch TV — he started withdrawing into himself, into dreaming in his armchair, which became more and more a throne of retreat.

For a while he hid, from Penina, the first abscess in his gums under his teeth. (He still had all his teeth and was proud he'd only had two fillings in his life.) One night, at dinner, she noticed he wasn't eating the hard taro crusts and asked what was wrong. Nothing, he said. Next morning she saw traces of blood in the basin after he'd brushed his teeth. At their mid-morning meal she saw the slight swelling on the left side of his face, said nothing to him but rang me. When I came and asked him about it, he said, 'Just a headache.' I got him some Disprins. He drank them, though he hated any form of medicine, so I knew something was wrong. 'We want you to see a dentist,' I insisted. 'I'll arrange it next week,' he promised, but didn't.

'He can't chew anything and the bleeding is bad!' Penina rang me a week later. I arranged the appointment, drove to their house, Penina got him dressed (he was angry but obeyed) and we took him to the dentist, who gave him painkillers and tried to clean out the abscesses. 'Everything is fine again,' Dad said on our way home. I rang and talked to the dentist, who said that the decay had reached the roots of his teeth. 'We have to extract,' he said. 'How many?' I asked. He hesitated and admitted, 'Most of the top and maybe some of the bottom.' False teeth. For a shocked moment Dad just sat on his throne staring at me, like a wounded creature. 'No!' was his total refusal. For almost two weeks we let him brood, until one night he switched on the light and clutching his badly swollen face, spat the blood into his cupped hand, crying, 'All right, then!'

He had to visit the dentist six times. He'd come home and hide in the bedroom, pretending to read. He refused to leave the house and insisted on eating alone. When I visited, his silent rage could have blown me out of the house as he grunted his replies to my questions.

I got his plate of false teeth, but for two days I didn't know how I was going to give it to him. 'I'll do it,' Fau, his youngest daughter, offered. 'Are you sure?' I asked. 'Yes, Finau'll like them,' she said. To this day I've never asked Fau or Dad how she'd handed over the plate and how he'd reacted: I've not liked to intrude on a secret they've wanted to keep to themselves. The next evening after Fau's visit, Penina found Dad in front of her dressing table examining his appearance with his false teeth in place. For almost three months, though, he didn't wear his teeth in public. We got his grandchildren to tell him how handsome he looked with them in. 'You think so?' he kept asking. 'Yes!' they'd chorus. One night I found him on his throne watching TV, his once caved-in face now full with his new 'pride'. He smiled when he looked at me. I nodded and said, 'Congratulations.' That Sunday he wore them to church.

Calamities never come in ones, they arrive in a series, our elders say. Since Israel, Dad drank the occasional beer, whisky or brandy. 'Good for my circulation,' he justified them to Penina and his church friends. Some weekends when I persuaded him to come and stay with us, he'd have more than one drink and end up humming to himself and have to be helped to bed. Now that the ravages were driving him into self-pitying protest, he drank more. Some evenings Penina and I would drink with him, then after dinner he'd escape into the mindless programmes of television, and fall asleep on his throne shortly after.

One night, after everyone had gone to bed, Penina woke him gently. As he struggled to his feet, he clasped his left hand and said, 'I can't raise my arm!' She helped him to bed. She rang and I rushed over.

'It's nothing,' he whispered when I pulled up his sleeve and started massaging his arm with coconut oil. 'I must've slept on it and it got numb.' I ignored his remarks. 'It's getting better already.'

We stayed with him until he fell asleep. 'Why him? Why does it have to be so humiliating?' Penina protested. 'He's very old. We've forgotten that; and for a while he did too,' I said.

In the morning he behaved as if nothing had happened, but I insisted he see the doctor. We argued. We compromised and got a taulasea, who massaged his arms and back with oil and herbs. The taulasea treated him every day for nearly a fortnight. He decided he was as good as new, but Penina and I discerned a slight paralysis in his arm even though he was good at disguising it. 'Now that you're fit again,' I played him, 'I've arranged for your doctor to give you a check-up once a month.' 'That's very thoughtful of you,' he took the bait. 'I'll have the check-up every month.' With that he hoped we'd leave him alone. 'I'm glad you've agreed to it.' And we left before he could protest.

Fau and Penina drove him to the doctor. 'He's okay,' Fau informed me later. 'He's really fit.' 'Is that what he told you?' I asked. 'Yeah, but I watched him and I can tell you Finau's well again.'

I saw the doctor as I'd arranged. 'He's had a minor stroke,' he said, 'but it's to be expected at his age, and he's healthy and strong enough to get over it. I've told him to stay in bed for a few days and not overdo the exertion. I've also given him some tablets to regulate his blood pressure.'

It was the school holidays and I instructed Fau to stay at his bedside and read westerns to him. 'But why?' she asked. 'He has to stay in bed and rest. And if you're there reading to him, he'll stay in bed.' 'Is that doctor's orders?' she asked. She saluted when I said yes. 'Do I have to read him westerns? I can't stand them!' she said. 'At the start, then I'm sure you can con him into liking those awful books that you read.'

'Ask him to tell you about Israel,' I said. 'God, Ola, I've heard enough about your trip!' 'And it's boring to you?' I asked. 'Any story's boring after you've heard it a hundred times.' 'Get Finau to give you his version of our trip,' I said. '*Pilgrimage*, not trip!' she mimicked me.

For three days Fau entertained him with extravagantly read-aloud westerns. (The grandchildren joined her audience in the bedroom.) On the fourth day, Dad insisted on following his usual daily routine: rising at 6 a.m., morning lotu, dressing and then gardening until about 10 a.m. and the first meal of the day. Fau and the younger children gardened with him, and they had to listen to his stories about astronauts and the Vanimonimo, the Space-Between-That-Is-Disappearing, Outer Space, to which we were rooted because of our beginnings. Stories he'd picked up from Pita before Pita had gone to America.

He became adept at disguising the paralysis in his arm. Exercise and work improved it, but he'd never regain full use of it.

After the first stroke, his speech and movements were slower. His body seemed to shrink in around his frame. His once lustrously black hair turned grey and started falling out. When we looked too sadly at him he'd catch his painful reflection in our eyes and look away.

'Ola, he can't control his body!' Penina cried over the phone. I calmed her down and got her to explain. 'For days he hid it from me. He kept telling the children not to leave wet things on the seats and chairs. This morning I caught him taking a wet seat cushion out to the sun to dry. There was a wet patch at the back of his lavalava . . . Ola, what are we going to do?'

Dad was prudish about bodily functions, so I didn't know what to do. For a week I avoided their house, afraid he'd see on my face that we knew. Fortunately he regained control and was visibly happy about it.

One day he was late for his morning meal and Penina went into the garden to get him. He was sitting on a tree stump, massaging the numbness in his left leg. He sensed her presence and stood up. She pretended nothing was wrong and returned to the kitchen, where, through the back window, she observed him as he approached. Though he was trying to disguise it, she could see the limp, the drag, in his left leg.

'My leg must've gone to sleep as I weeded,' he remarked as he sat down at the table.

'Friday's your monthly medical check-up,' she reminded him. She started washing the dishes.

'Don't tell Ola and the children,' he admitted. 'About the leg.' She caught the slur in his speech. She glanced at him. He was rubbing his top lip as if to warm it.

This time he had to spend a week in the hospital. He insisted on a private room. 'They mustn't see me like this,' he pleaded with us. Penina and I and his older children took turns at his bedside, reading or talking to him, filling his silences with our chatter.

On the second day I forgot a ballpoint pen, a letter-writing pad and some books on his bedside table. Next day he gave Fau the books to return to me. Nothing was mentioned about the pen and pad. I thought little of it until two nights later when I visited and he was writing what appeared to be a letter. He closed the pad. I kissed his cheek. We talked. He nursed the pad under his hand on his stomach. 'You want me to post that?' I asked as I was leaving. He shook his head.

On my way home the 'letter' stayed in my thoughts; it was obviously precious to him.

He regained almost full use of his leg, but the deadness remained in his top lip and slowed his speech further.

'I think his memory's going,' Penina told me at dinner. Finau was at a deacons' meeting at the church. 'He spent a long time last night telling me about when he first started working at Thurroughs, an excited and vivid account of it. This morning he said he'd spent last night telling *you* about it. When I told him it had been me, not you, he looked disbelievingly at me and then shrugged his shoulders and returned to his gardening. Not the first time either. A week ago he insisted he'd been talking to me about the church bazaar, but he'd been talking to Mrs Barnes. Two days ago he accused me of not ironing his shirt when he'd asked Fau to do it — only a few minutes before.'

'Old people forget things.'

'But you know how proud he is of his mind and its clarity, of his remembering. He'll . . . he'll fall apart if his memory goes.'

On Saturday morning, a few days later, after Penina and I helped him weed the taro patch, we talked in the shade of the old gatae tree behind the house, drinking the ice-cold orange juice Fau had brought us. Something reminded him of his first trip to Apia with his parents, and he talked about it. 'Lelefua, my mother, was more scared than I was. She clutched my hand so tightly it hurt and I had to tell her so, as we walked through town. She'd only been twice before and hadn't liked it, she told me. Fear, as you know, has a certain acrid, frantic smell — something like fresh blood. At least that's how I've smelled it. And my poor mother exuded that odour; it was worse when Lagona steered us — *forced* us — into our first Apia store. (Smythe's, I think it was.) I clutched her hand; she clutched mine as hard as she could. She dripped sweat. I looked up at her and she smiled and tried to look brave. She was *beautiful* in her fear, in her trying to be brave so I'd stop being afraid. The window light was like fire shining out of the bones of her face and defining her features sharply. And, as you know, she *was* very beautiful, though later, when I was a youth aspiring to the Palagi education Lagona wanted me to have, I was ashamed — yes, ashamed — of her, of her lack of education. You know the awful expression: *someone from the back*. I must've been a real fiapapalagi!

'Yes, Dad,' I joked, but he didn't hear, he was caught in another dimension.

'She was famous for the ietoga and mats she wove. As a child I spent hours, with my brother Pese, watching her hands, fingers, dancing with the strands, and out of that dance emerged a woven song, a mat. I wanted to learn so she started teaching me, "You're good at it," she told me. But I soon sensed that Lagona (and the other elders) were against my learning. As I became more adept at it, they started joking about my doing *women's work*. The other children, apart from Pese, joked about it too. So, one afternoon when she called me over to weave with her, I just shook my head and ran off to play with my friends. There was a hurt look on her face. That evening, during our meal, Lagona asked if I was still learning "to be a woman". The others, including my mother, laughed. "No!" I declared.'

313

Finau paused, his face aglow with sadness. 'If only we could undecide those decisions that we make that determine who we become without meaning to become,' he whispered. 'That *manly* decision not to learn women's work was critical to me, not in relation to my being a weaver but, more tragically, in relation to my mother and other women. That decision began my separation, my going away from her. After it, the umbilical warmth between us was gone, cut by my choice (and hers and my father's and our society) to be a man — and everything that entails.'

He bowed his head. In the rays of mellow sunlight filtering down through the foliage he appeared to be pure memory that had freed itself of bone. 'To the day she died I never again told her that I loved her. Men don't tell their mothers and sisters and other women that, not in public anyway.'

'Finau?' Penina tried to save him from his grief. 'Finau?'

He looked blankly at her, then at me. 'Well, as I said to Pita, don't you ever touch my carpentry tools again. I caught him and his friends wasting my nails and timber . . .' Penina and I looked at each other, alarmed by his disconnected stories. He talked for a few more minutes, staggered up and brushed the dirt off his lavalava, yawned as if we weren't there and ambled off into the house.

I tested him as we entered the kitchen. He was making a pot of tea. 'Dad, are we going to continue weeding the taro this afternoon?' He stopped dead still and we knew he'd already forgotten that we'd been weeding.

'If you want to,' he tried to cover up. 'But it'll be too hot.'

'How old was Lelefua when she passed away?' Penina asked him.

'Seventy-one. She was born on 27 March 1885, in the village of Malaelua, and died on 3 April 1956,' he recited. Perfect recall. Penina reached over and held his hand: he was pouring too much tea into her cup.

He steadied the teapot on the wooden stand and scrutinised us as if from a frightening height, a god afraid of tumbling into the raging sea and drowning. Penina made him sit down. 'It's all right,' she whispered to him.

'My remembering — it's going,' he said. 'What's going to happen . . . to me?'

'Old age makes you forget things,' I said without thinking.

'Don't patronise me!' he snapped.

'Drink your tea,' Penina said.

'Don't *you* patronise me either! I'm not a child — and I'm not yet a memoryless idiot.'

They had four children: Vailaau, who was about twenty-eight and married with four children, lived with them; Tala, the second son, was twenty-six and married with two children, lived with his wife's aiga;

Lemau, the youngest son, was also married with two children, and lived with them; and Fau, the only daughter, was nineteen and at teachers' college. Whenever I visited in the following weeks he got them to join Penina and me in listening to his memories of his parents, brothers and other relatives. He wanted to bequeath to us those memories he deemed important for our survival and continuation as an aiga. In remembering — his marvellous recreations — he didn't realise he was again falling in love with his Sapepe roots, which he had grown away from.

One night, when the others had gone to bed and he walked me to my car, he looked up into the dark bowl of sky that was pebbled with stars and said, 'Ola, every day I have to fight against the chasms in my memory, the abysses that threaten to drag me down into oblivion.' As he opened the car door for me, he added, 'The sky was just like this the first night we were in Jerusalem.'

'Yes,' I said. 'Shalom!'

'Shalom!' he called as I drove away.

I couldn't sleep when I got home. I sat in the sitting room, out of the wind, staring into the darkness of the bay, letting my thoughts wander through the house of my history, which now centred on my father and through him our village rooted in the eleele that encompassed our Dead and yet unborn in the Va, which lives in and around us and nourishes us with wisdom, the gift to be human.

'Can't you sleep?' Fusi's comforting voice came through the dark. She was standing at the top of the stairs.

'No,' I replied. I sensed what she wanted to ask. I waited. She waited. 'Aren't you going to ask?'

'Ask what?'

'About *your* brother.' She didn't answer. I heard her shuffling back towards her room. 'Fusi?' I called.

'Yes?'

'Aren't you going to ask how he is?'

'Does he ever ask how I am?'

His health improved noticeably, no lapses even in his memory. He hummed his way around the house, beat us at cards and outlasted us in watching TV, worked longer hours in his garden and was ecstatic about his new crop of long beans. He thrilled his grandchildren with oral versions of the westerns he'd read, surprised the church congregation with his sermons about political corruption in our country — that surprised me too as he'd never been openly condemning of our politicians. He spent from 5 to 7 a.m. writing and rewriting, the results of which he didn't show anyone; every morning he burnt the drafts in his garden. His cheerfulness infected us all. I couldn't remember a time our aiga had been happier.

In early September he reminded us about Children's Sunday, Lotu-a-

Tamaiti, which is the second Sunday in October and is celebrated more lavishly than Christmas throughout our country. He declared that his grandchildren and Fau (who protested to us but not to him) were to assemble in his house every afternoon at four o'clock. Under his tutorship, they were to learn hymns, biblical verses and recitations. On Children's Sunday children got new Sunday clothes (whether parents could afford them or not); they didn't have to serve their elders but were served by them, and were encouraged to almost kill themselves with overeating (so the parents could overindulge too).

We expected our grand family performance to be part of our English-speaking Protestant Church's Children's Sunday, and were puzzled when he distributed verses and recitations in Samoan. Fau, the rashly brave, asked him why. 'Didn't I tell you? We're having Children's Sunday at Sapepe,' he said.

I couldn't remember when we last attended church in Sapepe; it seemed we only did so when someone died.

For nearly three weeks, while the rehearsals were on, I rang Penina every night. She was high on happiness and she transmitted that to me. He was so alive, absolutely tolerant of the children who, under his expert coaxing (and consistent bribery), were learning two hymns (three-part singing — no bass) to Fau's guitar accompaniment. Fau was the only reluctant participant arguing (but not to him) that she was now too old for Children's Sundays. Her charming dad was flattering her unashamedly. Gifted, she was! He praised her; a really gifted musician who was wiser and more loving than even Pita, who was falling too much in love with the sciences and neglecting God.

Even Lopeti, three years old and the youngest, was learning his two verses and reciting them like an experienced miniature pastor, Penina said. No fears, no loss of nerve, not yet anyway, among the children. 'You should see Fau!' she laughed. 'Should be a missionary converting the heathens. She's just like her father when he preaches — solemn and serious, the permanent frown on her forehead.'

I couldn't resist seeing for myself and went on Friday afternoon.

Our family home sang with joy and laughter that swirled around the brilliant head of an inventive teacher who cleaned noses, flattered and pampered his pupils, promised sweets before the rehearsal and gave them generously afterwards, and threatened no food on Children's Sunday for anyone who failed to recite or sing properly. I was back in my childhood with a father (and family) who, I believed, would never age or die.

At the end of the rehearsal, he said, 'And children, I bet Ola can't remember any of the recitations I taught her as a child.' He looked at me, so did the children. 'Ola, as you know, doesn't go to church any more.' He was joking but he was being unfair: he was raising my nieces and

316

nephews to pity heathens, atheists, agnostics, Seventh Day Adventists, Mormons, the Holy Rollers and Christians who didn't attend church.

'I know Ola can!' Fau championed my cause. (She had great potential to be a heathen like me.)

I recited the whole of Psalm 23, and told them that was what Finau had taught me for Children's Sunday when I was fifteen. They applauded; Dad just smiled. I then recited (flawlessly) four verses from Genesis, and said it had been my recitation when I was five. they applauded louder. Dad smiled. '"And Jesus cried",' I recited. 'Dad taught me that when I was two and a half for my first Children's Sunday.' Their applause was thunderous. 'You want more?'

'Yeah, yeah!' Fau, my heathen ally, called. The children echoed her. I recited two more pieces.

'Are you going to be as good as Ola at saying *your* recitations?' Dad asked them.

'Yes, yes!' they replied.

Like children everywhere, ours were mad about sweets, but in the disciplined tradition of our aiga, were always polite in asking for and receiving them. So when I pulled out the large packets of toffees, mints and chocolates, they sat up, folded their arms and, with polite thank yous, accepted the sweets from Fau, my loyal disciple.

'You've got a fantastic memory,' Penina congratulated me when we were alone.

'Fantastic all right!' I laughed. 'I made it up, all of it. (Not the biblical verses, of course.)'

'But Finau never challenged you.'

'I knew he wouldn't; he doesn't remember what he got me to memorise, but he's not going to admit that to his heirs, is he?'

After my grandfather Lagona died, our aiga during a talatalaga at Sapepe offered Finau the Lagona title, the highest in the aiga, but he declined it, arguing that his cousin, Ma'alua, who lived in Sapepe and who'd served our aiga well, should have it. The aiga, however, conferred another matai title, Te'elagi, on Ma'alua, and left the Lagona title vacant in the hope that Finau would accept it one day. Our cousin Te'elagi Ma'alua and three other matai now ran our Sapepe aiga, but Finau, the eldest and favoured son of the aiga, was consulted about any important matter. Whenever he visited Sapepe, the village fono and our aiga accorded him the status of Lagona. He felt awkward about this but was proud that they *recognised* who he was.

We hadn't visited Sapepe for about three years, so Finau sent Vaila'au in the pick-up to inform Te'elagi and our aiga that we were arriving the Wednesday before Children's Sunday. On Saturday he called us together and explained the importance of our return. It was the first time we were taking his grandchildren to Sapepe, so we had to take appropriate gifts: money, as lafo for the matai who would arrive to greet us; cases of tinned fish, cabin bread and barrels of salted beef as sua; a large contribution of money to the pastor and church; foodstuffs, such as sacks of rice, sugar and flour, for our relatives; and cigarettes and tobacco for whoever came to see us. Dad had modest means and was frugal but, when it came to important aiga occasions, he spared little (and he didn't spare us, his children). Being the one with the most, I had to contribute the most.

On Monday I took Vaila'au, Tala and Lemau and and bought the food-stuffs we needed. They insisted on paying for some of it, even though as civil servants they weren't earning much. (A true Samoan heir is obliged to contribute whether she can afford it or not.)

Next day, Vaila'au took Penina and some of the women to Sapepe to prepare the main fale and house, which Lagona had built years before with our financial help.

I've not been one for the ostentatious display of wealth to prove, pub-licly, one's alofa for aiga, village or church, so on Wednesday morning, as I supervised the loading of Dad's pick-up and a truck I'd borrowed from Fano, I experienced accusing jabs of guilt. I kept telling myself, though, that I was doing it for aiga, for reaffirming ties to community, for our children to put their roots down in Sapepe. Besides, my father and I weren't poverty-stricken nobodies returning to a nobody aiga in a nobody village: we were the Aiga Lagona, and my father *was* Lagona and I *was* Meletasi, taupou to the Lagona.

In my car, with Dad ensconced beside me and Fau and Lopeti, his favourite heirs, in the back seat, I led our ostentatious fleet, which was cargoed generously with relatives, food and other goods, through the vill-ages. We reached Sapepe, at the western tip of the world, by mid-afternoon.

Not long after we unloaded the trucks and stored our 'cargo' in the back room of the house, Dad, Te'elagi and our other matai seated them-selves in our faletele to await the matai and aumaga of Sapepe.

They arrived as a group, led by Malo Tauilopepe Galupo, our highest ali'i. We, the women and the untitled of our aiga, started preparing food for them. Our neighbours and many of the aumaga came to help.

In and around the faletele, the aumaga and taupou, Malo's cousin, were pounding and mixing the ava. I recalled the long, sometimes tearful sessions I'd suffered as a girl when my grandparents taught me how to mix the ava and serve it; they were exacting teachers. After I'd per-formed it for the first time publicly — to welcome a concert party from Siumu — they'd blessed me with their praises. It had been worth it. How-ever, after my return from New Zealand I'd avoided the role; I knew it

318

was hurting my grandparents but hadn't cared. Now, as I listened to the high-pitched voice of the tulafale sharing out the ava, I wanted to show everyone — even my dead grandparents — that I still knew how to be the perfect taupou.

Penina reminded me about the money for the lafo. I got the bag of single dollar notes out of my bag, took off my jandals, and crept through the taulele'a on the back paepae and sat down behind Dad. Te'elagi, on behalf of our aiga, was thanking the village for their welcome to Finau and his children. Surreptitiously I pushed the bag of money against Dad's knee. As Te'elagi addressed each matai, Dad slipped him money, which he then gave the taule'ale'a who was serving to distribute to the matai; the tulafale who'd made the welcome speech got the most. Dad's very generous lafo worried me. 'Don't worry,' he whispered, 'I've got another bag.' (He could always sense my moods.)

Someone was observing me. I looked around the fale. The matai I knew smiled back at me. Only Malo Tauilopepe Galupo was deliberately hiding his scrutiny of me. He was the head of our two most powerful aiga, the unchallenged leader of our village and district, with a huge plantation, stores and businesses in Apia. (His father had been responsible for the 'modernisation' of our village.) Malo had come to Sapepe when I was at university in New Zealand. He was strangely *elongated* in everything that he was: elongated features and limbs; leanly elongated in his movements, gestures and speech, as if he was watching himself performing; and a charisma — that overused word — that was imperceptibly around you like a reassuring embrace. He was measuring me as a 'power', a possible threat? ally? and how he was going to fit me into his Sapepe. Malo was into power, into the controlling, using and manipulating of it; that was his kick.

In that gathering he said little, but we knew he was there, as if he'd always been in Sapepe, in the sea, bush, land, sky, rooted in our pre-Christian atua, in their grace, terror, wrath, alofa.

'Ola?' Finau said. 'Bring the sua: one for Malo, one for the pastor. And six barrels of beef, eight cartons of fish, and five cartons of cabin bread for the village.' I left with Malo lingering in the centre of my head.

Because I hadn't visited Sapepe often, I'd become a stranger to it. I wanted to belong like Pita, upon whom the people of Sapepe lavished their alofa. They treated my father and me with respect but a respect that kept us at a distance.

An hour or so after the ava, our aiga and the aumaga served the matai their food. I stayed in the back fale, talking to the other women.

'Why have you no husband?' Mate, my father's oldest sister and now a wrinkled crone, demanded of me.

'Because Ola's too tired!' echoed another crone. (It's forbidden for the

319

young to participate equally in such conversations.)

'Is that true, Ola?' Mate asked, peering at me through rheumy eyes that wept with mischief. The others tried not to laugh. 'Look, you're just a girl!'

'But she's been too long in the Palagi life!' her partner improved on the joke.

'You mean Palagi *tire* easily?' Mate asked.

'Ask Ola that question. After all, I've not *run* with a Palagi!' The others started giggling.

'Is that true, Ola? About Palagi?'

'Some,' I joined the mushrooming joke. 'But some can run a long, long mile!'

'What kind of mile? Samoan or Palagi?' Mate kept a straight face. Our bawdy lot ignored the fono and unleashed a shrieking cacophony of laughter. While Mate and the other elders were with us, not even Malo would reprimand us.

'Mate, ask Ola about Japan,' someone urged her.

'What about Japan?' she replied.

'Whether the Japanese are good at poula.'

'Are they, Ola?' she asked me.

'Yes, but they're not as fit!' I dared.

'Why not?'

I hesitated, hitched up my courage like a lavalava, and said, 'Because they're a little short!' Paused. Expectant silence. 'A little short — of breath!' Mate blinked, clapped her hands, and we all laughed again.

'Better not let the men hear us,' someone cautioned.

'Why?' Mate replied. 'Some of them are *really* short — but not of breath!'

And our laughter continued dancing around our compound and over to the faletele of puzzled matai and across the listening malae into the lagoon, which was as welcoming as on the day our ancestors first arrived, bringing voice to the wilderness. Mate cuddled me to her side. I was home again.

That night, Penina, the children and I slept in the sitting room while Dad and our matai slept in the faletele. His old friends came and he told them of our visit to Israel.

I kept waking, pursued by shadows and fears. A persistent dream blossomed to my grandparents robed in siapo tiputa and garlanded with oiled laumaile leaves, sitting like lava boulders at the door of my sleeping mats, with single teardrops sliding down their faces. Their eyes and hungry silence were the black oases of my drowning. Above our house the manuali'i, heralder of death, dared my frantic hand to chase it away. It was feathered with razor-sharp steel and lacerated my hand to the bone

320

when I waved it away. I knew it would cry death into our aiga, but I couldn't stop it, and wept in my drowning and bleeding.

The dawn light was tonguing its way through the slits and cracks around the windows and doors when I swam up out of that dream, sat up quickly and wiped the sweat off my body with a towel. I picked my way through the mosquito nets, sat down on the front doorstep and surveyed a world suffused with light and hushly still as in a technicolour photograph in a travel book about the mythical, romantic South Seas. Better that cliché than drowning in forebodings of death. But the manuali'i squatted in my breath, hatching its cry.

To my right, stretching from the house to our other fale under frangipani and breadfruit trees, were the stone graves of our ancestors, the Lagona and our elders back to the founding of Sapepe. In the early light the graves glistened like the black skins of eels. I looked again. Sitting cross-legged on a mat, Finau was weeding between the two central graves. His sleeping sheet shone like white fire. He was at home among our Dead, their keeper and custodian. Bent forward, his weight on his left arm, he looked as if he was scratching at the earth's skin in search of something. What?

I crept back inside, woke up Fau and asked her to go swimming with me. She agreed reluctantly. Her generation didn't like exercise, and females shouldn't exercise in public, but I was an elder, and well-brought-up children obeyed their elders.

Since my return from New Zealand I'd dreaded the lack of privacy in the village and within my aiga. I insisted on changing/dressing/ showering behind curtains or walls. (To lock yourself in a room is interpreted as a sign of dissatisfaction with your hosts or your aiga; to go for solitary walks or surround yourself with a shroud of silence is to be accused of being 'touched', anti-social, fiapalagi.) So I changed into my swimming costume behind a curtain, which I strung across the back of the sitting room, and wrapped a lavalava over me from breasts to modest knees. So much for the Hollywood/Margaret Mead myth of easy nakedness in Paradise. I joined Fau, who was in a T-shirt and lavalava, no Hollywood swimming costume for that native beauty: her dad — and the other elders — would have a fit.

On the empty beach I did some stretch exercises, to Fau's disguised amusement, and told her we were swimming half a mile out to the rock outcrop near the reef.

'Eh, I can't swim that far!' she protested. So much for the Hollywood myth of svelte Polynesian maidens swimming miles out, like happy dolphins, to welcome brave Papalagi explorers.

I remembered seeing a small paopao up by the hibiscus hedge on the roadside. 'Can you paddle a canoe?' I asked. She looked hurt at that insult.

So we went, pulled the canoe down and into the water. I picked up the paddle; she tugged it out of my hands, pushed the canoe further into the water, got in it, sat down with the paddle gripped across her thighs, and stared out to sea. I dragged the canoe out until the water was up to my ribs, then I started swimming while Fau, the expert paddler, paddled alongside me.

The water was a cool snug grip around me. Blue, grey, green over white sand and expanses of multicoloured coral. (I've never been afraid of the sea, even when I've imagined ferocious sharks and other creatures stalking me through the coral beds.) My lavalava became cumbersome so I pulled it off and dropped it into the canoe. 'Sure you can swim that far?' Fau taunted me. I dropped back into the water and swam faster, leaving her behind, knowing that most of her generation were frightened of being alone in the sea. 'Ola, Ola!' she called. I slowed; she caught up.

A short while later I tied the canoe to one of the rocks and we clambered on to the outcrop, sat down with our legs dangling into the water and looked back at the shore. 'You kids are bloody hopeless,' I said in English.

'Pita's not hopeless,' she countered in English. 'He's better at canoeing, swimming and fishing than . . . than . . .' She was scared to say it.

'Better than me?'

'I didn't say that,' she said, staring rigidly at the village.

'But that's what you *meant* to say.'

'But you're better than all the grown-ups I know,' she evaded me.

The sun was now a blinding disc on the summit of the range, casting an orange light that cancelled out the other colours. Our village, with the twin-towered church at its centre, stretched out under the vegetation along the curve of the bay, and then back up into the foothills of neat plantations. Malo's, the largest plantation, cut a wide strip right up through the bush on the range, like a runway to take off from into the Nine Heavens that comprised our pre-Christian cosmos. No wonder the sex-starved sailors and adventurers from a puritanical Europe of over-crowded squalor, gin, brutal justice and class repression had believed this to be Paradise. So easy to attribute to it the qualities your squalid society lacked.

'I'd like to go to university in New Zealand,' Fau intruded.

'Why?'

'To get a degree and be like you.'

I glanced at her. 'Fau, you don't want to be like me.'

'But we all want to be like you. We know Papa and the other elders don't like your not attending church and your drinking, but they admire you, and tell us we should try and be like you.'

322

'Fau, I've wasted almost a lifetime . . .'

'But you haven't!'

How do you convey the essence of your misspent life to a child who still had a future to discover and be? How do you explain that your possibilities were being replaced by a deadly cynicism and the sense of defeat that comes with middle age? How do you convince her that the journey to discover the infinite possibilities of the self may not be best done through exploring (and enduring) the Papalagi world? Fau's quest was that of the Third/Fourth/Call-it-what-you-like World's for the Western bourgeois dream of the self-replenishing new horn of plenty, the consumer society, an insatiable monster that hooks us on perpetual consumption so it can feed off us and keep itself eternally young and ravishing. Consume. Consume. Consume. Until our planet is a plundered husk reflecting our own spiritual bankruptcy. The quest can't be denied. Perhaps it is best that we try and live through it as quickly as possible, and hope to emerge from it not too badly ravaged, and with wisdom.

'. . . Will you persuade Papa and Penina to let me go to New Zealand next year? Will you, Ola? Please?'

'If that's what you *really* want.' I couldn't look at her.

The golden light was fading and up through it were emerging all the other colours, shades and shadows of our daylight world. Since the 1950s, our country had been emptying of our ablest and most adventurous people. Rising poverty, unemployment, corruption and our reckless refusal to live within our resources keep fuelling that emptying. (So much for South Seas paradises!)

The tide was rising.

I didn't have the strength to swim back to shore. Fau, who reminded me so much of the girl I had been, would paddle me back.

> *A sunbeam, a sunbeam,*
> *Jesus wants me for a sunbeam,*
> *A sunbeam, a sunbeam*
> *I'll be a sunbeam for Him . . .*

The children of your aiga sing to Fau's plucking guitar, and in English, so incongruous but it's your father's one step ahead of every father (and aiga) in Sapepe, this glorious Lotu-a-Tamaiti morning. (A few years back you would've cringed in shame.) As you bask in their performance in front of a capacity congregation and a sea of children in their new white best, and see your father, seated in the middle of the front pew conducting his brood of well-trained chicks, you turn mushy inside. You're a dropout from Christianity, but you've never rejected Lotu-a-Tamaiti, justifying that Sunday as the most important national celebration of childhood (and the alofa your father and aiga garlanded you with extravagantly). Like you, the other parents are here, reliving their Children's Sundays through their children.

At high school, Miss Flavell played you a recording of Dylan Thomas reading his 'Christmas in Wales'. You'd recognised it as the most apt description of your Children's Sundays. Since then, even when you've not gone to church on Children's Sundays, Dylan Thomas has sung in your centre, like a robust fire, each Lotu-a-Tamaiti. This morning, as you escorted your wards to the pastor's house, Thomas had sung again inside you. Wales. Samoa. The gifted poet son of a volcanic pastor, drunk on a wild imagery celebrating being 'young and golden'. The frightful cliché of sunbeams ain't Thomas but it's your way into your memory bank and the alofa that binds all aiga at Lotu-a-Tamaiti.

During your fourth Lotu-a-Tamaiti, while in the middle of your recitation, you remembered you didn't have a mother and started sobbing. Your father put his arm around you and whispered, 'Go on, go on, Ola!' (You can feel the warmth of his breath on your ear even now.) And you stumbled, with large sobs, through the rest of your recitation and had the elders (and not-so-elderly) in tears. At lunch your aiga heaped plates full of alofa on you, and you partook of their alofa until you were nearly bursting.

Falani, your oldest nephew, is now reciting. He's crazy about spanners, pliers and screwdrivers. Must be a Freudian explanation for it. His is a laid-back style, smooth, flowing gestures, well-modulated voice — the handsome bugger's going to break lots of hearts. He reminds you of cousin Semi, who ate so much one Lotu-a-Tamaiti he couldn't stand up and had to be rolled to the other end of the fale and ordered to sleep off his overeating. Semi, who later overate in the number of wives and children he had and had to be rolled into his oversized coffin, as prophesied by your grandmother.

Semi's overeating reminds you of that Lotu-a-Tamaiti when Aunt Fusi got diarrhoea and, that night, you had to keep chaperoning her to the draughty outhouse and shiver in the aitu-filled darkness and listen to her groaning and thundering and try not to inhale her stink. (Fusi refuses, to this hour, to mention that incident.)

Reciting now, in her little voice, is Felila, small like a bantam rooster and as feisty and smart. Direct heir in personality — if not appearance — to your cousin Moe, who, after out-performing every student at pastor's school in Lotu-a-Tamaiti rehearsals, refused to utter a syllable of her recitation at the service and was dragged out by her mother and slapped repeatedly for 'disgracing our aiga'. Her father threatened to break off her jaw and voice if she didn't go back in and fill the church with her recitation (and the unquestionable courage of their aiga). Moe marched back in, stood and, confronting the congregation, shook the church with her rebellious silence. When her mother rushed at her again, she ran over and sat against your grandfather, who almost slayed her mother with his glare. At lunch your grandfather sat and ate with Moe; you were jealous. Your grandfather then laid down a rule that became another aiga tradition: no one was to ever again hit any of his heirs during a Lotu-a-Tamaiti.

To this day you've never discovered why Moe refused to recite. But she's married to a merchant in Pago Pago, and whenever you visit them, she uses you as an excuse to out-drink everyone, and gifts you two cases of vodka to bring back to Upolu. She has no children. Does that have anything to do with that cruel Lotu-a-Tamaiti?

You can hardly hear Matagi, the shyest but brightest of your nephews, and he's not looking at grandfather. Eight years old and a disciple of Pita, who, before going to America, took him everywhere and taught him about TV, rockets, ET, time machines, computers, fish, whales, dinosaurs, Close Encounters, dogs, lasers and the other mysteries you know little about. Matagi, Wind, Breeze. Soft. Pliable. Able to shape his knowing to the shapes of what is to be known and discovered. He and Pita are the new tradition in your aiga. Your roots in the Vanimonimo. Finau is signalling to Matagi to speak up, but the Breeze, with lowered head, doesn't look up to obey.

And you recall Fiti, your one-eyed neighbour with continents of ringworm, a reputation for pig stealing, and a wife, Eta, who detested pork. While feeding frenziedly one Lotu-a-Tamaiti, Fiti collapsed and had to be loaded onto a truck to be rushed to hospital. 'Fiti, Fiti, I told you to stop stealing pigs!' Eta cried. (Rumour had it that Fiti had choked on a specially fatty piece of stolen pork.)

It was for Lotu-a-Tamaiti that Finau got you your first pair of shoes, brown leather ones with gold buckles. You were overjoyed because you were one of the few without shoes at the English-speaking church. But in Sapepe, where you went for that Lotu-a-Tamaiti, shoes were the conspicuous exception, and you were mortified to think you might be called 'fiase'evae! fiapalagi!' by the other children. Fusi threatened no lunch if you didn't wear them, and accompanied you to the pastor's house and put them on you so everyone could see. When the procession started, the shoes felt like precarious wooden platforms you had to keep your balance on, and you wanted to take them off, but you weren't going to let the others know that you weren't used to wearing shoes. You stumbled a few times. 'Shame, fiase'evae, shame!' some of the others jeered. You weren't going to let them win, so, despite the shoes causing you blisters, you wore them to church, during church and home after church. Your tormentors gave up, and some —your cousins — admitted they were envious. That night Fusi pricked your tight blisters and you cried with the pain.

Lopeti is looking directly at his grandfather as he hammers out his recitation, punching his left fist into the palm of his right hand to emphasise every word. (He's a lefty, considered a bad omen by his parents.) The congregation giggle and laugh (but not too loudly — it's church). Your youngest nephew isn't going to find life easy, because you're all spoiling him rotten. Like you, he's going to expect life (and everyone) to owe him a splendid living. But he's already got Finau's unbuyable honesty and that'll save him.

Semisi, the boy you had a crush on at pastor's school, eases into your remembering. Reticent, always anticipating blows that never eventuated, stutterer whenever adults were cross with him (which was often). Poor beautiful Semisi, you never revealed your infatuation to him but protected him against the other children. Semisi, who was never able to finish any of his Lotu-a-Tamaiti recitations without blubbering — and disgraced his tyrannical father, who later forced him into Malua Theological College. Semisi, once slim and supple and strong as poumuli, now strangling in fat and self-importance and rank and avarice as president of the Congregational Church. He doesn't stutter anymore: he's a loudly articulate, ruthlessly vindictive wielder of power.

Fau is now delivering her sermonette. Cool, calm and collected. (Uncanny — and flattering — how she resembles you in your photos at her age.) First Lady of the next generation of your aiga, if she returns from New Zealand, and if she returns with Finau's integrity, balance and tolerance. You look round the congregation. Many of the elders are weeping quietly as Fau sermonises: she has a way with platitudes, homilies and biblical clichés, of recycling them into new gold coins.

As she ends, she starts playing her guitar. The others stand up to sing their last hymn. You go up and, standing beside Fau, sing with them. Finau shuffles up and holds Lopeti's hand. Penina comes up too, then the rest of your Apia aiga. Unrehearsed. Just joy and pride as an aiga rejoining Sapepe, an aiga of many aiga, celebrating the annual renewal of its childhood.

As you sing, the dancing procession of Yemenite Jews at the Western Wall weaves its daring magic into your heart again, their joy transcending all pain and death, plaiting the rope of sanity across the terrible abyss of terror that is our century. To see that. To feel it. To be that. Is to know that everything is in harmony in the Va.

On Monday morning Finau told us he and Penina were staying in Sapepe for a while.

Over the following weeks, as we shifted more and more of their possessions to Sapepe, we thought their stay could be permanent but never asked them.

Vaila'au and his able wife, Loto, assumed the responsibility of looking after our Apia aiga. I went often to help them. They treated me as if I were Finau, head of our aiga. They consulted me even about the children's education.

Soon our house in Sapepe was a (larger) replica of our Apia home, with a radio, fridge, gas stove, beds, a gallery of family photos, even a coir front-door mat, and a thriving garden of indigenous plants and shrubs around it (and the graves). We built corrugated-iron walls around the outside shower to give it privacy, a flush toilet in the shelter of the breadfruit trees, and a garage at the side of the house.

Our faletele was rethatched at my insistence. (The other faletele in Sapepe had ugly corrugated-iron roofs.) Mate got the Women's Committee to weave the thatch (and for the first time, I learned how to weave one). Finau, Penina and our other elders slept in the faletele every night. The fale quickly became a club for Dad and his tribe of cronies, who our aiga fed and kept in cigarettes and other luxuries deserving of their rank.

One weekend his cronies hinted at a TV set like the one that Malo had. I glanced at Dad. He shook his head. (Must have been a difficult decision, as he'd been a TV addict in Apia.)

Penina kept reassuring me they were enjoying Sapepe, despite the usual jealousies, gossip and rivalries between aiga. Finau, she said, was handling our aiga problems with expert diplomacy. 'Is he going to accept the title?' I asked her.

'He's said nothing about it. But the elders, especially Mate, are putting pressure on him. You know what he's like though, the heavier the pressure the more stubborn he becomes.'

'And how are you finding it?'

'A bit difficult,' she said. I looked at her. Penina had a way of making her presence *obvious* when she wanted to: a silence, a pause, a slight raising of her eyebrows. 'I wasn't raised in my father's village; I was brought up in Apia. I like it here but it's difficult.' I waited for her to continue. We took her for granted, as always being there and coping better than any of us: whenever things got tough we turned to her automatically. She'd submerged her individuality in our aiga to become a major strength of it. How beautiful she was, I thought as I watched her.

The mellow morning light lay on her face, making her appear as if she was of polished dark-grained wood, with her mana shining through it. 'I'm quite happy with life here, but I don't think I'd like to adjust to it completely. It can get so confining I find it difficult to breath,' she continued. As she talked, I realised how much I'd needed and used her over the years, yet I'd not given much of myself to her. 'It's good having you to talk to, Ola,' she was saying. 'As you know, I find it difficult telling people how I feel. At times I get so full of worries I'm almost bursting with them. Then you visit and I lay them on you. It's not fair, is it?' She smiled. 'Sapepe is *small*; there is no privacy, no room to be alone . . .' It was as if I was listening to myself admitting to the limitations of village life, yet there was a difference: Penina accepted those and had the talent to live within and with them. I encouraged her to talk about Sapepe, then about her aiga, which, over the years, I'd sensed she'd been reluctant to discuss.

Even before she was born, her biological parents, Tu'ese and Sasa'e, had agreed to her adoption by her mother's sister, Sisifo, and husband, Mika, who were childless, said Penina. They lived at Lalovaea with Mika's aiga, in a small compound they rented from the Catholic Church. The land had been reclaimed from swamp. 'That's why even today I can describe at least fifty different types of swamp stench!'

Mika, a bulldozer driver from the Public Works, had to support his parents and five brothers and sisters, two of whom were married and with children. Throughout her life she would keep wondering how her parents ever made ends meet on his modest salary. But they did: it meant going without what her real parents, who owned a plumbing business, lavished on her other six brothers and sisters. Sisifo and Mika told her early about her adoption and they visited her real parents' branch of their aiga often. 'I got to know my *other* parents and brothers and sisters well but could never think of them as parents and brothers and sisters. They were friends, relatives, I visited and had fun with. And who gave me lots of money and things. But at the end of each visit — sometimes I spent weeks with them — I looked forward to going home to the frugality of my *real* parents.'

She went on to say that Sisifo and Mika quarrelled a lot, usually caused by the constant stress they experienced having to cope with a large aiga and endless fa'alavelave: they cursed the fa'a Samoa but always fulfilled their obligations to church, aiga and community. Endless debts, and Mika's salary was always overdrawn by the end of each month. Their quarrels, though, strengthened their love and their love for her. Strange, but that was how it was.

'Don't you want to go and live with your real parents?' Sisifo asked her one day. 'They have everything: money, good food, everything.' She said no, and skipped off to play with her friends. Sisifo and Mika tempted and tested her with that possibility at least twice every year, especially when they had to scrape money together to pay her school fees and buy her uniforms, or when Christmas loomed and they couldn't afford the presents they thought she wanted.

Whenever she was at her other parents' home, they treated her as their favourite child. She was embarrassed by this, because at times her

328

brothers and sisters resented her for it. She stopped going because of it, but they came and got her, and Sisifo and Mika encouraged her to stay longer and go to the Sisters' School from there. She stayed a whole school term, until she quarrelled with one of her sisters, packed her bag and fled for home.

'. . . Tu'ese, my other father, had a successful plumbing business which he'd struggled for many years to establish; he was strict and fair with everyone in our aiga; he was a respected deacon; fulfilled all his obligations generously; and so forth. Everything about him spelled success in the eyes of the community and our aiga. But I sensed a huge struggle within him . . .' Sasa'e, her other mother, got her to clean out the upstairs bedrooms of the house one Saturday morning while Tu'ese and the others were at the market. She wasn't to go into her father's workroom, even if it was unlocked, Sasa'e cautioned.

She turned the door handle just for the curiosity of it, meaning not to go into it, but her hand refused to turn the handle back and her feet pulled her towards the door, which her hand and arm were pushing inwards. Inwards. Until she was standing at his chair and desk and gazing round at the walls covered with old photographs of brass bands playing in front of churches and other buildings, brass bands seated in font of the Maota Fono at Mulinu'u surrounded by spellbound audiences. Photographs of choirs singing in various churches and celebrations. And leading them, his head held high, his eyes burning with a passionate intensity, his baton and arms raised to prescribe the shape of the world's heartbeat to his music, was the *other* Tu'ese, a young Tu'ese, one she'd not known and whom Tu'ese refused to talk about. '. . . And I experienced a huge sadness,' Penina said. 'That's the most apt way of describing it: I was almost overwhelmed by sadness. And with it came guilt. I had no right intruding into Tu'ese's secret self, into the secret of his guilt and what was wrong with his life. I turned and fled from it.

'I didn't mention my discovery to anyone until I met Finau, until there was love between us and I knew he would understand what I had done and what I had found out about Tu'ese and myself. For over a year I couldn't go back to my other parents' home. And when I did go back, I never again felt I belonged there. But I loved Tu'ese more: every time I saw him, the young musician and conductor with the magical baton and passionate eyes, stood beside him.

'Tu'ese was an extraordinary man who chose to be merely successful and respected,' Penina continued. 'He went on to take the highest title in our aiga, become a Member of Parliament then the Minister of Public Works, who promoted Mika to head of the heavy equipment section and made it slightly easier for my parents to make ends meet.' She paused, and remembering where she was, looked at me and said, 'How did I get to talking about my other father? And in Sapepe of all places.' Rising to her feet, she added, 'Got a lot of work to do.'

'Will you tell me more about your aiga later?' I pursued her.

'But they're unimportant.'

'I want to know, Penina,' I pleaded.

'But why?' She stood with her back to me.

'Because you're important to us.'

Since my divorcing Carl, I'd withdrawn almost completely from the social life of Apia. I still went to the odd dinner at my friends' homes, but I avoided the cocktail circuit. I spent my weekends in Sapepe. Because I was hardly there during the day, and spent my nights writing or reading in my study, Fusi didn't have anyone to fuss over. So she spent more time with our Apia aiga. She refused to visit Sapepe though.

For a while I avoided being a member of the Women's Committee, but I involved myself (and enjoyed it) in their collective activities: fundraising, health inspections, mat-weaving houses (I was hopeless at weaving), sewing workshops (I couldn't sew anything more complicated than a lavalava), cooking lessons (they enjoyed my incompetence in this: got a degree but can't even cook sapa sui), and in our quite famous cricket team, the Ainiuafa, Eaters of the Sinnet Coconut. I threw myself into the game, becoming the best batter and second-best bowler in our team. My performance helped in our string of victories against other villages, and won, for me, the unconditional affection of the women of Sapepe. Living in a prudish, puritanical Sapepe — at least in public behaviour — I had to make serious compromises with some of my vices and habits. For instance, I couldn't drink alcohol within the holy sight of people outside my aiga. (Fau, Penina and Dad were the only ones who knew I sneaked a vodka or three in the upstairs bedroom.) I refused to stop my running through the village and round the bay, but did so at dawn when the holy Sapepeans were still asleep (I'm sure some sneaked a look). I also wore a track suit that covered my tempting nakedness from neck to ankle and wrist.

Not even the fanatical members of our champion cricket team joined me in my training; they considered it unfeminine and masochistic, and women shouldn't exercise in public anyway. I was glad they didn't, because I couldn't run with someone else's rhythm. Lone running was also a healing withdrawal into solitude and my own pulse. In Sapepe I didn't have to wear make-up or fancy clothes — not that I wanted to. The safest philosophy was to be invisible, look like the group. When I became a member of the Women's Committee my individuality was cancelled out in our uniform: bright orange and red floral puletasi; and in our cricket uniform, a red floral lavalava and yellow T-shirt with 'Ainiuafa, Teine of le Vaiula' stencilled in red on the front.

Politely I refused (through my father) Pastor Simi's invitation (through my father) to be one of his Sunday school teachers.

Politely I refused (through Penina) my father's request (through Penina) for me to attend Pastor Simi's confirmation classes and be confirmed in the 'true church'. 'Remember, I'm forty-six — the rest of the class are teenagers,' I told Penina. 'One is never too old to be saved!' was Dad's reply (through Mate).

I resisted Mate's recurring advice that I marry again, preferably a 'rich Afakasi or merchant' and have lots of sons like Pita for the future of our illustrious aiga. When the Women's Committee put pressure on me too, I hinted I wasn't again providing free transportation, free food and free money for our trips to cricket matches and other functions, and the pressure vanished.

When our aiga had talatalaga I refused to keep silent (as the untitled and children are expected to), particularly if I didn't agree with the elders, who were mainly male and vain. And I refused to use the polite oratory expected by their rank (and repression). Dad didn't discourage my frankness, because some of our arrogant, boastful spongers needed deflating.

Politely (but with pride) I refused our elders' request that I again be the taupou of our aiga. I pleaded old age and recommended Te'elagi's eldest daughter. Later, when I was alone with Fau, she argued that, as Finau's only other daughter, she should have the taupou title. 'Don't you want to go to New Zealand?' I bribed her. 'The title is yours after you return with your degree.' She agreed with me. Ambitious people were so easy to buy!

In my lengthy celibacy, my determination to resist the 'delights of the flesh' (Mate's description) was extremely precarious at times. Masturbation, like habitual sex in a marriage, gets monotonous. And I don't agree with feminists who argue that lesbianism is the only cure for our 'male-enslavement'. Lesbianism isn't *my* preference, I've discovered.

Many men, mainly married and including some nearing senility, made advances. But I resisted them. Long punishing runs, cold swims and showers—remedies enforced at boarding school — came in handy. Back in my austere study at Fagali'i Bay, I 'sublimated' (what a word!) my temptations into exhausting bouts of writing. Though we never discussed the cause(s) of my listless, temperamental condition, Aunt Fusi recommended my becoming a nun — she was serious. I drank myself stupid laughing about it in my study. 'Sister Olamaiileoti Farou Monroe' had a sterling silver ring to it. More sterling still, 'Mother Superior Olamaiileoti Farou Monroe'.

*

I was fielding at the centre of the malae, that hot Saturday afternoon, when Fau rushed over, stood beside me as if nothing was the matter, and whispered, 'Papa fell.' I pretended dizziness from the heat, and our captain had me replaced. 'He tumbled down the stairs,' Fau said.

I tried not to run. Most of our aiga were in the sitting room. I hurried upstairs.

'I missed the third step,' he murmured from his bed. Penina and Mate were massaging his arms and legs, while Fa'atali, a skilled taulasea, was rubbing a herb potion into the left side of his face. 'Just a few bruises,' he added.

'Are you sure?' I asked. He nodded. The left side of his face was paralysed. Penina looked at me and I saw her desperation.

I got out his small suitcase and packed some of his clothes while they watched me. 'We have to go to the hospital,' I declared.

'Ola is correct,' Penina said to him.

'There's nothing wrong with me!' he said.

'Finau, it is best if you go to the hospital,' Fa'atali said.

'Do what Fa'atali has said,' Mate instructed.

'I am not going!' Final. I didn't bother to argue.

I broke all the speeding laws into and back from Apia with his doctor. (Fau, my co-driver, kept telling me to slow down but I ignored her.)

The doctor made us wait outside while he checked Finau. After a while he came out and told us that Finau only needed a good rest in bed.

Penina came with me to take the doctor home. 'I told your family what Finau wanted me to tell them,' said the doctor, son of one of Finau's friends, and who'd trained in Fiji. 'He's had another stroke, not a major one, but he won't recover fully from it — he's very old. The sight in his left eye is almost gone completely. He refuses to be put in hospital so you'll have to nurse him, give him the medication. Make sure he rests, and then, when he's able, takes regular walks. I'll come and see him once a week. And let the taulasea continue massaging him.'

When we returned home with his medication we told everyone that Finau just needed a good rest—no noise was to be made in the house or nearby.

Within a few days, against our wishes, he was out of bed and in his garden, then in the fale with his friends, playing cards and plaiting sinnet. But his speech was badly slurred and he wore his glasses everywhere; nor could he disguise the paralysis in his left leg, arm and face. He told his grandchildren, his leg and arm 'had turned into the super leg and arm of the Bionic Man'.

I was spending nearly every day at Sapepe. Fusi eventually asked what the matter was and I told her. 'He'll be all right,' she said. She asked me again two days later.

'He's all right!' I mimicked her. She burst into tears. I left for Sapepe.

'Are you *sure* he's all right?' she asked when I returned at the end of that week. I nodded and hurried upstairs to shower.

She followed me; waited for me to tell her. I let her suffer and went into the bedroom; she followed. As I dressed, I sensed her anger (and enjoyed it). 'And?' she demanded.

'And what?'

'Don't you talk to me like that!' She tried the mother bit on me. I brushed past her and went down to the kitchen. 'He's *my* brother, eh!' she shouted after me.

'So what?' I called back. As she thundered down the stairs, I turned. 'He's *my* father, eh!' I stopped her cold in the doorway. 'If he's *your* brother, why haven't you gone to see how he is?'

Turning her face away from me, she said, 'Because — because you've not asked me to come with you.' I rushed to her. We hugged, and she sobbed into my shoulder. And I wept too. 'He won't ever forgive me,' she repeated. 'All these years, gone!'

Later I cooked some bacon, eggs and tomatoes, and opened bottles of ice-cold beer. 'Tastes good,' she said. 'Didn't know you could cook.'

'Learned in Sapepe, *recently*,' I said. She chortled. 'He'll be all right,' I said.

As I washed the dishes she dried them and reminisced about my childhood and through that, Finau. It was as if we were back in that childhood before she had left with Esau.

'Does — does he ever mention me?' she asked.

'No,' I told her the truth.

'I don't know why and how it ever got that way,' she said. I waited for her to untangle it but she didn't.

Next morning I saved her by suggesting she shift in with our Apia aiga. She jumped at that offer and after she packed her suitcase and we locked the house (which now seemed an ever-expanding emptiness without family to give it life), I dropped her off and went to Sapepe.

We served Finau, his friends and our elders their mid-morning meal and sat back, ready to get them whatever they wanted. As usual they talked freely. Joked. Kidded one another. Finau sipped his tea but he was far away into the web of himself. Nothing to be upset about. The others talked on.

'. . . And I told Lagona, my father, not to be so tough on Pese, and Lagona got angry with me and told me children had no right telling off their parents.' His declaration was like an air bubble breaking up from depths unconnected to the flow and truth of the stream; it hit the surface and popped because it had nothing to do with what they'd been discussing.

'Fill Finau's cup,' I whispered to Fau.

As she was pouring tea into his cup, he looked up at her face. That brought him up from the depths.

'My remembering is going again; playing tricks on me,' he told Penina later.

That night he didn't sleep in the fale with his friends.

Each morning after that he got up early and wrote. We didn't know what he was writing but suspected it was what he'd started at the hospital. At midday, before he slept again, he locked his papers in his wooden trunk.

I didn't bring him any more books because the sight in his right eye was failing also. His arm and leg got more difficult to carry, but he struggled. Te'elagi gave him a carved walking stick that had belonged to his father. Finau couldn't refuse it and just carried it. However, the next Sunday as we walked to church, he started using it. From then on the stick was his inseparable companion, around which he gathered and wove and fastened his collapsing body.

He got Te'elagi to lead our evening lotu because his speech was so slurred it was difficult to understand him. His hearing was going too. Again he wouldn't admit it, but we now had to repeat what we said to him, and he talked louder.

Old age was unrelenting, but he didn't seem to mind now that he was inside Sapepe and his aiga again. Only when his memory faltered did he protest against his disintegration; only when he realised he'd disconnected again with the present did he curse Satan (not God) for taunting him with the lucid reminder that he'd once had an unfaulty remembering.

I always read him Pita's letters. He took special note of this: 'There's no time past or time future, all time is here and now in the ever-moving present.'

'That boy's getting too clever for my understanding,' he said. 'But in your next letter tell him that we humans die and become time past.' He started laughing to himself.

The first week of January was our special cricket tournament to decide the Champion of Champions. That year we hosted it in Sapepe, billeting eight teams (and their hordes of supporters) while the other seven teams travelled to us daily by bus.

Too busy with the tournament, I forgot Dad. However, whenever our team played, he sat with his grandchildren under our breadfruit trees and watched (and didn't seem to mind his wards being noisy supporters).

We managed to get into the finals. The fale and houses at the edge of the malae were packed with spectators. Our Women's Committee came and sat with us while we batted, and clapped and cheered us on.

Ours was a humiliating defeat. I made only six runs in the first innings, a duck in the second, and managed only six wickets in both innings. A miserable performance by our team. Our only excuse was that as hosts we had to house and feed our visiting teams and their hungry hangers-on until late at night, while our opponents had time to rest and replenish their energy with our good food. We were tired (and getting more tired as the tournament progressed) before each game. I hated losing and was therefore miserable.

It was the custom after each final for the winners to demand entertainment from the losers. We, and our Women's Committee, sat near one end of the pitch opposite our 'conquerors', and their captain, now a strutting martinet, ordered us to sing, dance, recite, hop-skip-and-jump, and imitate the crying of various creatures. She picked the soa from among us, starting with our youngest players. 'Ah, look at the creature's mouth!' we cursed among ourselves. 'Look at her bandy legs. Her face is like a crocodile's!'

'And now,' she announced, 'we want your captain and your New Zealand bowler to perform!' 'Drop dead!' I cursed to myself in English.

Our side, the Defeated, the Best Side, started singing again, clapping to the rhythm of the song as our conductor, as rotund as a short, overfed pastor, went through her repertoire of comic antics.

Our captain ran out to the front of the choir, bowed and started dancing. 'Swallow me up, ground!' I prayed, as my embarrassed legs pulled me forward, forced me to bow and started dancing, and I had to follow. It was the first time I'd ever danced in front of our village, never mind our haughty visitors and their demanding hangers-on.

Soon the women elders of my aiga and Malo's, led by Mate, were doing the aiuli around us, providing a background to our siva.

I danced and the ground wouldn't swallow me up and end my embarrassment.

Everyone kidded me about my 'awful dancing' (and batting and bowling) when I got home that evening. Dad said, 'You're a better runner than a dancer.' In his prayer at lotu, he said, 'Dear Lord, please bless our team, the Ainiuafa, give them more talent so they may win next year's tournament.' I fumed.

During our evening meal, our aiga picked our team to pieces and said I was the only good player in it (which I accepted). Mate boasted that in her youth *their* Ainiuafa never lost a game — well, just one, but she'd scored fifty runs. Dad reminded her that she'd sworn at the umpire and our aiga was fined three sows for it. Fau rolled her eyes (disbelievingly) at me, and Lopeti vowed he was going to be Sapepe's greatest cricketer.

That night we slept as if our good dreams would spin on forever.

*

335

Dad didn't leave his room the next day. Penina said he was busy reading and composing a sermon, and took his meals to their room.

He didn't leave his room the next day either.

The following morning I waited until Penina wasn't about and slipped into their bedroom, feeling as if I was returning to a secret hideout in my childhood.

It was nearly midday and a white light covered everything in the room, absorbing the other colours. The muffled murmuring of the sea rummaged through the room; wrapped itself around my moa.

Finau was asleep on the bed, the sheet covering him up to his waist. His chest rose and fell almost imperceptibly. Everything stopped still, as though someone had taken a flash photograph of it. I shut my eyes and turned away, but the black and white photograph wouldn't go away: the flesh was receding back into the gaps between the bones that were rising like a reef, the starkness of the skull was pushing up through the face in which I'd often read the truths of my life; slight twitches of veins in the right side of his face, refusing to die with the other half; so unjust that he was disintegrating into earth, air, memory — there was no grace in the body savaged by age without forgiveness. That was not my father. No. I remembered Nanny Mataao. And Gill and Karin and Aunt Grace and Shona. And . . .

Later, from the windows of my room, I watched the sea. I couldn't cry. I watched the sea. I couldn't hear it. I watched the sea. I watched.

It was evening when I drove into Apia. There was no need for Fusi and me to talk. She got into the car.

Locked in silence in the car, which was locked into the night, its head-lights pulling us ahead through a world without voice or sight, I watched again.

'He is upstairs,' Penina said to Fusi, who hesitated and looked at me. 'He's expecting you,' Penina saved her.

We stood at the bottom of the stairs and watched Fusi dragging her shadow, step by precarious step, up into the white light emanating from the doorway into his dying. Watched.

When her wailing wound out of the door and around and around the husk of our house and then, like a dolphin, swam with its magic forgive-ness through the body of our village, Penina and I followed it out onto the front steps, where we huddled and watched and felt the night flowing in to clothe us in robes as silk-fine as the most ancient ietoga.

'A year after he became Minister of Works, Tu'ese died of a per-forated ulcer,' Penina continued her story. I put my arm around her shoulders. 'The young musician, whom he had denied but who had lived

336

and struggled within him to be reborn, burst him open to death.' No sadness, she was simply describing what had happened, and what she had accepted. Yet I associated her story with Finau, and knew that Penina had intended that.

Her voice, her story, was now at the centre of the night. '. . . I wanted to experience the depth of grief that one is supposed to feel when a parent dies but I didn't,' she was saying. 'He was my father but then he wasn't. But I was sad for him, for his enormous loss of the gifted musician.' She was silent for a while, her shoulders were warm under my arm. 'After his death, I dreaded visiting my other home, because he was always there, in the very sinews of the house, watching me. And I didn't want to bear Sasa'e's grief, which she talked about and talked about to us, her children, whenever no one else was about.'

Penina explained that within a year of Tu'ese's death, Sasa'e was married to the foreman in their business and complaining constantly about everything. Nothing was to be trusted; God and fate were against her and her children; life was a plot against her and her family. To escape Sasa'e and her husband, who echoed her like a chorus, Penina stopped visiting them. Mika and Sisifo asked her why. 'I don't like her husband,' she lied, knowing they wouldn't again urge her to go. 'He doesn't like me,' she added just to make it more final.

A cool breeze brushed against our faces. I snuggled closer to Penina, into her coconut oil smell. '. . . Anyway, that year I completed standard six at the Sisters' School and persuaded my parents to let me go to work. The Sisters got me a job at Thurroughs.' She paused. We were again with Finau. The night breathed easily around us.

'For six or so years God was good to me: I was good at my job, your father and the Thurroughs liked and trusted me, I brought home my pay and gave it to my parents to help them support our aiga, I enjoyed church and playing basketball and flirting with a few of the boys of our church choir, and I could live with Tu'ese's memory — well, more a presence than a memory, especially when he tended to squat at the centre of my dreaming, gazing at me with those soulful eyes which were as large as breadfruit. Yes, I learned to live with that.' She paused again and pulled her sleeping sheet up to her neck.

'Innocent beginnings can have such devastating endings,' she whispered. 'Mika went to Savai'i for three months, at first, to help build the main road there. What could be more harmless than that? But when he returned I sensed he was hiding something from us and from Sisifo in particular. I mentioned nothing to my mother about it. I continued to believe that nothing could destroy the deep love between them: the blessing I'd been fortunate to grow up in.'

Penina hesitated and then said that after another three months in

Savai'i, Mika sent word through one of his workers that he had to stay on and try and finish the road quickly. Sisifo said nothing. Being their only child, onto whom they lavished their love, Penina refused to believe the rumours that Mika was living with another woman. And when Sisifo cried one night when they were alone and told her she feared that Mika was unfaithful to them, Penina reassured her that her father would never do such a thing.

'Funny how the building of innocent roads can lead to unexpected destinations,' Penina sighed. 'To shorten my story, the rumours were true. And I loathed my father for it. Yes, loathed him. When he returned, five months later, I refused to speak to him. A short while later, with the whole neighbourhood as their audience, my parents were screaming at each other, their accusations were monstrous and so hateful. She threw out all his possessions. He left for Savai'i that afternoon. Three days later, after trying to dissuade her, I followed Sisifo to live with Sasa'e and our other aiga.'

Now she had to live with the haunting presences of her two fathers, Penina explained. And two mothers who, despite their endless complaining about how badly life had treated them, carried the tragic pain of not being able to stop loving her fathers.

'Finau saved me from that intolerable situation. I agreed to marry him. My mothers said he was too old. "You shouldn't marry someone you don't love," they argued. I told Finau that, but he said that love would grow between us. Your father is so sure of everything — in his quiet way. And he was right: I did come to love him. I've been so lucky in my life with him, Ola. So lucky. I've never wanted any other man. Oh, at times I've had a second look at some other men. But I've never gone beyond that. To trust completely, to have faith in the person you love, he and I have always had that.' She turned and caressing my hair said, 'We've always had it, despite the fact that he has never stopped loving your mother. She's been the third person in our life. I've never been jealous of her: well, not permanently. I learned to trust her, and she, me. I know her better than I know most other people. Perhaps that's why I've never been jealous of you either, Ola. He puts you above me and his other children, Ola. But I've always accepted that because that's a very important part of who he is. And despite your many obvious failings, Ola, I came to love you.'

'What failings?' I joked.

The dark laughed with her as she itemised my failings. 'You're spoilt — blame Fusi, your father, your whole aiga for that. You're brainy and your aiga, because of that, keep expecting great things of you, but you're going to continue wasting your talent. You're beautiful and have the choice of any man you want, but you fall for the most hopeless men around . . .'

'What about some good points?' I interrupted.

Laying her head on my shoulder, she whispered, 'Your failings are so numerous and obvious we love you because of them; you don't bother to hide them, and they make you so vulnerable. Any idiot will have to love you because of them. And there are so many idiots round.'

'Such as?'

'Your father, me . . .'

'All right, all right!' I laughed, hugging her.

Next morning as the sun broke over the range, Finau wanted to be shifted to the faletele, where he lay on a bed of mats, propped up by pillows. I busied myself in the kitchen fale, cooking meals for his friends, relatives and the elders of Sapepe who came, throughout the day, to farewell him. Our aiga moved in an invisible sea of hushed quietness; even the children whispered.

Te'elagi summoned our aiga to the evening lotu. I lingered in the kitchen, pretending I was still busy with the cooking, but Fusi came and said, 'Please, Ola, come with me.'

We filled the fale, starting with Penina, Mate, Fusi and the youngest children circled around him, then the other concentric rings of our aiga tree, with the elders occupying the outer posts. I sat with the servers at the back. My fingers picked at the ragged edge of the mat I was sitting on; I watched my fingers as the lotu progressed.

After Te'elagi read from the Book, he asked Finau to give us his blessing and mavaega. I looked around the fale. Our elders were weeping silently; some of the children looked frightened.

'It is over,' Finau spoke from the depths of his breathing. 'God has brought me back to my aiga, and soon I will be going home to His house . . .' He stopped often to gather his strength. '. . . It is my wish that you remain a unified aiga, loving one another, nursing the Va between all of you and our village, church and country . . .' As his faltering voice bound us more tightly together, I recalled my first visit to Sapepe and how, alone on the beach at sunset, I'd discovered the I, Me, as separate from the Them and Everything Else.

Even before he started searching me out, I sensed it. 'It was the wish of our aiga that I become the Lagona.' Paused again. 'I've refused it up to now because I consider myself too old for it, too old to carry out the duties and responsibilities that go with the title.' His face, eyes shut, turned, like an upraised palm, towards me. I sank deeper. His eyes opened. I was caught in their clear depths. 'Ola, my eldest child, my daughter who questions everything, and who will question even my last wishes, who has never been content and happy with what is and what God has planned, Ola, it is my wish, and the decision of our aiga, that you *be* Lagona.'

Their thoughts were on me; they were as heavy as the world that had always expected more of me but I'd always escaped. He shut his eyes and, sinking back into the pillows, added, 'Ola, you are more than ready for it now.' Paused again. I could almost hear him laughing triumphantly, for he knew I knew he had me; he knew I knew that he knew it was unfair of him, in his dying, to bless me with the enormous burden of aiga, village and our Dead.

He started blessing other members of our aiga. 'Finau, I can't accept!' My challenge broke out before I could stop it. Their sobbing stilled for a moment. Sacrilege! Utterly unloving to reject the wishes of the dying, especially those of your beloved elders, and doubly unloving to do so in plain language.

His austere head rose up out of the pillows. Penina and Mate propped him up. The wheezing started shaking him; we thought he was choking. His mouth opened and the wheezing came out as mischievous chuckling. 'Ola, my rebellious daughter, will you refuse even the wishes of a dying old man who happens to be your father? And refuse him so inelegantly? I thought you were a poet.' He lay back.

'This person is unworthy,' I replied with bowed head, true to the role of the respectful daughter. 'Unworthy of you, our aiga, and the Lagona title.' My aiga loved me again, I could feel it. The game between Finau and me was beyond their comprehension.

'Ola, you were born out of Death, out of the love I had for your mother. Since that day, I have never been free of you. Do you hear me, Ola? I want to die free of you. This will free me of you.' He was trapping me more. 'Accept it — if not for me — for Penina, Mate and Fusi.' When he paused I knew he was ready to play his last card. I shut my eyes and bowed my head.

'*Accept it for the kidnapped boy who we executed in Israel!*' he whispered in English, into my head.

Later the fale blinds were drawn, the lamp was dimmed, and the others left.

Mate, Penina, Fusi, and I waited beside him.

He died at dawn on 3 December.

While they were preparing him for burial I ran the long curve of the bay and back.

We buried him the following afternoon next to his parents, as he had wished.

'He asked me to give this to you,' Penina said, handing me a long white envelope that was bulging with papers. It was the morning after his funeral, and Penina and I were alone in their bedroom, sorting through his clothes.

For almost two weeks I was too afraid to open it.

85

THE TESTAMENT OF FINAU LAGONA
OF SAPEPE (AND THE VAIPE, APIA)

Yes, I did write, rewrite, burn, write, rewrite, throw away many pages, starting with the pad you forgot at the hospital, until I thought I had twenty and a half pages of what I believed I needed to say to you and through you, as Lagona (and I pray you accept the title), to our aiga and our future (if there is a future for our tragic planet), but I realised my action — bequeathing to you what I deemed you should be guided by and, hopefully, be — was the thoughtless height of arrogance (and knowing you, you wouldn't heed it anyway!). So I've told Penina to bury my pages (of 'distilled wisdom') with me, in the inside pocket of my suit coat next to my dead heart, and to give you these twenty and a half blank pages of my 'testament' to do what you want with. As you well know, our aiga has sometimes not been able to afford toilet paper — I was brought up on leaves, coconut husks and smooth stones, but I hope you will fill our pages with your poetic discoveries and bequeath them to our next generation, who, led by the prophet Pita Lagona, will explore their roots to the Vanimonimo and the Atua who are rooted in the rich fertility of our moa.

Ia e ola manuia pea, lo'u afafine pele.
Finau

P.S. My heart wears the child's shoe of Yad Vashem. It is still a perfect fit.

343

86

I am Ola

I am Life

87

Today as I sit on the beach with my eyes shut to the sun's glare, my skin burning into the earth colours of Sapepe, the incoming tide hums in my head.

Today my bones, flesh, pores are being filled by the fertile weight of the tide.

Today the tide pushes before it a cool, flippant breeze with quick fingers that nip and scratch and flick gently at my skin.

Today I don't want to think of anything, least of all of happiness and the ravenous aitu who now inhabit the house that I am.

Today I want nothing, yet my aiga wants everything of me.

Today I need nothing, yet I need everyone.

88

I
I am
I am here

We
We are
We are here
We are here and
We are here and we
We are here and we are
We are here and we are one

Outou

Matou

Tatou

But where do I go from here?
Where do we go?

Afterword

*Wrapped up snugly in the truths of Ola's testament, as shaped by my
editing and arranging, I couldn't resist the temptation of finding out
where she came from and lived (or comes from and lives), so I took
our kitchen map of Samoa into my study and looked for Sapepe and
the Vaipe. They don't exist as such. I couldn't resist telling my wife
about my discovery, over dinner that night.*

*As she ate her lettuce and green-pepper salad she reminded me
that Sapepe and the Vaipe were 'creations of Albert Wendt's very
unSamoan imagination, in his novel* Leaves of the Banyan Tree'.
*'And remember,' she went on to make me feel more inadequate,
'Malo Tauilopepe Galupo is the melodramatically fascist heir who
returns, in Book Three, to take over Sapepe.'*

*So Ola in her story has played profound tricks with reality (hers,
mine and yours, dear reader), disguising her trail with fictions
borrowed from other practitioners of that magic, to give it other
depths of meaning, or, should I say, another* shape *of meaning. And,
through her creations, has added new dimensions to Albert Wendt's
Sapepe and the Vaipe and Samoa and ourselves.*

*All is real, whether borrowed or created or dreamed, or mixed
together with facts, fictions, strange sauces and herbs and condi-
ments in quantities peculiar to each mixer, dreamer, cook, creator.
We are all the possibilities of every creator.*

All is Ola.
All is Life.

Pati Tuaopepe
Tauese, Apia
3 April 1991